BOULDER CITY LIBRARY
3 1432 00205 42

D0053680

kissing **games**

ALSO BY TARA EGLINGTON

how to keep a boy from kissing you

kissing
games

TARA EGLINGTON

This is a work of fiction. All of the characters, organizations, and events portrayed in this novel are either products of the author's imagination or are used fictitiously.

www.wednesdaybooks.com
www.stmartins.com

Designed by Anna Gorovoy

The Library of Congress Cataloging-in-Publication Data is available upon request.

ISBN 978-1-250-07526-0 (hardcover)
ISBN 978-1-250-13142-3 (ebook)

Our books may be purchased in bulk for promotional, educational, or business use. Please contact your local bookseller or the Macmillan Corporate and Premium Sales Department at 1-800-221-7945, extension 5442, or by email at MacmillanSpecialMarkets@macmillan.com.

A different version of this book was published under the title *How to Convince a Boy to Kiss You* in Australia in 2013 by HarperCollins Publishers

First Edition: June 2018

10 9 8 7 6 5 4 3 2 1

For Greg,
my real-life Potential Prince,
who restored my faith and
thus brought Aurora back to life.
I hope you'll have all of my kisses, always.

ACKNOWLEDGMENTS

my US team:

Firstly, a special thanks overall to the St. Martin's team, for introducing Aurora to the USA! It has been such a special experience to see *How to Keep a Boy from Kissing You* released in the United States, with its gorgeous hardback cover, and to have new readers contacting me on social media to express their enthusiasm for the book. I feel very lucky to have the chance to publish this follow-up, *Kissing Games,* with you in 2018.

Alicia Clancy—thank you for your help and guidance in readying the novel for publication in the States. It's been fantastic to have firsthand advice on a new and wider market, and I really appreciate you looking over this novel many times, with an expert eye, and suggesting certain edits and changes.

A huge thank-you also goes out to my production editor, Jessica Katz, for all her hard work on *Kissing Games*.

My marketing and publicity team—Karen Masnica, Brittani Hiles, and DJ DeSmyter—you guys are fantastic at what you do! I'm so appreciative of all the time and effort you put into spreading the word about the Aurora Skye series there in the USA.

Kerri Resnick—BIG thanks for creating such a gorgeous, engaging, and fun cover for *Kissing Games*—I love it!

A special thanks goes out to Kat Brzozowski—who originally signed *How to Keep a Boy from Kissing You* and the sequel—I am so grateful to have had the opportunity to not only work with you, but to have had the chance to see the Aurora Skye series released in the States. Thank you for all the enthusiasm and assistance during your time with St. Martin's. I really hope you'll find your way to Sydney, Australia, in the near future so we can meet in person.

my australian team:

Elizabeth O'Donnell and the HarperCollins Australia legal and contract teams—thank you so much for the dedication and hard work that was put in from your side, in order for me to secure my contract with St. Martin's. It has meant the world to me to be able to have my books released in the American market, and to have the adventures of Aurora Skye and Co. embraced by new and enthusiastic readers.

Big thanks to the beautiful Lisa Berryman for guiding Aurora's second journey from start to finish here in Australia—it was absolutely wonderful to deliver the novel to such an enthusiastic recipient. Thank you for handling all aspects of the publishing process with such care and concern for not only Aurora and her story but also for myself as a writer.

My gratitude as always goes to my editorial team who worked so closely with me on the original manuscript, readying it for publication. Kate Burnitt—you are a wonder of organization, calmness, and all-around awesome! I am in absolute awe of your attention to detail and conscientious command of the overall editorial project. Thank you so much.

Nicola O'Shea—thank you for not passing out when handed a 160,000-word manuscript, and for expertly suggesting cuts and edits to whip the thing into slimmer shape! You are a fundamental part of ensuring Aurora's voice stays true to her readers and I thank you for that.

Emma Dowden—thanks for picking up on all of the finer details so that Aurora's world makes sense!

My family—I couldn't have gotten through the writing of this manuscript without you. Dad, thank you for taking the dozens of phone calls from one stressed-out-bordering-on-insane author—it's beyond reassuring to have a fellow creative cheering me on. My sister, Sarada, my brother, Rama, and my brother-in-law, Angus, thank you for being on the other end of the line whenever I needed you. It's been so wonderful to witness your support and enthusiasm for my books and to share in the joy of publication with you.

Greg—I gave you the dedication, baby! You were my rock through everything. I am blessed, blessed, blessed to experience the level of love, affection, and support that you give me. You are evidence that Potential Princes really do exist.

My wonderful fans—on Facebook, on Instagram, Goodreads, in bookstores—your enthusiasm for my books and support for me as an author is EVERYTHING. I can't tell you how much it means to me to receive your messages—they keep me motivated when I'm struggling with a difficult edit, or exhausted from too many hours at a computer. I really hope you love *Kissing Games*—I've had so much fun writing about Aurora, Hayden, and Co. for the second time!

I love to hear from readers, so please feel free to say hello via:

Facebook: facebook.com/taraeglington
Instagram: instagram.com/taraeglington
Twitter: twitter.com/taraeglington

1

For a girl who shares her name with a princess (Aurora from *Sleeping Beauty*), my present circumstances were fathoms away from a fairy tale. My kissing skills had left both parties maimed—one case worthy of the emergency room.

Our first kiss as a couple, and *my* first-ever kiss, had been a melding of everything I'd heard kisses could be, all the glorious clichés in action—weak knees, my heart a field of fluttering butterflies, life in Technicolor. Worth the wait.

With a start like that, I'd expected the second kiss to be as good. Or at least not to end in calamity.

Four hours ago I'd had no idea I'd be spending half of my Thursday night in the local hospital's emergency department, watching the on-call physician stitching Hayden Paris's formerly perfect lower lip.

four hours earlier . . .

I stood at my bathroom mirror, staring at my lips. I'd just applied red lipstick, taking a good five minutes to make sure that the edges were perfect. Now I was having second thoughts.

Normally I wasn't one to spend lengthy amounts of time pouting at my own reflection, but in the fifteen minutes before Hayden was due to arrive I was fixated on my own mouth.

It had started with the intention of making sure I had fresh breath. Three brushings and a lengthy flossing session later, I'd pinched the superstrong dental clinic–issued mouthwash used by my dad (otherwise known as the NAD—New Age dad), on the basis that it would work better than my Listerine. Figuring that if I used any more mouthwash I'd give myself acid reflux, I'd finally stashed a mini breath spray in the pocket of my skirt so I could do a last quick spritz after Hayden and I had finished dinner. Literally sharing breath with someone was nerve-racking.

I was now in a conundrum over lipstick. I'd automatically reached for the red, as numerous studies have proved that red lips are considered the most sensual, due to the way that lipstick mimics the way our lips flush when attracted to another person. But just as I'd finished applying the lipstick, I started worrying that it wasn't the best choice. It would inevitably kiss off, wouldn't it? What if I pulled away from the (hopefully) amazing kiss and Hayden was left smeared with red lipstick? Gloss wasn't an option, either—I'd overheard way too many guys complaining about how they hated goopy lips.

I blotted the lipstick, hoping to achieve a nice, subtle stain, like I'd been sitting in a field eating raspberries or something. Revlon had had that famous Cherries in the Snow ad campaign in 1953, so bring on Raspberries in a Field. I was obviously getting jittery if I was planning 1950s-esque cosmetic campaigns.

I hadn't talked about my anxiety with my best friends, Cassie, Jelena, Lindsay, and Sara. They were looking to me to be their dating guru—and hopefully the whole of Jefferson High would be, too, once I implemented my Find a Prince/Princess™ program. This is a program I designed to help guys and girls navigate the minefield that is the high school dating scene. As well as using the program to help Cassie find love with Scott (aka the ubercute new guy) and to help Lindsay win her ex-boyfriend Tyler back, I had also been using the program to weigh my own romantic prospects, with the aim of identifying my "prince."

A prince:

- has **P**rinciples. He stands up for what he knows to be right, instead of going along with the crowd.
- **R**ecognizes your worth. He understands how special you are and treats you with respect and kindness.
- possesses **I**ntegrity. He's genuine with his feelings and won't mislead you for underhanded or selfish purposes.
- **N**ever doubts you're the only one for him.
- is **C**onstant. He stands by you through the sunshine and the shadows, the good and the bad.
- possesses **E**ndurance. He is willing to overcome considerable obstacles to win your affection.

I know the "prince" thing sounds cringeworthy, like it's something from another century. But the program isn't about glass slippers or lying around until a prince shows up. It's about valuing yourself and saying no to guys with dishonest intentions or lukewarm feelings. Guys who lie or are self-involved or only looking for an ego boost. Guys who play around with our feelings like it's a form of sport.

What the program is really about is knowing what you are worthy of and accepting nothing less.

I get that some people might see this as idealistic. But if I listened to everyone else's cynicism, I'd never have stuck with the Find a Prince/Princess™ program for the past three years. I'd have given up and settled for a substandard guy. Instead, following my heart had landed me Hayden Paris, Prince Extraordinaire. After years of misunderstandings and miscommunication, Hayden and I had finally come together as a couple three days ago, after he'd revealed himself to be my secret admirer. I'd realized that he was *not* the bane of my life but actually the boy of my dreams. And after sixteen years and six months of not settling, I'd finally had that magical first kiss I'd been waiting for.

I'd once read that the term "French kiss" was derived from "soul kiss," because of an ancient belief that the sharing of breath was, in essence, the sharing of souls. It was a romantic notion, yet I had to admit, when I'd let Hayden touch his lips to mine the other night, I'd felt as if parts of me, tiny molecules at a time, had come close to dissolving in the intense closeness.

So when it came to tonight, I wanted the follow-up kiss to be just as legendary. I wanted utter elation, a moment of tenderness in which my heart would tremble inside my chest at how exquisitely beautiful it was to be so close to Hayden.

I shivered at the thought, and the tiny hairs on my arms stood up. Catching sight of my watch, I realized there was only about five minutes until Hayden was due to arrive. I had to turn my mind to practicalities.

My heart pounding, I ran downstairs to do a last-minute check of the living room. Thankfully, Dad had headed out to an event at the local meditation center, so I'd had some time this evening to prep the room for maximum ambience. Beyond emotional connection, romance was a sensory experience, so I'd aimed for soft light and scent. I placed oversize, velvety cushions on either side of the coffee table to encourage a more relaxed feel than the two of us perched at a distance from each other on my long couch, and then I set three large scented candles atop the coffee table.

After lighting the candles, I dimmed the light, just enough to heighten the mood but not so dramatically that I'd have difficulty making out Hayden's features.

Then I turned them up again a fraction of an inch. Yes, I was trying to create a sense of intimacy, but what if Hayden thought I was being overly forward? It was only our first date, and here I was getting out the candles!

Oh god, could I even pull this off? Yes, I'd readied the room, but was *I* ready? Could I take this second kiss to the dizzying heights required?

What if our heart-stopping first kiss had set a precedent in Hayden's mind that I couldn't equal the second time around? What if I instigated a kiss and it fell flat? What if Hayden was disappointed?

My basic plan was to move in close at some point during the night, ensuring that my intimate intentions were obvious to Hayden. But I had major timing trepidation. How would I know the opportune moment to get up close and personal?

For example, what if I moved in and he was tired or cranky or lip-fatigued from an afternoon arguing in the debate team? I pictured myself getting shot down midmove in the candlelight. Hmm . . . was rejection better or worse in low lighting? The lack of light would hide my extreme embarrassment, but I'd also be sitting there in a highly sensuous atmosphere. Hopefully not *too* sensuous. My hand went to the dimmer switch again.

Right. I was calling Cassie.

She picked up right away. "Hey, aren't you on your date?"

"About to be. As in, Hayden's probably heading toward my door right now and I'm doubting I have the courage to open it, let alone make a lunge for his lips later. Cass, what if I get the timing wrong and I'm left cast off in the candlelight?"

"Aurora, you know he's crazy about you. I'm sure he's planning to kiss you tonight. But if you want to be the one to make the first move, just look for the cues."

"Cues?"

"Kissing green lights. Physical indications telling you to go straight ahead."

"I'm a total newbie on the dating highway, Cass. Unless Hayden actually turns green, I'm going to be playing the yes/no game for the next few hours."

Cassie laughed. "I'm talking things like prolonged eye contact and sitting really close to you, not Hayden turning into a chameleon."

"Oh god, why can't he be a chameleon? You know the male actually changes color when he's in the mood? Just think—if Hayden's lips burst into stripes of blue and green, I wouldn't have any hesitation!" My voice rose a half octave with nervous tension.

"Aurora, I can hear you getting breathless. You have to breathe. If you don't breathe while kissing, you'll pass out. It happened to my cousin!"

"*What?*" I shrieked. "No one warned me about this!"

The doorbell rang.

"Argh! Hayden and his nonchameleon lips have arrived!"

"Focus on the feelings and you'll ace it," Cassie said. "I promise."

I caught sight of my face in the hallway mirror as I set the phone down and headed for the door. I looked like a rabbit staring up in terror at a farmer with a pitchfork. Fantastic.

I took a deep breath and opened the door. Hayden's smiling face greeted me. My whole body instantly relaxed.

"Good evening, Princess." He gave me a hug. "Any chance a wannabe knight bearing wood-fired pizza could cross the threshold?"

I smiled as I stepped aside to let him in. "Was it an epic quest?"

"It involved much gallantry," Hayden replied as we headed down the hall. "The guy at the pizza place was actually kind of a fire-breathing dragon. He had serious issues about half-and-half pizzas."

Hayden started turning right to go into the kitchen.

"Oh!" I touched his shoulder. "I thought we might eat in the living room. It's cozier."

My plan of action was to get Hayden comfortable. Get him comfortable and then pounce.

"Sure." He turned left then stopped at the entrance to the living room. "We might need a little more light."

Oh my god—the living room now resembled a dimly lit saloon where busty women of the Wild West were likely to slink by in skimpy corsets or recline languorously on velvet cushions. I must have accidentally hit the dimmer switch in my scramble to get to the front door.

"Sorry, I was, ah, setting the scene." Had that actually come out?

"The scene?" Hayden turned, eyebrows raised, his hand paused on the switch. His eyes were undeniably nervous. He probably thought he was about to be thrown down on the coffee table.

Great. I aim for ambience and wind up scaring my date.

"Setting the scene—for history!" I cried. "You know, the Middle Ages, living by candlelight? I was hoping it would help with my essay. I, um, was working on it while waiting for you."

My voice was increasingly resembling a chipmunk's—high-pitched, fast-paced, and bordering on panicky.

"Much as I love your imagination, I think the take-out pizza might destroy the illusion." Hayden laughed as he turned the dimmer switch up. "Let's skip ahead a few centuries so you don't drip sauce on that gorgeous dress."

I tried not to feel seriously insulted. Here I was, preparing to execute a major move, and my date didn't want to know about it. I flopped down onto one of the velvet cushions, trying not to let out a sigh as Hayden set out the pizza and filled our glasses with Coke. Why was this so easy in movies? I thought of *Cleopatra* and Elizabeth Taylor tumbling out of the rolled-up carpet. Caesar had been putty in her hands. I'd tried to set up a scene of seduction and instead I'd wound up eating pizza underneath blazing lights.

I looked across at Hayden, who'd picked up a piece of pizza but seemed to be waiting for me. I studied the pizza on the table in front of me. The second I took a bite, my painstakingly applied lipstick would be messed up. Then, as the smell wafted up toward me, I realized I had bigger worries—there was garlic on the margherita! No way was breath spray going to cover up that potent passion killer.

I looked up from the pizza and saw that Hayden was watching me with an amused expression.

"Here, my lady, let me choose the perfect piece for thee." He picked up a slice and put it on the plate in front of me.

His hazel eyes were so warm they were almost golden in the glow of the candles on the coffee table. Eye contact! That was one of Cass's green lights. Okay, time to up the ante.

My heart had accelerated within mere seconds. I had to push the rest of me to catch up with it before the opportune moment slipped by. I gave Hayden a long gaze and raised an eyebrow in what I hoped was a Cleopatra-esque expression.

He let out a nervous laugh. "Have I got sauce on my face?"

I started in surprise. "What?" Obviously my attempt at Cleopatra was more scornful than seductive. "No!"

My hands, still trembling from the extended eye contact, shook harder, and I dropped my pizza slice into my lap.

"You see! This is why we needed the light!" Hayden leaned forward, shaking his head in amusement, grabbed the pizza slice, and put it back on the plate with a smile.

He reached over and pressed a napkin into my hand, giving it a squeeze. Houston, we had contact. If I didn't do this now, I never would.

Hayden went to move his hand away, but I grabbed on to it. Before my fear could kick in, I leaned across the coffee table, meeting Hayden halfway.

"Sorry, blotting the stain will probably make it worse—" he began.

I placed my index finger over his lips, stopping his sentence short. His eyes widened.

Okay, replace finger with lips. With hopefully minty-fresh lips.

I leaned farther toward Hayden, closing the distance between us. The caramel aroma of the candles was intoxicating. I took a steady breath, trying to concentrate on my senses. I could feel my cheeks were flushed, although I couldn't tell whether that was from the warmth of the candles or the dizzying pulse of blood through my body. The room was in complete silence except for our breathing and the pounding of my heart, which thumped in my ears like the crash of the ocean on the sand when you lay your head down on your towel at the beach.

There were two inches left between our faces. I removed my finger from Hayden's lips and our foreheads touched. The gentleness of the gesture caused a pulling feeling in my chest.

Last step. Last tiny little step and the plan would be complete.

Focus on the feelings. Cass's advice floated back to me.

I touched his cheek with the fingers of my right hand. This was Hayden, my Potential Prince, my childhood friend, bane of my life turned boy of my dreams. I felt my lips relax into a smile, a smile that sank down through my skin and seemed to hover over my heart. I was so lucky. This thought tipped me over into the courage zone and, almost in a trance, I closed the minute distance left between us.

I pressed my lips to Hayden's, so lightly that the touch of skin to skin was almost imperceptible. Even the second time around, the sensation was so exquisitely unfamiliar that it was all-encompassing. I was lost to feeling—the exact pressure of Hayden's lips, his hair brushing against my fingers where they rested on his neck, the smell of his skin—a mix of soap and cologne with green-apple notes.

Hayden put his hand on my waist, pulling me closer and taking the kiss deeper. His breath was hot against mine. My pulse, already at high tempo, hit critical level. I now knew why Cass's cousin had passed out. The feeling in my chest as we kissed was so intense I almost couldn't bear it, yet I desperately sought more. I was like the candles, set alight with sensation, all thoughts dissolving in the heat of the moment. The feeling was so realistic that I could almost smell smoke.

I took another deep breath, hoping to dispel the phantom smell by inhaling more of Hayden's green-apple scent.

Wait a minute. Something *was* burning. The smell was unmistakable now, almost sulfuric. What on earth . . . ?

There were about five seconds of illogical agony, in which I wondered whether the mouthwash had failed me and the smell was coming from my own breath, before I realized what I was actually smelling. My hair was on fire!

The thought screamed through my brain, shocking me out of my kissing reverie completely. Forget the notion of "the heat of the moment"—I was literally going up in flames!

My eyes flew open, but I couldn't look down to see how much of my hair was on fire because Hayden and I were still in lip-lock. All I knew was that I didn't want the flames to reach my face. The hair spray I'd so liberally applied earlier was probably acting as an accelerant—I might only have seconds to spare!

I threw up my arm, trying to push Hayden away, and instead felt my hand make contact with one of the heavy candles positioned between us. I heard the clunk of the glass holder hitting the table at the same second that I felt boiling-hot wax spill onto my arm.

My whole body jolted from the searing pain. My teeth slammed together in an instinctual reaction and I bit down on Hayden's lips, which were still intertwined with mine. Hayden let out a muffled shout.

I ripped away from him and stared in horror at the gash in his bottom lip. But there was no time to apologize yet. I snatched the burning ends of my hair from the candle jar, then threw my glass of Coke over them, thankfully extinguishing the flames before they got any closer to my head.

My wrist was prickling with pain from the blisteringly hot wax. I needed ice. I needed liquid of any description. I snatched up Hayden's Coke and poured it on my arm. As my pain level dropped from all-consuming smart to a bearable throbbing, my attention snapped back to Hayden. He had leaped to his feet and was clutching his mouth. Blood was trickling between his fingers.

Blood. My kiss had actually drawn blood. And not in a sexy, *Twilight* way. I wanted to be sick.

"Hayden!" I leaped up from my cushion, too.

"I have to get to the bathroom before I get blood everywhere."

He pushed past me, his words muffled by his hand, and took off down the hall to the downstairs bathroom.

I ran to the kitchen for the first aid kit. I wanted to cry, from both the extreme embarrassment of having sunk my teeth into my Potential Prince and the throbbing pain of my wrist. I swiped at my eyes with the back of my hand, pushing away tears as I dashed toward the bathroom. I had to stay calm. I would have plenty of time to reflect upon my disastrous attempt at acting the siren once Hayden's lips weren't streaming blood. Right now I had to focus on helping him.

Hayden turned as I entered. He had one of our hand towels pressed to his lips. I gasped when I saw that the towel was no longer white but almost completely red, soaked with blood in the few minutes he'd been in the bathroom.

"It won't stop bleeding," he said. "I think I have to go to the hospital."

2

"Look on the bright side," Jelena said. "He's never going to forget your second kiss."

"How can he?" I wailed, and buried my head in a couch cushion. "Every time he looks in the mirror, the scar is going to be right in front of him. I have actually scarred him with what is, for most *normal* people, a straightforward action. Two sets of lips meeting! Simple!"

Jelena, Sara, Cass, Lindsay, and I were sprawled out across my living room. I'd sent the girls a text with a brief explanation of the debacle while Hayden was signing hospital release forms, so by the time we'd arrived back home and I'd said my mortified good-bye to the Parises and their lip-savaged son, all four of them were waiting on my doorstep, even though it was close to eleven p.m.

The hospital had called Hayden's parents. I'd thought my mortification couldn't get any worse, but seeing Mr. and Mrs. Paris choke back laughter after the doctor's highly unprofessional comment of "Nothing to worry about; just a bit of a perforation from some overenthusiastic necking" (who uses the word "necking" these days?!) had left me with a face as red as the burns on my wrist.

"A kiss normally *is* simple. You just had bad luck." Cass, sitting next to me on the sofa, gave my shoulder a squeeze.

"Odds of a million to one," Jelena muttered.

"Jelena, we are trying to be supportive here." Sara tossed a cushion at her. "I.e., make Aurora feel a little better?"

"I am!" Jelena tossed the cushion back at her. "I'm stressing how unlucky Hayden's night with the needle was! Aurora, consider it this way: you always said he looked too perfect."

"That was before I fell for him! How did my attempt at *Romeo and Juliet* become a scene out of *Fight Club*?"

"Don't stress. Men can pull off a scar," Sara said. "It's the rugged look. Think a cowboy in the Wild West—he's crossed paths with a coyote and lived to tell the tale."

"I don't want my Potential Prince to look like he's faced off with a coyote!" I put my head in my hands.

"Faced off and came out the victor, Aurora," Sara said matter-of-factly. "And now he's left forever brutish yet sensitive-looking."

Lindsay frowned. "Isn't that a contradiction? Can you *be* brutish yet sensitive?"

"Suffering makes a man complex, Lindsay." Sara shook her head and let out a sigh. "Like in *To Tame a Texan*. Carter Janson seems the rough type, but when he starts whispering to Eliza on the porch as the rain pelts down onto the dusty earth—"

"For god's sake, Sara!" Jelena interrupted. "You call yourself a feminist and you read that junk?"

"But Hayden's personality isn't brutish!" I protested. "This new look doesn't go with his student council–leading, animal rights–promoting persona."

Neither of them took any notice of me.

"A feminist is just someone who believes that women should have equal rights and opportunities, Jelena," Sara shot back. "It doesn't mean I can't read romance novels."

I lifted my head from my hands. "Can we please forget cowboy Carter?"

"Hayden's lips will restore themselves to their former glory," Jelena said. "If not, there's always plastic surgery."

I gave her a look.

"Aurora isn't concerned about that," Cassie said. "She'll love Hayden regardless of a scar. You'd never want him to get plastic surgery, right?"

I let out a groan. "No! Can we please assume that I haven't majorly disfigured the boy I'm yet to complete an entire date with?"

"Aurora, his lips aren't going to be permanently affected," Lindsay said reassuringly. "His lower lip might just be a little . . . bigger . . . than it was before."

"Bigger?" I wailed.

"For a while! The swollen factor. But it'll go down."

"And hopefully not leave a puckered scar," Jelena added.

I turned to her in horror.

"Five words for you, Aurora," Sara broke in. "Clark Gable as Rhett Butler."

"I don't remember Rhett Butler having a puckered lip," Lindsay said.

"He had big lips," Sara replied. "And a brutish appeal."

"Can we get off the Southern theme?" Jelena flounced over to her bag to grab her phone. "Mom's texted me. She's picking us up in five."

"You're leaving already?" I said.

"Aurora, if I were you, I'd be making an emergency appointment at the salon ASAP. Instead of stressing about Hayden's future physical appeal, can you please turn your attention to your own? Singed strands are so not hot."

"This is exactly what I'm talking about!" I followed my friends down the hall. "If Jelena's being harsh on my locks now, imagine the scrutiny Hayden's going to face from a whole schoolyard of taunters tomorrow!"

Jelena rolled her eyes. "Aurora, I doubt there'll be *actual* taunting. You're taking this a tad far."

"I'll meet you at the salon at seven thirty a.m. tomorrow," Cassie said, giving me a hug as she exited the front door. "I'm sure they can fit you in for a quick trim."

I gave her a weak smile.

Sara bounded past me as Jelena's mom beeped the horn. "Just keep reminding yourself, Aurora: Rhett Butler and his brutish mouth are still legendary, seventy-five years later. This could be a boon for Hayden."

"I ended up watching *Gone with the Wind* last night, after all of Sara's talk," I said to Cassie as we met at the school gate the next morning. "I kind of got the impression that Scarlett O'Hara was fooling herself once Rhett packed up and left."

"You watched through to the end?" Cassie's eyes widened. "That movie is like four hours long!"

"I couldn't sleep. It was a choice between my memory of Hayden's lip being sewn up by the doctor, while he grimaced in pain, and Rhett Butler's lips snarling, 'Frankly, my dear, I don't give a damn.' Epic Civil War–era costumes won out."

"Did it make you feel any better?"

"I guess it put things in perspective. I'm not having to defend my once-majestic-now-war-racked Southern plantation with a shotgun. My incisors severing Hayden's lip has to pale in comparison, right?"

Cassie grinned. "Now you sound like the bestie I know. The woe-is-me attitude so wasn't you.

"Any word from Hayden, post incident?" Cassie asked as we climbed the steps to our history classroom.

"He sent me a text with a smiley face and the words 'My lip isn't numb anymore, Princess!' at about seven this morning. So I guess he's not holding a grudge."

"That's sweet!" Cassie said. "He doesn't want you to worry. You guys are going to be fine."

"If he doesn't tremble in fear when he sees me approach his desk, maybe we'll eventually get to a second date," I said.

My eyes immediately leaped to Hayden's usual spot in the history room. He hadn't arrived yet, despite the fact that class was due to start in three minutes. He couldn't have passed out from blood loss, could he? I imagined his hazel eyes rolling back in his head as he collapsed in the schoolyard. My stomach flipped over. Could someone faint from the aftereffects of a split lip? I wouldn't have thought so, but he *had* lost a lot of blood last night.

"Cass, I'd better go see if I can spot Hayden," I said. "I'll leave my stuff here and come right back, once I know he's okay." I almost spilled the contents of my pencil case as I hastened to put my things down.

"Are you sure he hasn't decided to take the day off?" Cass's brow crinkled as she took in my presumably nerve-racked expression. "Maybe he's embarrassed about turning up with an obvious injury."

I shook my head. "No, he's not vain about these things."

Scott gave Cassie's hand a squeeze as he slid into the desk next to hers, then turned to me. "Hayden just texted me; he's on his way. What happened, anyway? All he's told me is that he's got a split lip."

Mr. Bannerman entered the room and put his books down.

"All right! I know the morning debriefing is akin to coffee in terms of vital rituals, but can we give it a rest now?" Mr. Bannerman clapped his hands above the cacophony. "Jeffrey!"

Jeffrey Clark, class clown supreme, paused in his reenactment of his most recent nudie run, thankfully not sans pants. "Seriously, sir? I was just getting to the best bit!"

"Or *bits*, if we're getting graphic." Travis Ela gave a hip thrust.

"OMG, ew!" Juliet Bryce threw her backpack at Travis's gyrating pelvis. "We all know the story by heart anyway. He does a nudie run almost every weekend."

"Technically, last weekend was all about mooning, not nudie runs," Jeffrey corrected Juliet in a serious tone.

"Just open a nudist camp already," she shot back.

"Ingenious," Jeffrey whispered, his eyes widening.

"I repeat! Will all talk of weekends, including future hypothetical ones spent at Jeffrey's nudist camp, please cease!" Mr. Bannerman shouted.

That very instant, Hayden strode in the door, and the female members of the class let out a collective gasp.

Any illusions I might have had that Hayden's lip had healed overnight were instantly annihilated. Lindsay had been right about the swelling. Coupled with the purple, indigo, and black bruising surrounding the stitches, the overall effect was horrific.

The room exploded in a chorus of *What happened?* I wanted to open my desk lid and stick my head inside.

"Seriously, man, what's the story?" Jesse Cook asked.

"A bar brawl, right?" Bruce Cornwell evaluated Hayden's lip critically.

"How'd he get into a bar?" Gemma Thomson sneered at Bruce. "He's underage, idiot."

"He got caught with a fake ID and the bouncers trounced him!" Travis said, leaping up from his seat to get a closer look, along with half the guys in the class. "Those jerks always go too far. Just last weekend—"

"Seems we can't get off the topic of the weekend, can we?" Mr. Bannerman shook his head, gesturing at the boys to resume their seats.

"I literally inflicted such a bad injury that people are hypothesizing it was the work of a professional thug!" I whispered to Cassie. "I am never pressing my lips against a boy's again!"

Scott tilted Hayden's jaw up. "I don't think it's that bad."

Not that bad? Was his assessment based on Hollywood-style grotesqueries like those sported by the soldiers in *Saving Private Ryan*?

"It's nothing," Hayden said. "Seriously, everyone, these things happen. Sorry, Mr. Bannerman."

"Thanks, Hayden." Mr. Bannerman walked back to his desk. "If you guys want to talk injuries, then let's take it to another level. Year: 1380; warfare exerted with trebuchets and flaming arrows."

Hayden dropped into his seat and turned to face me. "Hey, Princess," he said, using his old nickname for me, a throwback to when I was little and obsessed with fairy tales. He reached over and took my left hand, carefully avoiding the bandage around my wrist. For a second I felt as close to him as when our foreheads had touched the night before.

"Sorry for the unsightly appearance." Hayden sounded embarrassed.

"I'm the one who's sorry," I whispered, checking that Mr. Bannerman's back was turned. "I feel terrible."

"I told you, it's forgotten already," Hayden whispered back. The expression in his eyes was soft. "What happened before the biting was pretty much worth what came afterward."

"Only pretty much?" I said in mock outrage.

"Pain may have dimmed my memory slightly. The exact softness of your lips, for instance. You'll have to remind me once I've healed up."

I blushed. Even with all that bruising, he was still bowling me over.

"Wait a minute!" Jeffrey's shout shocked me out of my delirium. "She's injured, too!"

He pointed at my hand, the one Hayden was holding. Or, more specifically, at the bandage on my wrist. The entire class craned their necks to look. I hurriedly pulled my hand from Hayden's.

"There's more to this story!" Travis waggled his eyebrows.

Jeffrey let out an exaggerated gasp. "You punched him!"

"*What?*" I yelped. "How can you even think that?"

"Domestic violence—America says no!" Travis yelled.

"People, please!" Mr. Bannerman waved his arms at the front of the classroom.

No one paid any attention to Mr. Bannerman's shout.

"How did you come to that brilliant conclusion, man?" Travis asked Jeffrey, staring at him in mock wonder. "I'm still trying to unravel it."

"Elementary, my dear Travis." Jeffrey pretended to smoke a pipe and put on a British accent. "Hayden is sporting a lip the size of a small plum and Aurora has a bandaged wrist. She's obviously taken a slug at him and injured her own hand."

"Jeffrey, you're totally off base. Why would Aurora hit me?" Hayden was on the verge of cracking up with laughter.

"It's not even a question of why!" I cried. "I wouldn't slug anyone!"

"He was making inappropriate advances, wasn't he, Aurora?" Jesse butted in.

"I think it's time you dropped this ill-mannered cad," Jeffrey said, continuing his Sherlock Holmes impersonation. "Let *me* take you out. I'll advance on you only when you want me to." He waggled his eyebrows.

"That wasn't what happened, right?" Scott asked, looking concerned as he studied Hayden's lip again. He couldn't seriously believe Jeffrey's version of events, could he?

Hayden let out a laugh. "Of course not!"

"But you guys were at the hospital together?" Scott said.

"There are other ways of getting a split lip that involve two people," Hayden said. "Think about it."

I shot him a look. Yes, I wanted the rumor that I was an aspiring pugilist stamped out for good, but I hardly wanted the real story spelled out right in front of the class.

Too late. "Oh my god!" Jeffrey shrieked. "It wasn't your left hook that dealt that blow; it was your lethal lips!"

"There should be emotional leave available for students suffering severe humiliation," I said with a sigh as the girls and I headed into an accessories store. They had suggested after-school shopping in an attempt to cheer me up. "I can't believe the entire school is calling me Lethal Lips!"

"Aurora, I don't think the term's that widespread," Cassie reassured me.

I gave her a look. "When we had to select teams for softball, Sean Harper yelled, 'Lethal Lips, you're on our side! Get over here!'"

"I did hear them yelling, 'Run, Lethal Lips, run!' as you ran between the bases," Lindsay admitted.

"You see?" I flung my arms out, almost upsetting a display of statement necklaces. "Why did Hayden have to publicly allude to last night's events?"

"I'm amazed Jeffrey could be so insightful," Sara said.

"Jeffrey's got a radar for anything related to physical contact," Jelena said, pouting in one of the store's mirrors and reapplying lip gloss.

"Let's just hope the nickname doesn't cross school districts."

"Jelena!" Cass gave her a look.

"Don't worry, Aurora, I'll be the first to defend you," Jelena said. "Fervently, if need be. I'd just prefer not to have to."

"Thanks," I said wryly.

Jelena shrugged. "I might tell it like it is at times, but I've got your back. Seriously, though . . . Yes, the name's being used, but you don't have to acknowledge it. Rise above it like a queen."

"Jelena's right. Just hold your head high," Cassie said. "The Aurora I know always keeps her dignity in embarrassing circumstances. Remember that time you fell in a puddle after escaping Bradley Scott's embrace? Or when you and Hayden were nearly crushed by the holy-water stand in front of the whole cast of the play?"

I cowered with embarrassment behind the rack of headbands as the sales assistant, hearing Cassie's last remark, turned our way.

"I feel like my personal life's suddenly been made public," I said. "Not only does the whole school know Hayden and I have been kissing but they also know I'm completely hopeless at it."

"Is it really so bad that people know you and Hayden are dating?" Lindsay asked.

"We've only had one date. I hadn't even decided if I wanted to go public yet! I've been thrust into a high-profile relationship with no say in the matter."

Jelena raised an eyebrow. "Aurora, you're hardly Kim Kardashian."

"It's not like half the school hadn't already labeled you a real-life Beatrice and Benedick," Sara said, referring to the roles that Hayden and I had played in our school's production of *Much Ado About Nothing.* "The play hardly gave the impression you guys hated each other. Anyway, just for the record, if I was dating Hayden, I'd be parading it all over school."

"You are proud to be with him, right?" Cassie asked.

"Of course!" I cried. "All I'm saying is that I wanted to ease into it. Get a little more comfortable with us as a couple, *then* parade it around the school."

"Well, it's done now," Sara said. "All you can do is carry on from here."

"Exactly," Jelena said, stepping up to the counter to buy a heavy-looking statement necklace. "So a large number of people think you're accident-prone when it comes to mouth-to-mouth interactions—so what? You're still dating the guy who came in second in last year's High School Hotties poll. Stop whining already."

She had a point. A week ago I was agonizing over the possibility that I'd lost my chance with Hayden.

"So what now?" I asked.

"Well, the great thing is that Hayden's injured," Sara said triumphantly.

We all stared at her.

"And Hayden's lip being hideously lacerated is good because . . ." I gestured for her to go on.

"That baby's going to take a while to heal," Sara said. "So think of it as extra time to get your technique up and running. Then, in a couple of weeks, when Hayden's lower lip's hopefully back to its former state, you can make out with him and prove that kissing doesn't have to wind up lethal."

"Study the ancient art of lip-locking online," Jelena suggested.

"Do you know how much advice there is on the 'net for unkissed losers?"

I sighed. "Thanks, Jelena."

"How come you know that?" Lindsay asked her.

"Hey, I did my research years ago," Jelena said matter-of-factly. "That's part of the reason I am now Jefferson's equivalent of Helen of Troy . . ."

Sara rolled her eyes. "Jelena, your ego—"

I broke in before Sara could finish her obviously not-so-nice retort. "So the internet is my answer?"

"Expertise is a Google search away," Jelena replied. "Call me if you have any questions. We want to take you from Lethal Lips to Legendary Lips."

3

The girls and I parted ways and I headed farther uptown to meet my mother. She wanted to meet me in her favorite department store, as per usual. I felt guilty admitting this, but I experienced a constant low level of uneasiness whenever I was with my mother. It was hard to forget that she'd traded in the NAD and me for the glitterati set in Ibiza. There was nothing like being a twelve-year-old on the border of puberty and watching your dad Google Map a location where he thought your mother *might* be, after hearing her hurried voicemail from the international airport. Both the NAD and I had a rather negative relationship with electronic dance music for some time after her defection.

After three months went by and we both realized that Mom wasn't coming back from her impulsive vacation from her family, my normally unshakable dad broke down one night and threw our entire dance music collection off the back veranda. The next day, he arrived home with his arms full of meditation CDs, heralding the arrival of New Age dad. Unfortunately, many of our home furnishings also paid the price during the NAD's transition phase, meaning that our home was now a shrine to stark minimalism.

In the four years Mom was away, I kind of made peace with the fact that the beaches of the Mediterranean had claimed her forever. Mom was model-beautiful, and I guessed that parent–teacher meetings and school recitals were no match for lounging by the pool with her boyfriend, Carlos, one of Ibiza's most successful hotel and nightclub developers. She had her life and I had mine.

So when Mom and Carlos made the move back, three months ago, I honestly didn't know how to feel, much as I was the type to work toward forgiveness. Four years was a long time to gain back, and when I was around her I seemed to go instinctually into protection mode. Even so, the past few weeks had delivered a fair few knocks to my armor. Having her miss my theatrical debut in *Much Ado About Nothing* hurt far more than I'd expected, but that had been totally eclipsed on the emotional distress scale when I found out she hadn't even told Carlos that she *had* a daughter.

I shook my head, pushing away my annoyance as I entered the store. Mom *was* trying—she'd come clean to Carlos about my existence just this week. So I supposed progress was being made.

"Aurora!" Mom called from the Dior beauty counter. I gave her a wave as I headed over.

She was wearing an ivory silk camisole and beautifully cut slimline pants. Her hair was immaculate. My mother was the type of blonde that Alfred Hitchcock loved to cast in his films—impossibly elegant and ice-queen cool.

"You're looking well, darling." Mom put her arms around me.

I pulled away and tried not to look shocked. Mom was never a hugger.

"Carlos and I want you to join us for dinner sometime soon," Mom said, picking up her purchase and walking toward the store exit. "I can't say he's familiar with teenagers, but he's willing to put in the effort. I'm glad we've sorted out that nonsense from last week."

I tried not to feel insulted that my natural distress at being a nonentity to my mother's partner of two years was considered "nonsense."

"Why are we leaving?" I asked as we walked out of the store. Mom usually kept our catch-ups short, but this was pushing it.

"There's a boutique I want to take you to," she said, leading me across the road to a Victorian-style indoor arcade with lots of designer stores.

"Okay." This was familiar territory. My mother's way of showing her love generally revolved around ensuring that I was well dressed. She had prided herself on the fact that I was the only child in our neighborhood whose baby clothes were imported from Europe.

"I thought we'd try on some dresses this afternoon," she said.

"For what?" I replied, slightly uneasy. This wasn't another casting, was it? My mother was set on making me a model and had recently entered me into a Facebook modeling competition without my permission. I wouldn't put it past her to sneakily surprise me with a designer "go see."

"Don't make that face, darling." Mom pushed the button for the old-fashioned elevator. The door opened and she gave me a nudge inside. "It's a bit of a surprise, but I'm hoping you'll be happy about it."

Not again. I opened my mouth to launch into my *I don't want to be a model* monologue, but when the elevator doors parted again I lost my words. We were on the bridal level.

Mom swept out of the elevator.

"Obviously, you might have some mixed feelings about what I'm about to tell you," Mom said, "but I'm hoping you'll view my decision positively . . . You're almost seventeen now, and much more mature than when I first went away."

"Your decision?" My heart started pounding as I stared at the crystal-beaded bodices and Swarovski hairpieces twinkling in the shopwindows surrounding us.

"I'd like you to be happy for us, Aurora," Mom said firmly as she ushered me toward one of the boutiques.

"Us?" I was getting dizzy now.

"Carlos and me," Mom replied, sweeping me into the store.

I needed to sit down. Mom was getting married? The woman whose excuse for leaving her first marriage was that being a wife and mother "didn't come naturally" to her?

"He proposed on Bellbird Island the weekend I missed your play. We're getting married in six weeks. Bit of a whirlwind, but Carlos has got to be back in Ibiza for the European season."

Now I knew why she'd wanted to tell me alone. She didn't want me making a scene—i.e., staring in horror at the man I had no relationship with who was going to be my stepfather in approximately forty-two days.

"I suppose I'll have to tell your father, too."

"No," I managed to get out.

I pictured the NAD's face as he took my mother's out-of-the-blue call. Obviously, he'd moved on with his life in the past four years and no longer wanted Mom back, but the fact that she was reentering what she had formerly referred to as a "prison" (marriage) was totally going to throw him.

Plus, he was still getting over his recent breakup with the fickle Ms. DeForest, Jefferson High's interpretive dance teacher, who had not only made my life miserable with her highly embarrassing classes and enthusiastic issuing of detentions but had also brutally dumped Dad last Sunday after a tarot card reading. My mother's whirlwind nuptials were so not coming at a good time.

"Aurora, he'll have to know before the wedding. It's only fair."

Fair? She hadn't thought much about "fair" when she'd asked for a divorce via text message.

"I want to be the one to tell him," I blurted out, as the boutique assistant walked over to us. "Promise me you won't say anything."

"All right," Mom replied.

I could tell she wasn't thrilled but was willing to let me have my way if it ensured that I didn't throw a hissy fit. I didn't even feel capable of a tantrum. All the air needed for shouting had been knocked out of me.

"I want my daughter to try a few options for a bridesmaid's

gown," Mom said, as the assistant joined us. "This is the color palette I'm working with." She handed the assistant some samples in taupe, latte, and a light blush. "My gown is lace."

She already had her dress? Well, as I was yet to be introduced to the groom, it was only to be expected that my opinion wasn't needed on the gown.

I felt like I was under water as I watched Mom and the assistant (Annie, according to her name tag) walk along the racks, pulling out dresses for me. I could see their mouths moving, but my brain couldn't seem to process the words.

Annie nudged me into a fitting room with five or six dresses and began slipping the first over my head before I could protest. I tried to do up the little pearl buttons that fastened the bodice while she zipped up the back. My fingers trembled as the NAD's face popped into my mind. I didn't want to tell him. I wanted to suggest to Mom that she and Carlos get married in Ibiza—that way the NAD would never have to hear about it. Or see photographs in the social pages.

And yet the NAD was the only one capable of understanding how I felt right now. Mom hadn't wanted a family life with us, but Carlos was getting the go-ahead as husband? "Hurt" wasn't the word for it.

Annie pulled the door open so that Mom could see the first gown.

"Very elegant," Mom said, standing up from her seat and moving closer. "I like the length and cut, but I think I'd prefer a different material. What else do you have with the same low back?"

She and the assistant wandered away to look at more options.

We weren't going to discuss any of this further? I mean, obviously Carlos and Mom had made up their minds, but I'd have liked some time to come to terms with the idea. Instead, I was immediately being ushered into my new role as bridesmaid. Did Mom honestly think I'd be wholeheartedly toasting the happy couple in just six weeks?

I couldn't deal with the idea of standing around playing dress-up while my mind was close to meltdown, so I quickly slipped the dress off and put my own clothes back on. As I stepped out of the fitting room, I saw that Mom and Annie were in consultation over gowns on the other side of the showroom. I slipped out the door and took the elevator back down to street level.

As I walked away from the arcade and toward the bus stop to go home, I felt my phone pulsing against the side of my handbag. Mom had obviously discovered the empty room. I ignored the phone and got on the bus, slumping into a seat. Not answering was obviously going to irritate Mom, but right now I needed respite.

Unfortunately, when I got home the house wasn't empty. The NAD worked crazy hours, par for the course as the creative director of an advertising agency, so I was used to being home alone a lot of the time. But as I came in the door, I could hear that not only was the NAD home at a reasonable time but also he had company.

"Dad?" I called as I went toward the living room.

Two women and one man, plus the NAD, all wearing white, were sitting in a circle on the carpet. The NAD had set up on the coffee table the Himalayan salt crystal lamp that he'd ordered from YourSacredSpace.com.

One of the women, wearing a large turquoise pendant, was addressing the group. "So our aim today is to remind ourselves of the Acceptance Principles."

"Aurora!"

The NAD leaped up from his cross-legged pose as he spotted me in the doorway, presumably looking slightly unnerved. I'd become used to witnessing the NAD's and Ms. DeForest's alternative practices while they'd been dating, but a group session under our roof was new to me.

"Come join our sharing circle, honey!" the NAD said, and the group made a space for me on the floor. "This is Echo, Primrose, and Igneous."

I tried my hardest not to react to the names, but I couldn't help myself with the last one. "Igneous?"

"Like igneous rock, meaning 'born from fire,'" Igneous replied.

"My ex-wife burned the man formerly known as Ian down to nothing. Igneous was what was left in the scorched landscape that was the end of my marriage."

I sat down numbly after the besiegement of information about the volcanic end to Ian/Igneous's relationship. I wasn't sure what else to do. Leaving would be pretty insensitive.

The NAD reached over and patted my knee. "I should explain, honey. This is a sharing circle, so Igneous is in a state of total openness right now."

I gave him what I hoped wasn't an uneasy smile. Obviously, these people were, like the NAD, trying to come to terms with life's disappointments. I couldn't pass judgment on them, no matter how much the oversharing unsettled me. After all, it was healthier to express your emotions than to bottle them up. I just felt thankful that the NAD hadn't given himself a new name after he'd signed the divorce papers. Imagine if I'd had to start calling him Basalt or something.

Igneous let out a shuddering sigh. Obviously, the scorched landscape was still in pretty bad shape.

Echo took his left hand. "Igneous, we are interconnected in this sharing circle, just as we are in this existence. We have all known suffering. We all have known loss. What you are feeling is part of the larger human experience. Let's all join hands."

Suddenly I found my hands grasped by the NAD and Primrose.

"Coming to acceptance does not mean denying the pain we have felt in losing what was once precious to us," Echo continued. "Coming to acceptance means that we acknowledge the inherent uncertainty that is life. It means letting go of our attachment to expected outcomes and letting ourselves trust in the wisdom of the greater experience."

This was tough stuff. I wasn't sure if I was *able* to trust in the wisdom of the greater experience when it came to Mom's latest decision. Maybe I should drop the whole *Mom's getting remarried!* bomb as part of the sharing circle. The NAD was in a caring space here. We could all hold hands and get him through the initial emotional carnage.

"She took the dog!" Igneous said, weeping now. "And our Deepak Chopra collection!"

Okay, I'd wait until Igneous had finished riding the wave of loss.

"Igneous, I know what you're going through," the NAD said. "When Avery left, I felt like the ground underneath me had split open. The terror of moving forward kept me stuck straddling the fault line between my old life and my new one for a very long time."

I looked at him, shocked. The past was generally a no-go zone in this house. Obviously the NAD was entering fully into the spirit of the sharing circle. Maybe it was a sign from the universe that I should share too.

The moment the NAD stopped speaking, I would launch into an account of this afternoon's events. Otherwise I'd lose my nerve.

"The only way I came to acceptance of the situation was to see that her leaving wasn't a reflection on my ability to be loved," the NAD continued. "It wasn't *our* marriage Avery didn't want—she didn't want a marriage with anyone. She saw a shared life as an unwanted bond."

I snapped my mouth shut.

In just a few short sentences, I could have sliced through the ropes of the bridge the NAD had built to carry him safely into his new life! I wasn't going to destroy his illusions while his shaky self-confidence was still recovering from Ms. DeForest's decision to dump him.

"You've got to do the grieving work," the NAD said to Igneous, who was curled up into a ball, with his head resting on his knees. "And that takes time. Appropriately mourning the loss of the relationship will allow you to slowly cut the karmic cords between you and Lily."

Time. I should give the NAD a while longer to mourn the loss of Ms. DeForest before reopening the wounds left by my mother. After all, the wedding wasn't for six weeks. Perhaps I could use the time to slowly start hinting that Mom was now pro legally binding ties. Make some offhand comments about how happy she and Carlos were.

Ugh. I needed some time to adjust to the idea, too. It was probably best that I came to grips with my own negative emotions before I broke the news to the NAD. The last thing I wanted to do was saddle him with my pain on top of his.

The NAD got up from the circle. "I've got some rose quartz upstairs. It's a heart chakra crystal, so it helps clear pain related to separation and divorce. I'll be back down in a minute."

I stood up too and followed the NAD. I couldn't stay in the sharing circle—I felt like I was lying to the NAD's face by keeping Mom's news from him while everyone else was laying bare their soul wounds.

"Dad, do you mind if I excuse myself? I've got a history essay I have to start researching."

"No problem, honey. I know the circle can be an intense space for a beginner. I hope you'll join us again sometime—we're hoping to make it a regular Friday night thing. By the way, do you know what happened to the coffee table? I found big blocks of wax melted onto it."

I couldn't tell the NAD about my foiled seduction scene. Thankfully, he'd been traveling for business last night, so I'd been spared the embarrassment of having him drive Hayden and me to the hospital. I was pretty close to my dad, but not close enough to share my Lethal Lips moment with him. I gave him my blankest look.

He shook his head and sighed. "Must have been the cats knocking things over again. I should have listened when you suggested sending Snookums to feline obedience school. It would have been worth the hefty admittance fee."

What kind of person *was* I? I'd damaged our coffee table *and* my boyfriend's face and let my cats take the rap.

4

Despite the disaster of my second shot at kissing, I had high hopes for Saturday night. I was optimistic that a double date with my best friend and Hayden's best friend (i.e., Cassie and Scott) would help to dissipate the awkwardness between Hayden and me. I envisioned lots of laughs as we two couples respectively cozied up at an outdoor movie. However, here we were, lounging on picnic blankets, and Cassie's new shoes were closer to Hayden than I was.

Things had started well. Cassie, Scott, Hayden, and I had met up at the deli and bought picnic food, then had a great time laughing and talking as we walked through the botanic gardens and down to the bay, where the outdoor movie was to be screened. Lindsay and Tyler had decided to join us at the last moment, so we'd spread out two large blankets on a slope where we'd get a good view. Cassie and Scott had immediately intertwined themselves on one half of a rug—Cass lay back in Scott's arms and assembled Camembert cheese crackers on a plastic plate in her lap, reaching back intermittently to feed him. Even their feet were crossed over each other, so that every limb was in constant contact.

"That's impressive," Lindsay whispered to me as she started pouring soft drinks for everyone. "A week in and they've got synchronized snacking down to an easy art. You watch though—there'll be more whispering of sweet nothings and ear nibbling going on than actual eating."

"Ear nibbling?" I stared at Lindsay. "At this stage?"

"Time and experience teach you many things," Lindsay said, shaking her head. "The predictable course of early stage PDAs is one of them."

She nodded toward Cassie and Scott.

"This is what I call the domino effect. Watch—she's stroking his palm with her thumb. He'll take it up a notch in about ten seconds."

We watched as Scott pulled Cass's thumb to his lips and kissed it.

"She'll respond in kind now," Lindsay said, handing me my lemonade. "It's the unspoken rule of new relationships. It's like Newton's third law—every action has an equal and opposite reaction."

I was seriously impressed by Lindsay's perceptiveness. When I turned my hand to writing my dating guidebook, I was going to use her as a consultant. I was familiar with courting rituals, but I needed to develop my expertise in new-couple practices. So far, my own experiences would only provide content for a special section on "dating don'ts."

I watched as Cass took Scott's other hand and kissed the tip of each finger.

"Here's where the momentum quickens," Lindsay said.

Scott pulled Cass even closer, smothering the side of her neck with kisses. She giggled.

"And here we go," Lindsay said. "It's unstoppable now."

Cass turned her face up toward Scott's and *bang!* They were smooching. The plate of almost untouched crackers teetered precariously on Cassie's lap, then fell as she twisted herself backward in the throes of the kiss.

"Here's where they attract public disapproval," Lindsay said, pointing out an old couple who were frowning at Cass and Scott.

"The lovebirds won't pick up on the stares, though. They've disappeared into a bystander-free alternate-reality world where a five-minute snog equates to a quick peck in their befuddled minds."

"So you're officially no longer befuddled?" I didn't want to pry, but I was concerned about what was going on with Lindsay and Tyler. They'd gone from verging-on-permanently-fused finger lacing to negligible contact.

Lindsay shrugged. "I don't know. I haven't felt the high I used to since we got back together. There was the brief, heady relief of our reconciliation, but since then it's like the buzz has gone."

"A relationship doesn't have to be a roller coaster all the time," I said. "You and Tyler have transitioned over the years. Think of it this way: you've become a merry-go-round!"

Lindsay gave me a look. "We're the ride that triggers little to no adrenaline?"

"No!" I shook my head violently. "You've done the rounds of coupledom enough times to know each other's strengths and weaknesses, inside out.

"Love is more than just falling in love," I went on. I looked at Cass and Scott, who were now indulging in Eskimo kisses. "Anyone can be giddy in the first few months, thanks to the way nature throws all those potent *can't stop thinking about you* chemicals around, but to still get excited about seeing each other three years down the road—like I know you and Tyler do when you have a day or two apart—that's a beautiful thing."

"Linds!" Tyler called from the other picnic blanket. "The movie's about to start." He patted the spot next to him.

Hayden, who'd been having a chat with Tyler while they cut up the bread and cheeses, got up and headed over to our picnic blanket.

"I better get over there," Lindsay said. "Thanks for the pep talk, Aurora."

Lindsay took Tyler's drink over to him. He took it from her and put his arm around her waist to pull her in for a cuddle. Lindsay let him, but I could see she was distractedly scrolling through her phone. That was worrying. I let out a sigh.

Hayden gave me a concerned look as he sat down beside me. "Your hand isn't hurting, is it? I've got painkillers here if you need them. And some anti-inflammatories. And some burn salve, if you need to change the dressing. The hospital gave me a bunch of things."

Hayden pulled out packet after packet from his pockets. Any moment now I was expecting him to produce topical antiseptic in a hip flask.

"You've been on painkillers?"

"Only to help me sleep, the first night or two, and to take down the swelling a little. But I didn't want to get caught out tonight if I needed them."

My concern must have been obvious, because before I'd even uttered one syllable of *I'm sorry. What can I do?*, Hayden leaped to reassure me.

"Princess, it's nothing." He gave me a grin. "It's not like I'm sporting war wounds or anything."

"Mommy, why is that boy's lip so big?" A little boy, heading up the hill with his parents, who were heaving a huge picnic basket, pointed at Hayden.

"Ben! No pointing!" The mother pulled the boy's hand down and sent us an apologetic look.

Ben kept looking back at Hayden as his mom dragged him up the hill. "But it's huge!" He threw his arms out to demonstrate just how grotesquely swollen Hayden's lip was.

"Okay, obviously a small war wound." Hayden laughed awkwardly.

"No, Hayden—"

I stopped as a group of preteens wandered by and did a so-not-subtle double take at the sight of Hayden's face, which now wore no hint of his former grin. Did kids have *no* manners these days?

"Thankfully, the sun will set soon and the Hunchback of Notre

Dame will be hidden from view," Hayden said as the preteens finally passed by.

Less than a week of dating and I was officially responsible for Hayden deeming himself Quasimodo? Soon he'd be locking himself up in a tower. Should I take his hand? Try and talk him out of it? Tell him I was sorry for the twelve hundredth time?

Just as I reached out to take his hand, Hayden moved away from me, claiming the spot near Cassie's shoes. He was actually widening the distance between us.

Tyler and Lindsay both looked at me, surprised. I felt a lump appear in my throat and stared at the picnic rug as a flush bloomed over my face. I'd never imagined that any date would turn his back on me. Especially not Hayden, whose level of chivalry generally bordered on that of the uber knight, Lancelot.

Fortunately, the movie started at that moment and I willed myself to focus on the opening credits. Three days ago, watching *Love Actually* with Hayden, my bestie, and her date had seemed like a dream idea. Now I found myself cursing the fact that we'd talked the boys out of the action movie they'd wanted to see. All the *aw*-inducing moments being played out on the giant outdoor screen only served to highlight the awkwardness of the situation. My entire being seemed focused on Hayden's back, willing him to turn around, to exhibit some kind of recognition that I was his date.

I got my wish at one point—Hayden gave me a half-smile when he turned around to grab the mineral water—but it only served to make me feel worse than if he hadn't looked my way at all. I'd foolishly hoped he was turning to reach for my hand instead of the Evian.

I was selfishly relieved when Lindsay came crawling over in the semidarkness, halfway through the film.

"Tyler's chewing *so* loudly!" she said. "It's driving me nuts!"

Obviously, the flame of romance was far from reignited. I looked over at Tyler, who was obliviously munching away on a huge baguette stuffed with salami.

At that moment, the movie stopped for intermission, and the harborside lamps switched on, flooding the area with light. Cass and Scott, midkiss yet again, blinkingly pulled away from each other. Cassie giggled as she wiped berry-pink lipstick off Scott's cheek.

"Thank god." Lindsay stood up. "I'm going for dessert. Anyone want ice cream from the vendor guy?"

"We'll share," Scott said. He kept staring into Cassie's eyes as he absently handed over a fifty-dollar bill.

"Okay, well, that should just about cover the one ice cream," Lindsay said wryly.

"Drumstick, right?" I asked Hayden as I leaped up. No way was I staying here while Cass and Scott made out and Hayden and I pretended to study the halftime ads.

"I'll come with you." Tyler started wrapping the remaining half of the baguette in a plastic bag for later.

"No need!" Lindsay dashed down the hill, dragging me behind her, before poor Tyler could stand up.

"Obviously not just the baguette?" I asked as we got in line for ice cream.

"Salami-scented breath does not equal a happy date." Lindsay studied the ice cream choices on the board. "I don't understand how he can expect to have one arm around me and be brandishing a hideous-smelling sandwich in his other hand. He knows I hate salami. Does he literally think I'll put up with anything?"

Ah, so that was it.

"You're still angry that he broke up with you," I said.

"Yes and no. I don't know. I don't want to talk about it," Lindsay replied.

"But you can't ignore your feelings—"

"Four Dove bars and a Drumstick," Lindsay said as we reached the front of the line.

I gave up. I didn't want to upset Lindsay on our triple date. I'd just have to work out a subtle stirring-of-passions strategy to accelerate the TylerandLindsay merry-go-round just a little bit.

"Well, at least the date's going well for Cass," I said, as we headed back to the others.

Lindsay paused under one of the lamps lining the foreshore. "There's still another five minutes of intermission."

"You're right," I said, thinking of the three hundred awkward seconds I'd have to bear once I returned to Hayden.

We both let out a sigh.

"Well, we're certainly enthusiastic about our dates," Lindsay said with a short laugh.

"In my case, it's my date who's not enthusiastic about me," I replied. "At least Tyler's sitting beside you. I'm betting that Hayden would construct an isolation chamber if he had access to any materials."

"I'm the one in need of an isolation chamber," Lindsay said, opening her ice cream. "My entire picnic rug smells like a butcher shop."

"Dream date this is not." I opened my own ice cream and took solace in the chocolate shell.

"Aurora, I think Hayden's just self-conscious. Did you see how many people did a double take as they walked by?"

"Self-conscious, or just scared I'll deal out another blow," I said.

"No, it's the former," Lindsay said firmly. "Imagine if you were in his shoes, navigating a public picnic date with painful Mick Jagger–like lips."

"But why turn away from me?"

Lindsay shrugged. "He's probably worried that if he cozies up to you, you'll become the target of cruel stares as well, so he's bearing it alone on the outer edge of the picnic blanket."

Now I felt terrible for being annoyed at him earlier.

"But I'm proud to be with him!" I said.

"Then reassure him of that. Extend a hand; show him that you're willing to sit beside the boy with the swollen lip." Lindsay checked her watch. "We'd better go."

I walked up the hill with a newfound purpose. Compassion and care were my imperatives now.

I handed Hayden his ice cream.

"Thanks, Princess." His eyes brightened as he took the Drumstick from me and began to unwrap it. Seeing his eyes flicker from greeny-gold to almost topaz, I knew. He didn't want to be banished to sitting by Cassie's ballet flats. He'd done it because he'd believed that was best for me. Before I could overthink it, I sat down next to him, leaving a two-inch gap between us. If that didn't show him I was willing to join him in his humiliation, then nothing would.

Hayden's eyebrows went up a fraction in surprise.

"It felt silly to be over there alone," I said, "when I wanted to be here with you."

I felt slightly teary. Could Hayden really believe that I'd willingly separate myself from him because of a little public gawking? I supposed four years of me treating him like the bane of my life had left him with lingering doubts when it came to my regard for him. But after our highly emotional acknowledgments in the auditorium on Monday, I'd hoped he would see how much I was willing to lay my heart on the line for him. Our fledgling relationship surely wasn't so fragile that one not-so-ideal date could spell the end—was it?

I felt an overwhelming eagerness to share everything with Hayden, to let him in, little by little, to the world that was mine. It was a world that he'd known inside out, as my childhood playmate, before I'd drawn the curtains on our friendship, following my mother's sudden departure. Four years. It felt like yesterday and forever ago at the same time.

The last day my mother had been, in truth, my mother (i.e., residing within our family unit, not out of cell phone, email, and Facebook contact for twelve-month periods at a time), she'd asked me to spend the afternoon with her. It was an unusual request—she'd never been big on bonding time—but I'd chosen to go over to Hayden's instead. His pool had just been finished and he and I were dying to try it out. The next day, she was gone. A hurried message on the answering machine was all the NAD and I had left of her. After that, seeing Hayden, hearing his voice, or even the mention of his name, was a reminder of the oh-so-fragile moment when I might have kept my family together. Like the NAD, it had taken me close to four years to come to some kind of forgiveness—of my mother, but also of myself.

I felt like those four years of lost opportunities were there in my eyes as I looked back at Hayden.

His lower lip stretched into a smile—as much as it could with three stitches. "I've wanted to be sitting next to you for about an eon!"

"Well, we're here now," I said. "Let's not waste another second, in case the next date is four years coming!"

We laughed, but my words seemed to sit like a palpable presence between us.

"I'm not letting that happen ever again," Hayden said, his tone serious.

We held each other's gaze steadily, as if giving further confirmation to our assurances. Every other sound became just a low buzz somewhere beyond the seclusion of our shared world. Lindsay had been exactly right. The "alternate world" exclusive to couples really did seem to operate in a different time zone.

That is, until it was shattered by a third party.

"Great movie, huh?" Tyler said, popping up behind us. He grabbed our shoulders and pushed us forcefully together.

Hayden was thrown off balance. He threw out a hand to stop himself from body-slamming into me. Unfortunately, the hand he chose was the one holding the Drumstick. I tried to move, but there was no hope—seconds later I felt the cold ice cream smoosh into the side of my head. I flung a hand up to my vanilla-streaked hair and my Dove bar tumbled out of my hand and bounced onto Hayden's white shorts, scattering shards of chocolate onto his thigh and lap.

"Tyler, what is wrong with you?" Lindsay yelled, yanking a hugely embarrassed Tyler to his feet.

"I felt bad for them, babe!" Unfortunately, his whisper was loud enough for Hayden and me to hear. "You said you wanted to get them closer, so that's what I was trying to do."

"I never said for you to literally knock their heads together!" Lindsay hissed.

Now I felt even worse. Not only were Hayden and I an object of pity to other couples but also the mishaps of my love life were causing my friends to drive their relationship onto the rocks of blame and resentment.

"Sit down!" came a shout from behind us, as the second half of the movie started.

We probably looked like a bunch of teenage troublemakers, what with Cass and Scott's fervent PDAs, Tyler and Lindsay shouting at each other, and Hayden's swollen lip.

"Babe, I don't know," Tyler sighed, handing Hayden and me wet napkins to wipe the remnants of our respective ice creams off our skin and clothes. "All I was trying to do was make you happy. Just tell me exactly what you want me to do and I'll do it!"

Lindsay didn't answer. She sat down next to me, her arms crossed firmly against her chest. I could see her eyes had tears in them.

"I don't know what I want anymore," she whispered, just loudly enough so that only I could hear her.

5

"I want the date lowdown!" Sara said as she joined Cass, Lindsay, and me outside the auditorium. We were catching up on our respective weekends, prior to the start of the assembly. Sara was virtually shaking invisible maracas with enthusiasm.

I paused, at a loss as to how to sum up Saturday night. I glanced at Cass and Lindsay.

Lindsay and Cass looked at each other, but didn't open their mouths.

"Come on, Aurora," Sara said, rubbing her palms together in anticipation.

I just had to get this over with. "We ended up coated in chocolate and ice cream."

"Woo!" Sara semi-shrieked, punching the air. "Aurora! Way to start up the spice!"

A number of our classmates turned to look at us.

"You pulled out chocolate body paint on a group date?" Sara asked, fractionally lowering her voice.

"No!" I cried. "The chocolate wasn't intentional!"

"You had some Hershey's and got creative at halftime?" Sara closed her eyes and put on her best sultry voice. *"Aurora lifted up*

Hayden's shirt oh so slowly, revealing his chiseled abdominal muscles. He let out a low moan as she took the chocolate-dipped paintbrush and traced the bristles over his tanned skin—"

"Why would she have a paintbrush with her at the outdoor movies?" Lindsay interrupted.

Sara paused for a second. "Okay, start again. *Aurora lifted up Hayden's shirt oh so slowly, revealing his chiseled abdominal muscles. She reached for the rapidly melting row of chocolate beside her and traced it over his tanned skin . . ."*

I buried my head in my hands. One wrongly phrased sentence and my friends were off on a chocolate-themed fantasy sequence.

"Aurora warmed the row in her hands, then lifted a chocolate-dipped finger to Hayden's lips—"

I cut in. "Can I just bring us all back to reality before this thing gets really weird and say that there was no bare chest, chiseled abs, or chocolate-dipped fingers? The only place chocolate got smeared—and I'm using a nonsexy term for a reason—was on Hayden's pants."

Sara spat out the water she'd just sipped from her Evian bottle.

"How have you waited till now to spill this story?" she asked. "This is like sealed-section *Cosmo*."

She seriously thought this was what I got up to in public? I was the girl who'd never been kissed until last week!

"Tyler pushed us together, Hayden's ice cream went into my hair, and my ice cream fell into his lap," I said in a rush. "It was awkward, sticky, and the furthest thing from a turn-on."

Sara's face was the picture of disappointment.

"I spent more time with Lindsay than with anyone else at the picnic," I added. "Cass had to do the kissing for all of us."

Cass blushed. "Aurora, it wasn't that bad, was it?"

But I wasn't listening to Cass anymore. My attention was distracted by the sight of Jelena running toward us.

"This is it!" she said breathlessly as she reached us, her normally cool tones up an octave. "This is where it all begins!"

"Where *what* begins?" Lindsay asked.

"Seduction on a grand scale." Jelena's eyes were bright with excitement.

"You're targeting a guy who's in college?" Sara guessed.

"This has nothing to do with *boys*," Jelena said archly. "This is about swaying the masses."

We all looked at her blankly.

"I'm having serious doubts about allowing any of you fuzzy-headed people onto my campaign team," Jelena said, rolling her eyes. "School president elections?"

"The elections are starting already?" Lindsay asked. "How can you run for school president when you're a junior?"

Jelena stared at her. "You seriously know nothing about student government?"

"Not all of us are wannabe Napoleons," Sara said.

Jelena ignored her. "The changeover of school president happens at the end of third semester, when the seniors go into their study break prior to their final exams. Obviously, the outgoing president makes the graduation speech for their year and all that, but they don't have time to be as involved in the day-to-day politics of the school. So that's when the new president starts to take the reins a little more, before the school falls entirely under their command the next year."

"'Under their command'?" I raised an eyebrow.

"Well, in essence," Jelena said, examining her ice-blue manicure. "There's the usual tier of vice president, treasurer, class representatives, et cetera, but the main power lies with the president."

She noticed my expression. "Don't give me that look, Aurora. I'm not talking about despotism."

"Is Hayden running?" Cassie asked me.

I looked over to where Hayden had taken a seat with the other student council members. He'd been on the council pretty much since we'd started high school and had organized plenty of charity days, assemblies, and award nights over the past three years.

Sara sighed. "He'd look great on the electoral posters. Totally Kennedy-esque."

"Hey!" Jelena hit Sara with her leather-bound Tiffany notebook. "You can't be swayed by my political opponents' hotness. You're meant to be gunning for Team Jelena!"

"Hayden isn't running," I said. "He loves being on the council, but he thinks being school president is too much on top of aiming for a ninety-eight-plus score in his finals."

"What does he want the score for?" Cassie asked.

"International law," I replied. "You know, an extension of his whole James Bond, saving-the-world thing."

"Okay, Hayden's out of the running." Jelena rubbed her hands together. "Brilliant. One less adversary to slay."

Sara looked at her uneasily. "You sound like you're quoting from *The Hunger Games*. I'm not sure this is the greatest idea."

I pictured Jelena tearing toward the other candidates, scythe in hand, her eyes steely.

Jelena shrugged. "Hey, politics is a contact sport. It can get rough at times."

"Why now?" Cass asked. "You haven't run for class president in previous years."

"I didn't want to exert too much energy too early on," Jelena replied. "Plus, this way I'm a dark horse. Our schoolmates know that I've been involved in organizing everything from sports days to drama productions, but no one knows my personal policies, so when I finally reveal my agenda, I can blow everyone away."

"What are your personal policies?" Lindsay asked.

"You will see, my friends, you will see," Jelena replied mysteriously. "So, on to practicalities. Besides the duties I'd naturally expect my best friends to fulfill in the crucial phase ahead—"

Sara snickered. "*Duties* meaning 'slavedom.'"

Jelena didn't bother to correct Sara's probably accurate assumption. "I'm thinking I'll need two of you on a more-or-less full-time basis during the election period. Aurora, I'm psyched to use you because of your way with words. You know, Frederick the Great had Voltaire. Men and women in elevated stations need someone to keep them connected to the hearts and minds of the common people."

"OMG." Sara buried her head in her hands.

"'Common people' isn't exactly the best term," I replied, trying not to laugh. "We kind of want the student body to think you're *of* the people, not above them."

"You see!" Jelena grabbed my arm. "You're working your wordsmith magic already!"

All flattery aside, I had to admit that Jelena's enthusiasm was contagious. She was right: someone needed to lead the school in a positive direction. I hated to say it, but there was a lot of complacency among our student body. I'd seen Jelena's take-charge attitude in action in her recent role as stage manager of *Much Ado About Nothing*, and the production had been a spectacular success. A little tweaking of her tendency toward condescension and we would have a dynamic leader on our hands.

"I don't know about wielding words as masterfully as Voltaire, but I'm in," I replied, giving Jelena a grin.

"You won't regret this, Aurora. The schoolyard is a training ground for the boardrooms to come."

The bell sounded to call us into the assembly. But instead of following us, Jelena sprinted off in the opposite direction, toward the wood shop.

Knowing Jelena, she'd probably used her persuasion skills on the office staff to let her make more efficient use of the hour it usually took Mr. Quinten to deliver the results of the latest soccer match, summarize the highlights of the autumn fair, and run through the usual sprinkling of award giving. In other words, she was probably heading off to sit under a tree in the courtyard and listen to a motivational podcast while giving herself a manicure, and checking the time off as a study period.

"Okay, everyone, please take your seats!" Mr. Quinten's voice boomed over the microphone as we filed into the auditorium. "First matter on the agenda: the upcoming school president elections. I have the list of those campaigning to be our leader next year. Our first candidate is Julie Rivers!"

That wasn't a surprise. Julie had been gunning for school president since the day she'd learned the word "leader" in first grade. She had been school president at our primary school, class president in seventh, eighth, and tenth grades, and was already captain of the Endeavor athletic club.

We all applauded duly.

"Second campaigner: our always-gives-it-his-all Matt Stevens!"

Now, *that* was a surprise. I would have expected Matt Stevens, Jefferson's undisputed sports star, to spend his final year focusing on his goal of turning professional athlete. You almost never saw him without a protein shake in his hand.

"People, it's time to get motivated!" Matt yelled, doing a flying long jump over the two people sitting between him and the aisle. "On the field, in the water, academically, I'm all about results. Results are one percent inspiration and ninety-nine percent perspiration. And I can assure you, I'm gonna sweat for this school!"

"Ew!" Amber Jenkins, a couple of seats down from me, wrinkled her nose.

Matt did a backflip in the aisle as members of the football team leaped up from their spots across the auditorium and ran toward him. They got into a huddle before busting out into a triumphant group air punch and yelling, "Get motivated!"

"He'll probably do squats while he delivers his election speech," Sara said wryly.

"Okay, boys, exciting stuff, but let's keep it for the official campaign trail—there are several weeks ahead of us." Mr. Quinten gave Matt and his team an indulgent smile as he gestured for them to take their seats. "Third candidate is . . . Jelena Cantrill!"

The auditorium doors flew open to reveal Jelena, looking illustrious in a flowing imperial-purple gown, perched atop a Roman-style lectica—a chair with its legs lashed to long wooden poles—that had been spray-painted gold. Four members of the rowing team carried the contraption, and Jelena, on their shoulders. They were accompanied by two members of the school's orchestra, beating out a rhythm on bongo drums, and Meg Frankel, playing an Asian-sounding tune on her flute. Smoke rose from scented incense sticks positioned on either side of Jelena. After pausing for dramatic effect, the party slowly and ceremoniously made its way down the aisle, to cheers and whistles from the crowd.

Sara stared at the lectica. "So this is what the boys in my woodworking class have been working on for the past week."

I'd thought it odd when I found Jelena speed-reading Shakespeare's *Antony and Cleopatra* during break last week, but her reason for studying act 2, scene 2 was abundantly clear now. It might not be on a barge, but the golden lectica was certainly akin to Cleopatra's "burnished throne."

"Wow, I didn't know Jelena was running. Now I have to choose between Matt and the Goddess," said one of the football team members, sitting just to our right. He looked torn at the prospect.

"Matt's a great guy but, man, I have to admit I'd prefer to watch Jelena give all the speeches for the next year," another team member replied.

I was betting that although the football team had publicly pledged themselves to Matt, Jelena could count on a high number of secret votes from that sector.

The lectica reached our row. We all let out a cheer and Jelena tossed white rose petals our way as a tribute.

Jeffrey Clark bowed deeply as the lectica traveled past. "Thou shalt be my queen!"

Jelena blew Jeffrey a kiss and he mock-fainted. Travis Ela caught him and heaved him back into his seat, simultaneously bowing to the lectica in servitude. There was no doubt that Jelena knew how to win over a crowd.

The lectica reached the stage and the rowers lowered it to the ground. Jamie reached out a hand to help Jelena from her seat. As she made her way to the microphone, the drummers and flautist stopped playing. Jelena raised her hands to command silence from the cheering crowd.

"Seventy thousand two hundred," Jelena uttered as the auditorium went quiet.

"Is that a code?" someone whispered in the row behind us.

"This is all feeling very cultlike," Sara said, shaking her head.

"Hey, at least she's stirring souls," I whispered. This was the most enthused I'd seen our schoolmates since the day we'd won pre–summer break Ben & Jerry's ice cream.

"That's approximately how many minutes a year we spend at school," Jelena went on.

A chorus of groans rang out across the auditorium.

"Multiply that by four—the number of years we spend in high school—and that's two hundred and eighty thousand eight hundred minutes of our lives spent at Jefferson."

"Classmates, I have a dream!" Jeffrey shouted. "To live free!"

"Mr. Clark, this is Ms. Cantrill's speech, not yours!" Mr. Quinten looked uneasy. He was probably fearing a revolution.

"As Jeffrey says," Jelena continued, "we all have a dream to be free. But, for most of us, freedom will not come until we have a diploma. For some of you, that may be later this year. For others, it may be closer to four years away."

There were more groans.

"I can't bear it!" Travis mock-sobbed, his head in his hands.

"But, as your school president, I could offer you an escape!" Jelena cried, her voice triumphant. "We may be confined here at Jefferson for six hours a day, but I would transform the cage that encloses us." She paused for effect. "What I want to give you is a truly luxuriant high school experience."

Everyone was quiet.

"Yes, I care about amping up our charity work," Jelena said. "I care about ensuring the food choices available from our cafeteria give you the best chance for a hot body."

That was met with a cheer.

"But I also care about feeding your souls. Giving you moments of play and pleasure among the drudgery. That's why I'm inviting you to a decadent event this Friday night, to give you a taste of what a year under my leadership would be like."

"Oh, I'll be under your leadership anytime!" Rob Nelson bellowed from the row behind us. Sara clutched her ears in pain. "You just tell me your bidding, baby!"

"Not only will your senses be enthralled and your stomachs filled, but everyone who attends the event will also have the chance to participate in one of my beneficial programs," Jelena went on. "I am offering three attendees the opportunity to take part in the trademarked Find a Prince/Princess program, run by the brilliant and visionary Aurora Skye."

What?

Lindsay, Sara, and Cassie all turned to stare at me.

"I didn't know your program was part of the campaign," Cass said.

"I didn't either," I whispered, not wanting anyone to overhear. I might be in shock, but I was still on Jelena's election team, and I didn't want to suggest any lack of planning on her part.

"I don't know if it's a good idea to take advice from Lethal Lips!" someone yelled out.

The crowd erupted into laughter.

I wanted to hide under my seat. Instead, I used all my focus to stare straight ahead and appear poised, as if Jelena unleashing my program on the entire school had been jointly planned.

Sara craned her neck to see who'd yelled out. "It sounded like Daniel Benis," she said.

Okay, so Daniel *had* been stabbed in the eye earlier this year, during one of my Operation Stop Kiss maneuvers, so he might be lacking faith when it came to my dating practices. Still, he didn't have to share it with the entire school!

Jelena gave Daniel a disparaging look. "If you know what's good for you, you'll do away with that ridiculous nickname. Aurora Skye is responsible for bringing together two of this school's golden couples: the legendary TylerandLindsay, and our equivalent of Zayn and Gigi—Cassie and Scott."

A bunch of people turned to stare at Cassie. She blushed.

"Evidently Aurora knows her stuff," Jelena continued, and I heard people murmur agreement. "Her program will be made public in a few weeks, but before then, three lucky people will enjoy the benefits of her expertise, without the hefty price tag."

Hefty price tag? Sure, I had an empire to build, but I hadn't planned to start by charging through the nose.

"I offer you all the opportunity to see your school, as you know it, utterly transformed," Jelena finished triumphantly. "Thank you for your support, and I'll see you on Friday night."

She blew the crowd a kiss and took a bow. The auditorium curtains dramatically swooped closed. Mr. Quinten, unprepared, had to leap off the stage to avoid being hit by the heavy red drapes.

"Uh, thank you, Jelena," he said. "We hadn't planned on speeches, but that one was very theatrical."

Jelena gave him a queenly wave as she made her way down the stairs to the auditorium floor.

6

"Jelena, we have to talk," I whispered, as soon as she sat down with us. "That was a fabulous speech, but roping in my matchmaking program?"

"We'll discuss details after the assembly," Jelena said. "It's confidential material."

"That's what I mean! Only you guys knew about the program—I was waiting for the ideal time to launch it."

Jelena smiled. "Precisely! This is the perfect platform. There's a new movement sweeping in, Aurora, and you're a part of it."

"I know there's going to be a lot of attention because of the campaign, but in terms of ideal timing, I meant a moment when my dating foibles weren't still fresh in everyone's minds. You heard Daniel Benis."

Jelena rolled her eyes. "He's just bitter you wound up with Hayden—everyone knows that. Anyway, let's leave this till after the assembly. I don't want the masses having access to any of our brilliant ideas ahead of schedule."

Schedule? Just how detailed was Jelena's plan?

"Your entrance was captivating," Lindsay told Jelena.

"I loved your speech," Cassie said. "Except for the part about me and Scott—that was a little embarrassing."

"Cass, don't you want your love to spread its light and benefit others?" Jelena said. "You're a shining example of what the masses can hope for."

Sara shook her head. "Okay—masses? And that chariot thing you rode in on?"

"Lectica," Jelena said. "I was aiming for an ancient Roman feel—the ancient world is where democracy began."

"I thought you were meant to be of the people," Sara said, "not above them."

"Regal bearing shouldn't be taken for arrogance, Sara."

"You had *slaves* supporting your body weight!" Sara objected.

"They were willing participants," Jelena shot back.

Sara gave her a look. "Willing?"

"I hired them," Jelena replied. "The money came out of my campaign budget. I've been setting aside funds since seventh grade. I'm not about serfdom; fair wages keep people from rioting. I have Russian ancestry, remember? I think the revolution taught me something."

"People!" Mr. Quinten waved his hands to get the crowd's attention, which had waned now that Jelena had left the stage. "To round things up, our final campaigner, Alex West!"

We all looked at Jelena. Her elegant jaw dropped for an instant, but she quickly regained her composure. She knew full well that our gossip-loving classmates would be scrutinizing her face for a reaction.

Alex West's name had been taboo in our group following recent events. After courting Jelena—indisputably the Helen of Troy at Jefferson—for weeks, Alex had done a turnabout after finding out about my (short-lived) potential modeling contract. Not only had he pretended to be my secret admirer, but also, once rejected (like I'd *ever* go for a guy one of my friends was crazy about) he'd spread a rumor around the school that I'd passionately kissed him. He'd sullied my reputation, portraying me as a man-stealing woman, and had nearly driven a betrayal-shaped stake through my friendship with Jelena. Thankfully, Hayden had come to my defense and silenced the rumors, and Jelena and I had made up. However, a week later the whole situation was still pretty raw.

"He's no threat," Jelena scoffed as Alex darted up onto the stage. "He's blacklisted school-wide after his pathetic attempts at social climbing."

What she said was true. I couldn't believe Alex thought he'd actually win enough votes to be school president. Then again, he'd never had a problem with confidence.

"And here we go with another speech," Mr. Quinten said, checking his watch.

"I'm not about gimmicks," Alex said, taking the microphone from Mr. Quinten. "My policies are grounded in the real world, not some utopian fantasy." He sent a pointed look Jelena's way.

"Other candidates can idealize all they want, even to the point of promising you princes and princesses," Alex went on. "But we're nearly adults, so let's not pretend this kiddie Disney stuff is going to miraculously change our lives."

Okay, now I was seeing red. My program was grounded in reality! Why did people belittle love or put it into gooey pink boxes labeled "schmaltz"? Love could change lives!

"How about some policies that reflect the fact that we're on the verge of adulthood?" Alex continued. "I'm talking about membership for all junior and senior students at a real gym, with professionally guided workout sessions. Let's take our training to a level beyond doing laps around the track."

A roar of approval broke out from the section where the football and baseball teams were sitting.

"Think of the chicks we'll get after those workouts!" one guy yelled. He flexed a bicep, grinning.

Matt Stevens looked decidedly uneasy.

Sara let out a sigh. "He's pandering to male vanity. We're done for."

"Pure brawn alone never won a woman, as Alex should know," Jelena called out.

Laughs broke out across the auditorium.

"Aurora's program gives you the inside knowledge on the opposite sex, arming you with tips and tricks to win any guy or girl over," Jelena continued. "She's a personal trainer of the heart."

Alex smirked. "Cue the Disneyisms. I have a feeling my opponent's going to tell us to wish upon a star next."

Jelena stood up. She looked like she was ready to take to the stage and snatch the microphone from him. Mr. Quinten saved her the effort and stepped in front of Alex.

"Yes, it's set to be an exciting campaign this year! Fabulous to see that the candidates are so passionate about their policies. We look forward to hearing more from Mr. West and Ms. Cantrill on another occasion." He waved Alex off the stage.

"Why did they outlaw beheadings?" Jelena muttered when we met up for lunch. "Or putting someone in the stocks? Maybe I can make it my first ruling when I win the election. I imagine the boys who made my lectica could whip up some stocks. We could set them up in the courtyard near the fountain."

"Jelena!" Cassie looked horrified.

"What?" Jelena said. "It's not hurting Alex as such; it's merely allowing some public jeering. Are you saying you wouldn't like to throw a moldy orange at the guy who humiliated me *and* almost ruined Aurora's reputation?"

"I suppose." Cassie still looked uneasy.

Jelena took a dainty sip of her sparkling mineral water. "You might think I sound extreme, but if Alex gains control of this school, he will not have one iota of mercy. Therefore, our entire focus is now to stop Alex from ascending the first rung of the ladder of political power."

"On principle, I'm not going to stand by and watch him scoff at the holiness of the heart's affection," I said. After Alex's "Disney" insult, I was totally with Jelena.

"Now that's the determination my campaign party needs," Jelena said. "So, are you ready to launch the Find a Prince/Princess program on Friday night?"

My resolve faltered. Yes, I'd always intended my program to go public, but I hadn't planned for it to happen so soon. The union of Cass and Scott was testament to the program's success, but apart from reuniting TylerandLindsay, that was my only test case so far. Plus, the defining principles of the program were still a little shaky. Originally, I'd intended the program only for teenage girls. I knew what qualities a Potential Prince should have, but what should a guy look for in a Potential Princess? And what defined a successful love match? Chemistry? The *can't stop thinking about them* factor? Or was it common interests and ethics? Where did the paths of common sense and emotion cross? How many dates did it take to declare that a person had found their prince or princess? These were the foundations of the program, and I needed to nail them down; otherwise, how could I expect people to follow my advice?

"I just hadn't expected to launch it just yet," I admitted. "Like Daniel said, are people really going to want to take advice from someone rocking the name Lethal Lips?"

"Aurora, this election is everything to me," Jelena said. "Do you really think I'd be betting on you if I didn't think it would all end successfully? Have you ever seen me associate myself with anything less than stellar?"

Hearing her say that only made me feel even more hesitant. If my program was a core part of Jelena's overall campaign, there was even more at stake if it failed. The disappointment I'd feel if the program was unsuccessful was one thing. But what would happen to our friendship if she felt I'd cost her the election?

Jelena was still talking. "Even if there are some nonbelievers out there, the fact that they keep focusing on the Lethal Lips thing is actually a form of fascination. People want to talk about you and your love life. They always have. You know, yourself, how many people showed up at the *Much Ado About Nothing* rehearsal that fateful day when you and Hayden were supposed to lock lips. You always get the entire school talking. So, when this program is launched, they'll talk about that, too. That's what's going to drive my campaign to the finish line ahead of everyone else's."

That, or we'd overturn, hit a tree, and the campaign vehicle would explode into a fiery inferno.

I felt a twinge of guilt at the negative picture. I used to be such an optimist. What had my recent dating disasters done to me? Where was the Aurora who'd wanted to be cupid's wingwoman?

"I just wish I'd had time to help a few other couples before putting my techniques out in the public domain," I said. "Then I'd have more examples of my work to bring to the table."

Jelena shrugged. "Hey, you won Hayden Paris. No further proof needed. The entire female student body is in awe of how you got him to fall head over heels for you. They want some of that magic for themselves."

Unfortunately, that was exactly what it felt like—magic. As in something unexplainable. It was a struggle even for me to know how I'd won Hayden. Until he'd revealed himself as my secret admirer, I'd spent most of our contact time firing feisty words at him, scowling at him in class, and doing all I could to avoid him during the *Much Ado About Nothing* rehearsals. I'd just been lucky that, by the time I realized I was crazy about him, my behavior hadn't obliterated his feelings for me.

Jelena could tell I wasn't convinced. "Aurora, all you have to do is turn your original passion for the program into direct action. Think about it overnight."

"And just remember," Cass said, "most of us want a little fairy dust in our lives."

I smiled at her. It *was* amazing to see how my determination to ensure that she and Scott reached Couple Central had paid off. Cass seemed to float through the school day, the weight of her backpack or the burden of an upcoming assignment never dimming the halogen-light brightness of her smile. Imagine if more of our classmates were tapped on the shoulder by cupid. Senior-year stress levels would take a dive. I had to give this further thought.

Matchmaker. Fanner of the flames of love. *Amore* inducer. Love referee. How could I have so many synonyms for my chosen profession and still have no idea how to proceed?

I was sitting on my bed with my laptop that night, staring at the blank screen that should be outlining my Dating Doctrine. It had all seemed so simple in practice—coming up with tricks to help Cass catch Scott—but once I tried to put it down on paper, it sounded so clinical.

Out of desperation, I googled "matchmaking" and scrolled through the search results, which were all sites for established matchmakers. I didn't click on any links. I wanted my program to be one of a kind, totally different from what was out there already.

I tried another phrase: "love advice."

I started when I saw Ovid pop up among the results. A Roman poet as matchmaker—that was more my style. I didn't want to be just a relationship guru; I wanted to be a relationship guru who *wrote*. I clicked through, eager to learn how to meld my twin interests.

Ovid was the love guru of his era! The article described how he'd written three books that were collectively called *Ars Amatoria*, or *The Art of Love*. I scrolled down the page. Apparently his first book was a how-to guide for men on winning a woman's heart. Ovid had covered everything from ancient Roman hot spots for meeting a woman (book 1, part 2: "How to Find Her") to the fail-safe first date outfit ("Don't delight in curling your hair with tongs") to maintaining a positive outlook on your chances for love ("First of all, believe there's no one you can't get; you'll attract someone, simply lay the net"). Book 2 (published at the same time) told his avid readers how to keep the women they'd won. His advice included "Give her little tasteful gifts" and "Respect her freedom." Apparently, the Romans had gone wild for both books, so Ovid had quickly taken advantage of a hot market and followed up with a third one. This was aimed at the female market, with advice on everything from ways to handle a bad hair day to playing it cool with your admirers: "Don't be too anxious. Make him wait a little." Although scrolls had long been replaced by text messages, Ovid's tips were still straight up, two thousand years later. I excitedly searched for more quotes from *Ars Amatoria*.

"Venus favors the bold." The words leaped out at me, almost like a challenge. Ovid's statement didn't just apply to wooing and winning; it was about seizing chances—whether it was grasping the hand of the one you're crazy about or taking an unexpected opportunity to launch your truth upon the world. I snatched up my cell and dialed Jelena.

"Ovid," I said, before she finished the word "Hello."

"Influential Roman poet. Banished by Augustus in 8 AD. What about him?"

"He published dating guides on how to win over the opposite sex! He's my new mentor."

"Fabulous!" Jelena said. "This is totally in line with my theme."

"Theme?" I repeated.

"As you saw today with the lectica, I'm trying to evoke the glory of the Roman era. Audiences don't want boring schoolyard sermons; they want the theatrically compelling stuff.

"Politics and entertainment go hand in hand," she went on. "Think Julius Caesar. Before he was emperor he made his mark by re-creating epic sea battles for audiences. He threw a party in the streets, with twenty-two thousand tables! The Romans quickly realized that if he became leader, there'd be no end of enjoyable events. He became one of the most popular rulers in Roman history."

"Until he got stabbed," I said.

I hated to be a killjoy, but we had to be realistic.

"Hey, that was all to do with the haters in the senate, not public opinion," Jelena replied cheerfully. "High school is just as brutal as ancient Rome, and being popular is just as important as any policies I might suggest—probably more so, when it comes to our classmates casting their votes. I'm already unofficial party-planning queen, so now all I've got to do is take it up a notch and emphasize just how enjoyable my rule as president will be for all. That's what Friday night's all about—Rome in all its decadence."

Caesar aside, I had to admit that I did support Jelena's radical approach to modern politics. Anything that dragged our schoolmates' attention away from Snapchat and Instagram for a brief period had to be a plus.

"So taking Ovid as my muse is totally era-appropriate," I said.

"Genius," Jelena replied. "I have no worries when it comes to you implementing the Find a Prince/Princess program."

"You don't want to look through the guidelines once I've mapped them out?" I asked, surprised. It wasn't like Jelena to relinquish any iota of control.

"As I said, I trust you. My chief decree is that you have a solid breakdown of how the program will work over the next few weeks. Basically, we need the three 'matchmakees,' as I'm calling them, matched up and blissfully happy by the time election day rolls around. The details are your domain. All I ask is that the program runs seamlessly so we build a reputation for results."

Mere weeks to make three people's dreams come true. It was a challenge, if ever there was one.

"Spend the next few days on strategy," Jelena said. "Don't worry about the organizational aspects of Friday; I've got a team on it already. I can assure you, the night will be akin to something Ovid himself would have attended."

Jelena had a way of spurring you on. "I'm with you one hundred percent," I said firmly.

7

"You told me you were with me one hundred percent!" Jelena said, glaring at me.

It was the night of the party and we were in Hayden Paris's bathroom. I was sitting on the edge of the bathtub, wrapped in a purple towel and staring in horror at the outfit that Jelena was brandishing.

"I *am* with you! It just doesn't include appearing nude in front of my classmates!"

"It's not nude; it's flesh-colored!"

Jelena's voice was all optimism as she waved the string bikini back and forth in front of me. Maybe she was hoping to hypnotize me into agreement.

"It looks like the microkini Britney wore in the 'Toxic' video!" I grabbed the top and stretched the triangles out to emphasize the lack of modesty-preserving material.

"This isn't MTV video–style nudity," Jelena huffed, obviously insulted. "This is a nod to classicism. The sensuous beauty of Botticelli's Venus. With a little extra sparkle!" She gestured toward the iridescent Swarovski crystals that dotted the edge of the bikini bottom.

"I seriously doubt our classmates are going to make that connection." I crossed my arms over my chest, thinking of the snickers that had erupted when Ms. Collins told us to open our textbooks to Michelangelo's *David*. The boys had had a field day with nude jokes. "They're hardly art connoisseurs."

"Everyone knows *The Birth of Venus*, Aurora. It's ultra famous. Plus, you'll be floating on a giant clamshell! Like they aren't going to know you're Venus, goddess of love?"

I stared at the bikini again. I was fairly self-confident, but this was seriously pushing it.

Outside, the music pulsating from Hayden's backyard sound system went up a notch. However, it still wasn't enough to drown out the screams and shouts of the partygoers frolicking in and around Hayden's pool. The place was packed.

Jelena shook her head. "The plebeians are getting restless. Aurora, I have to be out there to manage this thing before we get complaints from the neighbors. You need to get your Venus on."

"I don't see why I can't wear an outfit like yours," I said.

Jelena was elegant in an aquamarine Roman-style dress. On her head she wore a laurel wreath, Caesar style.

"I admit my outfit is captivating, but for the launch we need conversation-stopping, all-eyes-on-you attention," Jelena said. "This bikini's the only thing that's going to do that for this crowd."

"You know how accident-prone I am!" I felt shaky just contemplating the possibilities for humiliation as I balanced on a giant floating clam in a microscopic bikini. "It's a wardrobe malfunction waiting to happen."

Jelena let out a giant sigh. "You aren't going to budge, are you?"

The music went up another hundred or so decibels. Any moment now the walls would be vibrating. I really didn't envy Cass and Lindsay, who were on crowd control for the first hour of the party.

"Are you guys ready?" Sara shouted through the bathroom door. "The place is full to capacity."

Sara was on door duty, welcoming partygoers and taking

the names of everyone who wanted to participate in the Find a Prince/Princess™ program. We'd constructed a special love-themed mailbox into which people posted a completed questionnaire that described their personal attributes as well as their ideal partner and relationship. The three lucky winners would be selected later on during the party. Jelena had bribed Jeffrey Clark into dressing as Cupid, complete with wings and heart-tipped arrows (painstakingly crafted during our art class). He would deliver the mailbox to Jelena and me once we were ready to do the drawing. I just hadn't known that Jelena had secretly cast me as Venus.

I held the bikini top up again, examining it. Perhaps I was being unreasonable . . . Nope. The top was about as big as two oversize triangular corn chips.

"Guys?" Sara shouted again.

"Fine. I'll be Venus, you take my outfit." Jelena snatched the bikini top from me and unzipped the back of her Roman dress.

"Thank god." I stood up, my knees weak with relief.

"But you aren't wearing the wreath," Jelena said. She took it off her head and placed it on the bathroom sink. "That's empress-only attire."

"Not a problem." I was willing to agree to anything now I was no longer expected to wear a top that looked like it'd been shrunk in the dryer.

"You realize this makes no sense?" Jelena said as she pulled on the bikini bottoms under her dress. "You're the spokesperson for the matchmaking program—the modern-day equivalent of Venus bringing love into people's lives. I had an ingenious association happening there."

"I just think people are more likely to listen to me when I'm wearing this dress," I said, picking it up off the floor and pulling it over my head, "rather than standing there wondering where I've lost my clothes."

"Seriously?" Jelena rolled her eyes. "This thing isn't even that sma—"

Her sentence died as she stepped in front of the mirror and took in just how little the top covered what needed covering.

I restrained the *I told you so* hovering on my lips.

Jelena pulled her hair over her shoulders to lessen the bordering-on-nude factor.

"I'm owning my gloriousness," Jelena said, giving me a superior look.

I noticed her eyes shifted instantly back to studying how the slightest movement threatened to destroy her strategic hair placement.

"Exactly. You are the personification of Venus! I'll go prep the others for your breathtaking entrance!"

"I've got my phone, so call me when you're ready," Jelena said, pulling her hair spray can from her handbag and giving it a determined shake. "I expect you guys to have the scene set in exactly ten minutes."

I shut the bathroom door behind me, simultaneously relieved and guilty about my narrow escape.

Sara was wearing a floaty emerald maxi matched with gold Roman sandals and a gold snake arm bracelet. She looked surprised. "Jelena gave you her clothes? Last-minute outfit freak-out?"

"Something like that." We didn't have time for explanations. "Jelena wants to make her entrance in exactly ten minutes, so we've got to get everything ready."

I dialed Bruce, one of the guys from woodworking class.

"Aurora, we're in the basement," he said. "Pretty much ready to go."

Lindsay and Cass rushed up. Lindsay's cheeks were flushed pink from exertion. "We need help!"

"Bruce, we'll see you in a sec," I said, and hung up.

"Hayden just confiscated a Roman jar filled to the brim with beer," Lindsay said. "Some of the soccer players smuggled it in. Tyler's being no help. I had to grab Hayden because Tyler was getting all uppity about telling off his teammates."

I got the feeling Tyler's scoreboard was approaching negative numerals.

"Okay, we'll deal with Tyler's unhealthy team bromance after the party," I said. "Right now we have to focus on clearing the pool. Jelena's ready for the next step of her plan."

Cass and Lindsay gaped at me.

"There's like fifty people in there!" Lindsay said.

"Everyone in the water right now thinks they're above pool law," Cass said. "Or at least the guys do. We might be able to get the girls out, but I know the boys won't listen."

"We need boys to do the ordering then," I said. "I'm going to grab Hayden. Wait here."

I'd seen Jelena's elaborate plans for the backyard area in art class, but the results were way beyond my expectations. A red carpet ran up to the twin six-foot-high papier-mâché columns that stood on either side of the pool gate, heralding the entrance to the party. Roman eagles perched on each stake of the pool fence, and fake vines were wound along its entire length. Stepping through the gate, I saw a long outdoor table heaving with gold platters of grapes, cheeses, and bread, Roman-style water pitchers, and plastic golden goblets and plates. Jelena had obviously utilized Cass's and Scott's artistic skills, because elaborate backdrops showing the Roman Colosseum, chariots, and gladiators stood behind the barbecue area. A projector screen hung from the veranda above the pool and flashed the quotes I'd found in Ovid's *Ars Amatoria*: "Kiss me with a thousand kisses"; "May he love tomorrow who has never loved before"; and my favorite, "Love conquers all."

Throngs of our classmates, decked out in Roman gowns, togas, or intricate gladiator armor, danced to the pumping music coming from the DJ's stand, which was set up on the veranda. On the lawn, partygoers competed in "chariot races" (using wheelbarrows), mud wrestling (Jelena had obviously gotten creative with Hayden's old sandpit), and a Roman ring toss.

I scoured the area for Hayden. There! He and Scott were

wresting guys down from a huge tree with branches stretching toward the pool—obviously too much of a temptation for daredevils.

"Hayden!" I ran over to him.

"Aurora! Thank god!" Hayden blocked access to the tree as Scott pulled down the last wannabe Tarzan. "I know I'm doing this as a favor, but it's getting crazy. I'm worried a neighbor will make a noise complaint."

"I know!" I said. "We need a plan. The girls are waiting inside. Let's take two minutes to brainstorm."

Hayden and Scott shot each other a look, obviously uneasy at leaving the backyard area unsupervised. They followed anyway as I dashed back to the house. Cass, Lindsay, and Sara were standing anxiously in the hall.

"We had to stop two body-painted slaves from making out on the living room couch," Lindsay said.

"I managed to get the henna stains out of the cushions with some spray from the laundry," Cass reassured Hayden.

He let out a sigh. "I really don't want my parents coming home to damaged furniture—or worse, the police."

"I know, it's totally unfair to you," I said, feeling guilty as I looked at his worried face. I had no idea how Jelena had convinced him to host the party, but somehow she'd locked it down on Tuesday, assuring me that Hayden was "totally cool with being host" and that Friday was ideal because his parents would be away.

"We need the pool clear," I went on.

"I vote we get out the hose," Sara said with a devious look. "They might like the pool, but they aren't going to like jets of water in their faces."

Hayden looked a little brighter. "We've got twin hoses. And my dad has a bullhorn in the basement."

"I think you're onto something there," I said. "Okay, Lindsay, Scott, and Sara, you get the hoses ready. Hayden, Cass, and I will head to the basement so I can organize the woodworking guys and Hayden can grab the bullhorn. He'll meet you on the veranda and then you can launch the clear-the-pool plan while Cass and I get the prop in place with the woodworking guys. Call me when you're done so I can cue the lights and music for Jelena's entrance."

Scott, Lindsay, and Sara darted down the corridor while Cass, Hayden, and I dashed down the basement stairs. I threw open the door and came face-to-face with Gary and Bruce from woodworking class, both looking proud beside a makeshift raft that held an oversize scallop shell carved out of thin plywood. It was painted a delicate shade of pink that glowed in the overhead light.

"I added the glitter," Gary said. "Jelena said I'll earn major points for this."

I wondered how long he and Bruce had labored over the prop. Knowing Jelena, her idea of a reward would be a couple of extra smiles thrown their way.

"I was the one who studied the engineering of flotation." Bruce gave Gary a pointed look. "Glitter won't do much if the vessel isn't watertight."

"Wait a minute . . . This is going to be launched into the pool?" Hayden asked. "I thought we were clearing everyone out of the pool so we could gain control over the party."

"It's a little bit of both," I said quickly, realizing just how unhappy Hayden was. "I thought Jelena had explained her plan to you."

He let out a sigh. "I think you and I had better have a talk later on. Jelena said tonight was all about you launching the program."

Obviously I wasn't the only one who'd been in the dark when it came to Jelena's Botticelli-inspired plan. How was I going to explain that a flesh-colored string bikini and an oversize iridescent shell *were* part of the program?

My phone rang.

"Aurora! It's been ten minutes!" Jelena was clearly unimpressed.

"It's been harder than we thought to clear the pool—" I began.

"I'm heading to the veranda in exactly three minutes," Jelena said. "The pool had better be clear by then." She hung up.

"Okay, everyone, grab the raft," I ordered. "We're heading for the veranda. Hayden, I promise I'll explain later, but right now I need you upstairs with that bullhorn. It's your house. We've got a stronger chance of people listening to authority if you're the one wielding that thing."

Hayden gave me a look, then grabbed the bullhorn from a hook near the door and dashed up the stairs.

Bruce, Gary, Cass, and I heaved the raft off the ground, up the stairs, and through the open glass doors onto the veranda. Jelena was standing near the steps leading down to the yard, wearing a white satin robe and holding two bags of pink rose petals.

James, one of the sound and lighting guys who'd worked with us on *Much Ado About Nothing*, was tonight's DJ. As well as spinning tunes, he was controlling the lighting, currently wrestling a giant spotlight into place. Jelena must have borrowed it from the school's theater department. I could see Hayden below with the bullhorn, valiantly trying to establish order.

"Jelena, Hayden needs help," I said. "No one's going to pay attention to him while music's still blaring."

"James, kill the track," Jelena instructed.

The booming electro beat died and protests broke out in the yard below.

"I repeat: everyone out of the pool!" Hayden bellowed.

Scott and Sara stood on either side of him, brandishing hoses. We watched as Sara turned her nozzle toward the stragglers in the pool. She placed her finger at the opening of the hose so a wide spray of water was unleashed across the area. Cries of protest erupted, but people began heaving themselves out of the water.

My phone flashed with Sara's number and I picked up.

"Okay, we've established control," she said. "We'll be switching the hoses off in exactly one minute, so you guys'd better be ready."

"Okay, James, be ready when I yell," Jelena said. "The rest of you, follow my lead."

Jelena darted down the back steps and toward the far corner of the pool, which was screened by lush greenery. We followed, setting the raft down out of view next to the pool shed.

Jelena called up to James. "Kill the lights now."

All the backyard lights went off, plunging the area into darkness.

"Time to get this thing onto the water," Jelena said, untying her robe and letting it fall from her shoulders.

Bruce and Gary stopped, the raft half into the water, and gaped at Jelena's costume. Relief washed over me once again that I wasn't the one wearing it. Somewhere above us, a smoke machine unleashed pale pink air.

"Position the raft!" Jelena commanded.

The boys hurriedly lowered it into the water, holding it in position so it couldn't float away before Jelena climbed aboard.

"Okay, so if you two give me a slight push—and I mean slight; if I end up in the water, I will *never* forgive you—this thing should float gently to the other side of the pool, right?"

Jelena gave Gary and Bruce a glance that made it clear that if they failed, all points gained from the creation of the shell would be forever lost. They nodded effusively in response.

Jelena handed them the bags of rose petals and carefully stepped onto the shell. As she took her position, she looked down to check that her hair was still in place over the bikini top. Her legs shook slightly as the raft stabilized itself.

"Cass and Aurora," she instructed, without turning, "head around to the other side of the pool now. I want you waiting there when I reach the shallow end."

I saw her legs tremble again and felt guilty leaving her. It wasn't like Jelena to show any semblance of nervousness. Then again, our classmates were hardly going to see her as their potential leader if she belly flopped into the pool off a glittery ride-on shell.

"I'm ready to go with the program as soon as you announce it," I promised, as I reluctantly headed for the steps back up to the veranda.

"Good luck, Jelena!" Cass shouted. "It'll be a triumphant voyage!"

"Release the rose petals!" I heard Jelena cry to Gary and Bruce.

As Cass and I ran along the veranda and down the steps that led to the pool gates, Rihanna's "We Found Love" started up on the sound system.

"Woo-hoo! Party's back on!" Jesse Cook, his gladiator chest plate dripping water, punched the air.

"What's with the pink smoke?" someone behind me asked, as Cass and I pushed our way through the crowd to the pool's shallow end. Hayden, Scott, Sara, and Lindsay were already there.

"Can you see her?" Cass asked anxiously.

I stared at the corner of the pool where Jelena's journey should have begun. Since it was an almost moonless night, it was hard to see anything in the shadows of the greenery.

"You don't think she's fallen off already, do you?" Sara asked. "What if the vessel sank under her weight?"

I envisioned the sparkling shell on the bottom of the pool and felt sick. Obviously Jelena could swim, but what if she'd lost her balance too close to the launch spot and hit her head on the edge of the pool?

"You guys saw her launch off, didn't you?" Hayden whispered.

"No, she sent us over here," I replied, wishing we'd insisted on staying until she was on her way.

"I'm going in," Hayden said, pulling his shirt off. "I want to make sure she's okay."

"No, wait!" Lindsay cried, pointing into the distance.

There, emerging from the pink smoke, the shell bobbing on floating pink rose petals, was Jelena. James turned the spotlight on and its beam picked up the crystals on the bikini bottom and the glittering surface of the shell. The way Jelena's hair flowed over the top of the bikini gave the impression that she was naked up top. The crowd let out a collective gasp at the spellbinding apparition, then cheers and wolf whistles broke out all around us. Jelena maintained a slightly mysterious half-smile, despite the overwhelming response.

A slow clap began, becoming more frenzied as the shell floated closer. As it neared the shallow end, Jelena's Victoria's Secret–like figure was highlighted even more magnificently. People began taking pictures on their phones.

"Jelena does realize these photos are going to be all over social media, right?" Scott asked Cass and me.

Sara answered for us. "I think that's the goal."

Jelena's clamshell gently nudged the edge of the pool step and the crowd stopped clapping, eagerly awaiting her next move.

"Cupid! I command thee to appear!" she called, her voice echoing over the pool.

Jeffrey, dressed in a pair of white trunks, with wispy white wings strapped to his back, danced toward her, flinging heart-shaped confetti at the crowd.

"Goddess! You called?" he cried, and took a heart-tipped arrow from the sling at his side, touching it to Jelena's collarbone, unable to resist making some kind of physical contact with the scantily clad Venus. "Cupid is here to do your every bidding. And I mean *every—*"

"Thank you, Cupid!" Jelena broke in. "Assist me in disembarking this vessel."

Jeffrey waded into the water and kneeled to form a stepping stone from the raft to the pool's edge. Jelena placed her hand on his shoulder and stepped daintily onto his thigh. Jeffrey's leg shook slightly at the weight, but his beaming smile never faded as Jelena launched herself to dry land.

One of the campaign team handed Jelena a microphone.

"Party attendees!" she cried. "Are you having a good night?"

Everyone broke into a cheer.

"Let me make it even better!" Jelena reached forward and grabbed my hand. "Torchbearers?" she called.

Three members of Jelena's campaign team stepped forward, each holding a flaming torch. Another pushed his way through the crowd, wheeling a huge heart with a giant *J* inside it. As it drew closer, I saw that the heart was made of sparklers.

"Tonight we light the fires of love," Jelena said. "Tonight I give you Aurora Skye's trademarked Find a Prince/Princess program, the first phase of a revolutionary plan to be rolled out over the next few weeks. I invite you to experience the fairy tale that will be Jefferson under my rule!"

Jelena clapped her hands and the torchbearers ignited the sparklers. The entire heart lit up, and I felt my own heart ignite with it as I looked at my schoolmates' faces, radiant with anticipation. This was a launch truly worthy of the Find a Prince/Princess™ program. Jelena had captured its essence. I squeezed her hand in gratitude as we watched the sparklers slowly fade.

"Roll video," Jelena called, as the last sparkler died. Above the pool, the projector started up.

An image of a heart, split down the middle, filled the screen, followed by a morose-looking girl. She was staring at her phone screen, which displayed the words "It's over." The image faded into a shot of the girl crying on her bed.

"Teenage love is a battlefield," Jelena said, her voice booming out over the pool. She paused for a moment, letting the statement sink in. "Our parents and teachers see it as puppy love—something light and fluffy and unlikely to cause much harm. We all know that's not the case."

A forlorn-looking guy appeared on the screen. He tore up a photo of himself and a girl, presumably his ex.

"You set your sights on a guy or a girl who's a love liability and you pay the price of having your mistake witnessed school-wide," Jelena said. Her voice softened slightly. "I know this firsthand."

At that, any whispers or soft giggles were silenced. The pool area became eerily quiet, as if everyone had stopped breathing. Hearing Jelena Cantrill admit to vulnerability was like Achilles exposing his heel—it just didn't happen.

"I've seen my classmates maimed by love, their dignity and self-confidence blown apart as if by a grenade. It doesn't matter if you're celebrity-grade gorgeous," Jelena gestured to herself, "have Einstein-like intelligence, or are a sports star. No one is immune.

"Say you've just begun dating someone," Jelena continued, as a shot of a couple laughing and sharing an ice cream flashed on the screen. "It started so promisingly. Maybe she smiled at you during a football game. Maybe he jotted down his number on your notepad after he helped you with an equation in math. Next thing you know, you're walking to school holding hands, texting each other before you go to sleep at night, and planning coordinated outfits for formal. It's official, it's on Facebook, you're a couple.

"Until . . ." Jelena paused dramatically. "One afternoon, he dumps you by text message. Half the school already knows and has been pitying you all day. Or maybe she's changed her Facebook status back to 'Single' without giving you any explanation, and all your shared friends have in-boxed you asking what happened." Jelena shook her head.

"Love is fraught with risk. As your potential school president, I care about your experiences at Jefferson—and that includes your love life. This is why I am collaborating with Aurora Skye on the launch of her Find a Prince/Princess program."

"Why do we want the program if falling in love means being put in the line of fire?" Juliet Bryce called out.

"You want the program because you're more vulnerable if you're making decisions on love solo," Jelena answered. "The brain is not to be trusted when it's in love and souped up on chemicals. You need an impartial third party, someone who can filter out the players and find you the guy or girl who not only makes you all tingly but is actually a good match for you."

"To be more precise, a *perfect* match for you!" I called out.

I'd spent my week devising what I called a chemistry calculator, which would highlight the crossover compatibility of two individuals. Everyone who'd attended the party had been required to fill out a questionnaire on the qualities of their ideal partner. My plan was to feed this data into the chemistry calculator to ascertain the perfect match for each of our three matchmakees.

"Exactly," Jelena said. "It's foolproof. Using Aurora's program to approach the dating scene is like entering the battlefield in a tank. It offers a level of protection that you just can't get on your own.

"So let's review Aurora's past successes," Jelena said, signaling to James.

The video switched to a photo of Lindsay and Tyler at eighth-grade school camp. A beaming, braces-wearing Tyler was triumphantly holding Lindsay's hand, next to the creek, the day that he'd officially asked her out for the first time.

"TylerandLindsay," Jelena announced. "You all know them well. The inseparability. The sentences uttered in unison. The bordering-on-sickening level of public affection."

I cringed as the screen flicked to a shot of them making out near the monkey bars.

"OMG." Lindsay looked like she was gritting her teeth as members of the soccer team punched Tyler on the arm, grinning like Cheshire cats. "Jelena!"

Jelena didn't stop. "Until January this year, when their relationship splintered."

A cracking noise echoed through the yard and several people looked nervously at the trees, unaware that James had hit a sound effect on the mixing deck.

"Shocked by this unexpected split, the school gave up hope of ever seeing Tyler and Lindsay reconcile," Jelena went on. "Lindsay's friends lost faith in love's happy ending. Tyler felt the anguish of dashed dreams after his foolhardy breakup decision."

A shot appeared of Tyler on his knees in the school library, begging Lindsay for a second chance. The real Tyler looked mortified at the public reminder of his desperation to reclaim Lindsay.

"How does she even have a record of this?" Lindsay whispered to Sara.

"Tyler *did* make a spectacle of himself that day," Sara whispered back. "I think some people got it on video, too."

Lindsay buried her head in her hands. I felt terrible for her. Why hadn't I insisted on being briefed before the launch of the program?

I would never have let Jelena use Lindsay's breakup as a platform for our agenda.

"But one person kept the faith," Jelena cried out. "One person knew that what Tyler and Lindsay had only comes once in a lifetime."

The next shot was of Lindsay and Tyler on the bus, Lindsay asleep against his shoulder.

Scott let out a laugh. "I swear she's had a video crew working full-time on this for years."

"Scott!" Cass shot him a warning look.

"That person was Aurora Skye," Jelena continued. "Her gifts are so great that not only did she heal Lindsay and Tyler's broken bond in a matter of weeks, but she simultaneously launched another epic love match—that of Cassie and Scott."

Their intertwined names appeared on the screen, hovering doves holding heart-shaped balloons on either side.

"Both genetically blessed yet bizarrely modest, neither one was game to make a move, despite the fact that Cupid's arrow had struck them both," Jelena said.

Jeffrey danced over to Cass and Scott and touched his arrow tip to their collarbones in turn.

"I shouldn't have laughed," Scott said wryly, as the audience turned its full attention on him and Cass.

"It would have been years of longing looks and shy smiles with no real resolution if not for Aurora's program. But with her Rules of Attraction guiding the two lovebirds, it was the start of something magical."

A montage followed: Cass and Scott working on a theater backdrop. Scott handing her a coffee and kissing her on the cheek. Cassie grinning as she threw her arms around him in the auditorium.

I looked at Cass, who was bright red.

"Oh no, she didn't!" Sara said dramatically.

My eyes shot back to the screen. Scott was down on one knee

on a picnic blanket, a blue Tiffany box in his outstretched hand, a shocked Cass staring back at him.

"Where did you get that?" I whispered in shock to Jelena.

"I tweaked the shot of him giving her the rose on Valentine's Day," Jelena whispered back enthusiastically.

"Oh man, Scott, you are whipped!" someone yelled.

"They're getting married?" a more gullible partygoer shrilled.

The screen changed to a shot of Scott and Cassie cuddling in front of a house with a white picket fence, a SOLD sign behind them on the gate. Twin toddlers, both with blond hair like Cass and Scott, hugged their knees.

"You actually Photoshopped in kids?" Cass murmured, mortified. She looked ready to run away.

"Could you get any cuter?" Jelena boomed over the mike, as girls in the crowd *awwed* at the shot.

I looked over at Scott and saw that he was laughing. Thank god he was taking it in good humor. Cass and Scott had only been together for two weeks!

"Obviously, all of this is yet to come," Jelena said. "But the montage demonstrates how, if I'm elected, my work at Jefferson will have benefits that stretch far beyond the schoolyard. So I ask you to think with your heart. Vote Jelena Cantrill!"

The presentation finished and the crowd burst into cheers.

"We're going to take a brief break to let you enjoy the party before we announce the three lucky candidates for the Find a Prince/ Princess program!" Jelena cried. "Remember, you must have filled out a questionnaire to be in the running!"

"Get your love on!" Jeffrey shouted, flinging more confetti into the air as James started playing Far East Movement's "Turn Up the Love." Centurions, Roman noblewomen, and slaves all started jiggling along to the music.

Jelena and I made our way over to the drink table. I poured us both a golden goblet of grape juice.

"I say ten minutes to build the anticipation, then we draw the names," Jelena said.

Hayden appeared at our sides, looking tense. "Jelena, can we talk?"

"Sure, Hayden." Jelena took a sip of her drink, seemingly unfazed by his stressed expression.

"I know I sound like a bore," Hayden said, "but the party I agreed to and the party that's happening right now are miles apart."

"Really?" Jelena replied. "I thought my brief was pretty detailed."

Hayden gave her a look. "You told me it was 'a small gathering meant to inspire.'"

I glanced at Jelena, surprised. She'd never mentioned the word "small" to me when we'd talked numbers over the phone.

Jelena shrugged. "I think this is pretty contained."

"Contained?" Hayden gestured at the guys now mud wrestling in his former sandpit.

"You aren't happy with the launch of Aurora's program?" Jelena sounded slightly hurt.

Hayden sighed. "I don't think it's fair that you're bringing Aurora into it."

"But you want her to be happy," Jelena replied breezily. "Now that she's in love, she's extra inspired to help others feel the same way. That's what tonight is all about."

"Obviously, I want her to be happy," Hayden said. "That's the only reason I agreed to the party, despite knowing Mom and Dad wouldn't be happy about it."

I had to speak up—first, because it wasn't right that Hayden should suffer the consequences of an out-of-control house party purely to make me happy, and second, because I felt really weird about Jelena announcing my feelings to Hayden like I was unable to do it myself.

"Jelena—" I started.

"So what's the problem?" she said to Hayden. "Aurora's happy, so you should be happy."

I tried again. "I'm not happy if Hayden's feeling uneasy—"

"I'm not sure how I feel about love with a political agenda," Hayden said, interrupting me.

I felt like a ghost—able to hear their conversation but unable to contribute.

"I know that sounds ironic for someone so involved with the student council, but love should go beyond policies," Hayden said firmly. "It's purer—"

"Love always has an agenda, Hayden," Jelena cut in. "Let me get you a mocktail. You'll feel better."

"The only thing that's going to make me feel better is clearing the party out," Hayden said.

"Seriously, right now?" Jelena shook her head. "We haven't announced the winners yet."

"So announce them and wrap it up," Hayden said. "If things were a little calmer, then I'd be happy to keep the night going, but you have to admit the mood's kind of out of control."

"Hayden, come on!" Jelena gave him a *You're overreacting* look. "Everyone here's just in high spirits because of the zeitgeist of love."

Her voice was drowned out by a retching sound. Travis, who had climbed out of the pool to get some grape juice, had thrown up on the formerly pristine outdoor couches.

"Ew!" A circle of girls who had been sitting on the couches leaped up, screaming, as purple vomit threatened their party costumes.

Jeffrey Clark appeared at our side. "Oh, jeez. I think I gave him too much."

"Too much *what*?" Jelena shot him a furious look.

"Um . . ."

"Spill it, Clark. Otherwise, I'm not paying you for tonight," Jelena said.

Jeffrey looked sheepish. "I may have slipped him a little something. Jack Daniel's never did a man wrong. Or not until now."

Travis retched again, and people darted away from the danger zone.

"It's a nonalcoholic party!" Jelena shouted. "I promised Hayden!"

Hayden sighed. "Really not cool, Jeffrey."

Jeffrey looked uber guilty. “I was just trying to help him woo a woman. You know, imbibing him with courage.”

“Okay, I admit it, you’re right, Hayden,” Jelena said. “We need to get this party under control.”

“I think it’s too late.” Scott put a hand on Hayden’s shoulder. “Hear that?”

We all fell silent. Over the booming music came the sound of police sirens getting closer.

8

"I can't believe we missed out on announcing the candidates while the party was at full capacity!" Jelena shook her head as she, Cass, Lindsay, Sara, and I headed to a booth at our favorite breakfast café the next morning. "Talk about a wasted opportunity. The only saving grace is that it's Saturday. I would not want to be seen at school with these." She gestured at the invisible-to-everyone-else bags under her eyes.

My own eyelids felt as heavy as the kettlebells in gym class. After the police had arrived and the partygoers had been sent home, the five of us, plus Scott and Tyler, had stayed up till one a.m. helping Hayden clean up. We were only three-quarters done when his parents arrived home. They'd driven the two hours back from their holiday house up the coast after they'd received a call from the police.

"I don't see why Hayden couldn't have waited till the professional cleaners showed up this morning," Jelena said as she studied the menu. "I'd prebooked."

"Jelena, we couldn't leave Hayden with trash all over the yard and body paint smeared on the walls," I snapped. Lack of sleep had stripped away my patience. "Seriously? It was the least we could do for him."

"Oka-a-ay," Jelena huffed, slamming her menu down.

"No, it's not okay!" I said, remembering Hayden's face when the police arrived on the scene.

Our neighborhood was one of the most respectable in Jefferson, so a single noise complaint from a neighbor had produced an entire convoy of officers eager to enforce the law on an otherwise quiet Friday night. Half the street had peered from their doorsteps while Hayden was questioned for twenty minutes by two officers. Meanwhile, the rest of the patrol hustled teenagers from the house and backyard.

"You realize that if Scott and Tyler hadn't hauled Travis over the fence to my place, the police could have charged Hayden with distributing alcohol to a minor?"

"He didn't buy it for them!" Jelena shot back. "Jeffrey was the idiot who smuggled in Jack Daniel's in a jam jar."

"It's Hayden's property," I explained, trying not to raise my voice in the busy café. "Meaning he's responsible for what happens there, and he faces the consequences if that activity is illegal. We're just lucky that the police only called Hayden's parents."

"Who were completely uncool about it." Jelena rolled her eyes.

"Their house was trashed by two hundred teenagers!" I cried. "Did you expect them to pat Hayden on the back?"

"My parents never have an issue with parties," Jelena replied. "They know that social events are key to stepping up a few rungs on the influence ladder. Come on, how many times have you visited my place when my parents have had the sound system up way louder than ours was last night?"

Jelena's dad was a high-flying producer for one of the TV networks. Their place was palatial—the outdoor entertainment area was bigger than the entire ground floor of my house.

"I don't get why you didn't host the party at your place, then," Sara said to Jelena.

"Our pool's being revamped," Jelena replied, sighing with relief as our coffees arrived. "Hayden's was the next-best option." She tore open a sugar packet and turned to me. "I never intended the party to get that out of control. I specified 'no alcohol' on the invitations, and I had Cass and Sara doing spot checks at the door. I can't help it if idiot Jeffrey smuggled JD in. And it's not my fault Hayden's parents are stupidly old-fashioned and have grounded him till Friday. Go blame them for putting the red light on any postschool make-out sessions for you and Hayden."

"It's not about make-out sessions!" I cried. Several patrons looked up at my impassioned response and I lowered my voice. "It's about the fact that you only got Hayden to agree to host the party by convincing him that it was his duty as my crush. That's not fair."

I took a deep breath before my temper could get the better of me. I didn't trust myself to lift my coffee cup, my hands were shaking so much from lack of sleep and extreme irritation. The guilt that I felt about Hayden's punishment and the Parises' trashed house had kept me from being able to sleep in the few hours available after we'd finished cleanup patrol. The girls had crashed at my place and Jelena had roused us all out in search of caffeine at nine a.m. Unfortunately, the NAD had given our Nespresso machine away just this week. Apparently, the group had labeled his morning coffee an "addiction to stimulants" and the NAD had filled the cupboard with dandelion and licorice tea instead—or "weak crap" as Jelena called it, when she saw the overpriced packages from the health food store.

My phone buzzed and I pulled it out of my bag. A message from Hayden.

> How are you and the girls faring? It's grim faces at the breakfast table over here.

What could I say? I'd already said sorry in about a dozen different forms when Hayden had walked us back to my place last night. I hadn't even been able to give him a hug, because his dad had accompanied us as well.

I started typing a reply, before realizing it was all wrong and immediately deleting it. I did this five times in a row, before putting the phone down, completely lost for a response.

What was wrong with me lately? Usually I was passionate and confident—words were my forte. But it was as if timidity had taken over since Hayden and I had started dating. It dawned on me: it wasn't just my classmates deeming me Lethal Lips; a part of me had actually started to believe I *was* a disaster in the dating game. And my every encounter with Hayden had become infused with self-doubt since.

"Aurora?" Sara's voice broke into my self-reflection. I looked up and saw the waitress patiently waiting for my order. The last thing I wanted was food—I felt sick to my stomach.

"Just raisin toast, please." Hopefully, I'd be able to nibble at it.

The table fell silent after the waitress had departed with our orders.

"So, what's up?" Jelena asked Lindsay and Cass. "You guys haven't said a word all morning!"

Lindsay shrugged. Cass fiddled with the ring on her right hand, avoiding Jelena's gaze.

"You know, maybe we should get Scott to give you a promise ring," Jelena mused. "It could be the next step in the campaign."

Cass looked up, her eyes slightly panicky. "Jelena, I don't think Scott—"

"Nothing tacky," Jelena said, assuming that was why Cassie looked uneasy.

"I'm thinking a promise ring from Tiffany," Jelena said, pulling out her iPhone and typing notes. "It would build on the little blue box concept that we introduced last night."

Cass looked pained at the reminder. "Jelena—"

"We could do a similar thing for Tyler and Lindsay," Jelena went on. "Except not Tiffany. It's got to reflect the overall feel of the couple. Tyler's not really a Tiffany type of guy."

"Why don't they get a tattoo of each other's name?" Sara suggested sarcastically. "You know, you could film a segment leading up to it. Lindsay pleading with her parents to sign the tattoo permission slip, her parents forbidding it, Lindsay being all *Romeo and Juliet* and disobeying them and jumping on the next bus with Tyler to the tattoo shop, where their eternal love is stamped on them for all time."

Jelena failed to heed Sara's sarcasm. "Hmm, that could be compelling viewing. Maybe instead of their full names we could just make the tattoo TylerandLindsay. Or T and L, if either of them's a little needle shy—"

"*No!*" Lindsay and Cass blurted out simultaneously.

"Cass, I don't mean you." Jelena laughed. "You and Scott aren't the tattoo type. This campaign has got to be believable."

"If it's meant to be believable, then you shouldn't be manufacturing content," Lindsay said, clearly distressed.

"Hey, your content was totally believable," Jelena said. "I showed all aspects of the TylerandLindsay dynamic."

Lindsay sighed. "I'm not even going to touch on the total invasion of privacy. But in Cassie's case you manufactured a whole proposal!"

"You completely embarrassed me," Cass said softly. "Now I'm worried Scott thinks I've been going on about Tiffany boxes to you. Boys always think girls are obsessed with getting married."

"Cass, you guys have only been together for two weeks," I reassured her. "Scott's not silly enough to think you're trying to lock it down already."

"It's not just Scott I'm worried about; it's the whole school," Cassie said. "Our dance class is performing Beyoncé's 'Single Ladies' at an assembly in a few weeks." She groaned. "Can you see me, front and center, enthusiastically flapping my hand at the audience and singing about putting a ring on it?"

Jelena burst out laughing, and we all glared at her.

"I'm sorry! It's just perfect irony," she spluttered.

"Perfect for your campaign, you mean?" Sara said, raising an eyebrow.

"I didn't want to have to talk about this stuff so early on," Cass said. "We've only just started calling each other boyfriend and girlfriend. Neither of us has even changed our relationship status on Facebook yet."

"I haven't changed mine back yet, either," Lindsay admitted. "I feel like the only honest status is 'It's complicated.'"

"That's going to have to change," Jelena said. "Both of you—let's do it now on my iPhone. What are your passwords?"

"*No!*" Cass and Lindsay cried again.

Cass shook her head, her delicate little chin looking unusually stubborn. "I'm not changing mine the morning after that slideshow."

"OMG," Jelena huffed. "What about you, Aurora? If you're heading up the Find a Prince/Princess program, you need to look loved up."

"I don't think you can call it a 'relationship' when one party's in solitary confinement due to the gross insensitivity of the other," I sighed.

"I get it. You don't want to be the instigator of the altered status," Jelena said. "How about I text Hayden and tell him to do it?"

"*No!*" the entire table cried.

"I really wish she didn't have any of the boys' numbers," Cass whispered to me.

"I'm just trying to help you people!" Jelena said.

"Hinder, more like it," Lindsay muttered.

"Oh my god! I didn't come to breakfast to sit with a table of people who are angry at me!"

Jelena grabbed her handbag and flounced out the door.

"I guess we're paying for her breakfast, too," Sara said wryly.

"You don't think Jelena will call Scott and talk to him about Facebook, do you?" Cass asked, as she and I walked home after breakfast. "Or worse, a Tiffany ring?"

I had a vision of Jelena marching an embarrassed-looking Scott into Tiffany and forcing him to leave with a little blue box for the sake of the campaign.

"No, of course not," I said in my most convincing voice. "She knows you've vetoed the idea, so she won't take it any further."

Cass still looked uneasy. "Scott sent me a text earlier, asking what I was up to. When I said we were at breakfast, look at what he messaged back." She handed me her phone.

U guys aren't picking baby names r u? ;-)

"Cass, he's totally joking!" I said, handing her back the phone.

"That's what I thought! And then I joked that we were choosing booties and he never replied."

"It's Saturday. Maybe he's gone for breakfast with his friends? Or he's playing sports or something. Plus, he's a guy; he probably thinks booties are high-heeled boots or something. Don't stress about it!"

Cass didn't seem to register my words. "Why did I say that? He was trying to make the situation less awkward and I totally reversed his efforts!"

We reached my place and headed up the driveway so Cass could pick up her overnight bag. She looked up at Hayden's window, which overlooked my driveway.

"I can't believe Hayden's trapped up there. It's like a male version of 'Rapunzel.'"

"I hate that his parents think badly of him for last night," I said. "Plus, imagine what they think of *me* now, after Tyler blurted out in front of them that the party was for the launch of my program? I know it's true and he was trying to get the heat off Hayden, but they're probably thinking, *Motherless teen leading our son astray.*"

"Aurora, you know that's not in any way true." Cass put a hand on my shoulder and forced me to look at her. "They were just upset last night when they found out their house had been taken over by hundreds of teenagers."

I nodded and smiled.

"And Hayden's not mad at you," she continued, as we headed to my front door. I opened it and grabbed her overnight bag from the hall. "I looked at his face when he said good-bye to you last night, and it wasn't angry at all, just sad."

"I hate that I made him feel like that," I said.

"Do something sweet for him," Cassie suggested, as she gave me a good-bye hug. "Maybe you could make him a card? You could leave it at the front door. That way he'll have something nice to look at while he's grounded."

I waved as she headed down the drive, then looked over at Hayden's window again, wondering what he was up to. I could hear the drone of a vacuum cleaner from inside. Mr. and Mrs. Paris had probably put him on further cleanup duties. Part of me wanted to knock on their front door, with a mop, as penance. Then again, just over a week ago, I'd damaged their son's face. Now I'd damaged their property. Any offer of help would probably be seen as a potential liability.

My phone buzzed in my handbag. I took it out and read the text message.

Quickly letting you know Mom and Dad are taking the phone off me for rest of wknd. Will work on Chemistry Calculator, don't worry! Be thinking of you too xoxo

My heart gave a little twinge. Here Hayden was, incarcerated at home, and still offering to spend the weekend creating the tool that would help me cross-reference all the data from the questionnaires last night. Although he'd made out that it was a simple thing to do on a computer, I suspected it wasn't. I'd really been looking forward to working on it together this weekend and had even bought ingredients for cookies, so we'd have something yummy to eat while brainstorming.

I sighed and took one last look at Hayden's window before heading into the house. Maybe Cass was right . . . I should do something sweet for Hayden—literally. I could bake some cookies and package them up for him! It was a small gesture, but at least making them would keep me from moping.

In the kitchen, I pulled out the ingredients and switched on the radio. An upbeat tune came on and I made myself hum along. I needed to stop wallowing and instead start believing that my life and its direction were entirely within my control. Like this weekend. Instead of moping about things going badly with Hayden, I could actively focus on improving the situation. I could bake the cookies and write a note to let him know just how much I appreciated everything that he did on my behalf, including lending his house for the night. And rather than stressing over the disaster surrounding the Find a Prince/Princess™ program debut, I could work on hammering out the steps needed to escort the couples down the road to Happily Ever After. No more Little Miss Meek. Hayden, my friends, and the program needed my positivity and confidence to thrive.

I cheerfully combined all the ingredients into the batter, shaped the cookies into hearts, and popped them into the oven. Just as I finished washing up, the timer went off. I pulled the cookies out of the oven and decided to take a nap while they cooled. I sank onto my bed; the cool sheets felt heavenly after the heat of the kitchen.

I didn't register a thing until something heavy landed on the bed. I opened my eyes and made out Snookums's yellow eyes in the darkness. He pushed his nose into my arm, letting out an impatient meow in his *Where's dinner?* tone.

Wait a minute. Snookums never got fed till sevenish. I sat up, shocked at how dark it was, and looked at my bedside clock. It was 7:30 p.m. I'd been asleep for hours!

I headed downstairs. The house was dark. I switched on the hall light, wandered into the kitchen, and saw a note.

Igneous is having a bad time of it tonight. Taking the quartz crystals around, then we're heading to a therapeutic Vinyasa class. Be back later this evening. Dad xx

I looked outside. It was really dark; the moon was only a sliver in the sky. How was I going to deliver the cookies now? Before, my plan had been to leave them on the doorstep. One of the Parises had been bound to step outside at some point and see them. Now, if the family had settled down for the evening, there'd be no reason for anyone to go out the front door. The cookies would sit outside all night. Even if they didn't get devoured by bugs, they wouldn't be discovered until tomorrow. I didn't want Hayden to be downcast for another twelve to fifteen hours. He had to get the cookies tonight. But how?

Three hours later, I stealthily climbed over the fence into Hayden's yard. That was a long time to get some cookies packaged up, but I'd gotten caught up choosing tracks for his mix CD. It had taken time to select a blend of upbeat, *you'll have better days* songs as well as romantic (but not too mushy) ballads that would hopefully make him think of me. And I'd drafted a number of notes before finally writing my best one, carefully, on my prettiest stationery. Choosing an all-black camouflage outfit had also taken a while. Anyway, the later I showed up, the less likely it was that Hayden's parents would be downstairs and hear me in their front yard.

Hayden's room was, thankfully, the only one that faced the front of the property, overlooking the basketball court. Mr. and Mrs. Paris had the master bedroom, which overlooked the pool out back.

I took the quietest steps possible across the basketball court, until I stood just below Hayden's window. The cookies had now become part of a hefty care package, which I'd loaded into a basket. I'd found some sturdy cord in the garage, which I planned to toss up to Hayden so he could heave the basket up to his room. But first I had to get his attention.

I grabbed a tiny stone from the border surrounding the flower garden. I held my breath, listening for any sound. The house was completely silent and there were no lights showing. I waited a second, then threw the pebble at Hayden's window. It made the slightest of clinks against the glass. I froze and listened again. The only sound was the thundering of my heart.

I picked up a slightly bigger stone. This one landed with a satisfying tap. I beamed, waiting for Hayden to come out onto his balcony. Silence.

"Carpe diem!" I whispered as I picked up a larger stone and flung it at the window. It hit with a massive *crack*. I flung my hands over my head, convinced the glass would splinter. I wondered if the bushes at the side of the house were high enough to conceal me if Hayden's dad came running into the front yard on intruder alert.

Thankfully, the only sound I heard was Hayden's balcony door sliding open.

"Aurora?" he whispered. "Am I dreaming, or is there a quarter-size dent in my bedroom window?" Hayden's voice was wry.

"Surprise?" I tried sheepishly.

He let out a muffled laugh. "Okay, don't throw anything else." He slid the door completely open. "I'm coming outside."

He stepped onto the balcony and looked at the glass, then whistled. "There's a fair amount of damage."

"It was meant with the best of intentions," I whispered.

"Oh, really?" He leaned over the balcony, just above me.

"I wanted to do something to say that I'm sorry for all the mishaps." I held up the basket. "I never meant for any of them to happen—like your lip, and the awkward date at the outdoor movie, and the party debacle."

"You don't think I'm still cut up about the lip, do you?" he whispered.

I winced at his words. "That's it, though. Your lip is literally cut up. And last night . . . I didn't know that Jelena had told you I was expecting you to host the party as proof of your dedication to me. I feel awful—"

"Okay, that's it." Hayden sounded incredibly unhappy.

I looked up to see him swing himself over the balcony railing, which was about fourteen feet up in the air.

"*What are you doing?*" I whisper-shrieked.

"I'm not letting you do this."

Hayden let his body drop down so he was hanging by both hands from the bottom rail. OMG.

I clamped my hand over my mouth to stifle a scream as Hayden let go of the rail and dropped through the air.

He landed next to me with a graceful thump. My heart felt like it had fallen several feet too.

He took my face in his hands. "I'm not letting you blame yourself for everything."

I was trembling, not just from the sudden stress of his fall but also due to the proximity of his face to mine.

"This is exactly what I'm talking about. I don't want you thinking you have to do crazy things to impress me or keep me happy. That includes leaping off the balcony."

"Princess, I don't do anything I don't want to." Hayden kissed my forehead, keeping his lips there for a full minute. "You need to realize that."

I didn't want to speak. I just put my arms around him. This was the first time I'd been in his arms since I'd discovered he was my secret admirer. Every tense muscle instantly unwound, the heat of his body melting away the stress in seconds.

"And I'm not unhappy," Hayden murmured in my ear. "I have you, so I can't possibly be unhappy, even if I am grounded and likely to face questioning over the window tomorrow."

"I'll tell them it was me," I said, pulling away to look him in the eye. "I'll come by tomorrow and explain—"

Hayden put a finger over my lips. "No. I'll tell them it was a chubby bird that misnavigated. Actually, make that a *clumsy* bird. More believable."

I laughed, batting him on the chest playfully. "Are you going to be able to keep a straight face?"

"I'll practice in the mirror," Hayden said, laughing with me. "But seriously, the pebble and the window? This sleek black espionage outfit?" He gave my leather-look leggings a thumbs-up. "What's going on?"

"I wanted to lift your spirits," I said, holding up the gift basket. "I know you have to stay inside till Monday, but hopefully this will keep you happy till then."

Hayden looked at the embarrassingly full basket.

"A book, CDs, a candle, cookies . . ." Hayden squeezed my hand in his. "But you realize this won't do the trick entirely?"

"What do you mean?" I looked at the basket. What else could he need? I'd even included some caramel-infused tea to go with the cookies.

"There's only one thing that's going to ensure I'm completely and utterly on cloud nine all weekend," Hayden said solemnly. "A kiss."

I felt my hands get instantly clammy with fear. "No, I—" I almost said, *I don't want to mess it up again*, but went with, "I don't want to rip up your lip again, now that it's healing."

"Haven't you heard . . . ?" Hayden's mouth was suddenly so close to mine. He kissed just to the right of my lips. "Kisses make everything better. They mend things. I don't know about the window, but I know that the tiniest touch of your lips makes my heart forget about anything painful. Even after what happened last time, I can't stop thinking about it."

"Hayden, we can't—"

"Aurora." The way he said my name was like a sigh. "Let me kiss you. *Please.*"

The word was like a magic key on a locked room. I lost all resistance. I closed my eyes, forgetting the calamity of the last time I'd attempted this. I felt Hayden's breath tickle my lips slightly and my knees shook in anticipation.

Suddenly, even though my eyes were closed, I felt a bright light shining in my face.

"Oh no." Hayden pulled away from me. "Dad."

"I thought your parents were asleep!" I cried, as the headlights of the Parises' car came closer. I put a hand up to shield my eyes and glimpsed Mr. Paris in the driver's seat. His lips thinned as he took in our illicit rendezvous.

"Mom is," Hayden said. "Dad had a dinner with friends. I wasn't expecting him back yet."

I wanted to put my head in my hands out of shame.

The car stopped in front of us. Mr. Paris opened the door.

"Hayden." His voice was displeasure personified.

Any hope of redeeming myself in the Parises' opinion vanished. I looked like a siren who'd lured Hayden down from the house and who had no respect for the Parises' rules.

"Mr. Paris," I said miserably, "this isn't Hayden's fault."

"Aurora, it's best you go home." Mr. Paris gave me a disappointed look. "I need to speak to Hayden."

I didn't dare disobey him. I handed Hayden the basket and walked back to the fence, resisting the temptation to break into a sprint. Funny how horrendously awkward it is climbing over a fence late at night while your crush's father is watching.

9

Sunday was torture. I was unable to see or speak to Hayden, so I didn't know what further punishment his parents had issued after last night's events. I dreaded to think what Mr. and Mrs. Paris would say when they discovered the dented window.

I played the events of last night again and again in my mind, imagining myself stopping at the fence, or not picking up that stone. But I always ended up with the image of Hayden standing in front of me, his face close to mine. I imagined his fingers entwined with mine and felt my face flush as I relived the feel of his lips on my forehead, his breath on my cheek, the warmth emanating from his skin as he moved closer and closer. I wanted that kiss. I wanted it so badly.

Only I couldn't seem to bring it fully to life. It was as if the trauma of our last lip-to-lip moment had wiped out everything else, leaving only blankness in its place. It was as if I had never experienced a kiss at all.

I opened my eyes with a start. What if the same thing happened when Hayden and I next attempted a kiss in real life? What if I completely froze, terrified of the accidents that might occur when our lips met? I imagined Hayden's mouth moving over my unresponsive one, and shivered. That would make me the worst type of kisser—the dead-fish kisser.

I couldn't let it happen to me. I had to become a kisser extraordinaire, stat! But how? I thought back to the advice Jelena had issued the day I was dubbed "Lethal Lips." The internet!

I had to admit, I was unconvinced that the electronic domain could act as tutor for such an intimate act. But when I wandered downstairs to find my laptop and googled "kissing tips," my doubts were erased by the innumerable results: "First kiss dos and don'ts"; "Nose placement know-how"; "The role of the tongue in the initial lip-lock . . ." I barely knew where to start.

I jumped up and grabbed a notebook, then began scribbling notes.

As more and more pages filled up, I started to worry. The basics didn't seem basic at all—in fact, they seemed overwhelming. I'd never considered the number of factors that made up a successful kiss. You couldn't just stick with your lips meeting his. Oh no. Terms like "pucker position," "yield and give," "over and under extension" were thrown around, and each was deemed crucial. Some descriptions made me think of scuba diving. "Don't forget to come up for air," one article warned. It seemed, just like Cassie had mentioned, that there was a real risk of expiring midact.

As I moved on to the pages on French kissing, my head clouded further with confusion. Part of me wondered if god truly intended tongues to be used in kissing. The whole idea of two slug-like things "dancing and curling around each other," as one site put it, was really unappealing.

And how wide was too wide when it came to mouths? Obviously, you couldn't come at someone with your mouth open like the shark in *Jaws*, but you couldn't gracefully maneuver your tongue out between your lips and into his mouth without a significant gap in the case of both parties, could you? What if you stuck your tongue out and his lips were closed at that very moment?

"Argh." I needed more intensive help.

I typed in "kissing demonstrations." I started with excitement when a video link popped up. A real-life tutorial—perfect!

I pressed Play. A youngish guy with an encouraging smile popped up on-screen.

"Hello, I'm Kai, the Kissing Guy. I'm here to ensure your introduction to the poetics of the pash is as breezy as possible." Kai's voice was super enthusiastic. "Today we're going to run through the fundamentals of a successful kiss, including head alignment, lip pressure, the technicalities of tongues, and the successful breakaway. We'll examine each stage in detail so you get a good feel for it.

"You may want to follow along, practicing on the back of your hand," Kai continued. "Some people practice on a pillow, but in my opinion the sensation of skin against your lips will help you to assess saliva levels."

I looked at my hand. This was straight out of some embarrassing eighties movie, where a teenage girl with a bad perm stared longingly at a yearbook picture of an unattainable quarterback.

"I encourage you to break away from your hand every so often and examine it," Kai said. "If there's no saliva on your hand, you know your kisses are too dry and your mouth should be more open. If your hand is trickling with saliva, your kisses are too wet. This is a result of having your mouth open too wide or of not engaging enough and merely letting your mouth hang open so the saliva seeps out."

My stomach churned. Maybe I could just watch.

"This may seem unappealing to many of you, but a bit of practice goes a long way," Kai continued. "Experts say that the first kiss can determine the eventual outcome of the relationship. If it's a good kiss, the couple will continue building their bond. If it's bad, the couple is extremely unlikely to form a significant relationship. In fact, in a recent study, fifty-nine percent of men and sixty-six percent of women reported that they lost their attraction to a formerly desirable partner after a less-than-perfect first kiss."

Saliva or not, I couldn't risk ruining a future relationship with Hayden due to my hesitation over using my hand as a make-out partner. I'd squeezed by with the first kiss, for whatever reason—luck maybe?—but judging by our second, I couldn't expect to wing it every time our lips met. I pressed Pause on the video and drew the curtains over the living room windows. Thank god the NAD was out. I sat back on the couch, sighed, and raised my wrist to my mouth. I turned the sound up so I could hear Kai's instructions while my hand was half over my face.

"So, the big moment has arrived," Kai said, in voice-over mode, as the scene changed to a shot of him and a girl standing close together against a white backdrop. "He or she is standing in front of you, their lips inches from yours. If this is your first time, you'll be asking yourself, *When do I shut my eyes?*"

That was a fair point.

"You don't want to shut them too early. Eye contact is key to building intimacy. Our pupils dilate when we're attracted to someone, and we are instinctively attuned to register this reaction in our partner's eyes. If pupil dilation is occurring effectively, you are likely to feel slightly dizzy and drawn in by your partner's gaze. This is when most couples move into 'pash position'—their bodies are urging them to get closer."

I paused the video and took up my pen. I couldn't do this half-heartedly. I drew a pair of eyes on my hand, then added a nose and mouth. I had to have some idea of where to place my lips; otherwise, I'd be roaming all over the place and end up making out with Hayden's chin. Having an outline made sense. No one could say I hadn't given my all to this kissing thing.

"Staring into your partner's eyes, move your face closer, inch by inch," Kai continued.

I looked at my hand. It was hardly giving off the look of love. I remembered the way Hayden's eyes had looked last night when he'd pleaded for a kiss. *Bam!* I got that hazy feeling. Pupil dilation was obviously kicking in.

"You're probably so close to your partner that you think you're going to go cross-eyed," Kai said, breaking into my delirium. "Close your eyes at this point. Some of you may be a little worried about missing your mark, now that you can't see. But if you've lined yourself up correctly and tilted your head to the right so as to avoid any collisions, you should meet your target easily. Do *not* keep your eyes open. I cannot emphasize this enough."

I shut my eyes, doing all I could to block the overwhelming sense of the ridiculous from my mind. *You are kissing Hayden. Not your hand. Hayden.* I repeated the mantra to myself.

"Relax your lips," Kai said. "Relaxed lips are kissable lips. It's easy to tense up when you're nervous, but that's exactly what you're aiming to avoid. Remember to keep breathing. Part your lips ever so slightly and make contact."

My lips met the skin on the back of my hand. I resisted the urge to jerk away.

"Move your lips gently over your partner's. Press your lips together and then apart. It's much like the motion you'd use to kiss someone on the cheek, but more drawn out. If you're practicing on your hand, you'll be able to feel how you can adjust the pressure of your lips. Try building up to a firmer pressure as the kiss gets more passionate."

I tried to make the lip-lock more intense, but without a pair of lips pressing back, it was extremely hard to ascertain the correct positioning.

"A great move is to place your upper lip just above your partner's upper lip, so your lower lip is nestled between their lips. Try nipping and lightly sucking at their lips, tilting your head accordingly. When you're ready, switch around so your upper lip is between their lips and you're nuzzling at their lower lip."

I'd totally moved off the marker guidelines and was currently nuzzling Hayden's ear.

"Okay, the kiss is going tremendously well," Kai said. "Now is the time to momentarily break away, without pulling back entirely from your partner."

I released my hand from the passionate embrace. Both of us were grateful for the break.

"Make sure you're still breathing steadily through your nose," Kai instructed. "When you're ready, commence the kiss again, but this time part your lips and allow your tongue to slip through them. Tentatively at first, trace your tongue along your partner's lips."

I resisted a shriek as I felt my tongue tickle the back of my hand.

"Not too fast now," Kai warned. "If your partner likes the sensation, they will mirror your action with their tongue. This is your green light to proceed. Slowly open your mouth slightly wider and push your tongue forward to explore your partner's mouth. Do *not* lunge your tongue into their mouth. Your tongue should be a tentative explorer."

I tried to imagine Hayden's tongue as a tentative explorer and got a picture of a nineteenth-century traveler hacking his way through the jungle. I burst out laughing.

"You should be lost in the moment at this stage," Kai said.

I looked at my hand and laughed harder.

"French kissing is the most challenging technique," Kai said. "It can go disastrously wrong or incredibly right, depending on how you execute it. It's the area where you're most likely to be deemed a good or bad kisser, so I'd encourage you to spend time practicing this one."

The idea of being judged on my ability with my tongue struck terror into me. I rewound the tutorial several times so I could rehearse from start to finish.

"I encourage you to watch my second installment, which goes to the next level," Kai said at the conclusion of the video.

The next clip popped up, entitled "Make-Out Mastery." What the heck; I'd gone this far. As I clicked Play, I pictured myself delivering a knockout kiss that left Hayden reeling.

"Mastery denotes extreme proficiency in a specific area," Kai began. "If you've watched my first installment, then you'll be feeling A-OK with locking lips. I'm now going to show you how to engage your whole body in the kiss and take things to the next level."

This was exactly what I needed. All of the sites had warned against letting your hands hang limply by your sides; you had to involve them in the kiss. I was confused about whether to put my hands around Hayden's shoulders or to place one hand on his cheek or to run my hands through his hair.

I heard a bang in the hall and shot up from my seat. I pressed Pause, then went to investigate. Snookums had stuck his head into one of my shoe boxes and was banging it against the front door. Bebe was attempting to knock the box off him. I returned to my laptop and pressed Play again.

"This is where we amp up the chemistry," Kai instructed. "So, we're kissing passionately . . ."

I turned my attention back to my hand and resumed lip contact. I was starting to get way more control over the pressure—my tongue muscle was adapting. I guessed these tutorials were the equivalent of bicep exercises.

Kai broke away midkiss to face the camera. "Here's where it heats up. You want to show your partner that this is one passionate kiss. Just warning you: this move can be tricky to pull off, and it's crucial to keep kissing as you do it."

I watched, almost hypnotized, my hand still at my mouth. There was another bang at the door. Probably Bebe, still wrestling Snookums for the box. I turned up the sound, super excited to progress to the next step. It was going to be groundbreaking stuff, from Kai's serious tone.

I watched as Kai pulled the girl closer to him and shifted his hand from her waist to her butt. OMG, this wasn't just kissing—he was going for the grope!

Kai turned his head to the camera again. "You see how I've amped up the sexy factor, simply by slowly moving my hand from my partner's waist to her butt?"

I was *so* not ready for any of this. Hayden didn't think he could grab me in inappropriate places during our third kiss, did he? He couldn't!

Just as Kai moved in for more intense kissing, the NAD and his entire support group came bustling into the living room. I frantically dropped my hand from my mouth and lunged at the Stop button, but instead of pausing, the video skipped back. I watched in horror as Kai groped the girl all over again, his detailed instructions blaring through the room. Why hadn't I worn headphones? More obviously, why hadn't I taken the laptop up to my room?

I shut the lid in an attempt to pretend the playback had never happened, but the faces of the NAD and the group made it clear they'd seen and heard everything.

What was the NAD doing home so early? I looked up at the clock and saw that it was four p.m. I'd spent hours hanging on Kai's every word!

"Aurora . . ." The NAD sounded as awkward as I felt. I saw his gaze go to my ink-covered hand.

"YouTube is a great platform for learning," Primrose said encouragingly.

"Evidently," the NAD said, opening the laptop and looking at the long list of suggested videos on making out. "Though you want to make sure you're learning the right things from it. Things appropriate for your age."

"The decision to embark on a journey of physical intimacy is not one that should be made without significant consideration," Echo said solemnly, sitting on the floor and crossing her legs lotus style. "The bonds that come from joining at a cellular level can be long-lasting. This is what makes it immensely painful for individuals if the relationship terminates."

OMG. They couldn't possibly think I was looking for advice on anything more than kissing, could they?

Igneous let out a shaky sigh. *Please, god, don't let him relay any memories of joining at a cellular level.*

"Young priestesses must be conscious of their choices involving energy exchange," Echo added.

I stared at her blankly. Priestesses?

"What Echo's trying to say"—Dad's voice was super serious—"is that there's no need to rush things. I'd like to think you and Hayden are sensible enough to realize that."

"Dad, I can assure you I'm not rushing into anything," I blurted out. The heat in my cheeks became a full-body blush. "I thought this was a kissing video. Kissing. Nothing else . . ."

Dad looked at me carefully. "Okay, honey. Well, you know you can always come to me for advice. I trust Hayden to do the right thing by you, but if you're ever uneasy that things are moving too fast—"

"Things are moving really, really slow," I cut in. "Like super slow. I'm talking snail's pace. Or maybe sloth's. Whatever moves slower! Anyway, I'm late to meet Cassie. We're having coffee. Be back later!"

"You might want to wash your face, honey!" the NAD called after me, as I dashed out of the room.

I looked in the bathroom mirror. Blue ink was smudged across my nose, cheeks, lips, and chin. I looked down at my hand and saw that my makeshift drawing was blurred. I had obviously been less precise with my lip placement than I'd thought. Why hadn't I used a permanent marker? Or, more obviously, why had I drawn a face at all? Sometimes I really wondered at the spectacular efforts I made to set myself up for extreme mortification.

10

"So, what was everyone up to yesterday?" Jelena asked, as we all headed over to the arts block for our early Monday art unit.

I stayed quiet. I really didn't want to relay in detail how the NAD's support group had outed me playing tonsil hockey with my own hand.

"Well, my Sunday was spent lying in the hammock reading *Capturing a Cowboy*," Sara said. "It's by the same author as *To Tame a Texan*. She's the queen of crafting spine-tingling chemistry. I had to force myself not to skip ahead to the part where Jeremiah and Georgia-May have to hide under an overhanging rock shelf after he rescues her from bandits."

"I'm sorry, but there's no way someone called Jeremiah can be hot," Jelena said. "It's like something straight out of *The Beverly Hillbillies*. You do not want to go lip to lip with a guy who eats road-kill."

"Well, Jeremiah *is* hot." Sara feigned a swoon. "He's got sinewy muscles and eyes the color of Colombian coffee beans. Plus, he doesn't eat roadkill—he eats squirrels."

"*What?*" we all chorused.

Sara shrugged. "They're trapped in the desert. They have to eat something, so Jeremiah shoots a squirrel to roast on their fire."

"I'm willing to bet you my new hair straightener that if a Jeremiah clone rocked up to that school gate, a roasted squirrel over his shoulder—"

"Jelena, do you have to get so graphic?" I felt like throwing up.

"With a roasted, not-to-be-named animal over his shoulder," Jelena continued dramatically, "you would not eat it."

Sara rolled her eyes. "Like I'm going to dig into a squirrel when the cafeteria's two minutes away. They only eat the thing because they're a two-day horseback ride from the nearest gold town."

"Even if you were in the desert, I know you wouldn't do it," Jelena said.

"If Jeremiah rescued you from bandits, you'd probably be so ungrateful and brattish that there'd be no way he'd lay you down and kiss your neck under the moonlight," Sara countered.

"With his squirrel-scented breath," Jelena shot back.

"Ew!" Lindsay, Cassie, and I exclaimed.

"Aurora, can we chat quickly?" Hayden was suddenly at my side. Hopefully, he'd missed the exchange about Jeremiah.

"Sure," I replied. "I'll see you guys in art in a few minutes."

Jelena gave Hayden a cool wave. He gave her one back. Thankfully, it seemed that Friday hadn't left them at odds with each other.

Hayden took my hand and led me over to the jasmine archway in the school garden. We'd stood here together once before, on the opening night of *Much Ado About Nothing.*

"Listen . . . about this weekend . . ." Hayden's voice turned serious, and he let go of my hand.

Why had he let go of my hand?

"I care about you, but I'm worried things aren't going to work—"

OMG. This was the *You're great but I'm just not feeling it* line that guys used to call it a day on a budding relationship. I was being dumped!

Maybe, during the long hours of his captivity, Hayden had decided he wanted a fresh slate dating-wise. An opportunity to woo a girl his parents would approve of. Though part of me could see the logic, another part of me was angry. We hadn't even had enough dates to ascertain whether things could work! How could you call off a relationship if you hadn't given it a fair chance?

"Hayden, I get it. You don't need to say anything more. I need to get to art class."

I was amazed at how cold I sounded. That numbness that had been my constant companion for a long time after Mom had left crept over me again. Coping with unexpected ends to relationships was my specialty.

I turned away from Hayden. I didn't trust myself to look in his eyes and hold it together. What I'd felt for him, even in this brief time, had been more than I'd let myself feel in many years.

"Aurora!" Hayden grabbed my hand as I tried to take off. He moved across the path so I was facing him again.

I looked at the ground and pushed his hand away. "I don't want to hear it."

"I haven't even finished my sentence yet!" His voice sounded agitated.

"You don't need to. I get it. I really do."

"No, you don't. Let me finish my sentence."

Hayden gently lifted my chin so I was forced to look at him. I willed all vulnerability out of my gaze as I met his eyes. They looked sad. Darn those autumn-leaf eyes and their ability to pull at my heartstrings.

Hayden started again. "I care about you, but I'm worried things aren't going to work—if you don't believe that I care," he finished in a rush. He let out a sigh. "I think I'm being crazy obvious about my feelings whenever I'm with you, but evidently it's not enough, if you're so worried you feel you have to sneak over at night."

"I know, I shouldn't have gone that far—"

"I loved you going that far."

Hayden took my hand again, and I felt the numbness lifting off me.

"You did?"

He smiled. "I'm all for spontaneous gestures of affection. Can't you tell from my track record as your secret admirer?"

I was totally confused now. Maybe I'd taken his words the wrong way. Sometimes I had a tendency to let my imagination run away with me. The thing was always boarding flights and jetting off before I knew the whole story.

"But I want those gestures to happen because you're crazy about me," Hayden went on, "not because you're stressing that you have to make things better in case I change my mind about you. Which I'm not going to, by the way."

"No?" I whispered. I felt my carefully concealed vulnerability show itself again.

Hayden dropped his hand from my cheek and reached for his back pocket. "I want you to have a visible reminder of how much you mean to me, and how permanent I intend this—us—to be."

He pulled out a Tiffany box. I stared at the blue and white packaging, feeling dizzy. I got a flash of Jelena's dismayed face at missing out on recording an actual Tiffany scene.

"I know most people would say I'm a total idiot for buying something like this so early on," Hayden said. "But you and me—it's not like we're two teenagers who just spotted one another in class the other day. I've known you—I've cared about you—for so many years now."

He placed the box in my palm. I looked up at him and could see his nervousness as he waited. I pulled at the perfect white bow and lifted the lid of the box. Inside was a delicate silver necklace with a tiny *X* hanging from it.

"It's a kiss," Hayden explained. "I wanted you to have one always, even if I can't physically be there. I chose the necklace so you can keep it close to your heart. You remember Peter Pan and Wendy?"

Hayden's dad had read us the story many years ago, and I'd almost cried when Wendy had been shot in the heart with the arrow. I remembered Hayden slinging an arm around me and saying, *She'll be okay. You remember the acorn around her neck—Peter's kiss will protect her. Plus, nobody dies in a fairy story. Not even Captain Hook, I bet.*

"Your kisses are everything to me, slight mishaps and all." Hayden took the necklace from my hand and fastened it around my neck. The slight brush of his fingertips on the delicate skin of my neck was the most tender thing I'd ever experienced. Half of me expected to wake up and realize this moment was all a dream.

I threw my arms around Hayden before it all melted away. "Thank you!"

He lowered his head to mine and we were on the precipice of a kiss before I knew it.

The bell sounded.

Hayden let out a frustrated sigh and pulled away from me. "The real world is calling. We'd better go."

As I dashed into the art room, all my friends looked up from their sculptures.

"So?" Sara bounced over to me.

"So, what?" I tried to be casual, but my cheeks were aching from grinning, a dead giveaway to my friends. "He gave me a symbolic kiss." I pulled out the Tiffany box.

The screams that erupted were enough to shatter glass.

"Girls!" Ms. Collins shouted from the front of the room. "Please attempt to focus!"

"Sorry!" Cass sent an apologetic wave to Ms. Collins.

"Open it now!" Lindsay said in a whisper, as we pretended to do work.

Jelena snatched the box from me. "I told you guys!" she said triumphantly, and sent Cass and Lindsay a look. "The little blue box is a realistic outcome! And you all pooh-poohed the idea on Saturday."

She opened up the box, and her face fell when she saw it was empty. She looked at me accusingly. "This isn't some symbolic thing, is it? You and Hayden are really odd with all that stuff."

"Well, it's a little like the acorn in *Peter Pan*." It was kind of fun to tease Jelena. "You know how Peter called it a kiss?"

"Hayden's calling thin air a kiss now?" Jelena stared at the box unbelievingly. "Are you sure he hasn't recycled an old gift box from an ex-girlfriend?"

Okay, now it was time to end the joke. "Guys—" I started.

"Hayden hasn't had a girlfriend besides Aurora, has he?" Sara asked. "That's why every girl's been sighing over him for three years with no luck."

"Maybe it's his mom's box?" Cassie suggested.

"No, he bought the box," I said, managing to get a word in.

"So he went to Tiffany and asked them for an empty box without making an actual purchase?" Jelena stared at me. "Can you even *do* that?"

"Jelena, don't be rude," Cassie said. "Tiffany is really expensive! That's why I've been saying that you can't go around pressuring Scott."

"I haven't!" Jelena protested.

"You stuck one of the ads on my locker today." Cass folded her arms, looking put out. "Scott came over to say hello and saw it."

"The man should know that you're worth the expense, Cassie," Jelena replied. "Same with Tyler. I'm doing you guys a favor. You have to set standards."

"Guys," I said, quickly interjecting, as Cass and Lindsay looked close to losing it with Jelena. "The box *wasn't* empty. It had this inside." I touched the charm on my necklace.

There was a mini stampede as all four of them lunged at my neck.

Lindsay stared at the necklace. "No way."

"It's a kiss," Cass sighed.

"Aurora, that's really special," Lindsay said seriously. "It took Tyler a lot longer to give me jewelry."

"You don't think Hayden's gearing up for the four-letter word, do you?" Sara asked.

"Don't be stupid," Jelena said. "This isn't a Harlequin romance. You can't drop the l-bomb after a grand total of two kisses."

"You guys have really only kissed twice?" Sara asked me. "If I was dating Hayden, I'd be lip-smacking nonstop."

"His stitches aren't due to come out till Wednesday," I replied, trying not to blush. "Plus, his grounding lasts until Friday."

"Are you ready for Friday, then?" Lindsay asked.

"I hope so," I said. "I've read everything I can on the 'net about kissing."

"Ah, so you took my advice." Jelena nodded approvingly.

I sighed. "How come you guys never told me how insanely complicated kissing is? Everyone makes it seem like it's the most natural, most easy thing in the world, and then I find out that a French kiss involves thirty-four facial muscles and one hundred and twelve postural muscles!"

Lindsay laughed. "You're thinking of it like an anatomy class. Or a gym workout. It's not like that."

"But the action's centered on anatomy," I protested. I'd done some reading on the science of kissing before bed last night. "It's all about mechanics."

Cassie looked curious. "Like how?"

"Like, in terms of what's involved in a kiss," I explained. "All emotions aside, the physiology is really complex. A kiss, if you ask scientists, is pretty much chemicals communicating."

"Communicating what?" Sara asked, looking confused.

"Well, philematologists—scientists who study kissing—say that it has a very practical purpose: it passes vital messages to both partners about their biological compatibility. It's like nature's ultimate test. If the kiss doesn't feel right, then it's no-go for lifelong coupledom."

"So what's involved in the test?" Lindsay asked.

"Saliva. One-third of an ounce of the stuff gets exchanged in the average kiss. Along with roughly ten million to a billion bacteria."

"Ew!" The whole group let out a cry. Ms. Collins glanced over disapprovingly, and we hurriedly pretended to focus on our work.

Jelena looked truly repulsed. She was something of a germophobe.

"Well, that certainly strips the romance from it all." Sara shook her head sadly.

"Gross as it is, saliva's apparently key," I said. "The chemicals it contains send a cascade—"

"No more watery adjectives, please," Jelena said. I'd never seen her look so unnerved.

"The chemicals send tons of info to your brain for processing," I continued. "And the brain uses the chemicals as scientific samples to determine your compatibility with your kissing partner."

"So what sorts of things does it look at?" Cass asked.

"Lots of different things. Like, apparently, on a cellular level, women prefer men who have a different genetic code in specific areas. There's this region known as the major histocompatibility system. If your histocompatibility system is too similar to that of the guy you're kissing, you'll be totally put off by him, because your body needs different DNA to make sure your offspring has a stronger immune system. That's why you usually know within seconds whether a kiss feels right or wrong."

"That kind of makes sense," Cassie said. "Remember Chris, that guy from my tennis lessons that I helped through his breakup?"

"One of the millions you've counseled, only to find yourself fending off their brokenhearted, desperate advances?" Jelena said. "Oh, we remember."

"Chris was perfect on paper," Cassie went on. "I was super attracted to him, too."

"You never told me this," I said, staring at her. We knew just about all of one another's secrets when it came to love stuff.

"I thought it was unprofessional to get involved with someone I was supposed to be counseling," Cass explained. "Anyway, one day we were sitting on the sideline, eating rainbow Popsicles. The wind was blowing my hair into my face, and the next minute Chris was pushing the hair out of my eyes and putting his rainbow-colored lips to mine. My heart was drumming like crazy, 'cause I'd been imagining kissing him for weeks."

"You had a secret crush and you never told me!" I blurted out. "What happened?"

"I didn't feel anything when he kissed me," Cass said. "Despite the fact that he had great lips, fresh breath, and was an extremely proficient kisser. I remember willing myself to feel something, but all I noticed was that our lips were sticky from the Popsicles."

"So that's why you quit tennis!" I said, putting the pieces together.

"Chris kept pursuing me," Cass said. "He kept asking me why I didn't like him, and I had no explanation for it. Now it's completely clear: he had a similar immune system!"

"Totally great excuse," Sara said. "*It's not you; it's your immune system.* Takes the personal out of it."

Lindsay's brow was furrowed. "Why wasn't Chris deterred, then? Wouldn't his body sense the incompatibility too?"

"Men aren't as programmed as women are to think about long-term suitability," I said. "Women are generally the ones in the driver's seat when it comes to whether the relationship goes to the next level.

"You know the weirdest thing I read? You've heard how guys are meant to like sloppier kisses? Well, supposedly it's biologically driven—their saliva contains trace amounts of testosterone and, through lots of tongue kissing, it's transferred to the woman, which increases the chances of her being in the mood for further make-outs."

"So men have an agenda with their brash brandishing of the tongue?" Jelena said, making another icky face.

"Totally true!" Sara said, stabbing the air with her index finger to emphasize her agreement. "Like Rob from math. When he kissed me at the spring dance, it was exactly like a drive-through car wash."

Sara's body convulsed in a shudder. "Water was flying everywhere and his tongue lashed me from nose to chin. The bristles on his upper lip felt like the cleaning brushes rolling over the car. Horrendous."

"I'm kind of having a slight problem with *Tongue horribilis*," Cass said softly.

We all turned our attention from Sara's theatrics to her.

"Um, repeat, please?" Jelena said, looking completely shocked.

"Currently?" I whispered, looking over at Scott, who, thankfully, was focused on his sculpture at the front of the room.

"How can you not have said anything?" Sara asked.

"I was embarrassed," Cass said, looking at the floor. "Plus, I was terrified that it'd somehow get back to him. We all know men have fragile egos."

"Scott's guilty of the car wash?" Lindsay looked like she couldn't believe it.

"It's not like a car wash," Cass whispered. "It's kind of like . . . I don't know . . . an overenthusiastic puppy."

"I.e., he's panting and slobbering," Jelena said matter-of-factly.

"Jelena!" we all cried.

"How come Aurora can talk about saliva and I can't say 'slobbering'?" Jelena asked.

"It's not over-the-top slobbering," Cass emphasized. "It's just that his tongue is too pointy. Slightly stabby."

Jelena looked like she was about to fall off her chair with mirth. "I'm so calling him that in secret! Señor Stabby!"

"Jelena!" Cass looked like she regretted saying a word.

"Has he had a girlfriend before?" I asked. "Maybe he doesn't have much experience and thinks the stabbing is par for the course."

"He said he dated a girl for two months last year," Cass said. "Her family moved overseas."

"No wonder she changed time zones," Jelena said. "I'm sorry, Cass. Puppies are cute, but they've got to be housebroken."

"How on earth have you put up with kissing him for hours on end?" Sara asked.

"I was kind of hoping he'd improve with extensive practice." Cass's face was stressed. "I've tried from the start to give him subtle hints. You know, keeping my lips tightly pursed to make it clear that his tongue's too enthusiastic. But he keeps poking it against my closed mouth, like an enemy charging at a fortress gate."

Sara shook her head. "Subtle never works. I ended up actually shoving Rob away from me when he didn't get the picture. Hopefully he won't unleash that car wash monster on anyone else."

"Okay, well, with Scott I suggest you snag a clothespin from home, and when he pokes his tongue out again, you clamp it," Jelena said, making a pinching gesture with her thumb and forefinger.

We all burst out laughing. Ms. Collins didn't even react this time; perhaps she had given up on us.

"I'm serious!" Jelena cried. "He'll never do it again."

"I think that might be a relationship deal breaker," I said.

"Don't get me wrong," Cass said. "It's amazing kissing—well, right up until the tongue comes into play. It'd be fine if the muscle was relaxed instead of pokey."

Her face scrunched up again and we all laughed.

"You see why I didn't want to bring it up?" Cass said to me.

"Cass, no." I felt relieved that I wasn't the only one floundering in the ocean of make-out mishaps. "We have to be able to talk about these things; otherwise, we can't help each other."

"Speaking of that . . . I'm going to do a Cass and let it all out," Lindsay said, her words coming in a rush. "I've gone dead to Tyler's kisses. I don't understand what's changed, because his kisses are totally on target technique-wise. As you can imagine, we've perfected our kissing over three years."

"We don't have to imagine," Jelena said. "We were witness to the training program in action, every lunch break . . ."

Lindsay ignored her. "I don't feel anything when his lips touch mine. The other day I zoned out mid–make out and imagined a whole showcase of my pieces on the Paris catwalks, shoes and all. I'm talking extensive detail. I only came to when Tyler accidentally pulled my hair while he was running his hands through it.

"I felt seriously guilty." Lindsay's face was red with embarrassment.

"I'm telling you, an upgrade's in order," Jelena said in a singsong voice. "This whole notion of an enduring high school romance is a myth."

"Hey!" Cass, Lindsay, and I all stared at her. She couldn't be serious.

"You're the one backing the Find a Prince/Princess program!" I blurted out. "You can't be lacking in faith about lasting teen love."

"Okay, I should put that more succinctly," Jelena said. "What I mean is, a lasting romance that started before you were a mature high school student is a myth. Lindsay and Tyler started dating at fourteen. Those three years are like a stratosphere when it comes to maturity levels. You think about what we were into at fourteen! You wouldn't wear the same clothes you did then, so why are you going to date the same guy? Whereas now we're approaching adulthood, it's way more likely that our tastes *might* be the same into our twenties."

"My parents met at fifteen," Cass told Lindsay. "Though they didn't actually become a couple until college. But I'm sure if they had taken the plunge in their teen years, they would still have lasted."

Lindsay looked slightly happier.

"You obviously don't want to call it a day," I said to Lindsay.

She nodded. I knew that whatever was going on for her was hugely complex. She wouldn't call it a day on Tyler until she was truly sure.

"You forgot the word 'yet,'" Jelena murmured.

"Jelena!" we all cried.

"Is it *so* wrong that I think Lindsay deserves a more mature man?" Jelena asked. "A senior maybe?"

"I don't understand why one minute you're holding them up as the Holy Grail of couples and planning for Tyler to present Lindsay with jewelry," I said, "and the next minute, you're encouraging Linds to toss Tyler away."

"First, I'm not saying drop him to the curb like trash," Jelena huffed. "More like gently hand him in to the thrift shop, like a dress you don't wear any more. You want someone else to be able to enjoy the item."

"I don't know . . ." Lindsay looked slightly green at the idea of another girl snapping up Tyler like a lucky thrift shop find.

"Second," Jelena continued, "as Lindsay's friend, I'm very aware of her dating market value. Why should she have to put up with something subpar? She's worth more. And finally, having an unhappy couple as a representation of the program completely undermines both the program and the election. I either want them madly in love or, if that's not possible anymore, not together at all. That's why, if Lindsay's leaning toward closing this chapter with Tyler, I want her to decide ASAP what she's going to do. Either end it completely so that Aurora can set her up with a fantastic new candidate in the next few weeks, or be considerate enough to hold off on dumping Tyler until I'm sworn in as president."

"You are truly selfless," Sara said, bowing in servitude to Jelena.

Jelena merely smiled as if Sara were serious.

"Lindsay, I don't want you to stay in a relationship that's unhappy," I said. "But I don't think that's the case. You love Tyler—and he loves you! There's a holiness in that—"

"And here comes the John Keats reference," Jelena interrupted.

I ignored her. "I just think you need to reignite the passion. I'll send you some links to the more advanced tips for stoking the fire."

"And me?" Cass looked at me imploringly.

"I could make a sculpture of a tongue-lashing creature?" Jelena butted in. "I'll make a plaque with Scott's name on it and, come presentation day, I'll slice the tongue off with my scalpel. Señor Stabby will totally get the point."

We all gave her a look.

"Jelena, besides Cass, you're the one who most needs this picture-perfect romance to work out," Sara said. "So let the love guru do her thing so you win the election."

Everyone turned to look at me. Wow. I couldn't believe my friends still saw me as the dating expert, after recent events. They had overwhelming faith in me.

"Cass, I think you need to be straight up with Scott," I said. "Otherwise, one day you'll be unable to take it anymore and the whole thing will fold in on you."

"But what can I say?" Cass asked. "I've imagined every possible scenario and there's never a right way to do it."

"The articles I read about bad kissers said that you have to focus on the positive, not the negative," I replied. "So, rather than saying *Scott, you suck at kissing*, you should say *I really love being kissed gently* or *I love it when your tongue is relaxed*."

Jelena, Sara, and Lindsay collapsed laughing.

"No!" Sara gasped between snorts of laughter. "You can't say that!"

"I *lo-o-ove* it when your tongue's relaxed," Jelena told Sara.

Sara stuck her tongue out and lunged toward Jelena. Jelena shrieked and tossed a piece of clay-streaked paper at Sara. The paper bounced off Sara's tongue and hit Lindsay on the shoulder.

"Girls!" shouted an irate Ms. Collins.

11

"By the way," Jelena said to me, as we headed out of art class half an hour later, "are you able to prepare a little statement for an announcement at two p.m.? I've cleared it with Mr. Bannerman—he doesn't mind if you miss five minutes or so of history so we can announce the chosen candidates."

"We're picking the candidates this afternoon?" I said, surprised. "You didn't want to make an event of it?"

From the discussion on Saturday, I'd assumed Jelena would have a follow-up party this weekend at her parents' house. The renovation was due to be finished on Thursday.

Jelena's voice turned furious. "Fricking Travis. His disgusting mess on the couches meant I had to compensate Hayden's parents the cost of their dry cleaning. And replace the expensive outdoor lamp he smashed. All of which ate into my funds considerably. Anyway, I've got bigger things in the pipeline for the next couple of weeks, so we'll have to resort to a free public announcement."

"I feel like I should have prepared this more thoroughly," I said, getting worried. "Two o'clock's only a couple of hours away."

Jelena shrugged. "I didn't want you building it up into a major thing and getting jitters. All I want is a brief introduction about how beneficial the program will be, just in case some people were unable to make the party. Then I'll draw names from the box and announce them with my usual flair." She shrugged again. "Easy. Then it's on to determining the best matches for the three lucky candidates, setting them up on a series of dates, then finally selecting their prince or princess. Presto! The election is won."

How could she see it that simply? Once the names were drawn, the romantic fate of those individuals would be in my hands. It was a heavy responsibility.

With this notion dancing around my head, I became immediately jittery. And stayed jittery until 2 p.m., by which time my jitters had reached a level akin to drinking three extra-tall coffees.

Jelena lightly kicked my left calf as she fixed her lipstick. We were sitting on a desk in the media room while the tech students set up for the filming of our segment. "Nip it in the bud. Live TV's all about poise."

"Okay, girls, could we have you in your spots, please?"

My heart became a jackhammer. I followed Jelena as she hopped up from the desk and headed over to take her place in front of the camera. She was wearing a blinding smile.

"Live in ten seconds," Andy, one of the camera guys, said. "I'll count you down to three, then I'll do a visual countdown with my fingers. The little light on the front of the camera will go green and you're safe to go. Okay, ten, nine, eight . . ."

Jelena gave me a nudge, frowning. My left foot was close to tap dancing. "Sorry!" I mouthed.

"Six, five, four," Andy said, then held up his fingers to indicate the last three seconds. The light on the front of the camera changed from red to green. We were live to all classrooms.

"Good afternoon, Jefferson High," Jelena said, her voice honey-smooth.

"It was wonderful to see many of you on Friday night," she said.

"I hope the party gave you a taste of the type of successful social event I would execute on a regular basis as school president. I'm talking school formals and winter dances on a scale never seen before. I should also remind you that, under my rule, not only will you have superior celebrations to look forward to, but three lucky winners will be attending those events with their dream dates.

"Yes, the time has come to announce who will take part in Aurora's revolutionary romance program. An overwhelming number of you filled in questionnaires at the party, which proves that finding that special someone is one of your top priorities. I'll be drawing the names right after Aurora's explained how the program will operate. Aurora?"

The camera zoomed in on me. I swallowed nervously, focusing on keeping the smile on my face. All I had to do was pretend I was selling the benefits of the program to one of my friends. I never had issues with confidence then.

"By participating in the trademarked Find a Prince/Princess program, you'll not only have access to a wide range of potential matches through our extensive database, but you'll receive personalized coaching throughout the dating process as well," I began brightly. "The dates will be tailored to the shared interests of you and your potential partner, which means no stress for you in planning that perfect rendezvous. There's no need to worry about accidentally taking a vegetarian to a steak restaurant or buying tickets to a romantic flick for a secret action buff. We also focus on post-date evaluation. If you aren't interested in a candidate after your date, we'll handle the embarrassing rejection process for you. If you are interested, we'll gauge the interest of the datee, and if they're similarly smitten, we'll arrange for the two of you to proceed to the next date. There's no danger of mixed signals and no need to agonize over whether or not to text first.

"We also aim to remove the time-wasting factors that hinder your progress toward finding your prince or princess. For example, in the real world, if you have what seems like a perfect date but then never hear from the guy or girl again, you can spend hours wondering what on earth went wrong. In the program, we can ascertain any performance blips that may be turning dates off, and provide you with helpful feedback. We also eradicate the fraudsters and cheaters before you waste time and energy on them. Jelena and I don't just want to get you to that glorious finish line in the race of love; we also want to get you there easily and efficiently. Let us do the difficult work for you."

I paused for a breather. I was amazed by how much passion had come to the fore during my spiel; it had completely knocked my nerves out of the way. I waved to the camera assistant, who rolled a whiteboard into the shot.

"Here are the three main aims of the Find a Prince/Princess program," I said, "set out step by step."

I indicated the first bullet point. "H(appily)—*H* stands for 'Helping candidates find a suitable match based on common interests and romantic goals.' This is where the questionnaires come in. We feed the data into our unique chemistry calculator to narrow down the three most compatible matches for each candidate."

I indicated the second bullet point. "E(ver)—*E* stands for 'Evaluating the suitability of selected candidates through a series of dates.' The evaluation process assesses physical chemistry, intellectual rapport, and shared goals and values. A third party is crucial here. Many of us mistake electrifying chemistry as a sign of true compatibility, but that's not always the case. Our program helps to identify whether you and your match share the crucial factors that contribute to long-term happiness."

I pointed to the final bullet point. "A(fter)—*A* stands for 'Arming the couple with the tools to maintain a healthy relationship into the future.' We aim to give you techniques for handling issues such as jealousy, money, and arguments, and we also consider your future goals. We don't just want to find your perfect match; we want to make things work for you both, long-term."

I paused again to let the invisible audience take in my words. I visualized them leaning forward in their chairs, super interested to find out more, all hoping their name would be drawn today.

"Jelena and I believe we have something truly special to offer in the Find a Prince/Princess program," I finished. "I'm incredibly excited to hand it over to Jelena to announce the three very lucky matchmakees."

The camera moved back to Jelena, and the assistant handed her a hat filled with scraps of paper.

"The level of attention given to these three matchmakees will be phenomenal," Jelena said. "For those whose names aren't drawn, you can still share in the fun. Aurora and I will be keeping you in the loop about the matchmakees' progress via the Aurora Skye: Find a Prince/Princess program Facebook and Instagram pages, along with regular Twitter updates. We can all feel like we're sharing in these love stories.

"I should mention now that, as part of their free-of-charge participation in the program, all candidates and their dates must sign a contract agreeing to the details of their experiences being documented in social media, advertising materials, and at school for the period of the campaign," Jelena added smoothly. "So, enough delay. Let's draw the first name from the hat."

One of the tech guys started rapping a desk as a makeshift drumroll. Jelena pulled out a scrap of paper with a flourish.

"And our first extremely lucky candidate is . . ." She paused for effect.

I felt as nervous as if I'd put my own name in for selection. I'd be working intensively with these three people for the next few weeks. I hoped they were people I would be able to build a strong rapport with.

"Chloe Butler!" Jelena cried.

I quickly forced a huge smile onto my face as the camera focused back on me. "Congratulations, Chloe! I can't wait to work with you," I said, hoping my momentary apprehension hadn't been apparent.

Chloe Butler? This was going to be more than a challenge. Chloe, also known as Crazy Chloe, had been on the dating blacklist ever since her breakup with her boyfriend Max at the end of ninth grade. Max had ended things with Chloe so he could date a younger woman (that is, a girl from eighth grade), and Chloe had gone slightly askew with grief over the betrayal. We'd been reading Virgil's *Aeneid* in English class at the time, and Chloe had found a historical kindred spirit in the wronged Queen Dido, whom Aeneas abandoned after totally making out that their relationship was on, during a pit stop in her city of Carthage.

Anyway, two days after the breakup, Chloe built a Dido-esque funeral pyre in the sports field, underneath an elm tree. She'd gathered as many of Max's belongings as she could (sweaters left at her place, soccer shoes stolen from his gym locker, all the gifts he'd given her during their one-year relationship), piled them up on the field, and set them alight, just as Max and his soccer team came onto the field. Chloe had then climbed the tree and made out that she was going to throw herself onto the pyre, just like Dido had.

The act had been more of a cry for help than a serious intention, as Chloe had willingly climbed down once the fire department arrived, bursting into tears when she regained the now rather charred ground. It had been over a year since the Dido moment, and Chloe had received extensive counseling. However, despite the fact that she was gorgeous, clever, and, these days, totally bright and cheery, she hadn't had a date since.

I had total sympathy for her. Max had been a complete jerk—he'd dumped her via Facebook on a Sunday night, and on Monday morning she'd had to walk past him and the eighth-grader making out by the school gate. It was enough to send anyone slightly loopy. I really wanted to help her find love, but I had no idea how I was going to erase that fire from the collective memory of all of the boys at Jefferson. I was going to have my work cut out for me, that was for sure.

"And the second name is . . . our very own lovable class clown, Jeffrey Clark!"

Jeffrey! I hadn't known he was searching for love. A make-out partner, sure, but an actual relationship?

Jelena winked at the camera. "Jeffrey, I'm sure you're fist-pumping in history class right now."

I just prayed he wasn't doing a triumphant nudie run. How was I going to get the girls at Jefferson to take a wannabe nudist colony owner and waterlogged-trunks-wearing cupid seriously? I'd always found Jeffrey hilarious, but it was hard to see him as someone's boyfriend. Like a fine wine, he needed maturing to become more palatable. Only I didn't have a couple of years; I had merely weeks to make him an appealing option.

"Time for the final draw," Jelena announced, her hand hovering dramatically over the hat. "This person will make up our trilogy of winners today, all of whom will go down in history as the forerunners of what is sure to become a legendary program."

She reached into the hat and drew out a slip of paper.

"Wow, this is a special one." Jelena looked thrilled. "I'm delighted to announce that the final matchmakee is the stunning Sara Sanderson."

"I'm not doing it." Sara's cheeks were a fiery red that matched her waist-length titian-colored hair. "You're going to have to do a redraw."

We were still in the media room. Jelena and I had been helping the tech guys pack up the boom mike and camera stands when Sara strode in.

"I am not doing a redraw." Jelena stood in a face-off with Sara.

"You have to," Sara said angrily. She turned to me. "Aurora, I didn't willingly put myself into the drawing. Jelena made me fill out the questionnaire at the party to encourage other people to put their names down."

Jelena shrugged. "You're an influencer. In marketing terms, it means that when you decide to take part in something, it becomes more appealing to others. Remember how everyone started wearing the ballerina bun after you rocked one last year? I needed people to see that entering the drawing wasn't something to feel scared about, that the program is legit."

"People were scared about entering the drawing because they didn't want their private lives made public," Sara snapped. "You promised you'd remove my name once more people had signed up. We had a deal."

"Did we?" Jelena looked blankly at her. "I don't remember that. I remember suggesting you put your name down—"

"By 'suggesting' you mean forcing," Sara said. "This is where your Russian heritage comes to the fore. You people 'suggested' political objectors go to Siberia."

"Guys." I stepped in between them. "Can't we talk this through in a way that isn't hostile? I'm sure we can come to a compromi—"

"I *suggested*," Jelena said over me, to Sara, "that you put your name down because I thought it would be a good opportunity for you. When was the last time you had a date with someone *actually* promising?"

I wouldn't have put it so bluntly, but Jelena was right. When Sara's name had been announced, I'd been thrilled. I was always hinting that she should veer away from her stock-standard dating prototype: muscled up, strong, and silent. From all my research into the science of dating, it was abundantly clear that men with excess testosterone were less likely to be the stay-at-home-and-snuggle type. Their brains were programmed to roam the land for as many females as possible. In modern terms, they were players. Sara always shrugged my hints aside, saying she found nice guys boring. Now was my chance to show her how dating outside the box could do wonders for her love life.

"Cass and Lindsay might let you play around with their love lives, but I'm not complying," Sara said, pointing at Jelena to emphasize her statement. "I don't want to date right now."

"Why on earth not?" Jelena looked shocked.

"I want to be a romance novelist," Sara said, smiling. "I want to have a completed manuscript by the end of senior year. It's my personal project for English class."

Jelena snorted. "Is writing the further adventures of Jeremiah a realistic career path?"

"Um, is being the next Stalin one, either?"

"Okay, enough with the Russian references," Jelena said.

"Guys!" I cried.

Neither of them blinked an eye at my attempt to break things up.

"I'll have you know that Mrs. Kent has had four romance novels published," Sara said. "That's why I went to her for advice. She asked me to write a short piece in that style, which I did, and she said I had real promise. That's why she's supervising my project."

"I can see where Sara's coming from," I said to Jelena. "She's too busy to date right now. Let's do a redraw. There were lots of names in that hat."

"I'm not redrawing," Jelena said, her arms staying firmly folded. "If Sara bows out of the program and she's our best friend, what does that tell the general public? It'll undermine their faith in us."

I paused. She had a point. "So what do we do? I don't want Sara to be unhappy."

The heat in Sara's cheeks faded slightly as she realized I was on her side.

"Well, neither do I," Jelena said. Sara's face softened further. "I'll make it worth your while," Jelena added.

Sara's cheeks bloomed red again. "You're going to bribe me?" she scoffed.

"I'm not bribing you, you idiot." Jelena looked insulted. "I'm just saying that there are further opportunities available if you take the one I'm offering you now."

"Like what?"

"Like getting firsthand material for your book," Jelena replied.

"The program will give you the chance to do firsthand research into romance. If you set out to write about sensual experiences without actually experiencing them, you're cheating your audience."

"Hey, Stephenie Meyer never made out with a vampire and she still had a worldwide bestseller," Sara said. "I have a great imagination and can write love scenes without having to make out with some guy. Plus, I don't want to be distracted from my writing. Look at what usually happens when I get a crush. I'm off daydreaming for weeks on end. I lose focus in my classes. And what have I ever gotten in return? Maybe some cute smiles from the guy—before he turns his attention elsewhere. I've been boy crazy since seventh grade and I don't want to be that girl anymore."

"But if you have a clear goal and the right type of guy, the relationship won't take over," I said.

"Love and levelheadedness don't go together all that well, Aurora," Sara said. "You'll learn that yourself, one day soon. Time becomes a casualty very easily."

I was sure that wouldn't happen to me. It hadn't so far, and my crush on Hayden was pretty hard-core. I could balance the heart and the head, I knew it. So could Sara, if she really tried.

"Sorry, guys," she said. "I think the program's great, but it's wasted on me. It's better if you give someone else the chance to benefit from it."

"Okay, what if I told you that if you take part in the program—just until the election date—I might be able to get your book to a publisher?" Jelena said slowly.

Both Sara and I looked at her in surprise.

"Jelena, don't be ridiculous," Sara said. "Your influence doesn't go that far."

"Oh, yeah? Want to bet?" Jelena replied confidently.

"Who do you know in the publishing world?" I asked. "And how do you know them?"

"Through my dad's media company," Jelena said. "It's not just TV; there's a print sector as well. Their publishing house is the third biggest in the country. Dad, being the networker he is, has buddies there. One of the fiction publishers, Marcus, came to our house for New Year's. One word to Dad and I can get that manuscript in the door."

"I can get it in there anyway," Sara replied. "Mrs. Kent's going to guide me on submission policies."

Jelena shook her head. "I'm talking skipping the slush pile. You send that thing in via the standard submission guidelines and it joins the hundreds of unread manuscripts that sit there for years on end. I know, because I've heard Marcus going on about it."

I could tell Sara was struggling to seem blasé.

"You take part in the program and, at the end of the campaign, I'll get Marcus's email address for you," Jelena said with a smile. "It's that simple."

"I just don't want to go head-over-heels gaga," Sara said. "The email's worthless if I don't have a manuscript."

Jelena sighed, obviously getting impatient. "No one's asking you to get married at the end of this thing. Just let Aurora find you some cute boys to take you out. Maybe you'll find one of them appealing enough to progress to a second date. Maybe you'll end up smooching him just before the campaign finishes—an uncomplicated moment of enjoyment for you, some great research for your book, and some good publicity for Aurora and me. Once the election is over, Aurora and I will distract the guy and get him to go for someone else. The public focuses on this new twist and you're free to finish the manuscript without the burden of a relationship."

"I don't want to fake a connection," Sara said. "My lips can't be bought, Jelena."

"It seems kind of dishonest," I added. "The program's meant to be for people who are genuinely seeking a soul mate."

"I don't want her to fake it," Jelena replied, rolling her eyes at me. "The public would see straight through that. I'm saying that the program is likely to deliver some great matches, so Sara probably *will* have chemistry with one of them, and our schoolmates will be witness to that. That's all I need for a positive campaign," Jelena assured Sara. "I'm not going to make you sign a contract that says you have to make out with anyone. If you feel like doing that, it's your choice, but there's no pressure."

"And if I don't have chemistry with any of them?" Sara asked suspiciously.

Jelena shrugged. "Then you've still participated and I'll hand over the email accordingly."

"What's the catch?" Sara said. "This seems skewed in my favor."

"There are conditions," Jelena said. "You forfeit the email if you show any kind of negative attitude. That includes bad-mouthing the program, refusing to go on dates, or presenting an unattractive, slovenly appearance to put people off."

Jelena had thought of all the loopholes.

"You have to be your naturally appealing self," she finished. "Do we have a deal?"

Sara hesitated for a second, then unfolded her arms. "Deal."

She smiled at Jelena and at me, then headed for the door, seemingly satisfied. She paused at the exit to call back to me, "Just make the boys cute, okay, Aurora?"

"I'm sure I can do cute," I said. "We were overwhelmed with responses."

Sara left the room with a spring in her step.

"Problem solved," Jelena said.

I shook my head. "I don't feel right about this. We're deceiving the public."

"No, we're not," Jelena said firmly as she picked up her silver handbag. "Sara just thinks she isn't going to fall in love."

I looked at her, puzzled.

"I want you to find her Potential Prince for real," Jelena said. "Yes, she's resistant, but think of this as the ultimate test for the program. I'm sure there are lots of unbelievers like Sara at Jefferson. You have something amazing here and it's up to us to prove it."

"But she doesn't want to fall in love. The only relationship she's seeking is with her muse."

Jelena made a face. "The only reason Sara feels apprehensive is because her dating experiences have been with players who can't sustain a relationship beyond the weekend. If you're constantly worried about being dropped, of course you're going to be distracted and unable to focus on school."

"I guess that's true."

"We owe it to her as her friends to show her that love *can* be a positive experience," Jelena said, getting out her lipstick in preparation for meeting the public postannouncement. "Plus, her ideal Potential Prince will help with, not hinder, her dreams. He'll be there at her side, proofreading the mushy chapters in all their glory." Jelena shuddered. "I'm just glad I won't have that task. I better run; it's almost time for next period."

12

As I headed out into the hall to grab my books for next period, I saw glossy, oversize campaign posters suspended from the ceiling all along the corridor. A shot of Cass and Scott entwined in a passionate embrace made up the top half of the poster; the bottom half was the now infamous shot of Tyler on one knee, pleading for Lindsay's forgiveness. Printed in bold black letters at the bottom of the poster was "The Find a Prince/Princess™ Program—It Works. Vote Jelena Cantrill for School President." The posters hadn't been here an hour ago. Jelena's campaign team had obviously been on the job while we were making the announcement.

"I'm fighting the urge to pull them down in protest," Lindsay said behind me.

I turned around to see her looking extremely unimpressed.

"The matchmakees and their dates might have to sign a contract, but Cass and Scott and Tyler and I certainly never okayed the use of our photos for promotional purposes. Tyler's hiding out in the nurse's office. The soccer team nearly fell down laughing when they walked along here half an hour ago. Apparently, every time Tyler tried to score a goal during practice, the goalie sank down on one knee. After about the fourth time, Tyler got so angry that he kicked the ball too hard, tripped, and fell flat on his face. He came limping into the library ten minutes ago, covered in dirt and totally furious at me."

"Why is he angry with *you*?"

"He asked me if I was letting Jelena embarrass him in public as some way of getting even with him for the dumping thing."

"What?" That was a really jerky thing for him to assume. "You're not like that."

"Exactly!" Lindsay said. "Even after everything I went through in the breakup, I'd never do something like this! You'd think he'd know me well enough that he'd have a little faith in me. But then, after three years of knowing him, did I ever suspect he'd break up with me out of the blue because he wanted to be 'free like an eagle'? No . . ."

We both fell silent. It was hard to know what to say. I'd thought that when Tyler and Lindsay got back together, things would go back to normal. But I was beginning to understand that something very precious had been smashed when Tyler ended things on a whim. Although they'd put their relationship back together, the cracks from that experience would always be there.

"I need to keep a closer eye on Jelena," Lindsay said, frowning up at the poster. "If this type of thing keeps happening, Tyler and I are going to be finished."

"Why don't you join the campaign?" I suggested. "Then you'll be in on the marketing plans. No more embarrassing surprises."

Lindsay looked wary. "I don't know if I want to be under Jelena's command. Have you seen some of her campaign team? Sheree's developed an eye tic from stress." She suddenly brightened. "Why don't I help you with the matchmakees? I'll tell Jelena it's in exchange for leaving Tyler and me out of her campaign from now on."

I was stoked to have her on board. "I'd love the help. It's kind of daunting playing cupid on my own. We've got some serious challenges ahead with our candidates."

"I still can't believe Jeffrey's name was chosen. Do you remember how shocked you were—we *all* were—when we thought he was your secret admirer? Jelena was nearly in hysterics." Lindsay looked guilty. "I shouldn't say that; it's kind of mean."

I sighed. "No, it's the truth. None of the girls see him as dating material. As do none of the guys, when it comes to Chloe. And Sara doesn't even *want* to date."

"What?" Lindsay said.

Sara not wanting to date was like a dog not wanting to go for a walk. It seemed against nature.

"I'll explain later," I said, as the bell rang for our next class.

"So where do we start with the setups?" Lindsay asked, as we hurried down the corridor.

"I need to meet with each of the matchmakees this week. Well, Chloe and Jeffrey. We already know what makes Sara tick. I suspect we know better than she does what type of guy would change her world. We just need to bring her around to seeing that nice guys can be a fun choice. With the other two, I want to get a clearer picture of what they're looking for in a relationship. The questionnaires are great, but I need as much information as possible to ensure I get the best matches for them."

"Okay, sounds great," Lindsay said. "Let me know the time and date of the meetings and I'll be there taking notes or doing whatever else you need."

She gave me a wave as she headed into chemistry.

"I want her to be bootylicious," Jeffrey Clark said, beaming across the table at me as he described his perfect woman.

Jeffrey had been like an eight-week-old puppy after the announcement. He'd bounded over to me the moment I'd arrived at English class. He'd begged me to start the search for his Potential Princess that very second, but I'd managed to persuade him to wait until Tuesday afternoon. We met at the picnic tables near the fountain after last bell. Lindsay joined us with her laptop so she could take notes.

"That's the first quality you look for in a woman? Bootyliciousness?" I asked, stunned. I knew boys generally rated attractiveness higher on the scale of importance than girls did, but still. We weren't casting for a rap video here.

Jeffrey took in Lindsay's and my displeased expressions. "Uh-oh. You think I'm just talking about jelly."

"*What?*" We both gaped at the word.

"You know . . . girl parts."

Lindsay gave me a panicked glance. Her hand was poised on the top of the laptop, like she wanted to slam it shut and run home.

"Jeffrey, a woman doesn't like her body parts being compared with food," I said, trying to be firm without showing I was mentally freaking out at the likelihood of him dropping that term on a date. "It's disrespectful. Yes, the word 'jelly' may have featured in a very popular Destiny's Child song, but it's totally not PC to use it in real life."

Jeffrey looked amused. "You ladies have got it *all* wrong. 'Bootylicious' is like 'Beyoncé-ish.' You know . . . a woman thinking she's all fine."

He reenacted Beyoncé's hair swing from "Crazy in Love."

"You want a woman who's highly confident about her looks?" I asked.

Jeffrey shook his head. "Ladies, this ain't about looks. I want a girl who knows she's all that," Jeffrey explained. "Confidence is the sexiest thing. You know the girls who are rocking it when they walk through the school gate. But she can't be arrogant."

"Confident, but not arrogant?" I said.

"And they need to be bold enough to tell me if I cross the line. I keep going on dates and apparently saying something wrong, but the girls never tell me what. Instead, they go all silent. Then they refuse a second date and I never know why. Women need to be straight up, like you just were. I'd never have known about the 'jelly' thing otherwise."

I nodded. "Okay. I'm getting a picture here. You want someone assertive. I'm assuming you also want someone funny?"

"Yeah. I guess." He sounded unsure.

"You're not looking for humorous?" I said, shocked. This was Jeffrey we were talking about here. His life *was* humor.

Lindsay stopped typing and looked up at us.

"I don't know." Jeffrey's face was serious. "Girls are always telling me *Oh, you're so funny*, but they never want to go on a second date. When I asked out Tess from math, she started laughing because she thought I was putting her on." Jeffrey looked hurt. "Aurora, I'm used to people falling over laughing at my jokes, but when it comes to that special girl, I want her to fall for *me*. Basically, I need you to make me Ryan Gosling instead of Jonah Hill."

I saw the edges of Lindsay's mouth twitch as she held back her laughter.

"Ryan Gosling is . . ." I tried to think of a nicer word for "unattainable." We had to be realistic.

Jeffrey whipped his shirt above his head. "I reckon I could get the abs. I'm lean, but that's a positive, right? It means if I get muscles, they'll pop out real good."

Lindsay and I both stared at Jeffrey's very un-Ryan-like chest. So did a group of girls coming from basketball practice, who were smothering laughter. I reached over the table and yanked down Jeffrey's shirt.

"Women like funny," I said, in an encouraging voice. "Sure, they talk about guys like Ryan Gosling, but in real life he'd be way too brooding. We don't want you pretending to be someone you're not. You're a humorous guy. We've just got to show your dates that you have a serious side, too."

Jeffrey smiled back happily. "I guess that saves me time at the gym."

"Physical characteristics of your ideal match?" I asked, before Lindsay lost her composure.

"I like blondes," Jeffrey said. "You know, cute, kinda like Emma Stone. Or those models from Victoria's Secret. Their curves are like *kapow*!" Jeffrey pretended he had whiplash.

"Why do men always think they're going to land a Victoria's Secret model?" Lindsay said. "I hate those parades."

"Hey, if Tyler's making you feel like you're lacking, you should know: you're not," Jeffrey told her. "You'd fill out those bras without any fill-it things." He took in her shocked expression. "I don't mean that in a sleazy way. I mean it in a *You should have confidence* way—Oh crap. Aurora, that's the look I get on my dates!"

"You weren't lying when you said our candidates would prove to be a challenge," Lindsay said wryly, after we'd finished Jeffrey's assessment. She pushed the laptop over to me so I could read the notes from the session.

"He's completely inappropriate at times, I know," I said, as I scrolled down the list of characteristics desired by Jeffrey. "But he's sweet, too. He's obviously super interested in a real relationship. I think he's just watched too many gross-out comedies over the years so his sense of male–female relations is slightly skewed. If we can get him to improve his filter, he'll start having better luck."

Lindsay didn't look totally convinced, but she nodded.

I looked at my watch. "Oops! We'd better get going to meet Chloe."

Chloe had added me on Facebook after the announcement, and had messaged me asking if we could meet at the coffee shop just around the corner from school at four p.m. When Lindsay and I walked in, Chloe was in one of the booths, focused on a textbook.

"Hey," she said, taking off her reading glasses.

I was always amazed by Chloe's eyes. They were like the violets in Mr. Paris's garden.

"Hey, Chloe," I said. "This is Lindsay. She's my assistant on the Find a Prince/Princess program."

Chloe smiled at Lindsay. "We don't have classes together, but I know you. I felt kind of a connection with you during the whole Tyler thing. Sorry if that seems too personal."

"Believe me, I'd rather people talk to me about it in person than behind my back," Lindsay said. "I got really tired of the whispers."

She slid into the booth opposite Chloe, leaving enough room for me to slide in next to her.

"At least the whispers were sympathetic," Chloe said. "The whispers about me cast me in the same light as that movie *Carrie*. Which I totally get—I do regret the decision to turn arsonist. I can't explain it. The pain of the breakup was so bad that I slightly lost the plot."

"I almost slashed Tyler's mountain bike tires the day after he dumped me," Lindsay said, letting out a giggle. "It's kind of normal to lose the plot. I know a lot of girls at school have fantasized about doing just the sort of thing you did. You were kind of an unofficial antihero."

Chloe's eyes became less intense and she let out a laugh. "*Psycho girl.* I should have had a T-shirt made up. Aurora, do you actually think I can take part in this program? I'm wondering if I should bow out gracefully. I don't want you to have to bribe boys to take me out."

"The incident *was* over a year ago," I said.

"Yeah, no one's discussing the whole Alex-betraying-Jelena thing anymore, and that was only a few weeks ago," Lindsay assured her.

"I'm sure everyone's forgotten about it," I said.

Sure, that was stretching the truth, but the more we focused on improving Chloe's situation instead of dwelling on the past, the better.

"I'd hoped so too," Chloe said. "But when my name was announced, the boys in my ancient history class literally gasped in horror. I swear the guy next to me pulled his chair as far from mine as he could get. And someone shouted that they were going to get their name removed from the program."

"That's horrible," Lindsay said, looking disgusted. "I'm so lucky I never had to deal with that when I was single."

"That's 'cause people saw you as the wronged party," Chloe said. "They saw me that way at first, until the bonfire. Then they felt sorry for Max. You know how popular he is."

"Only with the boys," I reminded her.

Max had insensitively dumped about five other girls since he'd ended it with Chloe. He'd had to start dating girls from other schools because the female population of Jefferson didn't want to be his next conquest.

"Mmm." Chloe's violet eyes had become the deepest purple-blue, like a storm cloud.

"Chloe, you can't let the incident define you," I said in my most encouraging voice. "You've got a ton of things going for you: you're so smart you'll get into any university of your choice, come graduation; you're as gorgeous as Elizabeth Taylor in *Cleopatra*—"

"Totally." Lindsay nodded furiously. "Richard Burton married her twice, he was so enraptured. He had no problem with a passionate woman."

"Lindsay's right," I said. "Yes, you took your emotions too far on one occasion, but there's nothing wrong with being a passionate woman. You're a person who cares deeply about things, and you shouldn't be ashamed of that."

"Don't let Max win!" Lindsay said loudly, as our coffees arrived. She thumped her fist on the table to emphasize her point.

"Okay, okay." Chloe laughed as the waitress uneasily backed away from our table. "I'll dip my toe in the dating pool, but on one condition: I only want you to set me up with guys who are emotionally intense. I want someone with depth, who can understand what I've been through."

"Of course." I could understand where she was coming from. Plus, I could see that, from a guy's point of view, you'd have to be pretty intense to handle staring into Chloe's eyes for extensive periods of time. There was a lot going on under their violet surface.

"He must be artistic in some way, too," Chloe continued. "Some of the world's most powerful poetry, art, and music have come out of deep suffering. Think van Gogh or Edvard Munch. I want to be able to take my date to the theater, switch on a symphony on the iPod, or visit an art gallery and know that he's experiencing the same rapture that I feel."

I was beginning to build a picture of her ideal man. He was a little like Hugh Jackman in *Kate & Leopold*—slightly not of this era.

"And I want him to have an impulsive side," Chloe added enthusiastically. "Max hated spontaneity—except for when it came to dumping me. I want someone who, instead of complaining about the rain when we come out of the movies, sweeps me up in his arms and kisses me while the raindrops fall around us."

"Wow. Right out of *The Notebook*," Lindsay said.

"A guy who stops the car to look at the stars." Chloe was grinning. "Who kisses me before I finish a sentence, because he just can't wait one second longer to have me in his arms."

She and Lindsay sighed simultaneously.

"We can make this happen," I said, assuring myself as much as Chloe.

We paid the bill and a very cheery Chloe headed off to her piano lesson, a hobby she'd thrown herself into following the breakup.

"I really like her," Lindsay said as we walked home. "She's done well to not end up cynical after what Max put her through."

"Yes, she has."

I had to admit, I was surprised that she hadn't seemed more apprehensive about returning to the dating game. Maybe the past year had taught her what she was looking for in a relationship. She obviously trusted Lindsay and me to help her find it.

"I get the feeling she's ready to fall hard again," I added. "But we have to be really careful to make sure it's the right guy she falls for."

Fall. It was a funny word for it. You never knew if you were in for a slight trip or a plummet off a cliff.

I stopped at the corner where Lindsay and I always parted ways. "Linds, what we're doing is actually pretty serious."

She took in my expression. "It's good that you're taking it seriously, Aurora. That's what matchmakers do. They know the magnitude of bringing people together."

"So do you," I said.

I suddenly realized, after meeting with Chloe, that Lindsay was highly invested in the program. She knew what lost love felt like, and she wanted to spare other girls the experience.

"So, now what?" she asked.

"I just have to wait for Hayden to finish up the dating database program so we can start using the chemistry calculator to derive the matches."

I was thinking I'd give him a call. He'd be sure to have some tips for improving Jeffrey's luck with the ladies.

After Lindsay had headed home, I pulled out my phone. I couldn't wait to tell Hayden about Jeffrey and Chloe and what they were looking for in a soul mate.

Wait a minute. I'd already gotten a text from Hayden.

Hey, Princess, so happy you liked the necklace. Didn't get a chance to tell you that my parents extended my grounding after we got caught on Saturday night. Am rationing the chocolate chip cookies so they last me through to Monday, when I'm a free man again! Mom and Dad only let me have the phone when I'm at school so don't bother texting back—just wanted you to know I'm thinking of you. At least the grounding has got me working hard—should have the database ready for you to run tomorrow. xo

Monday! He made it sound like it was right around the corner, not almost a week away! This coming weekend would be the second one we'd lost.

Maybe I was being too impatient. After all, Sleeping Beauty toughed it out for one hundred years before her prince came along. I guessed I should feel grateful I would still see Hayden at school. But it wasn't the same. I wanted time alone with him, so we could escape to a place where it was only us and we could say what we wanted to say without our classmates listening in on every word. If only I could go to sleep and wake up in six days' time.

13

I sat in my window seat when I got home, repeatedly touching the delicate chain and the tiny *X*. It was as if I needed to convince myself that they were real and the moment under the archway had actually happened.

My phone rang and I raced to answer, illogically hoping it was Hayden. Of course it wasn't. It was Mom calling. We hadn't spoken since I'd fled the bridal boutique. Part of me wanted to let the call go to voicemail, like I had the other two times, but, the longer I left things, the frostier she was likely to get.

"Hey, Mom," I answered, bracing myself for a telling off.

"Aurora." Her voice sounded unusually warm. "I wanted to apologize."

"You wanted to what?"

The word "apologize" generally didn't appear in the Avery dictionary.

"Apologize," Mom repeated smoothly. "I realize that my remarrying was big news to take in. I should have broken it to you in a more considerate way. The bridal boutique was meant to be a surprise, but I'd forgotten you're not partial to surprises anymore, for some funny reason."

I wanted to say that most people would have developed a distrust of surprises after their family unit had collapsed via an answering machine message, but I held back. I'd gotten an apology—that was as much as Mom was ever likely to concede.

"I was excited, I suppose," she continued. "I'm still hoping you'll be my bridesmaid?"

I didn't know what to say. I still felt overwhelmed.

"I know you'll be reasonable," she said. "Yes, there was an unfortunate breakdown of our relationship, due to your father bad-mouthing me—"

My jaw clenched. "Dad didn't bad-mouth you. He didn't even talk about you."

He hadn't been able to. His pain had been so deep that he'd had to communicate it through his home decor decisions. It had taken me awhile to realize just how shattered his soul was. One time, in English class, Mrs. Kent had read us a piece by an Aztec Indian: *Now I know / why my father / would go out / and cry / in the rain.* The words had made my chest so heavy it was like someone had piled stones on it. I'd avoided the NAD for days afterward, scared that he'd realize I could see his grief marked out in every new lamp or towel or fresh coat of paint he applied to the walls.

"It's the same thing," Mom replied. "He passed his bitterness on to you."

What did Mom expect—that the NAD would chatter brightly about her good qualities while we struggled to understand her preference for an Ibiza beach over her family?

Mom let out a sigh laced with irritation. "Your father needs to get past all of that. It was four years ago . . ."

"Things don't just magically fix themselves," I burst out.

I couldn't hold back anymore. Did she expect the NAD and me to just forgive and forget? Sure, I'd managed to go from never wanting to speak to her again to letting her back into my life, but that didn't cancel out all the emotions I'd felt over the past four years.

"I'm trying to fix things," Mom said. "Why do you think I came back to Jefferson?"

"You can't claim you're here solely for me. A weekly catch-up is hardly worth shifting across the globe for."

Mom sighed again. "I'm starting slow. Neither of us is ready right now for a regular mother–daughter closeness." She paused. "That's why having you as my bridesmaid is important to me. It's an opportunity for you to share in a significant part of my life."

I had the feeling that being her bridesmaid was just another form of pleasing her, like the school play and the short-lived foray into modeling had been.

"I don't even know the groom," I said.

"I want you and Carlos to meet as soon as possible. Next Tuesday night, to be exact. You can meet some of our close friends at the same time."

Even though her voice was upbeat, I could tell she was apprehensive about me meeting Carlos. After all, he'd been completely unaware she had a daughter, even after a year of dating. But I didn't feel like I could say no. I supposed I needed to develop some kind of relationship with my future stepfather prior to this whirlwind wedding.

"I'll text you the address, darling," Mom said brightly, before I could voice my agreement. "See you next Tuesday, seven p.m. Oh, and dress elegantly, please. Cocktail attire." And she hung up.

How could one call change my mood so fast? My daydreaming about Hayden had now turned into a picture of me sitting at a dinner table with Mom, Carlos, and their image-conscious friends, feeling uncomfortable and being ignored. I also felt uber guilty that I still hadn't broken the *Guess who's getting married* news to the NAD.

I stopped myself from sliding into a swamp of self-pity. If I wanted to stay upbeat and focused on the Find a Prince/Princess™ program, there was only one option: to not think about Tuesday night till Tuesday night actually arrived. I'd meet Carlos, and then at least I'd be able to describe him if the NAD launched into a series of *how, why,* and *when* questions. In the meantime, I would busy myself with the matchmakees. I needed to do some serious strategizing if this whole thing was going to have the outcome Jelena and I hoped for.

I sat down on the carpet and began pulling my extensive collection of dating guidebooks out of my bookcase. I was on the hunt for more information about how to make someone fall in love.

"I need a creaky bridge," I said to Jelena, when we met the next morning during break to discuss my progress.

Jelena, to her credit, didn't raise an eyebrow. "Oka-a-ay. Odd request, but you do have some novel tactics when it comes to setups. Can you explain why before I do my best to source one?"

"Oh," I said, momentarily stunned at the range of resources Jelena apparently had at her disposal. "It doesn't have to be an actual bridge. Just something that simulates the sensation of danger for the matchmakees and their dates."

"What happened to flowers and candlelight?" Lindsay asked, as she joined us, laptop in hand.

"It's from a famous experiment," I explained. "These scientists got a bunch of men to cross a river, one by one. One half of the group crossed via a broad, low bridge over a calm section of water. The other half had to cross via a spindly suspension bridge hundreds of feet above jagged boulders and wild rapids. At the middle of each bridge was a gorgeous young woman—one of the researchers. The woman asked each participant to fill out a questionnaire and, when they were done, she gave them her phone number and said if they had any questions they were welcome to call her at home. Out of the thirty-two men who crossed the scary bridge, nine were attracted enough to the woman to call her at home, whereas only two of the men who'd crossed the stable, unexciting bridge called.

"The scientists concluded that being on the treacherous bridge had spiked the men's levels of dopamine—the hormone related to attraction. The men believed their hearts were racing not because of the risky activity, but because of the gorgeous woman. There've been lots of studies since that have proved that couples who do novel and exciting things on their first date feel more bonded and are therefore more likely to proceed to a second date. Adrenaline's like superglue when it comes to couple bonding."

The theory had made sense to me the second I'd read it—the girls and I had always rated the severity of a crush by how dizzy and speechless the guy made you. Sara had once broken out into a full-body rash when she'd unexpectedly bumped into one crush at her corner store.

Lindsay grinned as I breathlessly finished my explanation. "Wow, that's pretty cool stuff. I suppose when you think about it, that's how it works in action movies. Like *Speed*—Keanu Reeves and Sandra Bullock make out at the end of the movie and, really, how long have they known each other? A couple of hours."

"It's the same with natural disasters," I added. "In any situation where fear or anxiety is heightened, the heart's more likely to be kick-started."

"How about a deserted island?" Lindsay said. "Like Harrison Ford and Anne Heche in *Six Days Seven Nights*."

"Okay, tornadoes, floods, and desertion on a tropical island are beyond the scope of my powers," Jelena replied. "Unless—"

"There's no need for us to go to those lengths," I said, cutting her off. "I'm thinking of arranging some dates at an amusement park—one that has super-scary rides."

Jelena shook her head. "I'm not doing this halfheartedly. We need happily-ever-afters for Sara, Jeffrey, and Chloe at the end of this thing. These aren't exactly straightforward setups, and I'm not taking any chances with Jeffrey. We need authentic adrenaline, people in fear for their lives. Creaky bridge it is."

"You're really going to find a bridge?" I stared at her.

"You really want to make people fear for their lives?" Lindsay said.

"So glad you brought this up, Aurora." Jelena pulled out her iPhone and began punching in notes. "It works perfectly with phase two."

"Phase two?" I tried to peer at her phone screen.

"You didn't see Alex's demonstration this morning?" Jelena asked, narrowing her eyes.

"Oh yeah, of course."

Alex had taken things up a notch, following Jelena's announcement on Monday. This morning he'd set up an obstacle course in the schoolyard and got guys and girls racing along monkey bars, sprinting between traffic cones, and lifting tires, all competing to win a brand-new iPad. Afterward, he'd handed out free protein bars, along with permission slips that would allow students to use the gym down the road during their PE period. Alex's motto, "Let's Get Real," was stamped on the bottom of each flyer.

"Not to mention stupid Matt Stevens's obsession with making boxing a PE sport." Jelena was virtually pounding her fingertips against her phone. "He's saying he can get a former Olympian in for the first session."

"But sports isn't your focus," Lindsay reminded her.

"I can't ignore the male vote," Jelena said, making a face. "If I do, I'm losing out on half the school. I need to focus on one-upping Alex—this gym thing is building momentum. Luckily, I know what appeals to men. Besides yours truly, of course."

I bit back a giggle while Jelena reached for her campaign folder. She pulled out a flyer and handed it to me with a triumphant smile. I read it out loud.

"'Think you're tough because you break a sweat at the gym? How about a real challenge? Test your true grit with activities like kayaking, canyoneering, rappelling, and more. Jelena Cantrill is campaigning to Take It to Another Level—a series of day trips and overnight camps where you can develop gladiatorial strength and have fun with your classmates at the same time.'

"Wow." Jelena had really hit the mark—sports plus a pass out of school? Guys *and* girls would be clamoring to be a part of it.

"You can see how it's perfect for the Find a Prince/Princess program, too," Jelena said, taking the flyer back. "I can't wait for next week. The three of us are going to have the best time."

"The three of us?" I got a sudden image of us riding rapids on inner tubes, Lindsay holding on to her laptop for dear life.

"Jelena," Lindsay prompted. "Spill."

Jelena smiled to herself. "I can't believe how well it's worked out. Sometimes my capacity for genius surprises even me."

"Jelena!" Lindsay and I cried in unison.

"Please let us know what we're in for," I added, trying to stay good-humored.

"Okay, okay." Jelena sighed at our impatience as she pulled another document from her folder. "I'd already prebooked a spot for forty students for next Wednesday. I'd assumed it would be mostly the school's athletes, but now we can get the candidates along too. Like you were saying, adrenaline will make the heart grow fonder. Think of the fantastic media angle. I'll have the campaign team video Sara, Chloe, and Jeffrey as they tackle the obstacle course of love." Jelena smiled happily. "*Love in the wilderness.*"

"Wilderness?" Lindsay looked uneasy.

"Okay, where are you taking us?" I grabbed the document from her hands.

"Impatient much?" Jelena rolled her eyes. "We're going on a three-day high-ropes course next Wednesday. Think walking a tightrope thirty feet off the ground—totally like crossing a creaky bridge!"

"Camping?" Sara wailed. "Like with tents? On the ground?"

Jelena had announced her plan over the PA system right after recess. I was amazed that she'd gotten it all organized so fast, but apparently she'd won Mr. Quinten over weeks ago. Being an ex-army lieutenant, he was all for it. In fact, he was so enthusiastic he'd signed on to be the trip's supervisor.

"Only for Thursday night," Jelena replied. "Wednesday night we have cabins. I've been told they're superior accommodations, considering the area's so remote. It's probably going to be just like glamping."

Sara shook her head firmly. "I don't like remote. It has all the makings of a horror movie. The wilderness is where all the escaped prisoners head to."

"For god's sake, Sara, it's a fully guided school trip. You did gymnastics for years. High ropes should be easy for you, seeing how you excelled on the beam."

"The beam's like three feet high, not thirty," Sara reminded her. "I didn't have to think about the possibility of plunging to my death."

"I really don't like heights." Lindsay's face was pale.

"The guy I booked with told me a group of thirteen-year-olds did the camp recently," Jelena said in her no-nonsense voice. "You're clipped in at all times. It's professional equipment of the highest standard."

Sara gave her a look and quoted from the permission slip: "'Insurance payment covers injuries sustained during activities, including accidental death . . .'"

"They have to put that in there, legally," Jelena said. "You have to sign a waiver for laser tag these days. It's all for insurance purposes."

"I agreed to go on a few dates, not damage my limbs," Sara said with a dramatic shudder. "If you want me to come along, you'll have to drug me."

"You agreed that you would fully participate in the program in exchange for that email address," Jelena said calmly.

Sara glared at her but didn't reply.

"Hey, it might be a great setting for one of your books," Jelena said. "You'll get a firsthand sense of how your characters would feel if they were inching their way across a rope bridge over a raging river."

Sara stomped her foot with frustration.

"Watch the shoes with the Rumpelstiltskin antics." Jelena made a face at Sara and Lindsay. "Both of you are being such downers. Just think of it as a three-day vacation from school."

The end-of-lunch bell rang. Sara threw Jelena another look and stalked away to class.

"Have the permission slip back to me tomorrow!" Jelena called after her.

"I'm really not good with heights," Lindsay said again, not moving from her seat, even though everyone else was packing up their lunch things.

"You won't be doing much high-ropes work," Jelena told her. "You'll be assisting Aurora. That's on-the-ground stuff."

Lindsay looked a little happier.

Just then, Hayden came out of the school office. I knew he'd been at a student council meeting. Jelena called him over.

"You're in for next week, right?" she asked. "Mr. Quinten suggested you as one of the group leaders."

Hayden gave my shoulder a squeeze. I held my breath as I waited for his answer. Three whole days together would totally make up for the two lost weekends. And the campfires and starlight would be sure to boost our relationship.

Hayden frowned slightly. No! He wasn't going?

"I'm totally up for it, but my parents have final say when it comes to the permission slip," he said. "I'm not exactly in their good graces at the moment."

"It'll be fine. I'll have Mr. Quinten give them a call." Jelena picked up her handbag from the bench and gave us a wave good-bye.

"I don't think any of us are getting out of this, are we?" Lindsay looked like a woman who'd been sentenced to the gallows.

Hayden brushed a lock of hair behind my ear as Lindsay headed off to math. "I don't want to get out of it. If I get my way, we'll spend the whole time side by side."

"I'll have to do a lot of fieldwork during the trip," I said, "but we'll definitely get lots of time together."

My voice sounded breathless. Did Hayden realize what he did

to me? I'd once had a tooth removed, and the dentist had warned me that the anesthetic shot contained a tiny bit of adrenaline. The racing of my heart and the super-heady exhilaration I'd felt back then were just like the sensations I experienced when Hayden stood next to me. Did I make him feel the same way? He looked totally calm. Maybe boys didn't get the jitters like girls did.

Hayden laughed. "So your candidates will be tightroping their way through their first dates, will they? That's a little worrying, considering first date nerves give most people the shakes anyway. You've got to hope those harnesses work."

"So if you and I were rope buddies, you'd be shaking in your shoes?" I asked.

I had to know. Hayden always seemed so confident—look at how he'd moved in for that kiss when we'd been standing in his parents' yard!

"Looking for compliments, Ms. Skye?"

Hayden gave me a poke in the ribs and I shrieked. He knew how ticklish I was.

"I'm just . . . I don't know. I'm wondering if you get nervous around me?"

"Let's just say, when it comes to you—"

The start-of-class bell rang, interrupting him.

"Yes?" He *had* to finish this sentence.

"I'd never risk a broad plank over a stream, since I'd wind up swimming within about seven seconds."

Hayden threw me a grin as he dashed off to class.

14

That evening, Lindsay and I sat in my living room, with my laptop open. The big moment had arrived: we were about to run the chemistry calculator to determine the ideal candidates for Chloe, Jeffrey, and Sara.

I'd handed Hayden the extra information gathered from my meetings with Chloe and Jeffrey only this morning, so he'd really gone the extra mile to finish the program for me today. I was super eager to get the matches. After all, I had limited time to get the matchmakees and their potential dates to agree to attend next week's camp.

Remembering Hayden's *seven seconds* remark earlier, I smiled.

"What are you smiling for?" Lindsay asked.

"Just Hayden and a comment he made about camp."

"I don't think Tyler's going," Lindsay said, a frown crossing her face.

"What? Why?"

"Most of the soccer team are going, and Tyler wants a break from them," Lindsay said. "Plus, he's kind of worried that Jelena might reveal more embarrassing photos or slogans on the trip."

"Well, you can reassure him that we're part of the campaign, so we can veto anything that we think is too much."

"He said he'll think about it." I could tell Lindsay was trying not to be annoyed. "Anyway, let's get on with the matches."

"Let's do Chloe's first," I said, selecting her name from the drop-down list of matchmakees.

Lindsay peered at the screen. "So all you have to do is choose a name from the list, hit the Match Me button, and the top three candidates will pop up?"

"Yup, it's that simple." I hovered the mouse over the Match Me button. "When we hit the button, the program runs through all of the matchmakee's character traits, plus their personal preferences for a mate, and cross-references all that with the information given to us in the candidates' questionnaires."

"Wait a minute, we need a soundtrack." Lindsay grabbed the computer from me, opened Spotify, and found the "Matchmaker" song from *Fiddler on the Roof.* "My mom made my sis and me watch this a couple of years ago," she said. She hit Play, then repositioned the computer between us. "Okay, go!"

I hit the Match Me button and the calculator began running through the data. Lindsay and I leaped up and danced around with excitement. She grabbed my hand and twirled me, and we did little pirouettes around the living room.

"It's done!!" I yelped as a Match Completed message flashed up on the screen.

I grabbed the laptop and we sat down on the couch again.

"First match for Chloe is . . ."

"Benjamin Zane!" Lindsay squealed. "His crystal-blue eyes and her violet ones—can you imagine how good-looking their children would be?"

I held back a laugh. I hated to be a downer, but despite the calculator giving them a ninety-six percent compatibility rate, I had my doubts.

"Linds, remember what Benjamin was like in the school play? Totally driven. He's dead set on making it to Broadway by the time he's twenty-one."

"I know he's all about his agent and his carpet-cleaning commercials, but a little bit of ambition isn't always a bad thing," Lindsay said sagely.

"Of course not. But don't you also remember when we thought he was my secret admirer? When I confronted him, he made it absolutely clear that his main focus was Benjamin. I don't know how a girlfriend would fit in with that."

Lindsay didn't look fazed. "Chloe's pretty driven herself. Plus, Benjamin's wild about drama and writing. He's got the theatrical temperament to understand Chloe."

I could tell she meant he was dramatic enough to not be put off by Chloe's "incident." Considering the guy had once pitched an all-out public tantrum because his *Three Musketeers* hat had an inferior feather to that of Hayden's (they had been thespian rivals since seventh grade), he couldn't really judge Chloe too harshly.

"I think Benjamin could be the type to get swept away if he falls in love," Lindsay said.

"Are you sure you aren't getting him confused with his former roles?" I asked, thinking of his impassioned performance as Romeo last year.

"Aurora! The system says he's the top match. Why are you so uneasy?"

I felt protective of Chloe. She'd had a rough time of it and I didn't want to risk any shaky setups.

"Let's give him a call," Lindsay said, reaching for our list of contacts.

She grabbed my phone and punched in Benjamin's number, then handed the phone to me.

"Lindsay, I just don't know—"

"Hello, Benjamin speaking."

Crap. He'd picked up right away. I'd kind of hoped to leave a voicemail so he could get accustomed to the idea of both Chloe and the trip before he called back.

"Hi, Benjamin." I put on my confident voice. "It's Aurora . . . You know, from *Much Ado*—"

"Aurora!" Benjamin sounded cheery. "I've been expecting you to call."

"You have?"

"We were going to meet and talk about signing you up to the casting agency I'm with, remember?"

"Oh yeah . . . As you would have heard from Jelena's announcements, I've decided to take the route of matchmaker rather than actress."

After I'd been chosen as the face of the Get High (Heels!) autumn campaign (thanks to Mom's unfailing desire to make me a fashion model), Benjamin had wanted to take me out to discuss career options. He'd assured me that although he'd started with crowd scenes, his agency had quickly landed him a regular role in cleaning commercials.

"See, this is why we need to meet. With looks like yours, there's more money in acting," Benjamin replied. "You land something like a Coke commercial and that's four months' income at once. I've been short-listed for a series of Japanese mineral water commercials. That's major. I could be the next Mr. Bubbly."

Lindsay looked at me curiously as I shoved my hand over my mouth to smother my amusement at Benjamin's potential new moniker.

"I'm kind of set on working in the realms of the heart," I said, standing and turning my back on Lindsay so I could resume my professionalism. "Which is why I'm calling, actually. You put your name down to be matched up, right?"

I wanted to check that he'd submitted the questionnaire himself and that someone hadn't filled it in as a joke.

"Yes, I did," Benjamin replied. "Though, if you're still up for a date, I'm more than happy to take my name out of the running. I thought you and I had a great connection in *Much Ado*, and I'd be up for exploring that."

This was awkwardly unexpected. I laughed nervously. "Oh, that's nice of you to say, Benjamin, but I'm kind of seeing someone."

Lindsay got up from the couch and moved closer to me so she could hear the other side of the conversation.

"Paris, right?" Benjamin's voice sounded like he was chewing something bitter. "Are you sure this isn't just leading-lady syndrome? You know, you were cast opposite him, so you think you have crossover chemistry? Remember, I was originally meant to play the role of Benedick. Paris nabbed it because of his fake audition—"

"I kind of thought you'd be too busy for dating," I broke in. "What with castings and all."

"Yes, I thought so too, but then I started reading a biography of Richard Burton. His passion for Elizabeth Taylor infused his roles in *Cleopatra* and *The Taming of the Shrew*. It's my duty as an actor to experience all the shades of this thing we call love. Listen, are you so sure you're stuck on Paris? Seems kind of an odd match to me . . ."

I quickly deflected the question. "Richard Burton! Wow! Benjamin, I have an Elizabeth Taylor stunt double that my chemistry calculator says you're perfect for. Chloe Butler?"

I held my breath, waiting for his reaction.

"Chloe . . ." He stretched the name out thoughtfully.

"She's really into the arts," I added. "She wants a guy she can take to the theater!"

"She's a stunning girl. And she certainly does look like Elizabeth Taylor in her prime. I just never considered her, because I thought she might not be into dating, after the whole Max fiasco."

"She's learned a lot since then." I thought it best to keep things vague rather than invoking the Dido reenactment in full.

"You know what?" Benjamin said. "I'm up for it. Anyone can write bitter Facebook posts or send nasty texts after a breakup, but it takes a true artist to draw from the *Aeneid* the way she did."

He was in! I spun back around to face Lindsay and gave her the thumbs-up sign with my left hand.

"Fantastic! So, Benjamin, we're bringing the matches together for the first time at Jelena's camp next week—you know, Take It to Another Level. We think it's the perfect place for the matches to spend one-on-one time together in an exciting environment. So if you can return the signed permission slip tomorrow—"

"I'm not big on these extremist things," Benjamin cut in. "You can break bones or get scars—not good when you rely on your looks for a living. Maybe Chloe and I could go on a date when you guys get back."

"Chloe's going to have a lot of competitors for her affections," I said, appealing to his competitive side. "I'd hate for this to be a *you snooze, you lose* thing for you. Plus, the camp isn't just sports. There'll be theater games by the fire at night. You're welcome to prepare a monologue."

I was hoping the opportunity of a captive audience would do the trick. Theater games weren't on the itinerary as of yet, but I was sure I could get Jelena to add them in.

"I suppose it could be considered part of my acting training for the week," Benjamin conceded. "Do you think anyone would mind if I did a longish piece?"

"No way! Go for it!" I said, pumping up the enthusiasm in my voice. "Chloe will be super impressed. Just make sure you give Jelena your permission slip first thing tomorrow—spots are filling fast."

I hung up, praying I'd won him over.

"Fantastic!" Lindsay said. "Okay, we've just got to convince the next two matches to come, and Chloe's set. I'll call the next boy."

"I can't believe he met someone over the weekend!" Lindsay said, as she put the phone down after calling Adam Brown. He was music mad and the lead singer in a band that was doing pretty well since forming a few months ago.

"How did he meet her?" I asked.

"Some family friend's barbecue. They've only been on one

date, but he's so smitten he wouldn't hear of even going out for coffee with Chloe. Apparently, this Alexandra girl looks like Charlize Theron and sings like Adele or something. Argh! He and Chloe had an eighty-nine percent compatibility, too!"

"That's okay," I said, looking at the matches on the screen again. "She has the exact same compatibility with this other guy—Hunter Greene. Do you know anything about him?"

"Wow. Okay, he's an interesting guy. He's an incredibly gifted violinist. My friend Lucy—you know, the clarinet player—is in the school orchestra with him, and apparently they were all in shock the first time they heard him play—even Ms. Fisher, the music teacher. He's won all sorts of competitions, here and internationally. He was at a full-time music school, but something happened over the summer and his parents decided to transfer him to Jefferson. Lucy says he doesn't say a word in class, but he plays so beautifully that all the orchestra girls are in raptures over him."

"Well, he fits the bill in terms of artistic nature," I said, intrigued by Lindsay's description. "I'll give him a call now."

I looked up his number and dialed. It went straight to voicemail. "Hi, obviously you've reached Hunter. Try not to leave a message if it's truly inane. Cheers."

I hung up. He sounded like a super-serious, slightly ironic type, and leaving a voicemail message just didn't seem right somehow.

"I'll talk to him in person," I said. "It's better if I get a sense of him, one-on-one, before we set Chloe up with him."

"So that's Chloe, then." Lindsay looked disappointed that we hadn't reached Hunter. "Do you think we should remove Adam's name and run the calculator again to get a third option?"

"Well, Benjamin's in, and if I can convince Hunter to come on the trip, then that's two," I said thoughtfully. "Chloe's the intense type, so I'm sure she's going to launch into 'deep and meaningful' right off the bat. Trying to juggle three candidates in the space of three days might be too much for her. She has a pretty high compatibility rating for both these guys, so maybe we should see how things go. If she doesn't have any luck with either Benjamin or Hunter, we can run the calculator again when we get back from the trip."

"Okay." Lindsay grabbed the computer and hovered the mouse over the matchmakee drop-down menu. "Jeffrey or Sara next? Let's do Sara—thank god we finally have some say over her dates. Some of her previous choices should have had warning labels attached to them."

Lindsay hit the Match Me button and we both held our breath.

"Johannes Alsvik," I read slowly, struggling with the last name. "Johannes . . . Do we know him?"

Lindsay let out a small shriek. "He moved here from Sweden at the start of the term. He looks like Alexander Skarsgård from *True Blood*. Don't tell me you haven't seen him! All the girls call him 'TB' as a code name."

"Ohh!" His face popped up immediately. "The very tall, slim guy? Often wears pale-aqua skinny jeans?"

We didn't share any classes, so I'd only had glimpses of him at assembly or in the corridors. He was definitely a ringer for Alexander.

"He's very fashionable. Sara is going to die!" Lindsay squealed. "I've seen her head turn whenever he walks into math. Call her *now*!"

We both giggled as I grabbed the phone and dialed Sara's number.

"Put it on speakerphone!" Lindsay demanded.

"Hey, Aurora," Sara answered.

"Hey! It's Aurora *and* Lindsay."

"We're doing the matches for you, Chloe, and Jeffrey!" Lindsay burst out. "And you're not going to believe who's come up as having a ninety-six percent compatibility with you. *Johannes aka TB!*"

"*What?*" Sara shrieked on the other end of the phone.

Lindsay and I grinned at each other. We had her.

"So, just think . . . Next week at camp you're going to have

Alexander Skarsgård, plus two other guys, fighting to win your affections," Lindsay continued.

Sara was silent. Perhaps she'd fainted.

"Sara?" I tried.

"I don't know," she said slowly. "Besides the fact that I'm determined to stay single so I can focus on my manuscript, Johannes is a little too . . ." Her voice trailed off.

"A little too *what*?" I wanted her to speak up if there was a problem with Johannes.

"Good-looking," she said.

I gave Lindsay a look. Sara sounded totally unconvincing.

"Isn't that your type?" Lindsay pointed out. "None of your dates has ever been beaten by the ugly stick."

"Yeah, but they, you know, look roughish. Johannes is . . . too coordinated with his clothing."

"You told me at the start of term that his aqua pants should be framed and auctioned off, they were so exemplary," Lindsay said.

What? I mouthed to Lindsay. She nodded, trying not to laugh.

"I think it's a little unfair to write Johannes off 'cause he dresses well," I said. It was obvious Sara was on a mission to avoid a setup. "Leave it to Lindsay and me to continue the matchmaking. We're going to get off the phone now."

"I don't get a say?" Sara wailed melodramatically.

"You don't get to veto all the options, you mean," I said goodhumoredly, and hung up.

Lindsay looked astounded. "I can't believe she said no to Johannes!"

"She's just stubborn," I said. "We're going to have to be cautious. She'll go hide up a tree at camp if we push it too far. I say we focus solely on Johannes for those first three days and then introduce the other two matches once we're home and she's warmed to the idea a little more."

Lindsay nodded and noted down the other two matches for later. Her phone rang.

"Tyler," she said, making a face. "I really hope he's not calling to whine again. My picture is up on the posters as well, but I'm not acting like a baby."

"Go ahead. Take it," I encouraged her. "I'll call Johannes from the kitchen while you speak to Tyler."

"Okay, Johannes sounds completely over the moon," I told Lindsay, as I bounced back into the room. "He totally knew who Sara was. His accent's sort of thick, but I'm pretty sure he compared her with some kind of Swedish goddess. He's up for the trip, too. It took him awhile to understand the concept of high ropes and camping and how it related to Sara, but as long as he's standing in the parking lot ready to board the bus on Wednesday morning, it's all good. He'll get the idea once we're there."

"Fantastic!" Lindsay looked happier. "Tyler was calling to ask if he'd left his sleeping bag at my place after the camping trip with Mom and Dad over the summer. So he's obviously done a turnaround on coming."

I beamed at her. "You'll see, this trip is going to be the beginning of a lot of good things."

"Even true love for Jeffrey?" Lindsay asked, looking at the laptop screen.

I sat back down next to her and saw that the cursor was hovering over his name, ready to trigger his top three matches.

"I have full confidence that we can do this," I said, boosted by my conversation with Johannes. "Hit the button."

This time, instead of jumping up and down with anticipation, Lindsay and I both tensely drummed our fingers against the couch.

"Jemima Brown, Ruby Jackson, and Piper Robinson," we announced together, as the names materialized.

I looked at the rating of ninety-four percent next to Ruby's name. "I'd never have thought to match her up with Jeffrey, but, you know, they might work really well."

"She ticks the *bootylicious* box," Lindsay said, making a Jessica Rabbit shape with her hands.

I laughed. Ruby had been the first girl in our class to move from crop tops to actual bras. "She does, and she walks that fine line of confident but not arrogant."

Ruby was one of those ultrabubbly types whose absence left a big hole in the class if she was away sick for a day.

"She'll probably be up for the camp if we push the wildlife aspect," I added. "The campground's in a nature reserve, so I'm sure there are oodles of lizards and native birds and possums to see."

Ruby was crazy about animals and wanted to be a vet, a wildlife conservationist, or a zookeeper. Her mind was usually on healing injured birds rather than fashion magazines or makeup looks, which was probably why she was so unconscious of her attractiveness.

"What do you think about the ninety-one percent rating for Jemima?" Lindsay asked. "Oh that's cute: Jemima and Jeffrey!"

"Jemima's kind of synonymous with cute," I replied.

"She's so tiny!" Lindsay shook her head. "I thought I was petite, but she's like a fairy princess. Except for those eyelashes. If she hadn't had them since grade school, I'd think they were extensions. So not fair."

"Even Jeffrey would have no difficulty sweeping her up in his arms."

"Do you think she's confident enough for Jeffrey?" Lindsay asked. "She's kind of quiet."

"That isn't necessarily a bad thing. When it comes to chemistry, it seems that, while it's important to have similar values and goals, you can have significantly different personalities and still be a great match. Jeffrey might love dating someone quieter, and Jemima might adore a lively boyfriend."

Lindsay laughed. "Let's just hope she sees the funny side of nudie runs. What about Piper? I don't know much about her."

"She's pretty," I said, thinking of her long, sandy-blond hair, which she almost always wore up in a ponytail, and the light dusting of freckles on her petite nose. "Jeffrey did say he's partial to blondes."

"Hope she's partial to him! Do you think these setups are going to work?"

"I guess we can only get them on the trip, watch their interactions, and observe the results," I said, shutting down the laptop, now that we had all the matches.

"Why do I feel like you and I are equivalent to Charles Darwin or something?" Lindsay joked.

"Hey, you never know . . . If this chemistry calculator is as precise as Hayden and I hope, then all the candidates could go gaga for Jeffrey, Sara, and Chloe," I said. "Maybe this trip will turn into a survival of the fittest."

15

The next morning, I made my way down to the kitchen to catch the NAD before he went to work. I needed him to sign my permission slip for camp.

"Hey, honey." The NAD took a sip of his now standard detox juice of chlorella, arugula, and kale and tried not to shudder.

"Dad, are you sure you need to detox? You're pretty slim and healthy already." I took my seat at the table. "Can you sign my permission slip? It's for a three-day camping trip next week."

The NAD smiled as he read the header, which had a photo of Jelena beside it. "Ah, Jelena's touch, of course." He grabbed a pen from his briefcase on the table.

"Yeah, all the girls are going," I said. "Lindsay's helping me with matchmaking. It's going to be such a romantic atmosphere . . . campfires and starlit nights—"

Dad looked up. "Is Hayden going?"

"I'm pretty sure, yeah."

I wondered if the Parises had signed Hayden's form. They had to—being a leader on something like this would look great on his résumé down the road.

"Hmm." The NAD's pen paused on the signature line.

I suddenly realized why. Stupid Kai and his Make-Out Mastery. "Dad! You aren't actually worried, are you?"

"No, honey, I trust you!" he replied, lightning fast. "I was just thinking . . . how would you feel about me coming as a volunteer?"

"You want to volunteer?" I looked at him blankly. Dad had never done a cafeteria stint or manned a fair stand in my whole time at school. "Don't you have work?"

"I have so many vacation days built up, my boss said I have to take some, pronto."

"And you want to spend them on high ropes with my classmates?"

It wasn't like I was embarrassed by Dad or anything, but his presence would obviously distract me from being able to focus one hundred percent on the program. Not to mention Hayden.

"Dad, Hayden's going to be in another tent, you know. The camp's completely boy–girl segregated—"

"Don't be silly, honey. It's not about that at all." The NAD grabbed his phone from his briefcase and punched in the principal's number, which was at the bottom of the form. "Hi, Mr. Quinten, this is Ken Skye, Aurora's dad. I'm hoping I can sign on as a parent volunteer for next week's camp? You're in need? Fantastic. Put my name down."

"Your dad? At camp?" Jelena blinked at me in shock when I handed over my permission slip.

I nodded.

"Climbing trees and walking on high ropes?"

I nodded again. I sure wasn't going to tell her the real reason for his sudden desire to volunteer.

She shrugged. "Okay. I suppose he's pretty cool for a supervisor. Maybe he'll take up a spot usually filled by one of those killjoy parents who are paranoid their kid's going to come to some gruesome end at the science museum or something."

"Oh, and here are the permission slips for Benjamin, Ruby, and Jemima," I added.

Piper couldn't come because she had a swim meet. We'd have to wait till we got back to set her up with Jeffrey. Jemima hadn't been crazy about the idea of roughing it, but fortunately I'd been able to convince her that it would make her college applications look more well-rounded.

"You should already have Johannes's form," Lindsay said, appearing at our side as we took our seats at the back of the art room. "I spoke with him earlier."

Jelena pulled her clipboard out of her bag and crossed off names from the Take It to Another Level list. "Check. So you told the girls they've been matched with Jeffrey?"

"Not exactly," I said, looking at Lindsay uneasily. "We kind of wanted to get them to the camp without preconceived notions."

"Meaning you didn't want to scare them off." Jelena didn't even look up from the checklist. "Smart thinking. Make sure you oversee his wardrobe selection. No tired T-shirts or too-short shorts."

Jelena sounded like she was telling me to check a six-year-old's backpack to make sure he'd packed enough undies. I was *not* approving Jeffrey's undergarments.

"Jelena, seriously?"

She looked at me with an arched eyebrow. "Aurora, let's not have the girls write him off on the first day of camp because of some mismatched socks. Women are particular about the details. You know, female birds tend to go for male birds with symmetrical feathers. Make sure Jeffrey's a symmetrical bird."

The next morning, I headed into school just a little bit early, hoping to cross paths with Hunter. Lindsay had told me that Lucy said he usually practiced before class, so I swung by the music room.

The most exquisite melody was emanating through the partially open door. I took a sneaky peek, careful to keep myself hidden as I watched a guy, presumably Hunter, eyes shut and brow furrowed reverently, playing with almost superhuman rapidity. He finished the piece, but his eyes remained closed. I half hoped he would begin it again so I could hear it from the start. I could see why the entire orchestra had been mesmerized.

However, instead of continuing to practice, Hunter opened his eyes and turned his gaze to the door, as if he could feel my presence there. I thought I'd better make myself known, so I pushed the door open.

"Hi . . . Hunter, isn't it? I really do apologize for interrupting you—"

"Do you play?" he said, staring at me unblinkingly. His eyes were the color of amber.

"Oh, no. I can't even count out a simple three-four rhythm." I laughed.

Hunter didn't crack a smile. "Do you need the room?"

"Huh?"

"You aren't a music student, then." He looked intrigued.

"No. I'm a matchmaker."

Hunter's eyebrows went up. "I remember now. You were standing at the edge of the pool when Jelena did her Botticelli number."

"You put your name in the drawing that night," I reminded him.

"Yes, rather a crazy moment." He looked as if he regretted it.

"Well, it came up."

Hunter laughed abruptly. "I'm not the lucky type."

"Why would you say that?"

I meant it lightly, but Hunter seemed to vibrate with intensity—his fingers were drumming the edge of his seat—and in that atmosphere, the question sounded penetrating.

His dark eyebrows drew together. "I don't know. Maybe I take the musician archetype too much to heart. Beethoven, Schumann, Shostakovich—they were hardly happy people. Freakishly talented, but not happy. Or maybe someone up there decided that it was enough to give me the blessing of musicianship, and every other sector of my life should be doomed to disappointment."

It had been a long while since I'd heard the word "doomed" in such a serious context.

"It's not an absolute rule that musical genius equals a life without love. Mahler married, you know," I pointed out, remembering the short bio I'd read in the program when the NAD had taken me to a symphony.

Hunter grinned. "Well, Mahler . . . Now, that's a long story." He stretched out the hand that wasn't holding the violin. "You're an interesting interruption to the everyday ritual. Aurora, wasn't it?"

I nodded as we shook hands. His grip was strong—obviously from extensive practice sessions—but his fingers were long and slim.

"I'm hoping to introduce you to the woman who's going to end your unlucky spell once and for all," I told him.

It took a good half hour to bring Hunter around to the matchmaking concept. Although he'd put his details into the drawing, a large part of him had assumed that his name wouldn't come up. Like Lindsay had said, it was clear that something had happened over the summer, and from his vague references while we talked, that "something" appeared to have been a heartbreak.

"Love is comparable to the myth of Icarus," he said. "Under your beloved's adoring eye, you feel invincible. You don't notice that you're too close to the sun until it's too late. By then, your wings are ablaze and you're plunging to the ground."

I was stunned by the mythological comparison; it was so similar to Chloe's reference to the *Aeneid*. If he'd hoped it would discourage me from setting him up, it had achieved the opposite effect.

I assured Hunter that we'd build him sturdy wings this time around.

Hunter paused for what felt like forever before nodding his agreement. I had no idea how his slender musician's frame would cope with three days of high-ropes activity, but I was bursting to see what his dynamic with Chloe would be like.

16

I spent most of Saturday helping the NAD pack for school camp, checking that we both had sleeping mats, water bottles, and enough socks and shirts to get us through three days. I doubted we were in for a *Survivor* experience, but I still wanted to be fully prepared.

On Sunday it rained, so the girls came around for an impromptu movie day. Sara, as part of her research for her novel, had downloaded *Vertical Limit* and *Sanctum* for us to watch. Jelena was busy with camp preparation, so it was just the four of us.

"What's with the sighing?" Sara asked me, when the movie had finished. "Is it a Hayden thing? He's allowed to come to camp, so why are you stressing?"

I sighed again. "I don't understand boys. Hayden was so enthusiastic about getting up close and personal before the stitches. But he's been stitch-free for about seventy-two hours and *nothing*. You saw him when he had lunch with us on Friday. Not even a kiss on the cheek. It's totally weird."

"But you said you'd decided you were a hundred percent not kissing him at school," Cassie said.

"And the poor guy's grounded," Lindsay added. "He's got no options for kissing you anywhere *but* school till next week. If he's of the same mind as you—i.e., not wanting to pucker up in front of everyone—that explains the nondemonstrative behavior."

"He could have asked to walk me home," I pointed out. "If he was really interested, he'd think outside the box."

"Aurora, you guys have three days together coming up. Give the guy a chance."

Sara had a point. I'd just have to wait it out. If Hayden was still acting distant by the time camp rolled around, then I'd know there was an issue.

"Isn't there a side street you could take?" I begged the taxi driver, on the way into the city on Tuesday night. Every lane of traffic was backed up ahead of us.

"Sorry, nothing but one-ways," the driver answered. "If you want me to drop you off at the hotel, we have to stay on this road."

I looked at my watch: 6:55 p.m. There was no way I'd be arriving in five minutes. Mom was going to be furious. It had been obvious from our conversation the other day that she was nervous about introducing me to Carlos, and my being late would only put her even more on edge. I pulled out my phone and dialed her number. It went straight to voicemail.

Was it normal to be *this* nervous about a simple dinner at a restaurant? I supposed meeting Carlos for the first time was rather major. What if he didn't like me? What if I didn't like him? My relationship with Mom was already tricky. If Carlos and I didn't take to each other, it would become even more difficult to maintain regular contact with her. Mom's role as my mother had always been far from traditional, but I didn't want to lose what we did have. It might not be the easy familiarity that Sara, Cass, and the other girls had with their mothers, but it was still something. I was her daughter.

By the time the cab pulled up in front of the hotel, I was sweating. I dashed into the lobby.

"Can I help you, miss?" a concierge asked, observing my stressed expression.

"I'm supposed to be meeting my mother and a group of her friends tonight." I gave the concierge both Mom's and Carlos's names. "Can you tell me which restaurant the booking's for?"

"Oh, this event is in one of our reception rooms," the concierge said with a smile. "Let me show you the way."

Event? Mom had told me it was a few close friends and Carlos.

The concierge led me to a large, glass-walled room. I could see lush greenery, exotic flowers, and twinkling lights through the glass—and about two hundred people.

The concierge opened the door for me. As I stepped through, I was enveloped in sound: music, chatter, laughter. People were mingling and drinking champagne. I stood on my tiptoes and scanned the room for Mom. She was near the back, wearing a sapphire-blue gown. As I moved closer, I saw her laugh and place her hand on a man's arm. He was dark-haired, roughly about ten years older than her, and very formally dressed.

"Mom?" I said as I reached her side. My stomach muscles tensed, hoping she wouldn't be angry.

She let go of the man's arm. "You're late, darling."

"Traffic," I said, as she leaned in to give me a kiss. Fortunately, her face was still relaxed.

"Ghastly, isn't it?" the man said with an ironic smile. He had a very English accent. "I don't think I knew what a traffic jam was until I came to this city."

Mom took in my curious stare. It couldn't be Carlos; he'd have a Spanish accent. It must be another friend.

"Aurora, I'd like you to meet Carlos," Mom said. "Carlos, my daughter, Aurora."

"I thought you were Spanish," I blurted out.

Mom looked horrified at my directness, but Carlos laughed.

"The accent trips everyone up," he said. "I was born there and am based there, but my father was English. I was educated in England—Eton and Cambridge, to be exact."

"Carlos's family have connections with the English peerage," Mom explained.

Carlos raised an eyebrow. "Essentially a bit of paper with a long list of names on it. They complain dreadfully at my making a living in hotels and nightclubs, although they don't complain about the lifestyle it affords them." He turned his attention to Mom. "Goodness, Avery, she's the image of you. I'd rather expected a child, by how you described her. Fifteen, correct?"

"I'm sixteen," I said.

Carlos shook his head, staring at me. "Well, that's certainly a relief. I'm not good with children. Your mother knows that, which is why I suspect she kept quiet about you. But I see we have a grown-up, thankfully."

Before I could think of a response, Carlos nodded to someone across the room. He gave my mother a kiss on the cheek. "Darling, excuse me. I need to talk business. Aurora, we must chat further. Your mother tells me you model. I know people in Paris and London—you could use Spain as your base. Much better to be in Europe if you want to establish a profile."

He was gone before I could tell him I had zero interest in catwalk work overseas.

"You see, darling?" Mom said, watching him walk away. "I knew you two would get along, once he was accustomed to the idea."

"So he wasn't pleased when he heard?" I asked, trying not to feel hurt.

"Oh, darling, as he said, he's not good with children. But this is working out wonderfully. He and I will be able to offer you the very best opportunities career-wise. I know you're not sold on the modeling thing, but he could get you a job working in international events, or the entertainment business."

I was feeling overwhelmed. I hadn't even worked out which colleges I wanted to apply for at the end of next year yet.

"Would you excuse me?" I said. "I need the restroom."

There were huge, soft-looking chairs in the open area near the sinks. I sank into one. From the few moments I'd spent in his company, I could tell that Carlos was very similar to Mom. Any relationship that developed between us would be about what he could do for me in terms of opportunities. The detachment both of them showed toward me made me feel insignificant.

I could see that Mom was happy to be marrying into a family with links to the English peerage. It trumped the NAD and the advertising agency.

The NAD. I put my head in my hands. How was I going to break all this to him? I'd told him I was going for dinner with Mom tonight, but not that I was meeting Carlos.

Fifteen minutes had elapsed by the time I felt more together. *You can do this,* I reasoned with myself as I headed for the door. I could smile politely, eat some canapés, and look pleased to be here.

Mom spotted me as I reentered the room, and she motioned for me to join her and Carlos, who'd returned to her side.

"Perfect timing," she said. "We're just about to make an announcement."

A staff member handed Carlos a microphone.

"Hello, everyone." Carlos's voice reached over the chatter. The room fell silent. "My first announcement of tonight is, of course, the launch of the Centaurus Group in this city. I've just met with the board and we've received full approval for the development of a new entertainment mecca, including a series of bars, dining establishments, and an exclusive nightclub. This is a whole new lifestyle-and-luxury investment, akin to those we have developed in Ibiza and London. These projects will be launching over the next five years."

Carlos paused and took my mother's hand. "I am also delighted to officially announce my and Avery's engagement. We hope to see you at a very special celebration in the near future. We will be keeping the details private for the moment, to avoid media interest, but you will receive invitations shortly, specifying the date."

He handed my mother the microphone. Mom looked the picture of elegance as she addressed the room.

"As Carlos said, I'm thrilled to share the news of our engagement with you this evening. Also, while we have your attention, I'd like to introduce you to my daughter, Aurora."

Mom stretched her hand out to me. I took it and stepped into the spotlight beside her, feeling every face turn to me. My heartbeat thundered in my ears. Having her acknowledge me as her daughter in front of hundreds of her friends, and at Carlos's side, meant so much to me that I felt as if I might cry. It was a proclamation of my existence in her world.

Was this a turning point for us? Was it a sign that she wanted to develop our relationship beyond weekly catch-ups? Part of me didn't want to hope, and another part of me couldn't help it.

By the time I got home that night, it was very late. As I headed up the stairs, I could see that the NAD's door was shut and his light off.

I felt guilt wash over me again as I stood outside his door. I had to do the right thing and tell him about Mom's impending nuptials. I couldn't do it tomorrow, though. To drop a bombshell this big just before the NAD was obligated to be a responsible adult presence for three days was not only insensitive, it was also dangerous. We were going to be carrying out activities on high ropes . . . What if the NAD was so devastated by the news that he forgot to clip onto the safety line or fasten his helmet?

I wasn't risking it. I'd tell him on Saturday, when he could go through whatever emotional trauma ensued, in the privacy of his own home.

17

The NAD and I arrived at the school parking lot on schedule at 7:30 a.m. the next day. Throngs of students stood around with their backpacks and sleeping bags, chattering excitedly. Mr. Quinten, decked out in camouflage attire, was loading bags into the back of the bus.

The NAD went to help him, and I made my way over to where the girls were standing. Jelena handed me a to-go cappuccino.

"I need you guys pumped full of energy," she said, beaming.

"Pleased with the turnout?" I asked.

Jelena shrugged. "Oh, the turnout's as expected. No, this stunning smile is due to my finding out that Matt Stevens has dropped out of the race for school president. So I only need to beat Alex and Julie now. I've got a way more interesting platform than Julie, and this camp will knock Alex's gym plan into insignificance."

Talk about a turnaround. Matt had held a major proportion of the athletic community's votes. Picking up some of those would give Jelena a good chance of winning.

"Can you guys hold the top of my pack together while I do up the straps?" Sara asked, huffing as she tried to wrestle with the almost body-size blue backpack.

"What have you got in there?" Cass asked.

"The usuals: waterproof mat, air sofa, solar light set, battery-powered fan, hiking boots, collapsible shovel—"

"A shovel?" Lindsay gaped at her.

"In case we need to build a pit for shelter," Sara said, unblinkingly.

Lindsay looked unnerved. "Aurora, I didn't bring a shovel. And I've only got my sneakers. I didn't know we needed actual hiking boots."

"Linds, it's fine." I felt like giggling, but I kept a straight face. "I've only got sneakers, too."

"Plus a microfiber towel, a heart-rate monitor, and a pack of antimosquito bracelets," Sara went on.

"Where did you get all this?" I stared at the assortment of items that she'd pulled out to reconfigure the space in her pack.

"I joined the Adventurer Club at the outdoor equipment store, so I got big savings," she said. "Plus I got a bonus headlamp."

"A headlamp?" Jelena spluttered. "We aren't going caving. The camp leader told us to pack light."

"Hey, who's the one who brought a self-inflating queen-size mattress?" Sara pointed at the huge box that Jelena's campaign team was heaving into the bus's baggage compartment. Mr. Quinten was frowning as he looked at it.

"OMG." Lindsay's face became a thundercloud as she checked her phone. "Tyler just *texted* me that he's not coming to camp."

"What?" we all cried in unison.

"He's loaned his sleeping bag to Paul from the soccer team. The coward!" Lindsay's voice was now a shout.

She marched over to the school gate. I saw her lips moving furiously, so she'd obviously called Tyler. She returned a couple of minutes later, her face still stormy.

"He's changed his mind again about putting up with the soccer team's jokes," she said, rolling her eyes. "Just about all of them are going to this stupid camp."

Uh-oh. My co-cupid wasn't backing out last moment, was she?

"Lindsay, I hope you're not going to give up on the camp too," I said.

"Your payment's nonrefundable," Jelena butted in.

"Of course I'm coming!" Lindsay snapped. "If Tyler wants to miss out on bonding time because of some teasing from a few guys, then that's his problem. He knows this trip was our opportunity to break out of the routine. Idiot."

She marched off in the direction of the bus. As she reached the door, I saw who was standing there, checking off students.

I grabbed Jelena's arm. "What is Ms. DeForest doing here?"

Ms. DeForest taught interpretive dance and had kept up a steady flow of criticism of me, which included giving me detentions, pointing out my supposedly black aura, and hypnotizing my cat. Worst of all, she was also the NAD's ex! We were talking breakdown instead of breakthrough! Even if the NAD kept his professionalism, like I hoped he would, Ms. DeForest was going to serve as a three-day-long reminder of his failed attempts at relationships. This trip wasn't going to help the NAD take charge of his life; it was going to spin him back down into a spiral of loss and grief.

Jelena winced at my death grip on her arm. "Mr. Quinten told me this morning. I have no idea what possessed him to allow her to be a supervisor . . . We don't need lectures on chakras while out in the woods; we need practical people who can make hot chocolate and lug food supply boxes. Plus, who wears *crushed velvet* on a school camping trip?"

"Oh no. He's spotted her."

I watched as the NAD made his way over to Ms. DeForest. I couldn't see his expression, but she had a pleasant smile on her face. The NAD gave her a hug.

"Your dad's really understanding," Cassie said. "I don't think I could hug my ex."

The poor man was obviously bewildered by the situation he'd

found himself in. I supposed he was doing all he could to apply the principles of forgiveness he'd learned through the support group.

Sara whistled. "That's one long hug."

I was one second from running over there and breaking it up. Any moment now, the NAD might start weeping on her shoulder. How on earth was I going to focus on my matchmakees when I had to maintain constant vigilance over the NAD's emotional well-being?

"You and I had better get on the bus first," Jelena said to me. "Remember, we want to get Chloe and Jeffrey to each sit next to a match." She turned to Sara. "Don't worry; we're not going to attempt the assigned seating thing with you. That's a battle I'm not willing to fight, this early in the trip."

Jelena headed for the bus and I followed her. The NAD and Ms. DeForest were still standing by the door, talking.

"That's so interesting that you've been doing forgiveness forums," the NAD said, his face lit with enthusiasm. "That's what my group's been focusing on, too."

The NAD saw me. "Oh, honey, isn't this great? Dana's lending a hand at the camp too."

"Ms. Skye." Ms. DeForest actually gave me a smile.

"Hi," I said, feeling slightly unnerved. I gave Jelena a look, and we boarded the bus quickly.

"I can't believe she smiled at me," I said, once we were inside.

"It was kind of like a crocodile," Jelena replied.

I wanted to laugh, but then got a horror movie image of the NAD being swallowed whole by Ms. DeForest's jaws, her beady eyes glinting in triumph. I shivered.

Jelena elbowed me in the ribs as Ruby got on the bus. "Here comes a candidate."

"Welcome, Ruby." I gave her a friendly wave.

"Hey, Aurora." Ruby's voice was full of enthusiasm, as always.

"Ruby, we've got you next to Jeffrey Clark today," Jelena said, pretending to read off her checklist.

“Oh, I didn’t realize it was assigned seating,” Ruby said. “I was going to sit with Samantha.”

“Jelena thought it’d be nice to do some bonding with people we don’t share classes with,” I explained, leading her down the bus to where Jeffrey was sitting in an aisle seat.

He had his headphones on and seemed to be asleep. I gave him a poke in the shoulder. He started with a fright, saw Ruby standing expectantly next to him, and leaped to his feet so she could get past. Unfortunately, in his haste to be polite, he stomped on her left foot.

“Ow!” Ruby’s smile faded.

“The lady is hurt!” Jeffrey threw himself down on the floor and grasped her purple sneaker in his hands.

Ruby looked seriously scared for a moment.

“I offer my lips to your fair sneaker as a humble apology,” Jeffrey said, puckering his lips.

Ruby let out a big laugh. “I wouldn’t put your lips there. I had puppies nipping at my shoes this morning.”

“Oh.” Jeffrey jumped up again. “They probably liked the awesome color.”

“Well, dogs can’t actually see color, so I figure maybe it was the suede material they liked.”

Ruby smiled at Jeffrey as he bowed elaborately and motioned for her to take the window seat. Fortunately, she didn’t hesitate.

“No way!” Jeffrey exclaimed, taking his seat next to her. “You’re telling me that David Copperfield can’t tell how much rainbow style I’m rocking on a daily basis?”

“David Copperfield’s his puppy,” I explained to Ruby. I’d met him during our wardrobe consultation. “A Great Dane.”

Ruby’s eyes lit up.

“He’s called that because he makes stuff disappear all the time,” Jeffrey said. “His food, of course, but also socks.”

“Does David Copperfield go to puppy school?” Ruby’s whole attention was on Jeffrey now. “It’s really vital that dogs learn about boundaries early on . . .”

I could tell they were off and running, so I headed back to Jelena, who was surreptitiously nodding toward Benjamin, who'd just boarded. He was wearing pressed pants, a blue and white button-up shirt, and a cable sweater tied perfectly around his shoulders.

"Benjamin, I'm going to put you next to Chloe for the trip," I said in a low voice, gesturing for him to follow me down the aisle. "I thought I'd let you establish a rapport with her before the other guys get a chance."

Sure, at this stage we only had one other guy lined up as a potential suitor for Chloe, but Benjamin didn't have to know that.

"Oh." Benjamin looked oddly affronted. "I was going to work on my monologue for the skits tonight."

"You don't want the first chance with Chloe?" I stared at him disbelievingly. He couldn't be that self-involved, surely.

Benjamin shrugged. "I was hoping my art would speak for itself. You know, my female fans usually spot me in a production, and that's where the interest starts."

"I think you should treat Chloe a little differently from your typical female fan," I said. "She's very intelligent—not to say your fans aren't—so she'd probably love a chance to chat about all things theater-related during the two-hour trip."

Thankfully, before Benjamin could respond, I saw Chloe coming up the aisle behind us.

"Chloe," I called, and watched Benjamin give her a full head-to-toe surveillance. Chloe's cornflower-blue top enhanced her violet eyes, while her dark denim shorts showed off her tanned legs. I could tell Benjamin's aesthetically demanding eye found her pleasing.

"Good timing," I said to Chloe. "I was just showing Benjamin to his seat, but, gentleman that he is, he didn't want to take it until you'd found yours. You're here, next to the window."

Chloe gave me a look that said she knew the whole assigned seating thing was a farce, but she was willing to play along. What I couldn't tell from her expression was how she felt about Benjamin being one of her matches.

Chloe held out her hand in greeting. "Benjamin, this is the first time I've seen you up close since I played the mermaid in *Peter Pan*."

"Ah, the siren." Benjamin lifted her hand and kissed it. "One of Mr. Peterman's better casting choices. Why no more drama club since ninth grade?"

"I guess I went all out on one performance," Chloe said wryly, obviously referring to the Dido moment. Maybe she wanted to get the awkwardness out of the way early on. "I figured I'd fulfilled my quota of drama for high school. That hasn't stopped me from going to a lot of theater in the city, though. My uncle's a theater reviewer, so I take full advantage."

"Ah, a critic. Is he the scathing type?" Benjamin stood aside to let Chloe into her seat.

I gave them a wave as I headed back to Jelena, but neither of them noticed. I had a feeling the next two hours could go very well, as long as Benjamin kept his ego in check.

"All good?" Jelena asked.

"Perfect. I think it's going to be a good trip for both couples."

"Fabulous. You take your seat with the girls and I'll finish letting everyone on."

Lindsay was in a window seat, staring pensively out at the parking lot. Cassie was next to her, thumbing happily through a magazine. Sara was sitting across the aisle, a romance novel in one hand, a pen in the other, and a notepad on her lap. I sat down next to her, leaving the seats in front for Jelena. She'd claimed two spots so she'd have space to stretch out.

I saw the NAD and Ms. DeForest take a seat up front, near Mr. Quinten.

"Why are they sitting together?"

Sara shrugged. "Aurora, I hate to say this, but maybe he was *hoping* she'd be on this trip. It's the adult equivalent of strolling by your ex's house in the hope he'll be outside. Maybe he's still hung up on her. Sometimes the flame refuses to die."

So the NAD was a moth and Ms. DeForest a lamp? As I watched the NAD laugh at something she said, I felt like yelling, *She dumped you over a tarot card! Back away from the flame!* Instead, I rested my forehead on the back of the seat in front of me.

"Let's not assume the worst, Sara, please."

"That doesn't sound good, Princess."

I pulled my head up and looked into Hayden's eyes. He was crouched down in the aisle beside my seat.

"Dad and Ms. DeForest," I whispered, subtly nodding in their direction.

Hayden looked. The NAD's and Ms. DeForest's shoulders were touching, they were sitting so close. "Seems like it's far from over." Taking in my pained expression, he put his hand over mine.

Sara stood up. "Why don't you sit here, Hayden? I was planning to sit with Jelena."

"No, no, that's fine." Hayden stood up, taking his hand from mine.

Jelena, Sara, Cassie, and even a sullen-looking Lindsay all exchanged glances. I could see *He's rebuffing her?* jumping out in fluorescent letters in their minds.

"Mr. Quinten asked me to sit up front," Hayden explained. "You know how crazy these trips can get. He's told me I'm responsible for maintaining a certain code of conduct among the students." He gave us a wave. "I'll see you at the campsite, Aurora."

Cassie reached over and gave my hand a squeeze. "Don't worry. You'll see tons of him over the next few days."

I knew it wasn't personal, but I still felt slighted. It was ridiculous how being in love exposed every nerve ending—any tiny knock felt like a major wound.

I was also bummed because Hayden was probably the only person capable of distracting me from scrutinizing my dad's every move for the next two hours.

"You should have asked Hayden to supervise your dad," Jelena said, following my gaze up the aisle.

Jelena raised an eyebrow as Ms. DeForest "accidentally" brushed her hand along the NAD's upper arm while reaching up to grab her handbag from the rack above the seats. The NAD's face lit up.

"This trip is going to be a disaster," I moaned.

"Tell me about it," Lindsay muttered. She violently stabbed out a text on her phone, then turned it off. "There. Tyler wanted to go into hiding. He's fooling himself if he thinks I'm going to come find him."

"Let's lose the negativity, please," Jelena said. "I organized this trip and it's an impossibility for it to be a disaster—cowardly boy-friend, flaky Ms. DeForest, and all."

She got out her iPod, selected one of her motivational podcasts, stuck the headphones into her ears, and pressed Play.

18

"This is a disaster!" Jelena wailed less than four hours later.

We'd reached the campsite safely, after two hours of my eyes burning into the back of the NAD's head. Mr. Quinten had instructed us to leave all cell phones and wallets on the locked bus, and we'd unloaded our packs from the baggage compartment. Rudy, the owner of the camp, who had a beaming smile and a boomingly enthusiastic voice, had told us that our cabins for that night were an hour-and-a-half walk away.

As the bus pulled away in a cloud of red dust, I'd seen from my classmates' faces that they felt like they'd been left in the middle of nowhere, metaphorically naked without their iPhones and tablets. Rocky ground, dry grass, and tall trees stretched as far as the eye could see. As we heaved our packs onto our backs and headed down the trail, Rudy explained that the area had been suffering from a bad drought for the past ten months.

He'd kept up a steady stream of information as we trudged along the track. By the time we were an hour in, most of us had been too red-faced and breathless to reply. It had been clear we'd all overpacked. Rudy, with his light backpack and compact sleeping bag clipped to one side, had bounded up the track in front of us, often walking backward so he could face the group while pointing out flora and fauna.

When we'd finally reached the campsite, there had been a collective sigh of relief as people dumped their packs onto the ground. Ten or so cabins circled the camp area, which consisted of a fire pit, a few wooden picnic tables, a covered kitchen area, and a barbecue.

"I have a feeling our accommodations won't make glamping standards," Sara had said, taking off her sunglasses and surveying the cabins. To describe them as "weather-beaten" would have been generous.

"I'm sure it's just some stylized rustification," Jelena had replied, looking unconcerned.

She'd marched over to our designated cabin and thrown open the wooden door. Her face had fallen immediately, and had continued to fall further with every discovery of the cabin's minimalism.

"There's no full-length mirror. There's not even a shelf for me to use my makeup mirror."

"There's no glass in the window, either," Lindsay said, pointing at the makeshift square cut into the wall. Some nasty-looking splinters poked out around its edges.

Jelena stared at the weatherworn and uneven floor, the cracks in the walls. "I was promised first-class accommodations."

"I guess this *is* first class, out here," I said, "seeing as there's no electricity."

Jelena didn't hear me. She was staring at the sagging canvas stretched over the rickety bunk beds. "This isn't a bed. This is barely even a hammock!"

"Um, Jelena? Hate to break it to you, but there's no real toilet," Sara said, as she came into the cabin.

Jelena froze. "What do you mean?"

"They're pit toilets," Sara said.

"Huh?" Jelena looked like she'd never heard of the concept.

"Long drops," Sara explained. "You remember, like in medieval castles?"

Jelena's mouth was frozen in an O of shock. "Rudy!" she yelled, leaning out the door.

Rudy came dashing over.

"I know you guys have to simulate a rustic experience, but, just between us, I'm assuming there are proper facilities for the camp leaders?" Jelena said. "You know, a shower room, with actual pipes and stuff?"

Rudy laughed. "Oh, sure. There's actually a tub, too. You can have a nice long soak."

Jelena looked overjoyed.

Rudy looked apologetic. "Oh dear. Sorry. I was sure you'd get the joke . . . No, the camp facilities are as you see them; same for staff and students."

"So you're saying we ignore basic hygiene for three days?" Jelena looked like she was on the verge of passing out.

"No!" Rudy laughed again. "You've obviously packed wet wipes, since they were on your camp checklist. We encourage everyone to do a full wipe-down twice a day. But I can show you how to draw up a great birdie bath with a metal bowl and some water from the tank, if you want something slightly more thorough."

Jelena had pulled herself together by lunchtime. We'd each been assigned to one of seven meal crews, each of which would be responsible for cooking a meal, and cleanup. Jelena had quickly ensured she was made "supervisor" of the lunch and dinner crews. This basically meant she positioned herself in a camp chair and watched the lunch crew's knife skills while filing her nails.

"Spam?" Lindsay's nose crinkled with disgust as we lined up to make sandwiches from the assorted canned ingredients assembled in the undercover area of the campsite. It was clear that there'd be no gourmet meals served on this trip.

"The creature is alive!" Travis shook a piece of Spam on the end of his fork at the girls behind him in line. They shrieked, and Travis dropped the meat.

"Back of the line," Mr. Quinten instructed Travis sternly. "In the army, we were grateful for what we got. We didn't throw food away."

"But is Spam a food?" Travis protested, as Mr. Quinten marched him to the end of the line.

As Lindsay and I sat down at one of the long tables positioned in the shade, I saw that Jeffrey and Ruby had taken seats across from each other. Jeffrey gallantly brushed down Ruby's side of the table before she put her plastic plate down.

"Setup number one is on track," I said to Lindsay. "As is number two."

Chloe and Benjamin were sitting side by side, just a few students down from us. I could see they were reading aloud from a play. Chloe looked up and smiled at me.

"Benjamin's convinced me to do a scene with him tonight," she called over. "He was going to do the opening scene of *Richard III*, but he wants me to play Lady Anne, so we'll do the scene where she's on the way to the funeral of her husband."

"It's a masterful scene, and Chloe's more than capable of pulling it off," Benjamin said, smiling at her. "I think she should consider doing drama senior year."

"Maybe," Chloe said.

"I wouldn't risk my thespian reputation on just anyone, you know."

Benjamin gave her a meaningful look, his eyes holding hers for what was longer than a friendly glance. Chloe lowered her gaze shyly and turned her attention back to the play. Benjamin gave me a thumbs-up and a grin. I'd never seen him so happy.

I gripped Lindsay's arm. "Did you see the look he gave her? I wasn't completely convinced they'd be a good match, when his name came up, but I'm happy to have cupid prove me wrong."

"I guess sometimes these things are instantaneous," Lindsay said, eyeing Benjamin as he moved closer to Chloe on the bench. "I feel bad for Hunter, though. He looks really at odds with the whole camping thing."

Instead of sitting at the tables with everyone else, Hunter was under a tree, on his own. He had a book in one hand and was studiously ignoring the laughter around him. Although he was wearing sunglasses, you could see by the expression of his thin mouth that he was equal parts uncomfortable and unimpressed.

"He has kind of a James Dean thing going on, doesn't he?" Lindsay said. "The whole loner vibe. There's a lot going on under the surface there."

"Can you watch out for him today?" I asked, worrying that one of our candidates was so obviously ill at ease. "I want to let the Chloe and Benjamin thing develop a little further before I bring Hunter into play tomorrow."

"No problem." Lindsay wrapped up her half-eaten sandwich and stood. "I'll go over and talk to him."

I watched as she went over and handed Hunter her untouched plastic cup of juice. He looked surprised at the thoughtful gesture. Lindsay sat down next to him and pointed at the book. Hunter handed it over and Lindsay asked him a question. His face, previously tense, visibly relaxed. That was a relief. I wanted Hunter to be the best version of himself tomorrow. If Lindsay could keep him talking and in good spirits, that would hugely benefit the program.

I was startled when Hayden sat down next to me, in Lindsay's empty seat. Finally! He'd been so busy dealing with broken water bottles, temporarily misplaced sneakers, and the removal of a giant spider from someone's cabin that we hadn't had time to exchange more than a few words since we'd left the parking lot hours ago.

"How goes the matchmaking? It's sort of a challenging environment for romance, isn't it? What with the heat." He wiped his forehead.

"Actually, I'm hoping that'll work in our favor," I replied, thinking of the creaky bridge theory. "The matches seem to be pulling together to make the most of the situation. Well, except for Sara, who's avoiding Johannes like anything."

Johannes had shadowed Sara for the entire trek to the campsite. He hadn't said much, but he'd kept darting glances at her. Sara had kept her focus entirely on Rudy and his monologue. I got the impression that Johannes was highly attracted to Sara but seriously intimidated by her standoffish attitude.

"Can you give me an update on my favorite two candidates?" Hayden asked.

I looked at him, confused. "Jeffrey and Ruby? Or Chloe and Benjamin?"

"You and me, of course." He laughed. "Is it looking promising?"

"I think you should tell me," I replied in all seriousness. Several days of minimal contact did make a girl doubt.

"Okay, people!" Mr. Quinten shouted. "We're heading over to the high-ropes course in fifteen minutes, so please ensure you've got your shoes on, water bottles filled, and sunscreen applied before we head off. We won't be returning to the campsite for around four hours, so make sure you have everything you need. Hayden, can I talk to you for a moment?"

Hayden gave me an apologetic look and walked over to Mr. Quinten. It was like our relationship was stuck on pause. Was I expecting too much to wish for a little progress? Or a conversation that lasted more than two minutes?

"So, if you look up at the ropes, you'll notice that they're divided into colored sections. Green denotes beginner, orange is moderate, and the black is our highest and most challenging course. The height of the ropes off the ground ranges from six feet to around seventy-five feet, which is the equivalent of a seven-story building."

Lindsay, standing next to me at the high-ropes course, whimpered softly.

"I'm sure you can stick to the six-foot parts," I whispered to her. "No one's going to make you do anything you're uncomfortable with."

"It sounds scary, but I can't stress enough how safe these courses are," Rudy said, over the group's uneasy murmurs. "Routine checks are carried out by health and safety professionals, as well as arborists."

I'd considered the possibility of a harness failing, but it hadn't crossed my mind that a tree could fall down or a branch snap off. Suddenly every creak of the pines towering above us seemed magnified a million times.

Someone, probably Travis, snapped a stick and let out a long "No-o-o!"

Nervous snickers broke out. Lindsay clutched my arm, her fingers wet with sweat.

"We are also fastidious about equipment," Rudy continued, unfazed. He was obviously used to high school students. "A team member will check every harness and helmet before you begin any part of the course. I'm now going to put you into groups so we can go through safety training. Everyone will be assigned a ropes buddy, and you'll monitor each other's safety throughout the afternoon. So choose your buddy, grab a helmet, and we'll fit you with a harness."

Rudy headed over to the equipment boxes and most of the students followed him. Lindsay still hadn't let go of my arm. She was like a koala clinging to its mother's back.

Hunter wandered over. "I'm not entirely sure about this seventy-five-foot thing," he said. "Lack of bravery is generally condemned in a man, but I'm confident enough to ask if either of you is willing to take on a buddy you'll have to baby?"

Lindsay's fingers relaxed. "I'm kind of hoping the six-foot-high parts make up most of the course."

"Our objective is to aim low, then. Rather ironic. I like it." Hunter looked pleased. "So you're mine for the afternoon?"

Lindsay nodded, blushing slightly.

Hunter laughed. "Sorry, that sounded rather inappropriate. Didn't mean to put it that way. I'll grab our helmets." He headed off to the boxes of equipment.

"He sounds like he's from another century sometimes," Lindsay said, still slightly pink.

"That's why I'm interested to see what happens when I put him and Chloe together," I replied. "They're both a little not of this time."

"That's if Benjamin and Chloe don't become a sure thing first," Lindsay said.

We both looked over at Benjamin, who was helping to fit Chloe's helmet. He brushed a lock of hair from her cheek as he fastened the strap under her chin. Her smile seemed to be etched onto her face—it had been a permanent fixture since lunch.

"It's looking promising, I know," I said, "but we still need a backup. Try to find out as much as you can about Hunter. He's not exactly the talkative type, but the more information we have, the more we can emphasize Chloe's complementary traits when we set them up tomorrow. We're working within a small window on this trip, so we want to maximize the opportunities."

Jelena came up to us. "Aurora, Ruby's been nabbed by one of her friends. Can you make sure Jeffrey's partnered with Jemima?"

"Will do."

I looked around for Jemima, who was standing alone. She looked way too nice to be camping, wearing a singlet with lace ruffles on the shoulders and shorts scattered with a tiny rose print. Her makeup was immaculate, despite the heat and the strenuous walk to the ropes course.

I walked up to her. "Jemima, perhaps I shouldn't say this, but there's someone here who's really hoping to be paired up with you. He told me he thought your exercise outfit was miles ahead of the other girls in terms of this season's trends."

Okay, I was stretching the truth, but Jeffrey did like bright clothes, so he'd probably go for Jemima's outfit. I quickly waved him over while I had Jemima's attention.

"Jeffrey?" Jemima sounded unsure. "Isn't he the one who's always talking about getting naked?"

I brushed off the question. "He's a really funny guy. He'll be a great partner for this exercise if you're feeling a little nervous. Good distraction."

Jeffrey arrived at our side. "Mr. Quinten's partnering with Travis. He thinks it'll keep him under control, but I think it'll be Mr. Quinten's undoing. Travis told me he's planning to let Mr. Quinten hang from his harness any chance he gets."

Jemima giggled. Jeffrey looked stoked.

"I won't let that happen to you, don't worry," he assured her. "And I'll go up the ladders first, so you don't need to stress about me checking out those cute shorts. You can eye me up anytime you like, though."

I held my breath. Thankfully, Jemima laughed and hit him with her helmet.

"I'm serious! I've been working out in preparation. Lots of squats."

Objective achieved, I returned to an unimpressed-looking Jelena.

"I'm going to have to talk to Sara," she said. "Johannes stampeded over to volunteer as her partner, but she won't say a word to him. She obviously considers 'enthusiastic participation' to be simply turning up. Are you pairing up with Hayden?"

I looked around for him. He was assisting Scott and Cassie with their gear. I gave him a wave.

"Hey, want to be my buddy?" I asked.

Hayden made a sad face. "Mr. Quinten wants me to supervise Jesse Cook—he's trying to separate him from Travis. He thinks they'll be swinging from rope to rope like Tarzan if we don't keep them on a short leash."

I tried not to pout, even though I knew Hayden couldn't help it. It wasn't like he could say no to Mr. Quinten's orders.

"I had no idea this trip was going to be so busy for you," I said.

"It's jam-packed for Aurora, too," Jelena said to Hayden. "She's on matchmaker duties, so she'd better get back to it."

She yanked me away from Hayden and back toward Jeffrey and Jemima.

"What was that about?" I asked her.

"Hey, if Hayden's busy, you're busy."

Did Jelena think I was being clingy?

"Plus, we can be buddies now," Jelena added. "This way we can stay a hundred percent focused on the matches."

"I don't know how easy that'll be while making our way across ropes strung seventy-five feet high." I would do my best to be on constant cupid duty, but we had to be realistic.

Jelena looked up at the ropes and made a face. "We won't be doing that stuff. I'm cocaptain of the camp, so I'm going to ask Mr. Quinten if we can stay on the ground and be spotters for any students in violation of the rules." She handed me a pair of binoculars. "I brought these so you can keep an eye on the matchmakees."

I took the binoculars and fixed them in the direction of the topmost ropes. The glasses were high quality. I'd be able to see the matches' every expression, whether lip curls of displeasure or twinkles in their eyes.

"Aren't they an invasion of privacy?"

"Think of yourself as Venus, goddess of love, keeping an eagle eye on the mortals," Jelena said. "This is going to be a totally breezy experience."

"Jelena, the only thing breezy about this whole experience is the wind up here!" I said, trying not to panic as I looked at the dizzying drop below. The rope I was walking along with very shaky steps was swaying from side to side. My hands, holding the line above me for balance, felt slick with sweat.

"Stupid Rudy," Jelena muttered. She was just a couple of paces behind me. "*This course is all about participation. You can't ask the group to challenge themselves if you're not willing to take on the challenge yourself!*" she said, mimicking Rudy's response to her suggestion that we should be spotters. He'd also told Jelena that it was her responsibility to go first, to set the example for the others.

"He thinks he can give me instructions on how to be a leader," Jelena went on. "You know, if your dad hadn't backed him up—"

"He only did it because Ms. DeForest was nudging him in the ribs," I cut in.

"She wanted you out of the way so you couldn't spoil her seduction plans. Your dad's already ensnared. She's just waiting for an opportune moment to enjoy her prey."

"Do we have to refer to my dad as 'prey'?" I stumbled slightly on my next step.

"You're shaking the rope!" Jelena's voice became panicked. "I do *not* want to fall. Yes, I'm wearing a harness, but I don't want all the boys below us witnessing the inevitable wedgie this thing will give me. Cut the shakes, stat!"

Suddenly a glass-shattering scream sounded from below. Jelena and I both looked down to see what had happened and simultaneously lost our balance. As we fell, I felt like my stomach dropped faster than the rest of me. Thankfully, the harnesses pulled us up within seconds. We sat, dangling midair, swinging above the groups at various stages below us.

"Who designed these things?" Jelena said, shaking her harness. "Ow!"

"I wouldn't play around with it. It's the only thing between us and a long drop."

I tried to keep my breathing calm. I didn't have a phobia about heights, but I wasn't wild about them either. I could hear the line above us creaking.

"Who screamed?" I didn't want to look down until my breathing steadied. I was already dizzy enough.

Jelena scanned the ground. "Lindsay—she fell all of a yard off that first rope. Hunter seems to have caught her."

Benjamin's voice drifted over to us. He and Chloe were making their way across the monkey bar section parallel to us. "I think with Lady Anne you've really got to show the audience the emotional transition she goes through."

"How's he managing to discuss theater?" I asked Jelena in a low voice. When we'd done that part of the course, we'd both been completely out of breath from trying to swing between the widely spaced bars.

"He's pretty fit," Jelena said, eyeing Benjamin's muscles as he swung from rung to rung. "During the *Much Ado* rehearsals, he told me he'd started working with a trainer to increase lung capacity so he could project his voice further."

"Well, it worked," I said, as words like "motivation" and "Stanislavsky" rang out through the trees.

"Jeffrey's guiding Jemima the whole way," Jelena reported. "I'm impressed."

Curiosity overruled fear and I reached for the binoculars, which were around my neck. About thirty feet below, Jeffrey was climbing the rungs of a tree ladder, coaxing a very nervous Jemima behind him. After hauling himself onto the wooden platform, he extended a hand to help her up, too.

"Nudie runs and crude comments aside, he's actually kind of a gentleman," I said.

"True. Okay, the sooner we finish this course, the sooner we escape this hell," Jelena said. "Let's go."

"Travis Ela! You do not leave a buddy hanging!" Mr. Quinten's enraged shout echoed through the trees.

I looked over. Travis sat on a platform, swinging his legs and eating a granola bar, while Mr. Quinten dangled in his harness. Travis had pulled the rope out of his reach and Mr. Quinten was stuck in no-man's-land.

19

By the time we headed back to camp, the sun was low in the sky.

After crawling through suspended barrels and falling off the ropes more times than we'd ever thought possible, most of us resembled the war-wounded. Bruises dotted arms, scratches ran up and down calves, clothes were stained red with dirt, and anyone not wearing long shorts had the equivalent of carpet-burned knees.

Strangely enough, Sara was in super high spirits as she, Jelena, Lindsay, and I trudged along the rocky path. Cass and Scott, holding hands, were several paces ahead.

"Rudy says he can't believe how fast I raced through the course today. He said it must be my gymnastics training that's given me superior balance."

"I don't want to hear anything more about Rudy." Lindsay looked drained. Four hours of facing her fears had taken their toll. "Thank god for Hunter. He barked at Rudy when he was pushing me to do the black course. I'd already challenged myself on the orange—I didn't need Rudy making me feel like a failure just because I know my limits."

"Did you learn anything more about Hunter?" I asked.

"He's quiet, but he can sure make a point. Rudy didn't listen to my protests, but Hunter's tone did the trick. Besides that, he's got a rather black sense of humor, though I find it pretty funny. Seems like his childhood was kind of a mess, but it's given him a depth that most guys at Jefferson are lacking."

"So it's clear why the system matched him up with Chloe," I said.

Lindsay hesitated. "Yes. I think she'll like him."

"Rudy says that I should think about doing some rock climbing, because I have the mental stamina for it," Sara said. "Rudy mentioned I could—"

"I'm finding it hard to understand why you're talking nonstop about a ruddy-faced forty-year-old and barely mentioning Alexander Skarsgård's doppelgänger." Jelena made a crazy sign near Sara's head. "You just spent four hours with Johannes. Don't we hear one word of feedback?"

Sara looked exasperated. "He couldn't do the course properly because his pants were too tight. We had to keep stopping and it totally messed up my time."

"Sara, he's from Sweden. His concept of camping could be totally different from ours," I suggested gently. "Maybe you're being a little hard on him. Did you chat with him, at least?"

"He kept asking me a million questions." Sara sighed and took a sip from her water bottle. "I don't know why he's trying to pry into my life."

"Whereas your dates in the past have been too stupid to construct sentences?" Jelena replied. "Or so self-involved it'd never cross their mind to ask you about yourself?"

I gave Jelena a warning look. Criticizing Sara's former dates wasn't going to endear her to her potential future one.

"Sara, the questions are a good sign," I said. "Johannes is trying to get to know you."

"I'm a writer and I want to be single—that's all he needs to know. Yes, Jelena, I promised I'd be on board," Sara continued before

Jelena could interrupt. "So I'll happily cozy up to Johannes in a campaign video when we get back home. But I'm not playing faux footsie on this trip. All of this extreme sports stuff is great inspiration for my male lead, and I want to focus on that."

"Must. Remove. Grime." Dinner was long over and Jelena stood in her bra and undies, scrubbing at herself with a washcloth and water from a bucket. She'd made her campaign team refill the bucket three times with fresh hot water, which they'd painstakingly boiled over the campfire.

"It's a lost cause, Jelena," Sara said, reading on her bunk. Thankfully, her massive lantern provided our whole cabin with more than enough light. Most of the other students had only flashlights. However, ninety percent of them were sitting around the fire outside, laughing and roasting marshmallows, so it seemed they didn't mind about their cabins being dimly lit.

There was a sound outside the door.

"Travis, if that's you trying to peek in again, I swear I'll sabotage your harness tomorrow!" Jelena shrieked.

"Jelena?" It was Mr. Quinten's voice. "Some of the students have pulled together some skits. We need you out here."

Jelena let out a whimper. "I only just washed my feet and now I have to go out there again?"

"You're camp leader," Sara said. "Just put on some UGG boots."

"They cost two hundred and fifty dollars." Jelena looked torn between the choice of dirt between her toes or ruined sheepskin.

I grabbed my sweatshirt. "I better get out there. I'm sure Benjamin's raring to go with his and Chloe's scene."

Jelena clenched her jaw with determination as she pulled on jeans, a sweatshirt, and her boots. "This camp will not be my Waterloo."

"That's the spirit," I said, and put my arm around her as we headed out the door.

I had to admit, there were some romantic aspects to camping. The fire crackled and the sky was a canvas of galaxies.

There were two groups on either side of the fire. One group, which included Benjamin and Chloe, was playing charades. The other group was playing Fluffy Bunnies, the age-old campfire game where you try to fit as many marshmallows into your mouth as possible while saying "fluffy bunnies." Among them, I was amazed to see Jemima, standing next to a cheering Jeffrey, her tiny mouth stuffed to the brim with pink and white marshmallows.

"Last one and you've set a new record!" Jeffrey pumped the air with his fist.

Jemima stuffed in one more marshmallow, successfully managed the phrase, then spat into a bucket. Jeffrey swept her up in his arms.

"Victory lap!" he shouted, and took off around the campsite.

Ruby looked put out. To have two girls going after Jeffrey was surely testament to the quality of the chemistry calculator, as well as to the creaky bridge experiment. Class clown to Casanova—unfathomable only days ago.

"This trip's really doing the trick, matchmaking-wise," I said to Jelena, as we sat down on a log.

"Aurora, we're ready!"

A confident-looking Benjamin and not-so-confident Chloe arrived at our side. I noticed he was holding her hand. Would they be cuddling by the campfire by tomorrow evening? All signs pointed to yes.

"Jelena, do you want to announce them?" I asked.

Jelena stood up. "Attention, everyone!" she shouted. "We've had a fantastic day—am I right?"

Cheers erupted from the students. The hearty dinner and cheery campfire had restored their energy levels.

Hayden ducked over and sat down next to me on the log. He handed me a hot chocolate. "There's only one person I want to watch Shakespeare with. It brings back good memories."

I took the cup from him, my heart warming along with my hands.

"Just think, if we hadn't been cast opposite each other, we'd probably have missed out on being friends," he went on.

I looked at him. Friends? That's all he considered us to be, all of a sudden? Had something happened since he'd handed over that little blue box? Had he changed his mind? Feeling tears form in my eyes, I quickly looked up at the night sky, blinking them away before Hayden could notice. I wanted to get up, but I was frozen to the log. I felt that any movement would cause my composure to collapse.

"Good, because I'm hoping to make this trip the first of many!" Jelena continued. The campfire highlighted her bright eyes and beaming smile, a complete contrast to the grin-and-bear-it expression she'd been wearing only moments before. She certainly knew how to mask her emotions. "Remember, if you're keen on white-water rafting, canyoneering, or rappelling, tell your friends to vote Jelena Cantrill!"

"Bring back the naked clam outfit!" Travis yelled.

There were whistles.

"I won't be removing clothes, but I will be giving them out!" Jelena yelled back.

She gestured to her campaign team, who were standing to one side. They began throwing T-shirts into the crowd. I caught one. The front of the shirt was emblazoned with "There's Only One Choice—Jelena Cantrill for School President!" in artsy red script, above a photo of Jelena as Venus. I turned the shirt over. "Bringing You the Find a Prince/Princess™ Program," it read in pink. Below were three hearts, holding a photo each of Tyler and Lindsay, Cassie and Scott, and Hayden and me.

I couldn't look at Hayden; I was too embarrassed. Especially as I was worrying whether he wanted to write "platonic" above our photo with a Sharpie.

"I don't suppose you have any boxers with your picture on them, do you?" Travis called out to Jelena.

"Ew!" all the girls chorused.

Jelena swiftly diverted the attention from Travis. "I now present you with two of our most talented classmates, Benjamin and Chloe, performing a scene from Shakespeare's *Richard III*!"

Chloe stepped out into the firelight. She wore a paper crown and looked very apprehensive. Mr. Quinten pushed four guys out to follow her—he'd obviously rounded up volunteers to pretend to carry the coffin of Lady Anne's husband, who'd just been killed by Richard.

Chloe stood in the firelight, not moving.

"What, you're scared of getting dramatic all of a sudden?" someone yelled. "You'd think you'd be right at home with the fire!"

There was laughter all around the campsite.

"Show her some respect!" I heard Hunter shout in Chloe's defense.

There was nothing like a man standing up for a woman's honor. Hunter had earned serious points in my eyes.

Chloe's jaw clenched. She turned to stare at the makeshift coffin and launched into a passionate lament. "Cursed be the hand that made these fatal holes! Cursed be the heart that had the heart to do it!"

"It's like she's completely choked up with fury and grief," Cassie whispered.

Benjamin entered, using two branches for crutches, his face twisted into an evil smirk. He'd brought a costume—a dark-blue robe that fell to his feet, a frilled white shirt and doublet, and socks that stretched to the knee.

"Wow, he's actually made himself a hump," Lindsay said, staring at the back of his robe.

Chloe became hysterical as Benjamin approached, begging god to avenge her husband's death. "Either heaven with lightning strike the murderer dead, or earth, gape open wide and eat him quick, as thou dost swallow up this good king's blood."

Benjamin looked bemused by Chloe's curses. As she circled

him, her eyes narrowed in fury, he flattered her, calling her the "divine perfection of a woman."

"And thou unfit for any place but hell," Chloe spat at him.

"Yes, one place else, if you will hear me name it."

"Some dungeon," Chloe flung back.

"Your bedchamber." Benjamin ran a finger across Chloe's collarbone and down toward her breastbone.

Wolf whistles erupted around the campsite. Everyone leaned forward, itching to hear more.

"This is so good!" Lindsay said. "I mean, I knew Benjamin was a great actor, but Chloe is amazing. Their chemistry is electric."

I glanced at Hayden. The same could have been said of us, only weeks ago. Had those fireworks fizzled out into a mere glow of friendship?

I tried to focus on the drama. Benjamin pressed behind Chloe, whispering in her ear, then moved his lips down the side of her neck.

"Your beauty was the cause of that effect; your beauty: which did haunt me in my sleep to undertake the death of all the world, so I might live one hour in your sweet bosom."

"Mr. Quinten, shouldn't you have warned us about sexual references?" Travis called out. "I'm filing a complaint. This trip has corrupted my mind."

Benjamin and Chloe finished to huge applause, the cheers for Chloe loudest of all. She was suddenly surrounded by students clapping her on the back and congratulating her.

Hayden turned toward me, smiling, but I couldn't mask my uneasiness following his comment. What if he asked me what was wrong? Did I have the guts to ask him for his definition of "us"? There was no way that wasn't going to be awkward. And if I got the answer I feared, I'd have to live with it for almost forty-eight hours of camp.

Before Hayden could open his mouth to speak, I made a dash for my cabin. I heard him call after me, but thankfully he didn't try to follow.

Half an hour later, Scott was standing outside our cabin, giving Cassie an extended good-night kiss. The contrast between Cassie's situation and mine hit home. I'd been daydreaming about Hayden kissing me good night outside my cabin, and now here I was, hiding from him *inside* it!

"He's really giving it his all," Sara said, her body hanging half over the edge of her bunk so she could peer out the door.

"You can kind of see the deep tongue-thrusting even from here," Jelena said dryly as she fastidiously moisturized her face.

She was sitting on her queen-size mattress, her magnifying mirror balanced upon her knees. The mattress was so huge that she'd had to wait till we were in our bunks to inflate it. The thing took up all of the floor space leading to the door, and its sides even edged up the walls slightly.

Lindsay, Sara, and I only just managed to stifle our laughter.

"Jelena, he'll hear you!" I whispered frantically.

"Oh, he needs to hear it." Jelena didn't lower her voice even fractionally. "That type of thing is akin to assault."

"Move along, young man." Mr. Quinten's stern voice came floating into the cabin. "Boys in one cabin, girls in another. Anyone in violation of the rule will be suspended. You are dangerously close to the entrance of that cabin."

"Sorry, sir." Scott sounded mortified. "'Night Cassie."

"We witnessed the atrocity," Jelena said to Cassie as she came into the cabin and shut the door behind her. "I'd wondered if you were exaggerating the extent of Señor Stabby's roaming tongue, but it's obvious that he's not picking up on your subtle hints."

Cass sat down on her bunk, below Lindsay's. She looked slightly depressed. "He's wearing a T-shirt with our picture on it in front of all the guys! He's amazing—except for that one thing."

"That one thing's a big part of a relationship." Lindsay was lying on her stomach, her arms propped up on her pillow. "If you guys kiss three times a day, five days a week on average, that's seven hundred and eighty kisses a year you have to deal with. If you aren't enjoying them, that's not a small problem."

"Can you endure seven hundred and eighty stabs of the tongue a year?" Jelena gave her reflection careful examination. "Probably more, 'cause he likely stabs ten to fifteen times a kiss, right? Or am I overestimating?"

Cassie gave her a look. "So you're saying I should be totally superficial and end it because Scott's a little off base technique-wise?"

This conversation was making me feel sick. It was too close to home. What if this was why Hayden was using the dreaded f-word? Now that he'd gotten his stitches out, the likelihood of being lip-lashed by me again had dampened his desire? What if he was sitting in his cabin, asking his friends if he'd made the right choice, and they were responding like Jelena and Lindsay?

"No one's ending anything." Jelena put her mirror back in her bag. "Not Lindsay, and not you. Those T-shirts were expensive. Don't make them out of date till I give the okay."

Cassie looked totally exasperated. "I don't *want* to break up with him. *You're* the one saying it's the only option."

"There are other options," Jelena said. "Just give me time to come up with something."

Cass let out a sigh and crawled into bed.

"Do you guys think that maybe Hayden just wants to be friends with me?" I asked softly.

Part of me hadn't wanted to put my fear into words, but I needed to know what they thought.

"What? Are you crazy?" Cassie gave me a weird look. "Is this why you ran away earlier? Hayden wanted me to come get you, but I told him you were probably asleep."

Lindsay frowned. "Why are you worried?"

"She's worried because he hasn't spent more than two minutes with her since last week," Jelena said. "Any girl would be."

My stomach dropped, exactly like it had when I'd lost my footing on the ropes. You could always rely on the brutal truth from Jelena. If she thought I had reason to worry . . .

Sara snorted. "Jelena, you're an idiot!"

"Aurora, Mr. Quinten's had him virtually enslaved this entire trip," Cassie said quickly. "It's not personal. Is there something else you're worried about?"

"Tonight, by the campfire, he said that if we hadn't been cast opposite each other in the play, we'd probably have missed out on being friends. Friends!" I burst out. "We've kissed! Twice! Is 'friend' what a guy calls a girl after all of that?"

"Some guys, yes," Jelena said.

Sara nodded her agreement. "The players."

"Hayden is not a player." Cassie tossed her pillow at Sara. "Don't listen to them, Aurora. Would Hayden really give you a necklace like that if he wanted to keep things platonic?"

I shrugged. I honestly didn't know what to think. The facts were: Hayden was stitch-free and he hadn't made one move.

Cassie yanked her pillow back from Sara and threw it at me this time. "Stop being paranoid! He was probably saying, in muddled-up guy language, *Thank goodness we became friends so I was able to tell you how I feel after four years!*"

"I don't know. Maybe he's changed his mind and is wishing he hadn't rushed into giving me a little blue box."

I touched the little *X* at my throat. It was sort of delicate for camp, but I hadn't wanted to take it off since he'd given it to me.

Cassie looked around for another pillow.

"All right!" I held up my hands in a surrender gesture. "I won't lose hope. I'll see what tomorrow brings."

The night was long. I couldn't get comfortable on the canvas bed (which was no surprise, considering it was pretty much a sling), and despite Cassie's reassurances, I had hypothetical situations running around my head like a group of joggers doing laps. Not to mention I was obsessing over the fact that the NAD and Ms. DeForest were sharing a cabin, along with the other adult volunteers. Obviously, you'd assume there'd be no funny business with Mr. Quinten around, but you never knew. Ms. DeForest was crafty.

I finally dozed off at what felt like two in the morning. At about three, I heard mosquitoes buzzing around my head. At four, I woke up sweating from a nightmare about a minuscule NAD screaming for his life while a giant velvety spider bore down on him. The air in the cabin was stifling; somehow the temperature had gone up since we'd gone to bed. I finally fell asleep as the birds started their dawn chorus.

I woke up to Jelena screaming.

"My eye!" she howled, clutching her makeup mirror.

Lindsay sat up in a panic and swung herself out of her bunk. Being half-asleep, she didn't place her feet properly and landed sprawled on Jelena's mattress.

"My beauty is ruined!" Jelena sounded like the Evil Queen from *Snow White*. Her right eye was red, the eyelid swollen. "*Ruined!*"

"Let me see." Sara made Jelena close her eye. "It's a mosquito bite."

"I had repellent all over me!"

"Not on your eyelids, obviously," Sara said. Jelena burst out crying. "No one's going to take me seriously. I look like Quasimodo!"

"Crying will only increase the swelling," Sara warned. "You need ice."

"Fat chance of that in this forsaken place." Jelena furiously wiped her eyes. "It's seven in the morning and it's . . . what . . . ninety degrees? It's a joke."

"Put this on it." Cassie handed Jelena some anti-itch ointment from her pack.

I passed her my medical kit. "Take an antihistamine."

Jelena swallowed the tablet shakily. I'd never seen her like this. She hardly ever cried.

By the time we headed to breakfast, at 7:30 a.m., the temperature gauge on my watch said ninety-three degrees. Jelena was wearing an oversize floppy hat positioned artfully over her swollen eye.

"Aurora, can I talk to you for a moment?" Chloe, wearing a serious expression, appeared at my side.

I led Chloe toward one of the cabins so no one could overhear.

"Is everything okay?" I asked. "Don't you like Benjamin? Has he said something to put you off?"

"Oh no, I really like him." Chloe looked embarrassed now. "He was so nice, helping me with the scene last night. Do you know how many people came up to chat to me afterward? I can't believe it."

"Aren't you attracted to him?" I was trying to figure out the problem.

Chloe beamed. "He's gorgeous. His eyes, and that voice . . . I get tingly whenever he brushes by me."

Maybe she just wanted to debrief? "I can tell he really likes you, too."

"Well, that's it." She looked worried again. "I thought so too. But he's been weird around me since last night. After our performance, when everyone was congratulating us, he wasn't smiling. And then this morning, when I got my cereal and headed over to sit next to him, he was totally silent the whole time." Chloe's eyes resembled bruised pansies.

"Maybe he's tired," I said. "It was a pretty big day—plus he usually puts a hundred and ten percent into his performances."

"Can you check?" Chloe asked. "I'd hate to think I did something wrong."

"No problem."

This was part and parcel of my role as matchmaker. I headed over to where Benjamin was sitting. His head was in *Richard III* again.

"Hey." I sat down next to him.

"Aurora. Good timing. This thing with Chloe and me isn't going to work out, so I need you to break it to her. I don't want to deal with any uncomfortable discussions."

"What? But everyone's talking about your amazing chemistry after last night!"

"I've realized she's not really my type."

"But she's gorgeous. And artistic. And talented."

An odd expression came over Benjamin's face at the last word.

"Exactly. Very talented. The thing is, I've done some hard thinking overnight. My career's about to take off with this Mr. Bubbly thing, and there's really only room for one dramatic talent in a relationship. I need someone who's happy to hang in the background while I'm midshoot. Someone who'll stand to the side when photographers want to take solo shots at a red carpet event. I don't think Chloe's that girl."

Now it all made sense to me. Benjamin felt threatened after Chloe's amazing performance. He wasn't used to sharing the spotlight. In his eyes, the most desirable woman was a supporting act, not a leading lady.

"All right, Benjamin. If you're a hundred percent sure you're happy to lose the chance with Chloe, I'll cross you off the list."

Benjamin nodded and picked up the play again. I turned away, rolling my eyes. I'd been hoping he'd realize how self-involved he was being, but, sadly, my original assumptions about his character had been proved right. I headed back to where Chloe was waiting.

She wasn't alone. Hunter was with her. Wow. I'd told him about Chloe when we first met, and here he was, so interested he hadn't even waited for an official introduction. I stopped shy of them, not wanting to interrupt.

"Promise you'll be my buddy?" I heard Hunter say. "I overheard Mr. Quinten saying it's a three-hour walk. Only first-rate conversation's going to keep my legs moving for that long."

Hunter gave me a wink as he went by. Chloe came over to talk to me.

"Did you find out what's going on with Benjamin?"

"He's not feeling well," I said. "Bad stomach. He's worried it's contagious, so he's asked you to steer clear for a few days. He'd hate to give it to you."

He was ill with envy, so the explanation did hold a shade of truth.

"Oh." Chloe looked concerned. "It wouldn't bother me, you know. If I get sick, I get sick. Benjamin helped me yesterday, and I'd be happy to help him if he's feeling bad."

"It's more male ego," I said quickly. "He doesn't want you to see him at less than his best. It's silly, I know, but maybe we should indulge him. Plus, it seems like Hunter's set on making you his partner for today."

Chloe hesitated. "I guess so. I've always thought that if you care about someone, you stand by them, even when they aren't at their best, but if Benjamin's really set on riding his bug out alone, I don't want to be a pest. I'll go tell Hunter I'll buddy up with him today."

After she'd gone, I let out a sigh of relief. I hoped Hunter would prove enough of a distraction to make Chloe lose interest in Benjamin. If she didn't, I'd have to come up with a nice way to tell her he just wasn't that into her.

20

The three-hour walk to our next camp was mostly uphill. An hour in, my watch read 102 degrees and the backs of our shirts were soaked with sweat.

Thankfully, Chloe and Hunter didn't seem too bothered by the heat or the trail. Or by Benjamin, who was just ahead of them, muttering about how the dirt and sweat were ruining his complexion for next week's callback. With the objective of winning a girl gone, Benjamin wasn't enjoying camp at all.

Chloe and Hunter were completely engrossed in conversation. I couldn't hear what they were talking about, but judging by their expressions, it was deep stuff. Hunter spoke for long periods while Chloe nodded as if her life depended on it. I turned around to check on Jeffrey. He was pulling both Jemima and Ruby up a steep hill.

"This is like Iwo Jima," Jelena said. The part of her face that wasn't covered by the hat looked outraged. "Their Web site is seriously misleading. I'm taking it up with Rudy's superior, the moment we get home."

"Why don't you think of it like a really intense cardio class?" Sara was holding her battery-powered fan in one hand and her face was completely sweat-free.

"You plan wisely, I see," Johannes said, appearing at Sara's side. "You bring useful things out here into the forest. Many of the other girls were not so sensible."

Jelena's jaw tensed. Sara's refusal to share the handheld fan with her had proved a sore point already.

Johannes had virtually stepped in front of Sara on the track, forcing her to make eye contact with him. Unlike some of the boys, who looked and smelled like a bunch of sweaty pirates who hadn't seen a port in weeks, Johannes resembled *True Blood*'s Eric after a fight with another vampire. The sweat, rather than seeming unappealing, made his T-shirt cling to every lean muscle of his chest and stomach. I watched Sara's eyes widen as she looked from Johannes's face to his body—until she shook her head and walked on.

"Yes, I'm very sensible," she said. "Including when it comes to my no-dating policy."

I didn't know if Sara's meaning was lost in translation or Johannes was simply pleased to have gotten a response from her after twenty-four hours of trying, but he didn't seem discouraged by her vow of singledom.

"Wonderful. I check path is clear ahead for you." He strode past us, kicking dead branches from the trail and looking back every so often to check Sara's progress.

I saw her eyes drift to his upper body again. It was obvious that if any guy was capable of wearing down her resistance to romance, it would be Johannes. As much as I supported Sara's future career as an author, Johannes did seem like a sweetheart. For the remainder of the hike, he held aside any overhanging branches so they didn't scratch Sara, he tied her shoelaces for her when we stopped for a breather, and he even gave her the last of his water when hers ran out. He was a gentleman. Sara could use a little more of that in her life.

"The camp is within sight!" Rudy called back to us, as the track started leveling out.

"Thank god," Jelena breathed. "I'm taking a power nap as soon as I reach those tents."

Jelena sank to her knees as she looked at the two tarpaulins, the rope, and the stones in front of us. "I didn't believe that our accommodations could get any worse, but how wrong I was. We have to construct our own tents?"

"Find two trees and string the rope between them, making sure it's secure," Rudy called out. "Building a tent may seem challenging, but it's one of the best skills you can learn. It'll be crucial for survival if you're ever caught out in the backcountry with minimum equipment."

Sara had pushed her way to the front to watch Rudy's demonstration.

"So, once you've got your rope secured and strung up at chest level, place your first tarp on the ground below," he continued, rolling out his tarp. "Then sling your second tarp over the rope so it's exactly midway above the bottom tarp. This forms a tent shape. Secure the edges of your second tarp with large stones. They need to be big enough to stand up to strong winds."

"Let's get this over with." Cassie grabbed the rope, taking charge. "Lindsay, Aurora, you get the tarps."

"I am not heaving rocks," Jelena said, her arms folded over her chest.

"Of course not; you're injured," Cassie said. "Go get yourself some water and a cookie from the supply boxes."

Sara made a face as Jelena walked away. "She doesn't have to help?"

"This will be five times faster without her complaining the whole time," Cassie replied. "Okay, someone help me secure the rope to this tree."

Jelena made a face when she returned, half an hour later, and stuck her head inside the completed tent. She looked like Louis XIV inspecting the progress of Versailles.

"You guys couldn't make it a little more spacious?"

"This was the longest tarp I could get, Jelena," Sara said, tearing open a protein bar. "I had to trade my battery-powered fan for it. Your mattress is a joke! There's room for, like, one sleeping bag in here now."

"Perfect. That's your spot." Jelena rolled out her mattress and pushed the Inflate button. She looked longingly at Sara's protein bar. "Can I please have a bite?"

Sara shook her head. "It's not my fault if you chose to bring dry shampoo over dehydrated food." She ate the last half of the bar in one bite.

"You know, I was going to offer you a spot on the mattress, but that settles it," Jelena shot back, "you are *not* sharing with me. Lindsay, Cass, Aurora, you may enter mattress territory. Sara, no closer."

Jelena pushed Sara's air sofa, which had been slightly touching her mattress, toward the entrance of the tent.

"OMG. Why don't you just draw up a treaty?" Sara stalked out of the tent.

"Let's all get some lunch," I suggested. "I think hunger's put everyone on edge."

"Canned corn isn't going to make me forget Sara's attitude." Jelena flounced out of the tent.

I barely had time to rest after lunch. Somehow, fate had assigned me to Ms. DeForest's evening cooking group, and apparently we had to start preparing the food ASAP.

"At twelve thirty in the afternoon?" I followed her and the rest of our cooking group to the kitchen area. "We aren't scheduled to serve dinner till eight p.m."

Couldn't we wait until it wasn't so hot? My watch now read 105 degrees.

"We're not using the barbecue." Ms. DeForest made a face as she said the last word. "It's a known carcinogen. I want us to prepare a meal based upon the principles of slow food. I've brought beans and legumes for a soup."

"Where are the cans?" I asked, looking through the crates containing the food supplies.

Ms. DeForest shook her head violently. "Nothing canned. Processing kills off the nutritional content of the food. We're going to boil the beans from scratch, but at an extremely low temperature—applying the principles of raw food. That's why we'll need ample prep time."

I looked at the sacks of beans she'd placed on the table, and pulled one out. It was rock hard. There was no way simple simmering was going to soften these. I was willing to bet Ms. DeForest's time estimate was way off.

"Five hours?" Jesse whined. "That's not kitchen duty; that's enslavement."

"I need someone to activate the almonds," Ms. DeForest said, ignoring him. "We're going to make paste to go in the soup, as we're keeping the recipe vegan. There's also going to be a beetroot and carrot slaw." She pointed at a bulging bag of carrots.

Ms. DeForest would have a revolution on her hands, come dinnertime. The most our classmates wanted to know about greens was seeing a slice of lettuce on their burger.

"Man invented fire for a *reason*," said Travis.

"Ms. DeForest, do you think the meal will supply enough energy after a long day?" I asked. "People will be in need of some carbs. There are pasta ingredients in the crates here, somewhere."

"Nonsense," Ms. DeForest said, pouring beans into a huge pot. "The Aztecs survived on legumes for centuries."

"Before they died out." Jesse looked despondently at the beans.

"Enough! I demand that you prepare this food in a positive way," Ms. DeForest said crossly. "Food absorbs your energy. All this whining means you're literally poisoning others when it's consumed."

If Ms. DeForest's theory was true, I was betting we'd wind up with beetroots infused with bitterness and carrots chock-full of resentment after hours of kitchen duty.

Over the next hour and a half, we took turns keeping a constant vigil over the beans. Ms. DeForest wanted them to be stirred frequently, and anytime they started to boil we had to take them off the campfire to ensure they returned to a simmer. In between stirring duties, we worked away at grating a mountain of raw veggies while shooing hordes of flies away.

Finally, when Mr. Quinten told Ms. DeForest we had to head off to the next high-ropes challenge, Ms. DeForest grudgingly released us and said she'd keep an eye on the beans.

"But I'll be drawing up a roster for your return at five thirty," she said, "so that the next three hours after that, until we serve dinner, are covered."

Thank god I was only signed on for one meal duty this trip.

"No way." Lindsay stared at the pole that stretched into the sky above us. "No. Not for anything."

"This is an opportunity to stretch your limits," Rudy encouraged her.

Lindsay was in line to make the Leap of Faith. This involved climbing a hundred-foot pole to a small platform, from which we leaped out to grab a trapeze bar several feet away. I was next, after Lindsay, and not exactly desperate for my turn, either.

"It's an opportunity *not* to die," Lindsay said to Rudy, her arms folded firmly across her chest.

"It's your fear that's creating the mental block here, Lindsay. You don't want to be a person who's afraid of life, do you?"

"I'm not afraid of life; I'm afraid of heights," Lindsay retorted, looking insulted at being called a coward. "There's a word for it. 'Acrophobia.'"

Rudy took no notice of Lindsay's protest. "You have a choice in how you view this."

Lindsay glared at him. "If we're talking about free will, I actually have a choice *not* to do this."

His *Feel the fear and do it anyway* speech was not doing the trick.

"Lindsay, this is getting embarrassing," Jelena said, moving over to us. "It's not that bad. I just closed my eyes when I jumped."

"Let's help Lindsay do this!" Rudy called out, punching the air enthusiastically. "Cheer her on, everyone."

"Go for it, Lindsay!" our classmates shouted.

"Don't be a coward!" someone added.

People were anxious to wrap the exercise up and get back to camp. It was approaching five o'clock now. The Leap of Faith had scared a lot of people, so it hadn't been a speedy undertaking.

"Positive reinforcement only!" Mr. Quinten instructed.

"Why don't you try climbing up there, no pressure to jump, and see how you feel?" Rudy said, trying to usher Lindsay closer to the pole.

"No." I could tell Lindsay was mortified by having her fear of heights made obvious to all our schoolmates. She looked like she wanted to cry. If she didn't want to do the exercise, then she shouldn't have to. She'd already braved the flying fox earlier, even though she'd told me she'd wanted to be sick the whole time. She wasn't a coward; she just had an issue with having her feet off the ground.

"Lindsay, don't make me look bad," Jelena said. "I need you to show support for the activities."

"No!"

"I'll go," I said quickly.

I started climbing the rungs up the pole in automaton mode. I just wanted to get back to the campsite, speak to Jeffrey and Chloe, and see how they were doing with their respective matches. I'd only come on this excursion to focus on the Find a Prince/Princess™ program, and the athletic activities were making it very difficult to find the time to do that.

As I climbed onto the platform and slowly lifted myself from kneeling position to standing, I looked down for the first time. I wanted to be sick. Sixty-five feet was one thing; one hundred was another. Every cell in my body commanded me to cling to the platform, to not launch myself off it like a crazy person.

"Fantastic, Aurora!" Rudy looked tiny, so far away from me. "Now all you need to do is approach the edge and jump for the trapeze."

I took a step and my heart twisted with fear. I tried to lift my other foot, but it was as if someone had superglued it to the platform.

"Take your time," Mr. Quinten called up.

"I might need an hour or so," I called down, trying to keep things light.

Maybe I could sit back down for a minute while I pulled myself together. I could use the time to do some strategizing on my matchmakees' behalf. Maybe by the time I'd finished brainstorming it would be time to return to camp and I could just climb back down the ladder. After all, Rudy couldn't keep us here all night.

A chorus started up below. "Jump . . . Jump . . . Jump . . ."

I eyed the edge again. I hadn't been all that lucky lately, what with the Lethal Lips thing and my failed attempt at subtly getting Hayden's attention when he was grounded. They say disasters come in threes. I didn't need the third one to be a faulty harness. "Don't feed the bear that is your fear!" Rudy shouted up to me.

I now understood why Lindsay had given him that death stare.

"Aurora!" The NAD's voice drifted up to me. "I know you have immense inner strength after so many years of being tested by the universe. Use it now."

There were shouts of laughter following his comment. I felt ashamed to give up, especially with the NAD's unfailing belief in me, but I couldn't do this. I was going to have to climb down.

"Princess!"

Hayden was shouting up to me now.

"Look at me."

I dared to peep down. Hayden was standing way behind the crowd, level with where the trapeze seemed to be, from my vantage point.

He gave me a wave. "All you have to do is pretend you're leaping out to me. It's that simple."

I took a tiny step.

I saw Hayden smile, even as far away as he was. "You know I'd catch you. Take another step and show me that you trust me."

Oh, man. Now what was I going to do? I inched myself to the very edge of the platform. My vision swam.

"Don't look down," Hayden called. "Look at me. I'm holding my arms out for you. I always will."

A lump appeared in my throat as I watched him lift his arms in the air, proving to me that he was ready and waiting.

"It's like Peter Pan teaching Wendy to fly. You just need to believe you can do it!" Hayden shouted, his voice full of assurance.

I wanted to believe. I wanted to show as much faith in him as he was showing in me. And so I leaped, keeping my eyes open, feeling my body launch through the air, toward Hayden, toward the bar, for what felt like forever. My heart, which had previously felt like it was going to jump out of my chest, seemed to stop.

Miraculously, my hands caught the bar, and suddenly I was swinging. Hayden still had his arms in the air. He grinned up at me.

"You did it, Princess!"

I started laughing from exhilaration and I didn't stop until they lowered me back down. The Leap of Faith *had* restored my faith. The support that Hayden had shown me during the exercise had given me fresh hope for our relationship. He couldn't have said those things if he didn't care a great deal for me, could he? All we needed now was some time alone together.

21

As soon as I'd completed the Leap of Faith, Rudy bustled us back to camp, as the sun was due to set within the hour. I was hoping to have a moment with Hayden before I resumed kitchen duty, but Ms. DeForest grabbed me the second we returned.

"Aurora, I need you to start chopping the onions." She pointed at three bags sitting on the table.

"Are they getting cooked?"

I knew what the answer would be but hoped I was wrong. Raw onion? Everyone's breath was going to stink.

"You children are having trouble grasping the word 'raw.'" Ms. DeForest sighed.

She went off to greet the NAD, showing a level of enthusiasm comparable with Penelope welcoming Odysseus home after his twenty-year voyage. I rolled my eyes.

As I began chopping the onions, Jeffrey came over and took a seat across from me.

"Hey, Jeffrey, how are you doing?"

"I'm feeling like the *man*! I've got two chicks making eyes at me!" Jeffrey's own eyes were wide. "They both wanted to be my buddy today, but I had to say yes to Ruby because I was Jemima's buddy yesterday. But then Jemima gave me a hug when I came down from the Leap of Faith. Aurora, she smells crazy good. Like strawberry-and-cream lollipops. But then Ruby asked me to help her put on sunscreen, and when I lifted her hair up to do her back and shoulders she smelled like coconut jelly beans." He groaned and put his head down on the table, right beside the plate of chopped onion. "I've gone from staring through the candy store window to frolicking around inside with the candy begging me to eat it."

"Don't repeat the candy analogy to the girls, will you? They might find it kind of insulting."

I poked Jeffrey in the side of the head to get him to move. Ms. DeForest was fussy enough about our negative energy contaminating the food. She'd have a fit if Jeffrey's hair wound up in her raw dishes.

"I know," Jeffrey said in a low voice. "But I need you to help me, Aurora. What candy do I choose? I kind of want both. I know it's wrong, but I do. Maybe I could kiss both of them—like at Baskin-Robbins, when you sample the flavors? Some taste testing before I choose which one to make permanent!"

I didn't want to be too hard on him, since he was obviously reeling with shock at the novelty of his situation, but I wasn't going to have him playing with the girls' feelings.

"Jeffrey, this isn't *The Bachelor.* You can't play them off each other. Plus, your choice shouldn't be based on pure physicality. You should choose the girl that you feel the best connection with."

"Jeffrey, you are not in this cooking group." Ms. DeForest was suddenly behind him. She gave me an irritated look. "Unless you have a desperate desire to join the cleanup session later?"

Jeffrey was up like a shot. "Aurora, I won't do any sampling, I promise. I'll try and work it out. They're both amazing. Either one of them would be a treat."

"All right, kitchen duty it is," Ms. DeForest said. "I'll see you after dinner."

Jeffrey was so high on cloud nine that he just shrugged and dashed off to his tent.

It became clear that the Leap of Faith had triggered people's appetites. We had a dinner line forming within seconds of the announcement that the food was ready.

"Mutiny!" John from the soccer team shouted, when he saw the raw food feast.

"We need protein!" Nathaniel yelled. "How are we supposed to build tone with rabbit food?"

"Protein, protein, protein!" the entire soccer team shouted.

"Legumes are protein." Ms. DeForest glooped some of the bean-and-onion mix onto John's plate.

He sniffed it and mock-retched.

"I'm starving!" someone down the line moaned.

"Sir, surely we can whip up something else for dinner?" Jelena asked Mr. Quinten. She looked extremely uneasy, as if expecting the hordes to rise up against her like the French storming the gates of Versailles at the start of the revolution.

"It's a little late for that," Mr. Quinten replied. There was a chorus of groans at his response. "By the time we prepare another meal, it'll be after ten. We need to be on schedule for bedtime so that everyone has enough energy for a day of activities tomorrow."

"How are they supposed to have enough energy with only grated carrot for sustenance?" Jelena said.

"This is a prisoner-of-war camp!" John shouted.

"Boys, cut the complaining," Mr. Quinten ordered. "I'll boil some rice quickly."

Most people ended up eating a plate of white rice with a drizzle of bean mix on the side. Hoping to talk with Hayden by the fire later, I deliberately avoided the raw onion.

After we'd eaten, the cleanup took a ridiculously long time, even with Jeffrey's additional help. Everything was stained with beetroot, and hours of simmering the beans had left a black, rocklike layer on the bottom of the massive pot. The heat hadn't let up, either. Though it was nine at night, sweat was trickling down my brow as I scrubbed at the pot base.

While I worked away, Ms. DeForest sat by the fire, her hands nearly touching the NAD's as they chatted. All personal issues aside, it was hard for me not to feel upset at the way he'd allowed her to monopolize his time on the trip. He'd claimed that being a volunteer would give us some father–daughter time, but that intention had completely gone out the window the moment he'd spotted Ms. DeForest.

When I'd finally finished cleaning the pot, I headed over to the fire. My friends called me to join them. They were sitting in a group with Hayden, Scott, Hunter, Chloe, and Johannes, some distance away from the flames.

"It's too hot to hang out next to that thing," Jelena explained, pointing at the fire.

Hayden waved me over to sit next to him. It was hard not to start beaming.

"We're playing Truth or Dare via spin-the-bottle method," Sara said, as I sat down. "It's Lindsay's turn. Lindsay, truth or dare?"

"Dare," Lindsay said.

"I dare you to go over to that tent and steal a pair of Travis's boxers." Sara was laughing before she finished the sentence. She pointed at Travis's tent, which was only a few yards away, and seemingly without occupants.

Lindsay hesitated. "Mr. Quinten said that if we step into a boys' tent, we'll get suspended."

"Mr. Quinten headed for the long drop two minutes ago," Sara replied. "Come on. You have a lot to prove in the bravery stakes today."

"Sara!" I chastised.

Lindsay marched over to the tent. She disappeared inside and we heard the sound of rummaging, until she emerged triumphantly, waving Travis's boxers in the air like a flag.

Travis spotted his *Family Guy* boxers from the other side of the common area. "Hey! They're my favorite pair! You know, Lindsay, I'd have given you the ones I'm wearing."

Travis came running toward us, unbuckling his belt. Lindsay let out a shriek and tossed the shorts at Sara, who screamed and batted them away. Fortunately, Travis tripped in his enthusiasm and sprawled flat, meaning he was embarrassed enough to head back to his former spot.

Lindsay spun the bottle and got Sara. "My turn. Truth or dare?"

"Truth," Sara said, obviously worried about what Lindsay might request if she chose a dare.

"Do you find Johannes attractive?" Lindsay asked.

We all held our breath. Cassie and Scott were giggling. I tried not to laugh myself.

"Well, you know . . ." Sara stumbled over her words, looking at the ground.

"Tell the *truth*," Lindsay said.

Johannes looked like he was only just holding himself back from nodding furiously.

"Well, when it comes to general opinion—"

"In *your* opinion, Sara."

"Fine. Yes, I do. In a completely impartial, *it doesn't make an iota of difference to me because I'm staying single* way, yes, Johannes is a hottie," Sara burst out. "Are you happy now?"

I knew it! A couple more weeks and she'd crumble.

Lindsay shrugged, giggling. "Well, I know Johannes is."

"The Swedish word for happy is *lycklig*," Johannes said. "And I am feeling it!"

"Okay, me next," Jelena said, and spun the bottle. "Cassie, truth or dare?"

"Truth," Cassie said. Last time she'd chosen one of Jelena's dares at a slumber party, she'd had to go pick up pizzas in her bikini. In winter.

"What's your ideal kiss?"

Our group seemed to go deathly quiet.

Cassie looked down at her fingernails. "This is kind of personal."

"Cass, you picked truth, and if you switch to dare I'm going to make you *demonstrate* your ideal kiss, so choose your poison."

Cass sighed and kept her eyes down, not daring to look at Scott.

"Soft and slow. Minimal tongue. If there is some tongue, then it should be relaxed—you know, soft, not pointy."

"I love it when your tongue's relaxed," Sara whispered to me and snickered.

Well, hopefully that was unsubtle enough that Scott would get the hint.

"Hope you're following those instructions, Scott!" Jelena elbowed him in the ribs.

Or so blindingly obvious he couldn't miss it if he tried.

Cassie looked like she wanted to elbow Jelena in the face. Thankfully, Chloe, who was next, sensed the tension and grabbed the bottle. She got Hunter, who chose truth.

"Why did you leave your music school for Jefferson?" she asked.

"I fell too hard for a girl and then lost my mind when she ended it," Hunter replied. "'Losing my mind' meaning I foolishly trashed a practice room one afternoon."

The circle was silent as we all studied Hunter. It was hard to believe someone so quiet could be so destructive. I was worried for a moment that he was going to get up and leave, but he seemed at ease with his confession. Maybe, like Chloe, he'd come to terms with his out-of-character behavior.

"That was an intense question, Chloe, so I'll ask one back. What do you honestly think of me?" Hunter looked at her like he could see through any facade she might put up.

To Chloe's credit, she didn't look frightened by the question. "I think I recognize a kindred spirit. And not just in a *losing your mind over your ex* way."

Hunter spun the bottle and it stopped at Lindsay again. This time she picked truth.

"Are you missing your boyfriend?" he asked.

Obviously, they'd talked while being buddies that first day. Still, that was a pretty personal question.

"Well, it's Tyler. I love him," Lindsay replied automatically.

"But do you know what love is?" Hunter pressed. "Because it

doesn't sound like there's passion there. A passionate woman is decisive—there's no hesitation in her answer or lack of emotion in her voice when she's questioned about the man in her life. Maybe Tyler hasn't been showing you the true meaning of love."

"One question per turn, Hunter," I said, trying to make the point in a joking way. I could tell Lindsay was shaken, even though she was trying not to show it. "Time to spin the bottle again."

Jelena gave it a quick spin and it stopped at Hayden.

Jelena clapped her hands together. "Hayden, truth or dare?"

"Dare. I can handle what you dish out." Hayden laughed.

"I dare you to kiss Aurora," Jelena said. "Show her the meaning of passion, just like Hunter was going on about."

My face was as hot as the fire. Everyone looked at Hayden and me expectantly.

Hayden gave me a long look. "I don't think it's appropriate for the situation," he said, and stood up. "I'd better leave you guys to it. I can see Mr. Quinten signaling."

"What were you thinking?" Sara hit Jelena on the head with her empty water bottle. "For someone who professes to be a leader, you don't put a lot of thought into the consequences of your actions, do you?"

"I'm sorry!" Jelena virtually yelled at Sara, yanking the water bottle away from her.

After what had happened with Hayden, I'd made a break for our tent and my friends had followed. We were now all sitting on Jelena's oversize mattress.

Sara gave her a wry look. "You might want to direct your apology to the person whose love life you've ruined."

"I didn't ruin anything," Jelena shot back. "Aurora, I'm sorry. I thought it would help you guys get a little closer. I wouldn't have said it if I'd had any doubts about him doing it. The whole thing doesn't make sense. What about the Leap of Faith? He was literally begging you to leap into his arms. So what the heck happened the moment I offered him an excuse to do just that?"

"The arms he was holding out were obviously platonic," I replied, trying my best to keep my voice from shaking. "It's not your fault, Jelena. Things have been weird all week. Hayden's obviously made up his mind that he's not interested in anything more than friendship with me."

"You know, being stupid enough to reject you is one thing," Jelena ranted. "I'd have forgiven him for that, because he'd deserve our pity for being severely short on brain cells and completely without taste. But I'm furious at him for publicly rejecting you."

To be honest, I was too. Scorning me in front of my friends, as well as Johannes, Scott, Hunter, and Chloe, was beyond embarrassing. If he'd lost interest in me, why couldn't he have told me in person? It was infinitely kinder than turning down a kiss in front of eight people!

Jelena twisted the corner of her pillow angrily. "He could have at least given you a peck on the cheek or the lips as a token gesture. He had no right to embarrass you that way."

"It doesn't seem like Hayden at all." Cassie looked as upset as I felt. "Maybe we're taking this the wrong way. I'll ask Scott to talk to him man to man—"

"No. I'll talk to him." Jelena's lips were thin with displeasure. "Not only is he rejecting my friend, he's messing up the romantic image of Aurora and Hayden that I'm trying to promote on those T-shirts—"

"Guys, don't bother," I broke in. "He flat out refused to kiss me in front of everyone! It's obvious: the Hayden–Aurora story is over."

I knew they meant well, but I was close to losing it. I was at a complete loss as to why Hayden would want to make me feel this bad. But that didn't mean I wanted my friends cross-examining him about it. There was only so much a girl's pride could take.

Sara turned to Jelena. "You see why I want to stay single? It's to avoid situations like this. You really like a guy, he seems completely into you, things are going great, and then *bam!* He hits you with a blow so brutal that you're left seeing stars."

"Guys, please." I got into my sleeping bag and lay down. My jaw was so tense my cheeks were aching. "I don't mean to be rude, but can you leave me alone for a while? I just want to go to sleep and forget about today."

And yesterday. And the last two weeks. And every moment I'd ever spent with Hayden. I'd never have them again, and that knowledge was killing me. I couldn't even take solace in the memories, because it hurt too much to know that Hayden had also experienced all of those moments yet obviously hadn't valued them. I'd given him my first kiss! That precious moment, which I'd never get back, had gone to someone unworthy of it. Someone who hadn't even had the decency to initiate an honest conversation with me, once he'd changed his mind about our relationship. He had that little respect for me.

I felt like a complete idiot. I'd been so caught up in my seemingly storybook ending that I'd been blind to the fact that my prince had been planning his exit for the past week or so! I almost started to cry, but held back. What Hayden had done proved he wasn't worth my tears.

I sat up and took a few deep breaths to calm myself. I wasn't going to hide in this tent like a victim of heartbreak. I'd lost confidence since the lip-lashing incident and hadn't been my usual forthright self the past couple of weeks, but that was about to change.

I thought back to when Hayden had just been my interfering next-door neighbor. I'd never hesitated to let him know my opinion of his behavior if I believed it was out of line. A month or so ago, I would have charged on over there and given him a piece of my mind.

I stood up and shrugged off my sleeping bag. Hayden might have rejected me, but I wasn't going to lie down and take it. For whatever reason, he'd decided to publicly embarrass me tonight, and that was *not* okay. It was demeaning and undeserved and I was going to tell him that face-to-face. After all, he'd already rejected me *and* humiliated me in front of my friends, so I had nothing to lose now.

I grabbed my flashlight, climbed out of the tent , and marched over to the campfire, where Hunter, Chloe, and Johannes were sitting. Hayden sat on a log, off to one side, having what looked like an intense discussion with Scott. Obviously, Cassie hadn't heeded my plea to keep her boyfriend out of my business. Well, I didn't need Scott to take control of this situation; I would defend my own honor.

Hayden looked up as he heard my footsteps marching toward them.

I grabbed his arm. "I need to talk to you *now*."

"Aurora, of course. I was just going to come find you." Hayden jumped up from the log. "Why don't you take Scott's seat?"

"I'm not talking to you in front of everyone." I gestured for him to follow me as I marched away from the campfire. "There are certain things that I have the sense"—I threw him a look over my shoulder to make my point—"not to conduct in public."

I switched on my flashlight and headed down the path toward the toilets, but instead of turning left, I turned right, into a clearing I'd spotted that afternoon. Sure, there might be bugs, but at least we wouldn't have to worry about busybodies listening in.

A huge moon had risen and the clearing we now stood in was drenched in its light. I *would* end up in the most romantic locale ever while wanting to kill my date.

"Aurora, be careful." Hayden grabbed my arm to steady me as I stumbled on a tree root.

"I don't want you to touch me." I pulled away. For some reason, the physical contact had spiked my infuriation levels to a new high. I felt hot tears forming and hated myself for it.

"Aurora, I know this is about the Truth or Dare. Let me explain—"

I turned to face him. "I don't care why you did it. All I know is that you did. You humiliated me in front of everyone, Hayden! Yes, I accidentally hurt your lip and got you into trouble with your parents and so you've decided you don't like me anymore. But you know what? Just because you've changed your mind about us doesn't give you the right to embarrass me. The things I did to you were accidents—I didn't mean for them to happen. But what you did tonight—you knew exactly how much pain you'd cause me."

"It's not like that." Hayden tried to take my hand and I snatched it away. "I didn't want to hurt you, I never would—"

"Then why didn't you talk to me in private?" I cut in. "I don't understand. I've known you since we were six, but now I feel like I don't know you at all."

"You need to hear me out, Aurora. The reason I—"

"No." Just standing here watching Hayden try to come up with excuses was making my chest ache. "You had your chance to talk to me privately, but you went with public humiliation. Now I'm telling you I don't want anything to do with you anymore."

"Aurora—"

"Nothing. In two minutes, when I walk away from you, it'll be like none of this ever happened. The play, the friendship, the kiss, the secret-admirer thing—you're off the hook, just like you wanted."

I reached for the necklace at my throat and hurriedly unfastened it. I wanted to be able to finish this conversation without showing Hayden just how hurt I was. I pushed my hand toward him, motioning for him to take the necklace from it.

Hayden looked furious. "I'm not letting you give that back. Aurora, do you really think so little of me that you believe what happened back there was me deliberately trying to hurt you?"

"I told you, I don't want to hear the reason." I grabbed Hayden's hand and forced his palm open. "Take it." I dropped the necklace into his hand.

"No." Hayden gripped the top of my wrist, leaving the necklace within our clasped hands.

"You don't want my kisses anymore, so I don't think it's appropriate that I wear one of yours permanently."

I wrenched my hand from his and we both watched as the silver *X* tumbled to the ground.

Hayden dropped to his knees. "Aurora, give me the flashlight!"

"What, so you can find it, return it, and get your money back?" I knew it was a mean comment, but I couldn't help it.

"So I can stop you from throwing away something precious!"

Hayden pulled me down to where he was crouched in the dirt and leaves, frantically scanning for the necklace. I sighed. Part of me wanted to march off as planned, but I couldn't leave him in the dark. There were snakes out here. Much as I was furious, I wasn't vengeful.

"Fine." I shone the flashlight on the area between our feet.

"Thank god." Hayden spotted the necklace and scooped it up, wiping off the dust with his shirt. He moved to fasten it around my neck again, his eyes intensely focused on mine. I held his gaze. Looking down would make me seem weak.

"I told you, I don't want your kisses." I tried to push him away.

"Because you think I don't want yours." Hayden fastened the clasp, but his hands remained on the back of my neck.

"Don't patronize me," I shot back. "I don't think; I know."

"You never like hearing this, but that overactive imagination of yours is both a blessing and a curse. It's frequently off base when it comes to me," Hayden said. "You won't listen to what I'm trying to tell you, so I'm going to have to prove your ridiculous assumption wrong some other way."

"I'm not sitting here waiting for you to prove some stupid point, Hayden. I'm going back to camp—"

My words were smothered as Hayden put his lips to mine, lightning fast. The *p* of "camp" became a puff of air exhaled from my mouth into his. I tried to pull away, but his hands at the back of my neck held me in position. His lips pressed mine with an urgency I'd never felt before, almost begging me to melt and meld into him.

"How could you *ever* think I don't want to kiss you?" Hayden's words were a vibration on my mouth.

"Because you *wouldn't* kiss me."

What was wrong with him? One minute he didn't want me, the next he did—it was completely unfair on my feelings. He was obviously one of those guys who was only interested in girls who weren't interested in him. I tried to move my lips away from his, turning my head to the side, but his mouth moved with me.

"Do you think I wanted them seeing this . . ." Hayden said, and kissed me even more deeply, his hands moving from my neck to my hair, stroking it like I was something precious. I felt my resolve come close to melting.

"What I've been daydreaming about for more than two weeks?" He pulled away and took in my skeptical look. "Yes, Princess. You might not believe me, for whatever crazy reason you've dreamed up since I gave you this necklace." He traced the *X* at my throat. "But I have. And I wasn't going to let our classmates steal this moment from us with their whistles and stupid comments about lethal lips."

"That's just it," I burst out. "They *were* lethal. Can you blame me for being freaked out that you might not give me a second chance, once the stitches came out? For being worried that our kiss would be a one-off?"

"Aurora, when are you going to get it?" Hayden's voice was almost harsh with insistence. "It's never going to be a one-off with you."

He pulled me to him again, and this time my lips matched his with equal urgency. My emotions were all over the place. Relief and confusion and joy all leaped about in my heart and were expressed in the almost desperate kisses we exchanged in the moonlight.

"What did you think that necklace means?" Hayden kissed down my neck to the pendant. "You and me . . . this is anything but impermanent."

His breath was hot against the hollow of my throat. I closed my eyes as he kissed his way back up to my mouth. I pulled him closer into my arms and, in doing so, lost my balance. My knees, weak from squatting, gave way, and I tumbled backward onto the ground. Hayden quickly put his hands behind my head to soften the landing, keeping our lips locked seamlessly as he fell on top of me. Ironically, losing my balance and winding up lying flat on the earth seemed the only way to regain some equilibrium in a moment when everything seemed to be spinning.

Hayden traced a hand down my arm. "I'm going to keep kissing you until you're convinced. How many kisses is it going to take? One hundred? One hundred thousand? I'm not shy about making my point, you know."

"Be quiet and kiss me."

I was too giddy for math or logic. I couldn't string a sentence together when Hayden's kisses kept stealing my breath from me. Not to mention that every time I opened my eyes I saw a sky bright with stars. The word "overwhelming" wasn't sufficient.

"Someone's changed their tune," Hayden teased.

"I need lots of reassurance."

As I said the words, I realized how true they were. Maybe it was because of my mother leaving, maybe it was because of the history that Hayden and I shared, but, for whatever reason, I was quick to doubt that anyone could really care for me.

"I'll give you every bit of reassurance you need, I promise."

I looked up into Hayden's eyes and noticed the gold flecks of his irises as they shimmered in the light of the flashlight, which was on the ground nearby. His eyes were a promise. He stroked my cheek with his left hand while his right clasped my waist.

"You tell me anytime you're unsure," he said, "and I'll do this . . ." His lips caught mine again.

The kiss deepened and I forgot everything—the ups and downs of the past few weeks, how angry I'd been at him, even the fact that sticks were jabbing into my back as we made out.

"It's so nice to be alone," I sighed, as Hayden kissed my neck again.

"Aurora?" a voice said, and suddenly a flashlight was in my eyes.

OMG, we were not alone!

22

The NAD was standing above us, wide-eyed with disbelief. I watched his gaze go from Hayden's hand at my waist to my arms around Hayden's upper back and then pause on my right shoulder. I looked down and saw that my off-the-shoulder T-shirt had become even more off the shoulder: my bra strap and almost the entire top half of my bra were exposed. Hayden realized this at the same time I did and quickly pulled my top back up to cover me.

"Mr. Skye."

I'd never seen Hayden look so guilty. He leaped up then reached down to help me to my feet. I could only imagine how disheveled I looked. A tiny part of me wished it had been Mr. Quinten who'd found us—to be caught making out in the woods by my dad was a source of shame neither of us would ever forget.

"You better fix yourselves up on the double." Dad's voice was the sternest I'd ever heard it. He focused on Hayden. "I'm not having my daughter suspended from school because you've lured her away from camp to do who knows what."

"Dad, it's not what it looks like!" This was a thousand times worse than the YouTube video. There was no denying we'd been kissing, but for him to think we might have done anything else was ridiculous. "This is like the third time we've ever kissed. I know I used the term 'snail's pace,' and this kind of throws that description into doubt, but—"

"Aurora, we'll discuss this at home, but I'm incredibly disappointed. I think I'm a pretty easygoing parent compared with most. All I ask of you is to be honest with me. We had a conversation about this very thing just over a week ago and you had the chance to be open about Hayden and your relationship. Instead, I'm left to literally stumble on how serious this thing is."

"Mr. Skye, you're right in one sense," Hayden said. "Our relationship is serious, in that Aurora's my girlfriend . . ."

I looked at Hayden in shock. He'd been thinking of me as his girlfriend? I really needed to start viewing my relationship from an unbiased standpoint. Maybe then I'd be a little less off base.

"Or rather, that's what I consider her to be." Hayden looked at me. "And I hope she thinks of me as her boyfriend. Therefore, I would never disrespect her or try to make her do anything she's uneasy with."

If the NAD hadn't been a six-foot-four thundercloud looming over us, I would have thrown my arms around Hayden. I was his girlfriend!

"This is a discussion for me and my daughter," the NAD said. If Hayden had been hoping to improve the situation by professing his dedication to me, it hadn't worked. "We need to get back to camp."

The NAD gestured for us to go first, back through the clearing and up the track to the campsite. Mr. Quinten was waiting, and he gave us a stern look as we approached. I was relieved to notice that everyone else had retired to their tents.

"Sorry, Mr. Quinten. Aurora got lost coming back from the bathroom," the NAD explained. "Her flashlight died. Thankfully, Hayden was making his way over there at the same time, so she wasn't alone for long."

"Yes, well, this is why we have the buddy system," Mr. Quinten said, looking displeased. "And I'd like to remind you that the buddies are meant to be same sex only. Boys and girls heading off into the dark together raises all kinds of questions and I won't have that. If this was anyone but Hayden, I'd examine the incident more closely, but I trust that he's upheld Jefferson standards."

The NAD nodded firmly. "Of course. Both Hayden and Aurora understand that something like this can't happen again."

"Good," said Mr. Quinten. "Now both of you, back to your tents."

Hayden and I walked over to the tents with the NAD right on our heels. He obviously didn't want me having one more moment alone in the dark with Hayden.

Hayden stopped outside his tent. "Good night, Aurora. Good night, Mr. Skye."

The NAD didn't reply. Hayden blew me a kiss and I blew one back.

The NAD and I continued to my tent. I'd never known him to be so silent. It was unnerving.

"I don't want any more moments like this, Aurora," the NAD said in a low voice, as we reached the tent. "It's stressful supervising this many teenagers. I never thought I'd find myself worried about you."

"Dad, I assure you, there's nothing to worry—"

"You are not to leave this tent until breakfast time."

"Of course!"

I hated being at odds with my dad. It was going to take months to win back his trust. I had no idea how Hayden and I were going to repair this situation, but we'd have to discuss it tomorrow.

The NAD stood waiting like a prison guard until I climbed inside the tent.

"Aurora?" Cassie whispered.

I peered through the dark and saw that she, Jelena, and Lindsay were all sitting up on Jelena's mattress. Sara was sound asleep on her air sofa. I carefully stepped over her.

I put a finger to my lips as I listened to the NAD's footsteps fade away. "Why aren't you guys asleep?"

"Because it's like trying to sleep in a sauna." Jelena switched on her flashlight and I saw that she was holding her water bottle to the back of her neck, trying to cool down.

"Aurora, you have a stick in your hair." Cassie pulled a long twig from the side of my head.

She, Jelena, and Lindsay stared at me with *What happened?* written all over their faces.

"Ew! There's dirt on the back of your T-shirt!" Jelena whisper-shrieked. "Step no closer! This mattress is a germ-free zone."

Lindsay and Cass sighed. I was sensing Jelena had forced them to prove their cleanliness before they'd been allowed on the bed.

"Okay, okay." I got out my wet wipes and stripped down, bagging my T-shirt and shorts. Looking at the state of them, it was a miracle Mr. Quinten hadn't hauled Hayden and me in for questioning. Thank god for Hayden's squeaky-clean rep.

"What happened to you?" Lindsay asked. "We saw you leave with Hayden, but we didn't want to tell anyone because we knew Mr. Quinten would go berserk and launch a search party. You didn't get into a fight, did you?" She looked like she believed I'd wrestled Hayden down to the ground.

"Not exactly." I relayed the details to the girls.

"*His girlfriend!*" Cassie high-fived me. "And you guys didn't have to have the talk or anything!"

Jelena shook her head. "Hayden's got to learn how to communicate better. How were you to know he was all PDA shy when it came to round three?"

"I've got to learn to stop jumping to conclusions," I admitted.

"I can't believe your dad caught you," Lindsay said. "Is he grounding you for a million years?"

"He doesn't really believe in traditional parental punishment systems."

I didn't know what would happen once we got home, but the weight of the NAD's disappointment was weighing on me.

"Ladies." We all froze as Mr. Quinten's voice came from outside our tent. "Time to quiet down now."

I crawled onto Jelena's mattress. There was no need for sleeping bags; the air itself was like a blanket. I lay there, listening to my friends' breathing become slow sighs of sleep, and relived the moments with Hayden in the moonlight. Every time the NAD appeared on the scene, I rewound to the beginning. Nothing could kill my buzz right now. I was Lethal Lips no more, *and* I was officially Hayden Paris's girlfriend! With that exquisite thought, I drifted off into dreamland.

I was on a date with Hayden. We'd been at the movies, but the theater filled with water and our seats became a raft. We bobbed up and down on our makeshift craft and tried to paddle our way to the exit. Water was dripping onto my hair. I covered my head but it didn't stop the drops from trickling down my face.

I woke up suddenly, realizing that water was dripping for real onto my head. Rain was thundering down onto our tarp, which was obviously leaking under the pressure. The unrelenting heat had been broken by a storm.

Jelena, who'd been sleeping next to me, woke up. Her shout jolted the others into alert mode. "Sara! It's pouring! Is the waterproofing on properly? You were responsible for it."

"Yes," Sara groaned from her air sofa.

"Then why am I virtually floating on a raft?" Jelena switched on her flashlight and motioned at the water lapping at the sides of the mattress.

Now that I could see properly, I realized the water was about four inches high. No wonder I'd been dreaming of bobbing up and down! I looked at my watch. It was 5:30 a.m.

"Rudy checked it." Sara's air sofa was afloat too, and she was gingerly balanced on it. "A tiny bit of plastic can't stand up to a storm of this level, though."

"OMG, the tent's moving!" Cassie gripped the edge of Jelena's mattress as the tarp below us slipped.

Lindsay gasped and Cass dug her fingers into the mattress as it slid toward the tent wall.

"The water's turned the tarp into a makeshift Slip 'N Slide," I said, grabbing my sodden belongings from the river developing next to the mattress. "We need to get out of here."

"Evacuate! Evacuate!" Jelena shouted in her authoritarian voice.

We all shrieked and leaped off the mattress into the ankle-deep water, the tarp slippery under our feet as it drifted down the incline. We pushed our way through the tent opening and outside, where we were hit by the full impact of the rain. The tarp slid away in the rushing water, taking Jelena's queen-size mattress with it.

"Let it go." Jelena's voice was hard. "We're the only survivors."

We made our way over to the kitchen area in the dawn light and joined the others whose self-constructed accommodations hadn't stood up to the violent storm. We all sat in a shivering huddle under the kitchen roof, clutching hot chocolates for warmth as lightning lit up the wrecked tents scattered across the campsite. Unlike most of us, Sara's cheeks were rosy. She'd pulled out an emergency blanket and was sitting wrapped up in the shiny metallic folds, with one of her hand warmers under her jumper, so she was toasty warm.

The NAD, Mr. Quinten, and Hayden were darting about in the storm, helping people move their belongings to the undercover area. Travis's bag had apparently been swept away; he was standing in the undercover area in just his boxers. He was in good spirits, though, pulling model-like poses while everyone laughed.

Within two sips of her hot chocolate, Jelena was besieged by students complaining of ruined shoes, lost flashlights, and, funnily enough, a bad hair day. Benjamin's tent had collapsed in on him and his cheek had gotten scratched by a tent pole. Despite the cut being about an eighth of an inch in size, he was apparently seeking a compensation payment for reconstructive surgery and potential loss of income.

"I am the next Mr. Bubbly," I heard him saying.

I noticed Lindsay was sitting with Chloe and Hunter. From what I could hear, Hunter was making some rather dark jokes about current events.

"Never fear. I'll look after you ladies," Jeffrey said. I looked over to where he was sitting, between Ruby and Jemima.

I watched as Jeffrey wrapped his sweatshirt around Ruby's shoulders and Jemima sent a glare in her direction. Ruby raised an eyebrow back at her. For a second, I wondered if Jeffrey was completely blind to the rising antagonism between the girls, but as Ruby's gaze turned even steelier, he seemed to finally register the tension.

"Come on, ladies, cheer up. The storm will be over before you know it," he said. "Oh, look, Ruby, you'll love this." He crouched down and picked up a baby green tree frog from the wet cement. It was obviously seeking shelter from the storm. "Here, have a hold."

It was unclear exactly what happened—whether the frog actually leaped or Jeffrey pushed it toward Ruby with a little too much enthusiasm—but the next thing I knew, the frog had tumbled down the space between Ruby's generous breasts.

Ruby let out a scream—the first negative reaction I'd ever seen from her in response to any type of wildlife. Quick as a flash, she turned her back to the group and whipped off her tank top. I ran over to help as she pulled at the cups of her bra, trying to free the frog.

"Let me help!" cried Jeffrey, looking incredibly guilty.

"Not the time, Jeffrey!" I stressed, as Ruby finally freed the frog and struggled to adjust her bra again.

Within seconds, she'd spun around and started yelling at Jeffrey.

"You aimed it right at her breasts!" Jemima said indignantly, joining Ruby in a face-off with a terrified-looking Jeffrey.

"This wasn't about breasts at all!" Jeffrey protested. "For once in my life I can claim that to be true!"

"What is *wrong* with you?" Jemima looked even more horrified by Jeffrey's attempt to protest his innocence.

"I mean, I believe the human body is something to be proud of!" he said. "That's why I do the nudie runs!"

Jemima looked more uneasy. "Aurora, you told me that was a joke!"

"I can't believe you picked up a green tree frog," Ruby said furiously. "Do you even know what the chemicals on your skin do to theirs? Completely ignorant . . ."

"And insensitive," Jemima threw in.

Both girls stalked away. In the space of twenty seconds, Jeffrey had blown his chances with two formerly eager candidates.

He sat back down on the bench, his head in his hands. "Aurora? You know I didn't mean it, right? Surely we can get them to see that!"

I could hear the girls' angry voices from the other side of the undercover area, even through the thundering rain.

"I think we're going to have to start from scratch," I said gently. "Thankfully, there's one remaining candidate. You and I are going to prepare for this final round very carefully once we're back home."

"Okay, people, head office is telling us the rain is easing," Mr. Quinten announced at about one p.m. We hadn't left the undercover area the whole morning because the rain hadn't let up and Mr. Quinten didn't want anyone out in the open while there was lightning. "To make it home by five p.m., we need to start walking now."

Half the group cheered and the other half groaned.

"I know the weather's still pretty miserable, but the sooner we get going, the sooner you'll be back on the bus," Mr. Quinten said. "You've got your raincoats, and I have a large number of trash bags here if anyone wants one."

Fifteen minutes later, a line of plastic trash bags traipsed down the mountain. Pretty much everyone had opted for full body cover, casting aside any fashion concerns.

"I literally feel like garbage," Jelena said gloomily.

"No one at school will ever believe you wore head-to-toe trash bags," Sara giggled. She was wearing her snazzy purple waterproof pants and matching jacket.

"Sara, let me give you extra shelter." Johannes came rushing over with a garbage bag stretched above his head like a canopy.

"No, it's fine. I've got my protective gear—it's all-weather," Sara said, and gave him a little push away.

Unfortunately, the push set Johannes off balance on the slope. Sara's eyes went wide as she watched him flail at the edge of the trail. "Johannes, no!" She grabbed for him as he fell, but it was too late.

We all watched in horror as Johannes tumbled down the craggy rocks and landed several yards below with his weight on one foot. A loud crack echoed through the trees.

Sara, Rudy, and Mr. Quinten dashed down the trail to Johannes, who was clutching his ankle, white with pain.

Mr. Quinten took his foot gently and felt it. "It's broken."

Sara burst out crying. Johannes's face went even whiter and he passed out.

Sara was still crying when we finally made it back to the bus. She'd insisted on waiting with Johannes on the track while Rudy radioed for a four-wheel drive to bring a stretcher to carry Johannes back to head office, where he was picked up by an ambulance.

"They wouldn't let me go to the hospital," Sara sobbed. "All I wanted was to keep holding his hand and they tore me away. Hayden and Mr. Quinten got to go, instead."

"They're the designated crisis management contacts," I said. "It wasn't personal."

"I'll take you straight to the hospital the second we get back to school," Jelena said. "I'm going over there, too. Poor Johannes."

We boarded the bus and, for the first time in hours, felt dry.

"Heaven," Lindsay said.

She snuggled into her seat and pulled her phone out of the storage compartment. A chorus of message tones went off as the phone got signal.

"Tyler's been texting you?" I asked.

"About a million times," Lindsay said, unimpressed. "It's weird . . . the three days feel like three years."

I saw Hunter, sitting two seats ahead with Chloe, look back at Lindsay. What he'd said the other night during Truth or Dare was written all over his face. Lindsay quickly looked out the window.

"Well, the trip certainly brought some people together." Cassie sounded the most upbeat of us all. "Scott says it's like we've lived through a disaster."

She lowered her voice. "And he got the point after last night!" Cassie threw Jelena a smile. "The pokey tongue is no more! I know I was mad, but thank you. Plus, Aurora, the best news of all is that you and Hayden are back on track. That was worth all the suffering, wasn't it?"

"It was," I answered, without hesitation.

I was bummed Hayden wasn't around for the ride home, but maybe it was best we didn't cozy up in front of the NAD, after last night's events. Hayden had told me he wanted to come around to our house to talk to Dad properly this weekend.

"Creaky bridge worked well," Jelena said. "I wouldn't want to live through it again, but it's done more than cement Cass and Scott and you and Hayden. Look at Hunter and Chloe."

"And my dad and Ms. DeForest," I said wryly, pointing at Ms. DeForest, who'd fallen asleep on Dad's shoulder.

"Hope it's a temporary delusion of your dad's," Jelena said. "A man on rations in survivalist conditions is in no fit state to make a decision about repairing a relationship."

"I hope so." I shut my eyes to prevent myself from peering at them with morbid curiosity.

23

When we arrived back at school, it was still raining. I grabbed my pack from the back of the bus and raced over to our car. The NAD was swinging a purple backpack into the trunk—Ms. DeForest's backpack, to be exact.

As the NAD took my gear from me, I peered into the car and saw Ms. DeForest in the front passenger seat. I let out a sigh before opening the back door. She couldn't be coming home with us already, surely?

Ms. DeForest glanced back at me as I climbed into the car, but she didn't say hello. Thankfully, the NAD opened the driver's door, saving us from an awkward silence.

Dad laughed as he pulled out of the parking spot. "I really admire your commitment to sustainable travel, Dana, but this deluge is too much for any bicycle."

Phew. It seemed we were only dropping her home.

When we pulled up at Ms. DeForest's place, I put a polite smile on my face as she opened her door to get out. "See you at school, Ms. DeForest."

She frowned slightly. "Oh, I'll be back in a minute. Didn't your father tell you?"

I suddenly had a very bad feeling.

"Dana's going to be staying with us for a while," Dad announced, as we waited for her to return with "some supplies." "Her place is undergoing renovations in the next two months, so I thought she'd be happier out of the way of the plaster dust and saws."

I gaped at the NAD. Maybe I'd heard wrong. He had to mean two *days*.

"Sorry, Dad, I think I heard wrong. Two months as in eight weeks?"

I waited for the NAD to realize his mistake and start laughing. Instead, he nodded.

"Yes. I'd go in to help her with her things, but she's too tired to grab anything but an overnight bag. We'll come back tomorrow and pick up the rest of the stuff."

"Dad, she just dumped you, and now you're inviting her to come live with us rent-free?" I realized how rude that sounded, but I was completely thrown for a loop.

The NAD turned around to look at me. "Aurora, you're on thin ice at the moment. You know I don't dish out groundings, so the way that you're going to make amends in the next few weeks is by being as welcoming to Dana as possible. I'm expecting you to make extra effort on this one."

The heater might have been blasting but the car felt icy cold. I shivered as Ms. DeForest came scooting back, a huge suitcase bumping along behind her. Overnight bag that was not! Was Dad going to relocate the entire contents of her house tomorrow?

The NAD leaped out of the car to help Ms. DeForest. Together, they heaved the suitcase onto the seat next to me, then ducked back inside the car, both laughing. The NAD's blue eyes were sparkling like raindrops caught in the sunlight as he fastened his seat belt.

"Let's head on home!" he said cheerfully.

What had creaky bridge *done* to my father? This relationship was careering along at the speed of a rocket ship.

The weather was still stormy the following morning when I

headed downstairs for brunch. The NAD had made the token gesture of putting Ms. DeForest's "overnight bag" into the guest room last night, along with sheets and a towel for her, but when I'd headed up the stairs to bed last night, I'd seen her pulling the NAD's door shut behind her as she entered. Ms. DeForest was clearly more than a temporary housemate—Dad had plunged headlong back into the relationship.

I caught myself grimacing in the hallway mirror and quickly forced my face into a more pleasant expression before I entered the kitchen. If the NAD considered welcoming Ms. DeForest to be my penance for the Getting Busted Making Out at School Camp incident, then I was going to make her feel right at home. Starting with preparing breakfast for them both. Hayden had texted me that morning to ask if it would be okay if he came over to talk to Dad this afternoon. I needed Dad in a good mood so that their man-to-man talk started on a good note.

I started pulling kale and ginger out of the fridge. If Ms. DeForest wanted raw food, I'd make her the most potent antioxidant juice there was. I opened up one of the cookbooks Igneous had lent Dad. There was a juice named the Mean Green Monster, the king of detox concoctions. I hit the On button and the juicer roared into gear.

"What's this?" the NAD asked, as he and Ms. DeForest entered the kitchen. Ms. DeForest was wearing his bathrobe.

"The Mean Green Monster," I replied, switching the blender off. I poured the liquid (which, in my opinion, smelled and looked like pond scum) into two glasses. "I thought I'd make you guys some breakfast. I started with the juice, since I don't know your preferences meal-wise."

Knowing Ms. DeForest, I should have started activating almonds last night.

The NAD looked surprised. "That's thoughtful of you."

"Yes." Ms. DeForest took a suspicious sip of the juice, then, to my surprise, she smiled.

"Happy, Dana?" the NAD asked.

"I'd have added some more ginger, but it's certainly tolerable."

This was as enthusiastic a response as I was likely to get from her. The NAD opened the weekend newspaper, as he and Ms. DeForest sat down at the kitchen table with their juices.

"Toast, anyone?" I asked. "Meaning sprouted bread with nut butter?"

"Yes, please." The NAD was pulling out the various sections of the paper.

"No, thank you," Ms. DeForest said. "I like to allow the juice time to produce vital stomach enzymes before I have my first meal for the day."

"Okay, toast for me and Dad, then."

I turned my back on them and made a face while loading the toaster. How was I going to get through two months of this?

The toast popped up, and I took it over to the bench facing the kitchen table and started spreading the nut butter on it.

"I don't know why you read the paper, Kenneth," Ms. DeForest said, as Dad frowned down at an article. "It's full of negativity."

"I like to have an awareness of what's going on in the world," the NAD answered, turning the page. "If we stay ignorant of the suffering of others, it's hard to be a truly conscious individual."

"But don't you think," Ms. DeForest put her hand over Dad's to stop him turning to the next page, "that a focus upon negative events only lends them power? By reading this, you are helping to spread a plague of fear. Newspapers are the genesis of disease. Look at this, for instance: the social events page—an entire section devoted to materialism and self-interest."

She took the paper out of Dad's hands and shook it in the air for emphasis. I nearly gasped out loud when I saw photographs of Mom and Carlos's engagement party filling a whole page. I raced over to the table for a closer look. To my horror, a photograph of my mother and Carlos had "Recently engaged and soon to be wed" in bold letters above it.

Thankfully, the NAD hadn't seen it yet; he was focused on what Ms. DeForest was saying.

"These are people in positions of power, able to make a real difference, but their notion of charity is to attend a ball wearing a dress, the cost of which could have provided a hefty donation to whatever cause they pretend to be interested in."

Ms. DeForest waved the paper in the air again. I couldn't let Dad spot Mom. Not when I hadn't told him the news yet.

"I agree," I said, and gripped the corner of the paper, motioning for Ms. DeForest to let go. "It's really reprehensible. Dad, I think you should listen to Ms. DeForest and stop reading the paper immediately."

Ms. DeForest looked taken aback by my support. "Not yet, Aurora. I don't think your father's getting it." She flung the social pages down on the table and thrust her finger right at the photos of Mom and Carlos. I wanted to scream. "Look at this: people smothering their consciousness with alcohol and hedonism."

The NAD, recognizing my mother, choked midsip and sprayed green juice onto Carlos's and Mom's faces.

"I knew you'd be horrified!" Ms. DeForest cried triumphantly.

"That's my ex-wife!" The NAD pulled the damaged paper closer. "Aurora, look at this! The paper says she's getting remarried." He stood up, looking furious. "This is typical of Avery. Doing what she pleases and never letting you or me know about it, as if it doesn't have an impact on us at all."

Would it be totally heinous of me to pretend I hadn't known about the engagement? To make the NAD feel like he wasn't alone in his ignorance?

"'The lovely couple were joined by Ms. Skye's stunning daughter . . .'" Ms. DeForest read aloud, as she took a closer look at the photographs.

The NAD sat down again and grabbed the paper from Ms. DeForest.

"Dad—"

"You knew about this?" He looked up at me, the hurt on his face unmistakable.

"Yes, but not for long; barely any time, in fact—"

"And you deliberately kept it from me." Dad's voice was very quiet. He shut the paper.

"No! I wanted to tell you—I was going to, this weekend—"

"This is the second time this week you've chosen not to share an essential part of your life with your own father." Dad stood up, folding the paper under his arm. "The person who stood by you when the woman you've been keeping this secret for ran out on our family."

The words stung like I'd been slapped in the face.

"Kenneth . . ." Ms. DeForest reached for his hand. "Let's go to a meditation class."

"I don't want to meditate on this." The NAD strode over to the kitchen trash and threw the paper into it. "Let's go get your furniture."

I heard him grab his keys from the hall stand and open the front door. Ms. DeForest dashed after him without a glance back at me.

As soon as I heard the car leave, I grabbed the paper from the trash can and headed out to the front to dump it into the recycling bin. I wasn't going to risk having the NAD see the photos again later. Hayden was outside, putting the garbage out.

"Hey," I called, and he turned around with a smile. "Do you mind putting this one in your bin?"

Hayden looked down at the paper as I handed it over the fence to him. Even through the splatter of Mean Green Monster he recognized my mother's picture in a second. His eyes scanned the caption and he dropped the garbage bag in shock. "Aurora!"

I nodded. It was hard to know what to say.

He leaped the fence in one quick move, pulling me in close. "This is how she told you? I know what she's like, but still—"

"I knew," I said miserably. "I've known for a while. I was trying to come to terms with it before I broke the news to Dad. It just never seemed like the right time, and so he found out from the paper instead."

I felt so ashamed about what a coward I'd been, but Hayden's hug only grew tighter.

"Your mother should have told him. It was completely out of line for her to hand that responsibility over to you."

"She offered. It's just . . ."

"She wouldn't have been as kind."

Hayden looked at me like he understood everything.

"Listen, did you ask your dad about me coming over for a chat?" he asked.

"I was about to, and then he saw the photos."

"I'll drop by anyway," Hayden said. "Probably around five?"

"I don't know if it's a good idea today."

The NAD wasn't the shouting type, but at the rate things were going, he'd likely show Hayden the door.

"Your dad's going through a lot right now," Hayden replied. "And so are you. Removing one worry from his shoulders might help the situation—and mean that he eases up on you."

"I can deal with it," I protested.

Hayden shook his head. "Nope. Not taking no for an answer. Every prince is, by law, required to fight a dragon before winning his princess. Your dad's not even a fire-breathing one, so I'm getting off pretty easy."

I laughed, knowing that Hayden couldn't be stopped once he was on a mission.

"Okay, fine. But if I see his nostrils flaring, I'm pushing you out the door for your own safety."

I headed back up to my room and dozed on my window seat for the remainder of the day. I woke up to the sound of furniture being shifted. Ms. DeForest's belongings had officially entered the premises. Even though I didn't want to, I knew I should go down and help.

As I stepped into the hall, my toe connected with a concrete dragon that had materialized there.

"Oww!" I wailed as I hopped on the spot.

"Aurora?" The NAD's head suddenly appeared from the living room. "Are you okay?"

"I think I nearly broke my toe, but I should be asking *you* that question."

I tried to put my own suffering aside and focused on Dad's face. To my relief, his brow was relaxed and his mouth curved upward instead of down.

"I'm great," he replied brightly. "Dana's helping me redo the place."

I felt a twinge of horror. Not again. I tried to peep into the living room, but the NAD was blocking my way.

"I was so blinded by anger and old wounds this morning that I couldn't see the situation for what it was," he said, and shrugged.

"Which is . . . ?" I asked tentatively.

"The universe is commanding your father to move on," Ms. DeForest answered for him, as she joined us in the hall. "Your mother chose to do what she's done in a karmically unconscious way, but, for Kenneth, this is an opportunity to step purposefully into a new future."

I didn't mean to be a downer, but I didn't see what was so revolutionary about the latest room makeover. Dad's tried-and-tested method for dealing with the unexpected was to replace the furniture.

"I couldn't believe he hadn't done a sage-burning ceremony in here." Ms. DeForest shook her head. "The walls were dripping with energies left behind by Avery. So much so that they permeated our clothing during the ritual. We had to strip off and have cleansing salt baths."

Ms. DeForest sounded like an exorcist describing a house possessed by evil. Thank god I'd slept through that part of the process.

Dad put a hand on my shoulder. "I apologize if I took my frustration out on you this morning, honey. Your mother put you in an impossible position."

"However, it's important for Aurora to learn that this household is trying to vibrate at a certain frequency and dishonesty will not be tolerated."

Ms. DeForest obviously didn't want to let me off lightly.

"Shall we show her?" the NAD asked, looking proudly at Ms. DeForest.

She nodded, and gestured for me to enter the living room.

I blinked in shock as I took in the scene in front of me. "What happened to the sofas?"

The NAD pointed to where the four-piece set was squashed into a corner. "We drew on Dana's feng shui expertise."

"Furniture should never be positioned underneath overhead beams," Ms. DeForest said. "It's a negative influence upon your health."

Having the sofa two feet from our flat screen TV wasn't exactly healthy, either, but I held back from commenting as I looked around the rest of the room. Quartz crystals lined all the windowsills, and intricately beaded screens separated the dining and kitchen areas. Huge potted shrubs were everywhere, creating a veritable jungle of greenery. The coffee table was lost somewhere in the undergrowth. As I stepped forward, I bumped into a heavy wind chime.

The NAD gestured around him. "Isn't it fabulous?"

What had Ms. DeForest done? The living room was a wreck. If we ever misplaced anything in here, forget locating it. The Amazonian jungle would have swallowed it.

"What do you think?" They both turned to me.

Ms. DeForest stopped smiling and arched an eyebrow, obviously expecting my disapproval.

The universe was clearly testing me, what with my mother's imminent nuptials and now the NAD's own version of "moving on." I hadn't been able to soften the blow of the former for him, so there was no way I was going to be anything less than super supportive about the latter.

"It's completely transformed."

Thankfully, I was saved from further elaboration by the doorbell. I raced to answer it, leaving the NAD and Ms. DeForest rhapsodizing over their creative collaboration.

Hayden stood on the front step. The NAD came out into the hall. His beaming smile faded when he spotted Hayden.

"I wanted to come over to clear the air, Mr. Skye." Hayden's voice was confident, but I could see the nervousness in his eyes.

"Perfect timing!" I reassured Hayden before Dad could reply. "Dad and Ms. DeForest have been doing that all this afternoon!"

"All right, Hayden, the universe is obviously commanding us to have a chat." The NAD motioned for Hayden to follow him toward his study.

They emerged forty minutes later, the NAD looking much happier. I'd been trying not to pace the hall the whole time.

"You two feel free to hang out in the kitchen," Dad said, as he and Hayden joined me in the hall. "Dana and I need to put the finishing touches on the living room, but I've told Hayden he's welcome to stay for dinner."

"It went well, then!" I whispered to Hayden, as we headed for the kitchen.

Hayden caught sight of the living room as we passed it, and did a double take. "You could say that."

"How did you appease the dragon?"

"Your dad told me that although it would be a challenge, I had to learn to control my baser urges and focus on relating to you via my heart chakra."

Despite my best efforts, I snorted as we sat down at the kitchen table.

"I tried to convince him that my baser urges weren't a threat to your innocence, but he wasn't buying it, after finding me sprawled on top of you the other night. Then we did a guided meditation together."

The NAD came into the kitchen as Hayden finished his sentence.

"Nothing like a deep-breathing exercise to resolve conflict," he said, smiling at us as he went over to the electric teakettle. "I told Hayden that, as a requirement for dating you, he needs to attend our men's circle on a weekly basis, to ensure he's relating to you in an evolved way."

OMG. I didn't want Igneous offering Hayden advice on relationships.

"Dad, that's not necessary—"

"As I said, it's a requirement for dating you," the NAD said firmly.

The NAD was definitely sterner than he had been pre-camp. I wished he'd have a little more faith in me.

"I know you're both aware that relationships must be taken slowly," he finished, and headed out of the room.

"Slowly? He's the one letting his on-off girlfriend move in," I whispered to Hayden.

Hayden squeezed my hand. "As long as I'm allowed to see you, I don't care how many guided meditations I have to do."

"Just don't give a guy called Igneous your phone number," I warned. "Trust me on that one."

24

"Jelena, you didn't have to come. Lindsay and I have this under control," I said on Sunday afternoon, as the three of us sat in Jeffrey's living room waiting for him to bring us a drink before we got started on his matchmaking workshop. "I don't want Jeffrey to feel overwhelmed with three women trying to overhaul his approach to dating."

Jelena waved my concern away. "Relax. Jeffrey looked totally stoked to have three girls showing up at his front door. Plus, it's time to get real. We're two weeks from election date, come Monday, and Jeffrey's lost two of his matches. If the third one doesn't work out, my campaign's going to be in serious trouble."

She fell silent as Jeffrey entered the room with three glasses of Coke and ice. He served the drinks, then sat down on the couch and looked at us expectantly.

Jelena launched into business. "So, strategy: Ruby and Jemima are officially out of the picture, so it's time to try a new approach. Aurora, the DVD."

I reached into my bag and handed the disc to Jeffrey. He looked at the DVD case. "A nature documentary? You want me to bring out my animal instincts?"

"*No*," Jelena almost shouted.

I hurriedly explained the strategy. "We noticed you were extremely discouraged after what happened with Jemima and Ruby."

Jeffrey looked bummed. "Yeah. Neither of them will talk to me. I even left a message on Ruby's home phone and her mom called back, totally freaking out that I'd referred to her daughter's boobs on the family's voicemail." He took in our horrified faces. "I didn't mean to! I was trying to apologize and the word 'boobs' slipped out! I'm a guy; it happens!"

"Okay, moving forward . . ." I quickly changed the subject. "The DVD should demonstrate that you're not alone when it comes to letdowns. In the animal world, it's generally the male of the species that does the chasing, and it's hard work."

Jeffrey pressed Play and stared at the underwater scene that materialized on the screen.

"The male sea horse finds it far from easy to woo the female," the voice-over began. "He repeatedly intertwines his tail with hers, changing color to indicate his interest in her—a complex dance that often lasts for days at a time. The male also takes on the responsibility of gestation and gives birth several weeks later via his birthing pouch. Exhausted from the lengthy courtship ritual and birth process, the male often dies shortly afterward."

Jeffrey looked uneasy. "Aurora, I don't know about this. Death seems a pretty high price to pay for a regular Friday night date."

"Jeffrey, don't be a beta male," Jelena said. "If you want to get lucky, you've got to think outside the box."

"What Jelena means to say," I added, before Jeffrey could take offense, "is that, like the animals in the documentary, you need to persevere against the odds."

"We want you to put more thought into the courtship ritual," Lindsay added. "We think it's important for you to consider what women really want."

Jeffrey looked as bewildered as Freud probably had when writing upon the subject after a lifetime of study.

"Chocolate?" he tried.

"That's true, a lot of the time," I admitted, impressed by his insight. Jeffrey looked happier. "But when a woman is observing your courtship dance, there are two main things she's evolutionarily programmed to look for, whether she's conscious of it or not. Lindsay?"

"If you want to impress a woman, it's all about *protecting* and *providing*," Lindsay said. "Obviously, in this age, we're not saying women can't look after themselves both financially and emotionally. The protection and providing they're seeking are a little different from what they might have been traditionally. Protection might be listening to a girl talk about her bad day or lending her your sweater if she's cold. Providing might be buying her popcorn at the movies or getting her a bottle of water if it's hot and you can tell she's thirsty."

"Providing can be material, let's face it," Jelena said. "Girls like gifts. Even in the animal world, the male often presents the female with elaborate offerings. Aurora, can you skip ahead to the bowerbird part?"

I hit the Fast Forward button and stopped at the beginning of the sequence showing a male bowerbird gathering bits of grass and straw for his bower. A time-lapse sequence showed the nesting quickly progress from humble beginnings to a tentlike shape resplendent with blue objects scattered here and there.

"Once the structure is complete, the male bird begins his wait," the voice-over noted. "Until a female appears, he will fuss over the decorative elements, often painting the walls of the bower with smashed berries, doing his utmost to fine-tune all elements so that a potential mate will be impressed."

"Now *that* is effort," Jelena said, as a female bird showed up and inspected the bower with a critical gaze. "If a guy built me a house and decked it out with shiny things, I would definitely say yes to a date."

"I'm saving for a house, but that's kind of like fifteen years away, what with how much I earn from working at the supermarket. Am I going to be single for fifteen years?" Jeffrey looked terrified at his inability to provide to the level of Jelena's expectations.

"Maybe—" Jelena started.

"No!" I cut her off. "Jeffrey, neither Lindsay nor I are dating guys who've presented us with fully furnished apartments. But Jelena's right in one way: girls like effort and planning. The best way to demonstrate this is by asking them out on a date."

"And the more thoughtful and unusual the date, the more the girl knows that you don't see her as a hookup." Lindsay said.

"Unfortunately, even though it wasn't the case, that was what Ruby and Jemima got suspicious of," I explained to Jeffrey. "So, in order to avoid a repeat situation, we suggest you ask Piper out on a special date."

"Okay, so plan a romantic and interesting date. What else?" Jeffrey, to his credit, had grabbed a notepad.

"Be a good listener," I added. "Girls will give you all the secrets about what they truly want if you focus on what they say and don't tune out. Say a girl mentions she likes strawberry ice cream. When you invite her over to watch a movie a couple of weeks later, you can have a pint waiting. Major points scored."

"It's when boys stop talking to their girlfriends that things go wrong," Lindsay said sagely.

I looked over at her, wondering where she was at with Tyler.

Jeffrey nodded furiously as he scrawled down our tips.

"Women want romance, conversation, commitment, and consideration," I summarized. "It's pretty simple, really."

"Did you get all of that?" Jelena said, looking sternly at Jeffrey. She was keenly aware that her election hung on his adoption of these courting essentials.

"How was your date?" I asked Lindsay, as she took the seat next to me at Monday morning assembly.

She'd canceled our post-Jeffrey catch-up because Tyler had planned a surprise for Sunday afternoon.

"We went to a restaurant on the beach."

"Sounds lovely."

"It should have been. It's funny . . . When I was sitting there watching the waves crash higher and higher up the sand, I started thinking of the weirdest thing. Do you remember that speech from *Julius Caesar* we did for English last year?"

"'There is a tide in the affairs of men, which, taken at the flood, leads on to fortune'—that's the one, right?"

"The last few lines kept running through my head: 'On such a full sea are we now afloat, and we must take the current when it serves, or lose our ventures.' I feel like last week's camp was the high tide for me and Tyler. He should have gone with the current while it was there."

"But that's the whole thing with *Julius Caesar*, remember? It's all about fate versus free will. Do you think fate is guiding you and Tyler? Or do you think you can turn the tide yourself?"

"I don't know," Lindsay said. "I'm going by what I'm feeling, and I feel so different from this time last week."

We fell silent as Mr. Quinten took the stage. "Well, it's a musical extravaganza today, as we've got Hunter Greene and the school orchestra performing something very special."

The orchestra members filed onstage and Hunter approached the mike.

"Good morning. Today we'll be performing a piece by Hector Berlioz. I thought I'd tell you a little bit about it before we begin, so you can understand the work in its context. Berlioz, a French Romantic composer, is one of my favorites to perform, not only because of the emotional power of his compositions but also because he was inspired by other art forms of his time, notably literature. Last week, I was telling someone the story of Berlioz and how he was simultaneously introduced to Shakespeare—whose work would become a defining inspiration for him—and the love of his life, Harriet Smithson, on the same night."

The audience, which had seemed distracted and bored when Hunter started speaking, had gone quiet, waiting to hear more.

"In 1828, when Berlioz was a struggling young musician, he attended two Shakespeare productions—*Hamlet* and *Romeo and Juliet*. Not only was he completely enthralled by Shakespeare's genius, he also saw Harriet Smithson, an Irish-born actress, playing the parts of Ophelia and Juliet, and fell head over heels for her. Berlioz was a pretty intense guy by nature, and he set about pursuing Harriet relentlessly. He sent love letter after love letter to the hotel where she was staying, but his heavy-handed approach scared her and she rejected him.

"Berlioz poured all of his unrequited feelings for her into the *Symphonie Fantastique*, which is the story of a young artist who falls hopelessly in love with his dream girl. The work was a tremendous success; however, Harriet and Berlioz didn't meet again until four years later, in 1832, when *Symphonie Fantastique* was performed in Paris. Berlioz sent Harriet tickets for the best seats in the house, hoping she would attend. She did show up, and when she realized that this remarkable piece was based on Berlioz's regard for her, she began crying. A year later, she and Berlioz were married."

A chorus of *Ahhs* broke out among the girls, including me. I couldn't believe I hadn't heard this story before. To have a man so in love with you that he created a symphony—now that was a Potential Prince!

Hunter continued. "Today we'll be playing the first two movements for you. I hope you enjoy them. And to the person I first shared this story with last week: this is for you."

Hunter sat down with the orchestra and put his violin to his chin. I scanned the room for Chloe. It was obviously meant for her—I'd overheard her and Hunter rhapsodizing about classical composers while at camp. There she was! Her eyes were glowing as she watched Hunter.

Jelena, sitting next to me, had also turned to look at Chloe. Now she swung around and gave me a thumbs-up. I gave her one back.

Even though I had faith in the Find a Prince/Princess™ program, I was shocked at how fast it had worked. For someone as quiet as Hunter to be making a public declaration, he had to be enraptured with Chloe. Just like Berlioz, he obviously fell hard once presented with the right girl. And my program was responsible for delivering that girl. As I sat there, letting the extraordinary music wash over me, imagining Chloe and Hunter holding hands, come election day, my heart squeezed happily. Finding true love for other people gave me almost as great a thrill as knowing Hayden was mine.

When the piece finished, everyone sat in silence before breaking into enthusiastic applause. It wasn't every day that classical music got high school students excited, but Hunter's story had set the scene, helping us understand the emotion of the music.

Lindsay looked absolutely blown away. "I can't believe it!"

"I know!" I said. "I never saw this coming!"

"Aurora . . ." Lindsay looked like she wanted to either cry or say something hugely important. "You know how Hunter was talking about passion—"

"Linds, passion means different things to different people," I cut in. "Tyler might not write you symphonies, but he does love you to pieces."

For some reason, what I'd said seemed to make Lindsay unhappier rather than boosting her spirits.

"Aurora, I can't work with Hunter and Chloe anymore."

"What?" This was out of the blue.

"I don't feel comfortable, not after what happened."

"Hunter's comment the other night? Lindsay, you can't let his take on passion make you doubt your own relationship choices."

"Trust me on this one." Lindsay's face was troubled. "I'm happy to keep helping out with Jeffrey and Sara. I wouldn't bow out unless I knew that you were more than capable of assisting Chloe to find the right man."

I wanted to press her further for an explanation, but something told me not to. "Which is evidently Hunter," I said, instead.

Lindsay remained silent.

"You don't think he's a good match for her?"

I was really worried now. Had Lindsay found out something negative about Hunter during their time together at camp? Was that why she didn't want to be around him?

"No, he's very compelling," she said. "It's just—"

"Good morning, everyone."

Lindsay and I looked to the front as Alex's voice came over the microphone. He'd come onto the stage while we'd been immersed in our conversation.

"I thought I'd use today's assembly to update you on a policy that I'm introducing as part of my campaign. Three weeks ago, my fellow candidate Jelena Cantrill discussed how many hours we spend at Jefferson."

Jelena immediately sat bolt upright.

"I believe it came to two hundred and eighty thousand eight hundred minutes," Alex said. "That got me thinking. As you know from the group workouts we've been conducting at the gym, I'm all about efficiency—that is, using your time wisely to maximize results. What I want to propose today is that we start to think about our school day like we think about our workouts. Just like exercise, more time spent doesn't always equal better gains. That's why I'm not proposing social events or excursions as part of my campaign. These things really only maximize the amount of time you spend at Jefferson, and honestly, if you've got a healthy life balance, there should be plenty of after-school activities that you're excited about attending anyway. I'm all about making the hours when you are required to be at Jefferson work more efficiently for you. Playing with time, if that's what you want to call it."

"Oh, don't go with the *I have godlike powers* angle," Jelena muttered under her breath.

"You all know how blurry you feel when you arrive at school at eight a.m.," Alex continued. "The coffee hasn't kicked in and you're already being asked to work out math problems. But what if it didn't have to be this way? Recently, detailed studies have shown that at least twenty percent of high school students microsleep at least once during their school day."

"More like once every ten minutes!" Travis yelled out.

Alex laughed. "Scientists know that the teen brain is still developing and requires about nine hours of sleep a night, which many students, due to travel and the early start, miss out on. This affects their performance at school, which in turn has an impact upon their grades. The consequences of this can be severe in senior year, when your final grades are crucial to winning a spot at your university of choice. So, what if we rethought the school day? What if seniors had an extra hour of sleep and began at nine a.m.?"

His suggestion caused immediate chaos. Students were cheering and stamping their feet in approval.

"Many parents on the school board may find this revolutionary, but it's their children's futures at stake!" Alex shouted over the microphone, as teachers tried to regain control of the room. "What I'm talking about isn't a first. The One Hour Later approach has been tested at a number of schools, and scientists found that not only did teachers report their students were more alert and focused throughout the day but also depression among students dived.

"Now, I need to be straight with you," Alex warned. "This isn't a change that can happen the very day I get voted in."

"The day *I* get voted in!" Jelena was gripping the arms of her seat, visibly restraining herself. "He might want to remind himself that there are two other candidates in the running."

I could tell how upset she was. Alex's suggestion was the most radical to ever be put forward by a school president candidate. Even though Jelena was undeniably popular and had run a compelling campaign so far, it was hard to compete with what Alex was offering.

"In most schools, the introduction of the program took about a year to trial and officially approve," Alex said.

There were groans, and Jelena looked slightly appeased.

"But we're talking about great change here, people, and that takes time. Let's face it, this is way better than extra class trips or vanity items in the girls' bathrooms. Ladies, hair straighteners might be a nice lure, but your looks are going to benefit more from extra beauty sleep. For all you guys who've been coming to the gym with me, this is the extra rest time that your bodies need to repair torn muscle fibers and build that physique you're training so hard to achieve. So, by jumping on board and voting for me, most of you will gain yourselves a year of extra sleep-ins throughout senior year. If our school year is roughly thirty-nine weeks, then I work that out to be about eleven thousand seven hundred extra minutes of sleep gained. Not bad. So vote Alex West for school president!"

The applause and cheers were ear-shattering. Mr. Quinten was barely able to wrap up the assembly.

Jelena was almost purple with suppressed rage as she marched out of the auditorium. "What a bunch of lies. There's no way he'll get that type of thing passed, what with teacher-and-parent politics!"

"Actually . . ." Alex popped up behind us. "As I said, this type of change has been implemented in a number of schools."

"Mr. Quinten's never going to let this get through to the school board. He's an army man. He's all about discipline and rising early," Jelena said.

She stopped walking and wheeled around to face Alex. Alex stopped too, and a crowd gathered to watch what looked like a showdown.

"Funny you say that, because Mr. Quinten's actually really interested in One Hour Later," Alex replied coolly. "He's concerned about the stress levels among our senior students. I've already set up a meeting for him on Wednesday with my uncle, who's on the board of education. He's overseen many of the schools that have decided to reconfigure their school days." Alex smiled, looking like a cat that had backed a mouse into a corner. "You know, you can't let my personal rejection of you color this entire election, Jelena. Remember, this is about the students, not your dented ego."

Jelena's eyes resembled Medusa's—I was surprised the fury in them didn't turn Alex to stone.

"That's enough, Alex," Hayden said. "If you want to know the opinion of someone who's on the student council, it's going to take considerable effort on your part for your fellow students to see you as the honest type."

"Everyone will realize, before long, that my reputation was unfairly blackened," Alex replied, before heading off to class.

Jelena shook her head. "He's delusional. Thanks, Hayden."

Hayden gave her a smile, then ducked around to give me a quick kiss on the cheek before he headed off to his math class.

Sara wandered up, pushing Johannes in his wheelchair. She had spent most of the past two days by his side.

"Alex won't win," she told Jelena. "Everyone remembers what he did to you and Aurora. Do our schoolmates want a leader who's capable of things like that?"

"For an hour more sleep, most of our schoolmates would forgive anything!" Jelena looked infuriated.

"Maybe you could campaign for the same idea?" I suggested.

"And look weak to the entire student body?" Jelena replied. "Everyone at school will just assume I have no confidence in my own platform and have to copy his as a fail-safe. I'm not going there." She let out a frustrated sigh. "You know what's going to happen if he gets in. He'll be a complete tyrant and make our lives hell."

"Well, we can't let him," Sara said. "Just let us know what we can do to support you. Posters, badges, slogans—whatever. We're behind you one hundred percent."

Jelena and Sara might butt heads occasionally, but I knew Sara didn't like seeing Jelena bullied by an alpha male.

"Are you fully on board with the Find a Prince/Princess program, then?" Jelena asked Sara. "It's crucial. There are a number of people at Jefferson who value what we have to offer, and I want to prove to them that Aurora's ideas work."

"I promised I'd act loved up with Johannes if you needed me to," Sara replied, without hesitation.

Johannes looked put out. "Act?"

"Johannes, you know that my focus is my career," Sara said, squatting down next to his wheelchair. "I had so much fun hanging out with you this weekend, and I'm sure you would make a perfect boyfriend for any girl, but I'm not looking for that. I want to be your friend, though, very much."

Johannes looked glumly at the ground. It was obvious he'd gotten his hopes up after having Sara as his nurse all weekend. I could tell Sara had developed an affection for Johannes, too, because her lips turned downward as she watched his face fall. She quickly moved closer and pressed them to his cheek. Johannes looked up with a start.

Sara put her hand on his arm. "For the greater good of Jefferson High, we need to ensure Jelena wins." Sara looked at Johannes with pleading eyes. "Some hugs and kisses while we pretend to be a couple for two weeks can't be that bad, right?"

I couldn't tell what was going through Johannes's mind after Sara's offer. Maybe he was insulted at the idea of playacting as her boyfriend when he clearly wanted the real thing. I felt kind of guilty running a program where we promised love and then delivered a facade. But who was to say that Sara wouldn't be won over? This was Johannes's chance to convince Sara how great a boyfriend (and how understanding of her career) he could be.

As I watched him nod his agreement to Sara's proposal, I realized this was probably his thinking as well.

"Okay. But this kissing you speak of, it must start now," he said. "We have to build support for the campaign quickly."

Sara shrugged. "Okay." She pecked Johannes's cheek again, happy to have gotten her way.

Johannes shook his head, looking disapproving. "That is never going to win us the election, Sara. If we are a couple—a *new* couple—then there are no pecks. It should be kisses that are . . . like what you call snogging."

And with that, his lips landed on Sara's.

I clapped a hand over my mouth to smother a gasp. Lindsay

wasn't so discreet—she let out a soft shriek. Jelena smiled her first smile since Alex's announcement. We tried not to stare as Johannes put his all into this very public kiss. Throngs of students started whispering and pointing as the kiss stretched on. Sara's hands were tensed against Johannes's chest, as if to push him away, but as his mouth caressed hers, her fingers relaxed. Johannes pulled her onto his lap in one quick motion, so they were cuddled up together on the wheelchair.

"Break it up!" Mr. Quinten said, tapping Johannes on the shoulder as he went by.

Johannes pulled away. Sara's mouth was red from the passionate kiss. She sat in his lap, looking stunned.

"That's a kiss that will win us an election," Johannes said firmly.

"Sara, I got a shot of the kiss," Jelena said. "I'm uploading it and adding tags of the two of you. It's so good to know I have your support! Johannes, are you happy with the picture? We could always repeat the kiss if you aren't."

"We're late for class." Sara leaped up from Johannes's lap and started pushing his wheelchair down the path.

"Okay, I'll tag this one then!" Jelena shouted after them. "Album: Find a Prince/Princess Program: Successes!"

"You're thinking the same thing I am, aren't you?" I said to her. "Sara's going to start feeling it for real."

"I'm just happy that we have one sure result from the three couples," Jelena said matter-of-factly.

She could make out that she was all about power and position, but I could tell that matters of the heart were just as important to her as they were to me.

Chloe came running up and threw her arms around me. "I hope you can add a second success story to the list. Aurora, I nearly cried like Harriet did during the *Symphonie Fantastique*. I couldn't believe it. I mean, we basically spent the whole last two days of camp together, and he was texting me almost every hour over the weekend, until we had our date yesterday—"

"You guys had a date?"

I felt totally out of the loop. I'd kind of hoped the candidates would allow me to arrange any meet-ups, like I had originally proposed. That way, I'd be able to tailor the location and activity to the couple.

"I didn't have your number," Chloe said. "I messaged you on Facebook, hoping you'd give me some tips, but I didn't see a reply, so I ended up going."

"I'm really sorry, Chloe," I said.

With everything else happening over the weekend, I'd completely forgotten to check my texts, let alone my Facebook.

Chloe laughed. "Don't be silly! He took me out on the family sailboat. We talked a lot about our former relationships. It's so great to hang out with a guy who's open about his past and his relationship wounds. I was able to be honest in return. And then, today! He's told me several times how cautious he is, after what he went through with his ex, so that public mention of Berlioz and Harriet was a huge thing. Aurora, I don't want you to set me up with anyone else. I think Hunter might be the one."

Seemed like Hunter wasn't the only one who fell fast and hard. "Are you sure?" I said. "You've only been set up with two of your three matches. Benjamin's decided to focus on his career for the time being, but I'm more than happy to arrange things with a third candidate. That way, you can ensure you've evaluated all your options."

I was hardly the type to discourage the notion of love at first sight, but I felt a responsibility. I hadn't organized their date or held a postdate analysis with either Chloe or Hunter. I was supposed to be an impartial third party, ensuring that the essential elements of a successful relationship were present.

Chloe brushed away my worries. "Aurora, I don't need to. I have this amazing feeling."

"Aurora's just modest," Jelena replied for me. "She's a little stunned by how effective her techniques really are."

"I have faith in the program's fundamentals, but are you sure it's wise for Chloe to throw out her other match?" I asked Jelena, after Chloe had virtually skipped off to class. "We're still two weeks from the election."

"Aurora, that performance at the assembly this morning said it all. Hunter's crazy over Chloe, and she feels the same way. So why worry?"

"Let me think about it overnight," I said. If I was still concerned tomorrow, I'd have a chat with both Chloe and Hunter.

25

"So was Johannes's kiss like this?" Hayden asked. "Fast and furious?" His lips moved over mine frantically, as if we were a hero and heroine reunited after a lengthy wartime separation. "Or long and lingering?" His lips traced mine with agonizing slowness before he deepened the kiss.

How could kissing be so much fun? Now that I'd finally stopped almost hyperventilating every time Hayden moved close to me, I felt like I was addicted to it. As soon as he'd arrived at my place after school (the NAD and Ms. DeForest had gone to their Monday *prana* yoga class then out for dinner afterward), my lips had met his before they'd even formed a hello. Now I was sitting on his lap on the couch and kissing some more.

When we finally broke away from each other, I looked at the clock and gasped. "How is it seven p.m.? I put this clock here so I'd know to stop kissing you after fifteen minutes! Three hours have passed!"

"That clock is no fun." Hayden hid it behind a couch cushion.

I grabbed it back. "We're running out of time to watch the movie."

"I warn you, John Keats is only going to heighten the romance."

Hayden pulled away from me reluctantly, got up, and reached

for his schoolbag, taking out a DVD. Since Keats is my favorite poet, Hayden had told me we had to watch *Bright Star* together.

As we cozied up together on the couch, I was transported to a world where a young, impoverished Keats courted the object of his affections, Fanny Brawne, and created poetry about the sacredness of young love.

"Breathtaking, isn't it?" Hayden whispered, as we watched hundreds of butterflies fluttering about Fanny's room.

Hayden had to grab the tissues at the end, though, as Keats and Fanny were forced to say an agonizing good-bye. Keats was leaving for Rome in the faint hope that the warm weather would improve his health, despite the fact that he was suffering from incurable consumption. It was clear they both knew they would never see each other again in that lifetime.

"I think you're close to the end of the box," Hayden teased, as I wiped my eyes for the umpteenth time after the film ended, trying to pull myself together.

"It was so unfair," I whispered, barely getting the words past the lump in my throat. "Think how many people nowadays give up on love or treat it lightly. Keats and Fanny would have given anything to have the chances that we do, to live their lives out together."

"Life is always fragile," Hayden said seriously. "You never know what might happen. That's why you and I have to promise each other never to take things for granted. We have to seize every moment."

"I promise," I said, taking his hand. "I know this is only the beginning, but you mean so much to me."

Hayden kissed me, taking my other hand and entwining our fingers like a bond against whatever might come.

"What happened to your face?" Jelena said in horror, as we all sat down at a picnic table for lunch the next day.

"I know, I know." I shook my head.

Last night's kissing session had taken its toll, despite how romantic it had been. The film hadn't intensified just our emotions; it had seemed to do the same thing to our kissing. We'd remained on the couch in the dark, kissing and whispering to each other as the film played on in the background, until Hayden's mom had called. She hadn't seemed happy—I'd heard her reminding him that it was 10:30 p.m. on a school night.

Waking up this morning with a red rash across my entire chin and upper lip area had been a rude shock. Although Hayden didn't have much facial hair yet, the friction of his skin against mine over what I estimated to be five hours of kissing was enough to make my face feel as if it had been sandpapered.

"Didn't Hayden come over last night?" Cassie asked mischievously.

"Even your nose is peeling," Sara said, giggling. "Isn't that slightly off the target?"

"We watched *Bright Star*," I said. "It's the most beautiful film I've ever seen." I pulled out my iPad. "Listen . . . I downloaded the soundtrack."

"*I never knew before, what such a love as you have made me feel, was; I did not believe in it*," Keats said, as the film's score played in the background.

"It's beautiful," Lindsay said, listening again. "I totally get it."

Jelena was still staring at my face. "How long did you guys make out for?"

"Five hours?"

The girls all cracked up. Sara nearly toppled off the end of the picnic bench.

"I know, it seems ridiculous," I said, "but it was our first actual date after Hayden's grounding."

"A little self-control, maybe?" Jelena sounded bemused. "Your skin's not going to stand up to another session like that between today and the weekend."

"I was all set on self-control, but now that I've seen that film, I don't want to waste any moment that could be spent feeling the way I do when I'm with him."

I'd always held Keats's proclamation "Love is my religion" as my mantra, but now that I knew the details of his story, the words had taken on an even greater meaning for me. What I'd also realized overnight was that I shouldn't caution Chloe about putting all her eggs into one basket when it came to Hunter. Carpe diem. They both knew what they wanted and they were going for it.

"Aurora, that's a big risk to take," Sara warned. "There are other important things in this world besides love. What if your relationship with Hayden falls through? You might regret making him your entire focus."

"She won't do anything too silly," Cassie told Sara. "It's natural to be somewhat obsessive at the start. I felt like I was floating instead of walking, when Scott and I first got together."

"So, do you think I should watch the movie?" Lindsay asked me. She'd looked it up on my iPad.

"Everyone should watch it," I said, as I closed my eyes and concentrated on Keats's voice again.

"I haven't stopped thinking about you all day," Hayden said to me, later that afternoon. We were lying on our backs on a picnic blanket in the park. It was the most beautiful autumn day and we were watching the clouds sail by, their whiteness startling against the crisp blue sky. "I think you've broken my brain."

I couldn't resist. "Wasn't it already broken?"

He rolled over onto his side and poked my shoulder. "It'd have to be, to fall for you. Four years of unrequited advances. You know, my dad once said the definition of madness is repeating the same action again and again, expecting a different result. And yet I hung on, teasing you day after day, hoping my witty comments would bring you around."

I reached for his hand to kiss it. "Maybe you were like a piece of sand in an oyster's shell. You annoyed me and annoyed me until I realized you were a pearl."

I winked at him, and he made a face.

My phone rang. I sat up to grab it from my handbag.

"Nope." Hayden grabbed the phone from me. "We've only got an hour until we both have to be home for dinner, and I don't want to share even one of those sixty minutes." He looked at the caller ID. "Jeffrey can wait, can't he?"

"I promised to be fully available to my matchmakees during the campaign period," I said. "I have to take this."

Hayden handed me the phone.

"Jeffrey," I answered the call.

"Babe," Jeffrey said. "I think I have my courtship dance all choreographed."

"So you're ready to make a move on Piper?"

When we met on Sunday, I'd let Jeffrey know who his final match was. Turned out they shared a chemistry class together and Piper's lab area was right next to his. Jeffrey had long been hoping to cause a non-school-based reaction of his own.

"I've kicked butt on that already, Aurora. At the start of chemistry today, I offered to help Piper set up her Bunsen burner. You know, this chivalry thing really works with chicks. She's never noticed me before, but when I started pulling out the beakers she was totally grateful.

"Anyway, I let her go on about all these girly things, without interrupting, like you advised. Most of it was kind of confusing, like how her best friend bought the same dress as her for this music festival and Piper thinks it's totally bad or something. Anyway, after all of that, I found out she has a thing for French food. My dad went to some fancy-schmancy place recently, and when I said the name, she flipped out. I saw my chance and asked her if she wanted to check it out Friday night. I was expecting her to say no, but you're not going to believe it—it worked! For the first time *ever*!"

"Good job, Jeffrey!" I was so proud of him.

"I did good, right?" He sounded thrilled. "So, do you have any other tips for Friday?"

"Take her flowers," I advised. "Not red roses or a big bunch, because they're a tad much for a first date, but maybe a few lilies or something that smells nice. Something that says *This is a date*. Once you get to the restaurant, make sure you open doors for her and pull her chair out. Let her do a lot of the talking during the meal, like you did today. I've been out with so many guys who go on about themselves the whole time."

Hayden let out a snort. I knew he was remembering a few of my previous lackluster dates.

"That said, you have to make sure you talk about yourself enough to allow her to build a positive picture of you."

"Okay . . ."

I could tell Jeffrey was confused. "I'll come over tomorrow night and do some role-play with you, okay? We'll get it down pat."

I smiled as Jeffrey hung up. He might be the class clown, but he was certainly endearing in his way. I was hoping that Piper would realize that, too.

"Ah, the inside story on what impresses women," Hayden said. "Jeffrey's going to have an edge with all this coaching. I never knew when to stop going on about myself, back when I was courting you. You thinking I was arrogant and a know-it-all seemed to be the only thing that got a passionate response."

"You bumbled your way through it."

I put my phone down beside me and reached over to kiss his forehead. Hayden tried to turn it into an actual kiss.

"Hayden, I'm sorry, my face is killing me . . ."

"Now *I'm* Lethal Lips." Hayden sighed, wrapping me up in his arms instead.

I'd never felt safe like this in my whole life. Being in someone's arms was like a warm bath on a cold day or sheets fresh out of the dryer. Utter reassurance. Since Mom had left, I hadn't had a lot of cuddles. Sure, Dad and I had a great bond, and he always gave me a quick hug before I went to bed, but it wasn't like this. My brain, always in chatter mode, overanalyzing every aspect of my life, seemed to slow to a pleasant hum while I was encircled by Hayden's arms. My breathing became a steady rhythm and I felt like I might drift away to dreamland any minute. I yawned and realized that my lips were in permanent smile mode.

The phone rang again.

"Don't get it." Hayden's voice sounded sleepy, but he loosened his grip around me, obviously resigned to the fact that I was on matchmaker duty.

"It's Tyler." I was mystified. He'd never called me on my cell.

"Tyler, is Lindsay okay?"

"I'm calling you because I was hoping *you'd* be able to answer that question." He sounded miserable. "She's been so weird lately. I know I messed up by not going to camp, but I tried to make it up to her with the lunch, and I was planning on surprising her with Taylor Swift tickets—I know Lindsay's desperate to go. I bought two tickets the second they went on sale."

"Tyler, that's really sweet."

"I was going to give her the tickets tonight, but then we got into a totally weird fight. All over some film about a poet."

Uh-oh. "*Bright Star*?"

"That's the one. I was having a hard time following it, because I'm an action movie guy. I was trying because Lindsay seemed so into it, and then I made this comment about not getting why the poet guy—"

"Keats."

"Yeah, Keats, was so morbid. He was saying something about wanting his hour of death and that girl at the same time. He's like a vampire or something."

I got an image of John Keats and Edward Cullen side by side.

"Keats felt battered by the world," I explained. "He didn't mean graves or coffins when he talked about death; he envisaged escaping to a place with less suffering, accompanied by the one he loved."

Hayden was staring at me. Tyler was the last person you'd expect to be discussing John Keats.

"Well, Lindsay could have said that." Tyler sounded put out. "Instead, she leaped up from the couch, shouting that I didn't understand anything about passion."

I'd been right on yesterday with my suspicion about what was behind Lindsay's request not to work with Hunter. She'd obviously been hugely affected by his comment at camp.

"I don't get poetry, but I do know what I feel when I look at Lindsay," Tyler said. "I want to be around to cover her with a blanket anytime she's cold. I want to be cheering her on when she stages her fashion shows. And I know that when she laughs it makes me happier than anything else. Yes, I was an idiot at the beginning of the semester, but I learned my lesson when I lost her. Aurora, you need to help me. She won't even pick up the phone since she left my place. I tried driving around to hers, but her mom said she hadn't come home yet."

"Of course, Tyler. I'll call her right now," I said. "I'll call you back."

I hung up and immediately called Lindsay. No response. I didn't want to leave a message, because this was something we needed to talk about in person.

"Tyler and Keats?" Hayden asked.

"Let's just say Lindsay and Tyler's viewing of the film wasn't as successful as ours."

I kept calling Lindsay all evening, but the phone continued to ring unanswered. I even called her home phone, but Lindsay's mom said she was at a friend's. After texting around, I knew she wasn't at Jelena's, Cass's, or Sara's. Maybe she was hanging out with one of her other friends from school, someone who wasn't so involved with the TylerandLindsay saga. I could understand how she might need some cooldown time after the *Bright Star* fight.

The next morning, I waited for her at her locker.

"Aurora, I know you were trying to reach me all night," Lindsay said, before I could even form any words. "I'm sorry. I was watching a DVD with a friend and I'd put my phone on silent after having a fight with Tyler."

"Tyler called me, which is why I was worried about you . . ."

"Tyler complained to you?" Lindsay sighed as she got her books out of her locker. "I'm really sorry."

"Linds, it's no problem. I'm happy to talk about things with both you and Tyler if—"

"That's exactly what I don't want," Lindsay interrupted. "I need to come to my own decision about my relationship. I don't want to end up holding anyone else responsible if I make a choice based on their advice. After all, nobody knows what truly goes on in a relationship except the two people involved."

"I'm worried that you might not realize how passionate Tyler is about you."

It was so easy for self-doubt to cloud your evaluation of your partner. I knew that firsthand. If Lindsay heard what Tyler had told me . . .

"Aurora, I know you're a matchmaker, but this time I really need you to butt out."

Lindsay shut her locker with a bang and headed off down the hall. I watched her, shocked. Even during the breakup with Tyler, she'd valued my opinion.

"She's not herself at all." Tyler joined me at her locker.

"She wants me and the girls to keep out of it," I said. "I think you're on your own with this one. I mean, I'm more than happy to advise you, but I can't plead your case with Lindsay."

"I'm not losing her again." Tyler's jaw was set.

"Why don't you wait till Friday, so she can calm down, and then give her the concert tickets?"

Tyler nodded. "I'll book a nice dinner for before the show, too. I need to bring out the big guns."

"Good luck, comrade."

It was hard to take a step back from being Ms. Relationship Fix-It, but I had to have faith in Tyler. He'd originally won Lindsay's heart, so he should be able to recapture it, right?

26

"Me! Hauled into the principal's office!!" Jelena ranted, as she joined Sara, Cass, and me at the school gate at the end of the day. "How stupid can people be? *May be insulting to people's religious beliefs*—they were buttons and bracelets! We aren't even a Christian school! Do Christians even own the acronym WWJD?"

Jelena had made some bracelets with the letters standing for What Would Jelena Do? instead of What Would Jesus Do?

"I think they took more offense at the banners paraded near the school entrance while the ice-cream truck was parked there," I said. "Apparently, some parents who were driving past to go to Saint Andrew's saw them and called Mr. Quinten to complain that the school was using Jesus for a political purpose."

"How many times do US presidential candidates talk about god in their campaigns?" Jelena pointed out. "I told Mr. Quinten that, but did he listen? No!" She let out a huge sigh. "Now we can't use the buttons *or* the bracelets. Money completely wasted."

"Small minds can't grasp great ideas, can they?" Alex said, approaching us.

"Buzz off, Alex," Jelena ordered. "I'm not in the mood to tolerate your gloating."

"This isn't gloating. I actually agree with you," Alex said, without a hint of sarcasm.

We all looked at him, wondering what twisted point he was trying to make.

"Before Mr. Quinten spoke with you, he was in a meeting with my uncle," Alex continued. "He thinks One Hour Later is a brilliant concept, but my uncle told me in confidence that Mr. Quinten said I was unlikely to get voted in. When it comes to the presidency, the student council counts for a third of the votes, and they have serious doubts about me because I haven't been at Jefferson for even a full term yet."

"Well, boo-hoo." Jelena's foot was tapping impatiently, like she was seconds from walking away. "I don't understand why you're telling me this."

"They have doubts about you, too," Alex said. "They did a preliminary poll yesterday, and Julie Rivers apparently has half the student council votes tied up."

"Julie? She's had no innovative ideas so far."

"She's the safe vote," Alex explained. "Her policies aren't controversial and won't cost very much, which is their concern with you. Hair straighteners, extreme sports trips—they all cost money."

"So what? The money comes from student fund-raising."

"Which the majority of the board members feel would be better spent on things like new carpets for the music room or IT resources. Basically, Julie's going to become school president unless either of us wins the student vote by a landslide."

"Hey, that could happen," Jelena said confidently.

"Currently, as my political spies tell me, our respective voters are torn between you or me. Half the guys are hyped up about my gym program, the other half are on board to do your Take It to Another Level stuff. Plenty of the girls want an extra hour of sleep and intend to vote for me, but an equal number say they won't vote for me because I'm seen as chauvinistic."

"Imagine that," Jelena shot back.

"So say, come election day, that there's an equal number of voters for you and me," Alex went on. "There's probably another third of kids at Jefferson who are just apathetic and will vote Julie in because they don't care. So, by my calculation, the votes will be around a third each, which gives it to Julie, if the student council swings her way. You and I have both been campaigning our butts off—I don't think there's anything more either of us can do on our own to win more votes." Alex paused. "Our only option is to join forces."

We all stared at him. Ever since he'd first announced he was running for president, he'd been dead set on beating Jelena.

"You mean you want me to join the dark side?" Jelena looked disgusted at the idea.

I didn't blame her. Working with the person who'd publicly humiliated her would seem like she was admitting defeat.

"I'm offering you the opportunity to be copresident of Jefferson. I understand if you're suspicious of that, but I can assure you this isn't an underhanded attempt to beat you. To prove it, I'm willing to draw up a legally witnessed document with Mr. Quinten to certify that our platforms will be equally implemented. That way, you'll know that I'm not going to do the wrong thing by you."

"Right. Because prior circumstances would never lead me to suspect that."

Jelena was far from convinced, and neither were the rest of us.

"Look, I know I was a jerk to you. And to Aurora." Alex turned to me. "If you want to know the truth, my parents announced they were divorcing the same week all of that stuff went down. If I'm honest with myself, I was a pretty foul person because of it."

Jelena, Cass, Sara, and I all looked at each other. It was hard to know what to think about Alex's new revelation.

"All personal stuff aside, you and I are very similar," Alex said. "We both want to be leaders. We're the Napoleons of the world. You know this already, Jelena—that's why, before all that stuff happened, we got along remarkably well."

Jelena's poker face remained. "I need time to think about this."

"You'll need to think quickly," Alex said. "The election date's twelve days away. We need to use that time to build support for us as a couple." He turned and walked away.

"Jelena, no. You can't!" Sara cried, as soon as he was out of earshot. "A couple? Ugh. If he behaved without honor when you guys were dating, he's not going to be trustworthy once you're both voted in."

"That thing about his parents was major, though," Cass said, quick as always to forgive those suffering misfortune. "I mean, he's far from the sensitive type, but maybe the way he acted was exaggerated by stress."

"Plenty of other people's parents separate and they don't do what he did to Jelena. It's no excuse." Sara's tone was absolute.

I didn't know what to think. I'd been a wreck when my mom left, and what had I done? Immediately pushed Hayden away. I'd been pretty cruel, and it had taken me a long time to see that. Maybe it was hypocritical for me to cast Alex as a total villain. Then again, he'd devastated my best friend. He'd pursued her publicly, then dumped her for me as soon as he heard about my (short-lived) modeling contract. And then he'd lied about us both, and the majority of our classmates had believed him. Why should we give him another chance to do something equally bad down the line?

"This isn't a debate about the motivations behind his past behavior," I said. "This is about the next year and a half and whether it's a good idea to have Alex by your side, Jelena. I don't think you should be so quick to assume that you can't win this thing on your own. So you and Alex currently have equal votes—that could change in the next twelve days. Maybe you need to propose some more practical ideas, make the school board realize that you have a grounded approach instead of being all about glamour."

"I need to think about this." Jelena pulled her sneakers out of her bag and hurriedly put them on. "I'm going to the gym."

The only time Jelena ever used her family's membership at the health club was when she had major things to ponder.

"We should talk about this further!" Cass called after her.

"Can't! Too confused!" Jelena shouted back, breaking into a sprint.

"She can't agree to a copresidency with him," Sara said.

"She won't," I assured her. "Jelena will see it as conceding defeat. She'll want to win or lose on her own terms. You wait . . . She'll march up to Alex tomorrow and tell him so."

The next morning at break, Cassie, Lindsay, Sara, and I sat waiting in one of the library booths. Jelena had texted us to meet her there.

"She obviously wants to reassure us that she's continuing to campaign alone," I told the girls, who all seemed edgy. "She'll have come up with some kick-butt ideas to put into practice over the next eleven days."

"She'd better." Sara was biting her nails.

Jelena swept into the room. She was smiling. I knew it! She'd obviously reworked her campaign approach and felt confident of its success.

"I know you won't be happy about this," she said, as she sat down, "but I've decided to run alongside Alex. I wanted to let you all know before Mr. Quinten makes the official announcement in twenty minutes."

"*What?*" It was a unanimous cry.

Ms. Carraway, the librarian, looked over at us, frowning.

"Jelena!" Sara's voice was a drawn-out moan.

"Why?" I asked. "You have a strong platform, the Find a Prince/Princess program is going great, and I'm sure we could have added a few appeasing options for the student council."

"You can still go back and tell Mr. Quinten you made a mistake," Cass said.

"Heck, *I'll* run down and tell him you made a mistake," Sara said, looking ready to bolt. "Because that's what it is—one very ugly, soon to get uglier, mistake."

"Jelena, we all pledged to help you," I said. "You don't need to do this."

"I do." Jelena's face was determined. "Being school president has been my goal ever since I set foot in Jefferson High, and I'm not risking a loss. The next year and a half is my time to establish my leadership credentials. From that point on, I'll be able to claim *I headed up a high school* on college applications. So I'm not spending my senior year watching Julie Rivers take the opportunity that should have been mine. If I go with Alex, I'm guaranteed to win."

"But it's Alex!" Sara tried to keep her voice down, despite her unhappiness. "You must feel, on a gut level, that teaming up with him is wrong?"

"This isn't about emotions," Jelena replied. "Yes, I spent half of last night convinced I couldn't spend the next year and a half sharing the decision making *plus* the glory with him, but you know what? Sometimes great challenges are demanded of true leaders. You know, Sun Tzu, who wrote *The Art of War*, was almost dead set against alliances? He believed they weakened a kingdom's rule and made it vulnerable to false friends. Except in one circumstance: when an alliance furthered the opportunities of both parties and increased their overall position. He suggested that a leader should use an alliance like a man crossing a river uses stepping stones—as a way to move toward your absolute goal. This situation with Alex, it's only a minute part of my overall grand plan."

"Okay, I get it," I said. Jelena had obviously given this a lot of thought. "But a year and a half might not feel like a short amount of time if you guys are constantly at loggerheads. You get infuriated by his attitude now, so how is it going to be any different when you're trapped in a stalemate during a student council meeting?"

"Jelena, it's Alex!" Sara wailed again. "A misogynist is going to be leading this school!"

"Coleading," Jelena said firmly. "I'm strong enough to hold my own against him. Plus, we've got a contract. We had it witnessed by Mr. Quinten."

"What did Mr. Quinten say?" I asked.

"He was surprised when I proposed it, but by the end he'd embraced the idea. He likes the idea of a boy–girl team as opposed to a single candidate. He thinks we might be more effective as a duo."

"No, no, no," Sara muttered under her breath.

Cassie and Lindsay looked depressed. My stomach was in knots. I knew there was no hope of talking her out of it now.

"So our Find a Prince/Princess program falls under Alex's control?" I asked.

I couldn't think of anything worse. The idea of having to report to a relationship cynic made my spirits sink further.

"No, that part of the campaign's my jurisdiction." Jelena got out her notebook. "Alex is happy to leave you, me, and Lindsay to manage it. Here's a copy of the contract so you feel reassured. You'll notice we're combining the sports elements into one—the gym memberships will become a regular thing, while the extreme trips will be once a semester. One Hour Later is a key factor and will need both of us focusing on it."

"You can be practical all you want, but this is a disaster waiting to happen," Sara said, looking absolutely miserable.

Jelena shook her head. "Ye of little faith. I'd better head back to the office. Mr. Quinten wants Alex and me to explain our decision after he's officially announced it."

After she left, we all let out a collective sigh.

"I guess we've got no choice but to believe her when she says she can handle it," I said. "She's tough, and I'm sure that tenacity will see her through all of this. Still, I don't envy her the senior year ahead. Alex is going to present a whole heap of challenges for her in the next eighteen months."

27

Hayden had bought us tickets for an action thriller on Friday night. I was so engrossed in both it *and* not spilling my popcorn in a three-foot-wide radius, like I usually do, that I was shocked to see I had three missed calls on my phone when the credits rolled on the screen.

I looked at the caller ID as Hayden and I filed out of the theater. "Uh-oh, it's Jeffrey. I hope nothing's gone wrong on his date."

"How could it?" Hayden said. "You were over at his place prepping him for two hours on Wednesday night. Plus, didn't he text you to say that she was on her way, earlier? She obviously didn't cancel on him."

I could tell by Jeffrey's hello when he answered the phone that everything wasn't okay.

"Aurora, it's happened again. They all think I'm obsessed with hooking up or something. Can you come over?"

When Hayden and I reached Jeffrey's house, he opened the door, looking serious. It was odd to see him without his usual wide smile.

"I hope you don't mind Hayden being here," I said. "We were at the movies, so we've come straight from there."

"Can you be understanding of a brother's suffering?" Jeffrey asked Hayden, as he ushered us through to his living room.

"Hayden's the sensitive type," I assured Jeffrey, shooting a glance at Hayden as he tried not to smile at Jeffrey's melodramatic tone. "So, what happened during the dinner?"

"It's what happened *after* dinner that made things go kaput." Jeffrey collapsed onto a couch. "I never get anywhere with chicks!"

"Jeffrey, if you got shot down for a good-night kiss, believe me, it happens all the time," Hayden said, sitting down on the couch opposite him. "As Aurora can tell you, girls are picky with kisses."

"Definitely." I sat down next to Hayden, feeling more reassured. "These things take time. Boys often see kissing as just a little fun, whereas girls see it as proof of a connection. Give it another couple of dates."

"The only part of her that wanted to get close to me was the palm of her hand." Jeffrey lifted his own hand to his cheek and winced. It was then I noticed that the right side of his face was redder than the left.

"She slapped you?" Hayden and I said in unison.

"I did everything you said, Aurora! I pulled her chair out, I let her do the talking, I paid for the meal. I was killing it! She totally cracked up when I made a chicken out of my napkin. Then, after we left the restaurant, I asked if she wanted to come back to my place so I could show her some of the comedy DVDs I'd been telling her about. And she said yes! To top that off, Mom and Dad are away. Home alo-o-one! So we get home, we watch a DVD, she's curled up on the couch next to me, and I feel like a king instead of a joker."

"And then?" It was painful listening to Jeffrey's excitement, knowing that he was literally about to get a slap in the face.

"Then she asks where the bathroom is. I pointed her down the hall, and while she was in there I had a revelation. Like, this girl is totally bangin'—she's funny, she's hot, she's actually on my couch. Now's the moment to do the bowerbird."

"The what?" Hayden looked confused.

Jeffrey shook his head. "Oh, man. How did you ever land a woman? You know, putting yourself out there for the ladies? Showing them your best courting action?"

"We watched a documentary on animal courtship, focusing on the efforts made by the male," I explained to Hayden.

"So I thought, what's the human equivalent of the bowerbird's nest? And then it hit me. I wanted to provide comfort and romance at the same time, so why not the hot tub?"

I was starting to get a bad feeling about this. "You have a hot tub?"

"In our backyard. It's a beast. Completely decked out with jets. Piper told me at dinner that she was all achy from basketball practice, so while she was in the bathroom I grabbed some of my mom's tea lights. There was a bunch of red roses on the kitchen sill that Dad had given Mom on Monday, so I pulled the petals off and scattered them around the tub. I loaded the CD player with some choice music. I'd been thinking Beyoncé, but there was already a CD of Mom's in there called *Mood Music*. So, perfect, right?"

I inwardly groaned. Hayden shot me a look. He knew as well as I did that Jeffrey had set himself up for disaster.

"Piper came out of the bathroom while I was trying to catch my breath. No wonder all those animal dudes end up dead, Aurora—romance is exhausting." Jeffrey flopped back on the couch again. "Anyway, she gave me a funny look, 'cause I was breathing hard, and she asked what was up. I was worried about leaving the tea lights unsupervised near the wooden tub, so I told her I had a surprise. When I led her outside, she was blown away.

"She was all smiley for a moment and said she couldn't believe I'd done all of this for her."

That meant *Successful gesture* in girl language. What had gone wrong?

"Then I hit the hot tub lights, which are all different flashing strobes. It kinda makes it look like the grotto in the Playboy

Mansion. I said I wanted to get in the tub with her . . . I don't know what was wrong with that, but she suddenly looked scared and said she didn't have a suit. So I told her not to worry, she didn't need one. I'd turn down the lights so I wouldn't be able to tell she was naked."

I was horrified. "You told her she should get naked?"

I could see Hayden's shoulders shaking as he struggled not to laugh.

"Well, she didn't have a suit!" Jeffrey protested. "I wanted her to be able to get into the water. The jets are freaking amazing. So I hit the Play button on the portable dock, hoping some music would relax her, only . . ."

"What?" We might as well hear the catastrophic ending.

"It was that song with the line 'Let's get it on,'" Jeffrey finished, looking nervously at me. "I didn't know that song was on there, I swear!"

There was no recovering from this situation. I was going to have to call Piper to apologize. Nope, that wouldn't cut it. Jelena and I would have to send her flowers to apologize. Even then, we'd still have one very traumatized student on our hands.

"The next second, she slapped me, saying I had no respect for her and that inviting her for dinner was a ploy to get her naked." Jeffrey looked completely blindsided by female logic. "And worse, when I texted her later, she said she should have listened to Jemima and Ruby and that the three of them were going to post a warning about my 'Casanova tactics' all over social media so no other girl would make the mistake of falling for them. I just checked Facebook and it's true! Aurora, this is as bad as when Chloe set fire to that dude's stuff!"

"He was following the material; he just went slightly too fast," Hayden said, as we headed back down the front path. Jeffrey's place was only a few streets from mine, so we'd decided to walk home in the moonlight.

"But we practiced his approach! Never, during any role-play exercise, did Jeffrey use the word 'naked.'"

"No matter how many rehearsals, you can't control every aspect of the real thing," Hayden pointed out. "Jeffrey's real personality is always going to come to the fore in the end. He's quirky and a little bit of a smart aleck, and the right girl is going to get that about him. His perfect match would have laughed the whole thing off and told him he needed to make a bikini part of the surprise next time."

I gave Hayden a skeptical look. "I don't know. Most girls would have been pretty unnerved by the situation."

"You can't shape him into someone else to win over his matches. Sure, it might work for a while, but they're going to figure it out eventually. It's not fair to Jeffrey or the girls." Hayden reached for my hand. "There's nothing wrong with your program, Princess. You just need to realize that you can't rush these things."

"But I am in a rush." Didn't he get it? "It's ten days till the election deadline. Our classmates aren't going to wait around for months to see the matchmakees find their happily ever after; they want results on election day."

"You can't force what's unnatural," Hayden replied, like he hadn't even heard what I'd been saying.

"But quick chemistry can be natural. It worked perfectly fine for Chloe and Hunter."

"Well, I didn't want to say this, but in my opinion they're rushing in."

I stared at him. "Why are you being like this all of a sudden? It's my program and it hurts me to have you say you don't believe in it."

"I do believe in it, but—"

"What happened to your whole speech about seizing the moment?"

"I was talking about us. We aren't rushing in. We've known each other more than half our lives."

"If you know me so well, you should know that I believe in love at first sight," I said. "Extraordinary connections do happen. People are always making out like romantics aren't practical. It's insulting."

"Aurora." Hayden's voice was super serious. I could tell he was upset that we were fighting. "The reason I caution people about rushing in isn't because I think romantics are foolish. It's because there are some guys and girls who take advantage of other people's openheartedness. One of the reasons I'm crazy about you is that you have this innocence. You see the good in everyone and believe their hearts to be as loving as yours is. But the world isn't entirely made up of people like that."

"I know," I said. "But I believe that love can transform people. If it's great love and all encompassing, it takes away their cynicism and softens their hearts so that they're kinder and more compassionate to anyone they come into contact with. I want that for the world. And I need a boyfriend who supports what I'm trying to do."

"I created the chemistry calculator, Aurora. Of course I support you."

"Then start having a little faith in what could happen," I said. "That a guy and a girl can meet, and feel the way we do, and want to seize it without hesitation."

"Okay, for you, I will," Hayden said, as we reached my driveway. "Starting now, we're the carpe diem couple."

"Agreed."

I put my arms around him and it was as if the argument had never happened.

"You're at home today, aren't you?" the NAD asked, when I came down to breakfast the next morning.

Ms. DeForest placed a bowl of papaya at my spot at the table. "The enzymes are great for digestion."

I thanked her, then turned to Dad. "Well, Mom texted me. She asked if I had some time between one and five today. I'm not sure what she has planned, but I said that was fine. Why?"

I hadn't wanted to say the word "Mom" after last week. The NAD, Ms. DeForest, and I had point-blank ignored last Saturday's events. I was actually looking forward to seeing Mom. Things had felt different since the engagement party. She'd sent me a link to the inspiration boards that her wedding planner had put together, and she had actually asked my opinion. To be included in a major part of her life was a significant step forward in our relationship.

"We're having some people over today for a special ritual, and we'd like you to play a part in it," Dad said. "I texted Hayden this morning and he said he's happy to join us."

"We were planning to hold it at twelve thirty, since it's the most opportune time astrologically." Ms. DeForest's mouth was pursed, as if she'd discovered her papaya was rotten. "If you're leaving at one, then we have a problem. Can you tell your mother you're busy?"

"But it could be something to do with wedding preparation," I started, then stopped.

God, this was awkward. I'd already promised Mom, two days ago, that I was free. The NAD and Ms. DeForest could have said something earlier if they'd blocked out an appointment with the solar system.

"I'm sure she can handle it on her own," Ms. DeForest said. "Your father said she cancels on you all the time."

For some reason, even though that was the truth, it seemed harsher coming from someone of similar age to my mother. And realizing that the NAD had discussed with her my disappointments—which I'd never even shared with my friends—made me feel exposed and vulnerable.

The NAD could tell I was hurt. "What Dana meant to say is that this is a special occasion. We should have let you know earlier, but sometimes spiritual realizations come knocking at inconvenient times, like late last night. We've been lucky to round up the majority of our friends after only inviting them this morning."

"Fine," I said. "I'll see if she can pick me up at two thirty."

"I can't see why you can't give your father the whole afternoon," Ms. DeForest pressed. "He's given you his whole life as your full-time caregiver."

She made it sound like I was karmically indebted to him. He was my dad, after all; I hoped he didn't see sticking around as some burdensome sacrifice.

"Your loyalty should be to him, not to a woman who didn't want to be a mother," Ms. DeForest went on.

That was enough. She might be living here, but that didn't give her the right to judge my personal relationships. She'd crossed the line. I got up from the table, feeling like I'd been kicked in the chest.

"Dad, I know she's our guest, but I'm not sitting here listening to this. She's got no right to make comments about the situation between me and Mom."

The NAD quickly pushed his chair back, the legs screeching against the kitchen floor as he tried to stop me from going. "Dana doesn't want to see you get hurt again. She knows about loss firsthand."

I wasn't staying to hear some sob story about Ms. DeForest's past.

"If she doesn't want me to be hurt, then why is she saying things that leave me feeling like I'm bruised?"

I charged out of the kitchen and up to my room, locked the door, and turned on my iPod dock. I heard the NAD knocking on the door, but I turned the music up louder. I wasn't up for a *Show respect to our guest* lecture.

I almost didn't hear my phone ringing.

"Aurora?"

"Tyler, it's not exactly the best time. Can I call you back a little later today?"

"No!"

Tyler was prone to dramatics, but this sounded like it couldn't wait.

"I went over to Lindsay's house this morning to give her the concert tickets and tell her about our dinner plans, and she started crying. At first I thought it was because she was happy, but then, while she was hugging me, she asked if I'd be able to be friends with her if we broke up."

"*What?*"

They couldn't break up! Yes, they'd had some speed bumps recently, but there was no reason why they couldn't start coasting again, if they were both set on working through their difficulties.

"She said it was only a hypothetical question, but, Aurora, I'm scared out of my mind. I don't know what to do anymore. You have to talk to her. I know she didn't want you to, but *please*. I feel like I'm on my way to the boyfriend execution block."

"Tyler—"

"Maybe I should head over to her house. I could write another poem and perform it. It worked last time!"

I shuddered, thinking of Tyler's former attempt at the poetic form. Keats he was not.

"Now's not the time for rashness," I said. "Too much heavy-handed pleading could push her over the edge. Lindsay's made it clear to me that she needs thinking time, so we need to step back."

Cupid was certainly not on duty today. Right after I hung up from Tyler's call, I got a call from Jeffrey, who was distraught at being persecuted on Facebook. Apparently, Ruby's, Jemima's, and Piper's comments had unleashed a torrent of links to anti–sexual harassment articles and images on Jeffrey's wall. He'd managed to antagonize everyone further by launching into a defense of the naked body and the value of streaking. I ordered him to stay off Facebook, as a form of damage control. Jelena would have to issue a public statement on Monday, before the situation got worse.

The only positive news I got was Chloe checking in to tell me how Hunter had serenaded her with his violin over the phone last night. He'd also asked her to take the ferry with him over to Indigo Bay on Sunday afternoon.

Just after I'd concluded the call with Mom to reschedule the pickup time, there was another knock at my bedroom door. "Aurora?"

It was Hayden. I lowered the music for the first time in two hours and opened the door to see him dressed all in white.

"Your dad requested that I wear white. Everyone downstairs is, too. How come you aren't dressed?"

I was still in my Garfield pajamas.

"I feel like these ceremonies happen every week," I said. "Why do we need to dress up for this one?"

"Um, judging by the backyard, this seems a lot more elaborate than your dad's usual living room sessions."

Hayden left the room while I went into my walk-in closet and quickly changed into a white blouse and skirt, then dashed across the hall to the bathroom, which had a window that overlooked the backyard.

I peered through the screen. It looked like there were white roses covering a wooden frame at the back of the garden, and throngs of people were assembled to its left and right.

"Is that a floral archway?"

I ran for the stairs, Hayden following me. As people made their way through the sliding door into the garden, they took a white feather from a basket held by Igneous. White shells lay on either side of a makeshift path leading to the archway.

I marched up to Igneous. "Have you seen Dad?"

Primrose, wearing a flowing white gown, appeared. "Your father is inside, preparing himself."

"Thanks." I turned to go find him.

Primrose caught me by the arm. "I promised Kenneth I'd show you to your spot."

She guided me toward the archway, where a line of chairs was set up. None of them had been taken by the guests, who were all standing around talking about *prana*-enhancing foods and recent soul challenges.

"Primrose," I said. "Dad only told me about the ceremony this morning. What's this all about?"

Hayden had followed us, and Primrose gestured warmly for him to take the chair next to mine.

"Uncertainty is the only certainty in life," she said, smiling at us. She waved at someone near the house. "Excuse me."

"I'm going to find Dad," I told Hayden. "This whole thing is weird. There are, like, fifty people here."

"I stopped at your dad's bedroom door on my way to your room," Hayden said. "There was some group chanting going on inside. No one responded to my knock."

Just as I was about to head back to the house, music started playing over the speakers, which had been dragged out onto the backyard patio. Everyone quickly organized themselves in standing rows. A Chinese gong sounded and the crowd turned their heads toward the house.

Then I spotted Ms. DeForest and the NAD, arm in arm, coming down the path. Ms. DeForest wore a white lace gown and had a coronet of white baby's breath on her head. My heart stopped. I tried to reach for Hayden but my arm wouldn't move. I opened my mouth but no sound came out. It was like all those dreams where I'd tried to tell my mother how angry I was that she'd left—my vocal cords only made strangled sounds.

Hayden grabbed my shoulders. He looked almost as shocked as I felt.

All I could do was stare at the NAD and Ms. DeForest, their radiant smiles burning into my retinas. They stopped at the floral archway and faced each other, like a bride and groom at an altar. This. Had. To. Be. A. Very. Bad. Dream.

My vocal cords unclenched and the words came out as one continuous horrified whisper. "Itcan'tbehecan'tmarryherIknewnothingaboutthis."

"There's no way your dad would get married again without asking you," Hayden breathed into my ear.

His words and his hands on my shoulders were the only things that kept me steady on my feet.

Primrose appeared next to the NAD and Ms. DeForest with a microphone in her hand. "*Namaste.* Just to assure everyone, this is not a marriage ceremony."

She let out a little laugh of amusement. I released a sigh of relief so loud that the people nearest to me looked over.

Thank god. The NAD and Ms. DeForest were probably the designated priest and priestess for some ritual. It could be an ancient druidic ceremony of autumn, for all I cared, as long as it wasn't the legal binding of two people.

"I'd like to invite those with chairs to sit, and those without chairs to find themselves a place on the lawn," Primrose said.

"This is not a marriage ceremony," she continued, when everyone became quiet, "but it is conducted with the same intent. Kenneth and Dana want to share with you all the fact that they have commenced a significant relationship. I'll let them speak now."

I turned to Hayden. I felt like my face was frozen into a picture of anguish, like Edvard Munch's *The Scream*.

"It's not a wedding ceremony," Hayden whispered, putting an arm around me. "Keep telling yourself that. You can talk to your dad straight after; just hold it together a little longer."

"Thank you, Primrose." The NAD turned to address everyone assembled in the garden. "The reason why people have wedding ceremonies is so they can pledge their dedication to each other in front of their friends and family. Dana and I suffered some setbacks at the beginning of this relationship, which many of you will remember. Both of us were quick to find reasons why the relationship was too hard, hiding the fact that it was our emotional baggage that prevented us from being able to bring our lives together in a holistic way. After crossing paths again, we have realized that this is a connection that we want to commit to.

"Last week, Dana made the symbolic shift of coming to reside in this house with me and my daughter, Aurora. What the past eight days have proved to Dana and me is that we want to move forward with our relationship. After initially considering a private ritual, we realized that we wanted all of you to feel like a part of our decision."

This ceremony had to have been Ms. DeForest's idea—she knew she was onto a good thing with the NAD and wanted to make it permanent. Just the other morning, I'd heard him suggest that she could cut down to part-time work if she wanted, since he was happy to support her focus on her spiritual growth.

I watched her take the microphone from the NAD. "As I said to Kenneth last night, having witnesses lends this occasion a sense of accountability. You'll hear our promises to create a future together, and we want to honor those promises, both to ourselves and to you."

The ceremony continued with a Kahlil Gibran reading, the NAD's and Ms. DeForest's individual pledges of intention, and a sand-pouring ceremony.

The NAD called for me to join him in pouring the sand that represented his past into a hurricane lamp, but I knew if I got up there, my calm would break. I didn't move from my chair. The NAD quickly told the disappointed crowd that I was still a little shy when it came to alternative rituals. Thankfully, everyone nodded understandingly, except Ms. DeForest, who gave me a look before resuming her pleasant expression.

A cloud of butterflies was released into the air at the end of the ceremony, and then the NAD and Ms. DeForest virtually skipped back down the makeshift aisle. As the cheering crowd surrounded them with congratulations and spiritual blessings, I sat motionless in my chair.

I felt Hayden nudge me. "Aurora? Tell me you're okay?"

"My dad just conducted his version of a marriage ceremony with a woman I can't stand!" I burst out. "Of course I'm not okay!"

Fortunately, no one was within earshot to hear Kenneth's unsupportive daughter. I'd had not one but two parents spring life-changing choices on me in a matter of weeks. Of course, I was glad that they were both moving on, but couldn't they at least consult me about things that shifted the axes of my life? It hurt me that they believed my opinion was of no consequence or value.

"I can't believe he sprung this on me in my own home!"

"I'm sure he meant to fill you in," Hayden said, looking anxiously at me. "Aurora, I know if it was me in this situation, I'd be totally confronted by it, too. But, like you said last night, sometimes people fall in love and they move quickly."

I stood up, seeing red. "I can't believe you're using carpe diem as an excuse for my dad's insensitivity!"

I was so angry I didn't stay to hear his response. I headed down the garden path and into the kitchen. Dad was there, opening a bottle of organic wine.

"Aurora!" His face brightened as he spotted me.

"You know, for someone who advises his daughter against rushing into relationships, you set a pretty bad example."

I felt pathetic for how the words came out, trembling instead of cool, but composure was fast deserting me. Before he could reply, I headed for the front yard. I didn't know where I was going, or how, but I had to get out of here.

Almost miraculously, Mom's car pulled into the drive.

As I opened the door and jumped in, I saw the NAD, Hayden, and Ms. DeForest at the front door, witnessing my harried exit.

28

"Your father's making odder fashion choices as he gets older," Mom said, as we swung out of the driveway.

"Believe me, the odd choices go beyond clothing," I muttered.

Mom peered in the rearview mirror at Ms. DeForest. "That spiritual garb comes close to crossing the line into bridal wear, doesn't it?" She shook her head disapprovingly. "There's a time and a place for long white lace."

As we headed toward the city, I switched my phone off. I needed space from Hayden, Dad, Ms. DeForest . . . everyone. My head was throbbing from tension.

"Where are we going?" I asked. "Florists? Cake tastings?"

"Jefferson College. It's their open house."

"You're enrolling?"

Life had thrown so many surprises at me recently that the prospect of my mother returning to school wasn't unbelievable.

Mom let out her tinkly laugh. "You are a silly child sometimes. No, of course not. Carlos has been talking to me about fostering your potential. He was rather impressed after meeting you. We thought you could do a year here while staying at home with your father and then transfer overseas to a top college. Perhaps

Cambridge or somewhere else abroad. Carlos suggested we could buy you an apartment to live in."

Instead of our catch-up being about red-velvet versus chocolate ganache, or South American roses versus peonies, it was all about me. This was a first.

"After all, you'll be applying next year," Mom continued. "I want to be a part of that."

As she pulled in to the university parking lot, I realized I was breathing again.

After spending several hours picking up brochures and touring campus facilities, Mom took me back to her and Carlos's apartment for the first time, made tea, and served it in impossibly fragile china. I was terrified I'd drop my cup or saucer on her matching set of black-and-white-striped chaise longues, which looked like props from the film *Marie Antoinette*.

"You liked attending Jefferson College, right?" I asked her. "I know you met Dad there, but you've never told me what it was like academically."

"The business course was very comprehensive, but my studies were broken up by my modeling work. I was flying in and out of the country. Never anything truly glamorous, like Parisian shows—I was a little too short to do catwalk—but commercial work paid really well. Your father followed me to Japan only two weeks after he met me. He's the type to jump in quickly, as you'd know."

I let out a laugh before I could stop myself. He certainly hadn't changed.

"Tell me about what happened in Japan." Dad never wanted to talk about the early days.

"At the time, I had no idea he'd got it into his head to come after me. We'd been on three dates, and I'd told him I had to go away for work. He managed to track down the hotel where the agency had put me up and booked a room on the same floor as mine. The night after I arrived, I heard this knock at the door. It was about nine p.m., and I was annoyed because I'd specified to the front desk that I wasn't to be disturbed. Anyway, I flung open the door, ready to give a staff member a dressing-down, and there was your father, with a huge bouquet of white roses. He told me I was too sophisticated for red roses. I was at an age where I desperately wanted to be sophisticated and was completely won over by the gesture."

Mom's voice sounded like she'd been drinking honey tea instead of the green that was in our cups.

"Speaking of your father . . ." Her voice became practical again. "We should get you home."

"I'm not in a hurry."

"Something's going on back there, isn't it?" Mom said. "I saw your face when I picked you up."

I nodded. I didn't want to go into it; it would only make going back even more formidable.

Mom sighed. She obviously thought I was being difficult. And then she said something that was far from the mom I knew.

"Why don't you stay here for the night? Carlos is away. I can give you a nightgown and a spare toothbrush to use. I'll drive you back tomorrow morning."

The guest room was bigger than my room back home, and our place wasn't exactly small. Mom told me she had to do some work on one of Carlos's proposals but I was welcome to help myself to books from their library. I flicked through a few books, not really absorbing anything; instead, I listened to Mom typing away on a computer in the next room. It had been four years since I'd slept in the same house as her, and knowing that I could call out and have her answer me within seconds was almost surreal.

I finally switched on my phone at nine p.m., knowing I needed to tell Dad I wasn't coming home. He certainly wouldn't be expecting Mom to keep me overnight. My phone lit up with missed call after missed call. Dad, three times. Hayden, about ten times. Jelena. There were texts, too. Jelena had seen Jeffrey's Facebook page and wasn't happy. Tyler had sent three texts asking if calling Lindsay still counted as giving her space. Hayden had obviously told Cass what had happened, because there was an *R U OK???* from her. I felt exhausted just looking at all the messages. I sent an *I'm staying at Mom's, I'll talk to you tomorrow* text to both Dad and Hayden before turning the phone off. I felt guilty about Hayden, but I knew if I called him in this mood, we'd only wind up in another argument.

Mom had left a towel out for me, so I headed into the en suite bathroom. I washed my hair, hoping that, by some kind of magic, it would strip my mind clean of all the stress.

When I got out, Mom was sitting on my bed. I stood there in my towel, wondering if she was going to ask me to go home. The little girl in me felt like clinging to her skirts and begging to stay.

"I thought you might need a comb," Mom said, holding one up.

She gestured for me to sit down at the dressing table, then gently ran the comb through my hair.

"You're such a beautiful girl, Aurora." She studied me in the mirror. "I always said to your father that I wanted a child other mothers would be envious of, and that's exactly what I got."

"You *wanted* a child, then?"

It felt like a forbidden question, but after what Ms. DeForest had said, I wanted to know the truth. It wasn't like the question hadn't gone through my mind a million times since Mom had left.

She raised an eyebrow. "I wasn't silly enough to get pregnant accidentally, if that's what you're thinking. I suppose someone's told you I left because I never wanted children."

Mom stopped combing and met my eyes in the mirror. The question hovered between us for what felt like minutes.

"I didn't know what mothering was really about, to be honest," she said. "You have to remember, the English way is to send your children to boarding school. I only saw my own mother about three times a year for most of my childhood."

Mom's parents had been English. I thought of how she'd once told me she'd come here because it was the other side of the world and different from everything she'd ever known.

"Unlike your father, who'd race to you the second you let out a tiny murmur or whimper, I'm not good with small children," Mom said. "That's why my relationship with you has improved. You're becoming mature enough to understand me as a person rather than simply demanding things of me as a mother."

A few months ago, I would have been insulted by this. Now, I found myself trying to understand what she was saying.

"I'm looking forward to fostering a friendship with the woman you are going to become, Aurora." Mom stopped combing and bent to kiss my forehead quickly. "There's a hair dryer in the bathroom cupboard. Sleep well."

When Mom dropped me back home the following morning, I realized something. The odd feelings I got whenever I said good-bye to Hayden after a date, or after walking back together from school, were the same feelings I had now. An unease, a slight lump in my throat, a worry that I couldn't quite name but which floated around in the back of my mind for a good hour or so before I managed to sufficiently distract myself. It was so obvious now that I couldn't believe I'd missed it. I hated good-byes, even the ones that were part of the normal routine. I seemed to equate good-bye with an unconscious sense of dread that this could be the last time I'd see the person for years.

I didn't want to feel like that anymore. After all, Mom had come back into my life. Maybe I needed to stop living on guard, believing that all the people I cared about would inevitably leave without warning.

As I opened the front door, I saw the NAD and Ms. DeForest coming down the stairs with suitcases. I had to appreciate the irony—just when I was attempting to rework my take on good-byes.

"Aurora." Dad stopped at the bottom of the staircase, Ms. DeForest behind him.

I could tell by both their faces that they were unhappy about yesterday.

"I tried to call again this morning," Dad said. "Dana and I are going on a retreat in the country. We'll be back Wednesday evening. I've left the fridge full of supplies, and I've written our number next to the phone in the living room, if you need to reach us.

"We need to talk, but Dana and I have a long drive ahead, so I think that's best left for when we return."

"You stayed with your mother," Ms. DeForest commented, as she and Dad moved toward the door.

I nodded. I didn't need to explain myself to her.

"That's one of the things we need to discuss," Dad said. "Obviously, it's good that you and Avery have reconnected. But you need to realize it could be a temporary thing."

"Individuals like your mother aren't the type to forge stable relationships," Ms. DeForest added.

"Maybe she's changed," I said, feeling angry that they seemed to want to take away the tiny seed of faith that had started blooming in my heart. "Maybe this time it's different."

"I've seen eighteen years of this pattern," Dad replied, opening the front door. "Your mother loves you—I've always told you that—but she is who she is. Family isn't her priority. It's a tragedy, and she'll probably regret it one day, but she'll never change."

I remembered her kissing my forehead the night before. "Well, she's my mother and I want to give her the benefit of the doubt."

Dad didn't reply. He shut the front door behind him, and I heard the car start soon afterward. Then I was left, in the quiet, alone.

29

"All three candidates eliminated in under two weeks! We need to fix this."

Monday morning art class hadn't even started yet and Jelena was already laying into Lindsay and me about Jeffrey's matches.

"Jelena, have you seen his Facebook page? It's the equivalent of a feminist rally," Lindsay said. "He didn't do anything, of course, but no one is going to convince the girls of that."

"We can't tell everyone we couldn't get him a match." Jelena sounded frustrated. "Aurora, aren't you embarrassed? This is going to reflect badly on you."

I tried not to feel insulted. "As I said, we need you to release a press statement. Then I'll try to talk some of the girls around."

Lindsay sighed. "It isn't going to work. I hate to be a downer, but we have to be realistic. His locker was covered with antiharassment posters this morning. Someone even photocopied pages from *A Vindication of the Rights of Woman* and stuck it up there."

"What about a match with a girl from another school?" Jelena wasn't giving up. "Between the five of us, we have to know a few girls who might not have heard about Jeffrey yet."

"The girls on Facebook aren't all from Jefferson," I said. "They're from all over—the Catholic high school, public high schools in neighboring suburbs—"

"Excuses. Start working on it," Jelena commanded. "In the meantime, I'll try to hire someone to play the role of starry-eyed girlfriend."

"You can't lie to people like that!"

Lindsay let out an ironic laugh. "She's technically already doing that with Johannes and Sara. This program doesn't seem to be working for anyone."

"That's not true." I gave her a confused look. "What about Hunter and Chloe?"

"Shh!" Jelena furiously motioned for us to keep our voices down, as someone opened the classroom door.

Sara stepped in, glaring at Jelena. "You told us you were only associating with Alex in order to advance your political career. And then I see on Instagram that you guys went to the movies together on Saturday night *and* had lunch over by the harbor yesterday. Did you spend the whole weekend together?"

Jelena didn't look embarrassed, despite Sara's accusing tone. "Yes, most of it. We were ironing out the details for this last week of campaigning."

Sara's eyebrows were raised. "He keeps glancing over here every five minutes. He finds power an aphrodisiac, Jelena. I know it's flattering, after he was the one to dump you, but you should tread very carefully."

"It's Alex's problem if he lets himself be ruled by attraction instead of intellect," Jelena said. "That type of weakness is pretty typical for a man. After all, Napoleon commanded the whole world, but you know who commanded him? Empress Josephine. He would be in the throes of agony every time she chose not to write to him while he was away on a military campaign. Alex may think that we'll be reigning jointly next year, but I knew from the moment he came seeking my help that the power dynamic would turn around quickly."

"Jelena," I said, "you and I both know what happened to Josephine."

"She let herself become vulnerable. I'm not going to do that."

On Wednesday afternoon, I was sitting in one of the private study rooms in the library, working on a science paper, when I was interrupted by Tyler.

"Aurora, things are no better," he burst out. "Lindsay won't even answer her cell, either for phone calls or texts. You know, I've been pretty understanding this past week, but there's a point where her attitude gets plain rude."

"Aurora, I think I need to go into a protection program," Jeffrey said, pushing past Tyler. "There are girls booing at me in the halls. Someone threw a banana at me at lunch! What if they start throwing harder stuff? Like a mango or something? I'd be knocked out!"

A sob came from behind Tyler and Jeffrey. Both of them froze.

"Chloe?" I stood up when I saw her distraught face.

"Everything's gone wrong, Aurora. It's my fault. I always get too hung up on guys too soon. It scares them!"

She folded herself into a chair, crumpled, like a piece of paper that had been too roughly handled.

"I'll come back later," Tyler said, freaked out by tears, as usual.

"I'll get her some water," Jeffrey said, and dashed out.

"Chloe, what happened? I thought everything was going great."

"It was! The dedication at the assembly, the conversations that went on for hours, the violin sonatas he played for me—Aurora, he was texting me like every twenty minutes since we got back from camp. Sending me pictures of paintings he loves, and excerpts from *Romeo and Juliet*. After the story of Berlioz and Harriet, *Romeo and Juliet* was our thing."

Chloe looked up as Jeffrey came back into the room. She violently wiped the back of her hand across her eyes, looking mortified to have someone she barely knew witness her breakdown. Jeffrey handed her a paper cup of water.

"Sorry, I'm a mess," Chloe said, looking up at him, her eyes smeared with mascara.

"Babe, no probs," Jeffrey said. "I know how brutal dating can be."

He sat down beside Chloe, looking at her with concern. To my surprise, Chloe didn't ask him to leave. She plunged back into her story.

"He even tagged me in an Instagram picture he posted of Plato's *Symposium*—the one that talks about soul mates! Aurora, who posts about soul mates with another person if they aren't feeling that way themselves?"

She broke down crying again. Jeffrey reached over and squeezed her hand. Strangely, Jeffrey was the right man to have around in a crisis. I sat stupidly in my chair, waiting for Chloe to reveal why she was so upset.

"You have to tell me what's gone wrong," I said. "Like you say, it's obvious Hunter's crazy about you. I'm sure we'll be able to sort this out."

"*Was* crazy about me." Chloe hiccuped. "Until Sunday."

"The date you told me about? You went, right?"

"Yes! And it was picture perfect. We found the ideal picnic spot looking out across the entire bay. We had lunch, and then Hunter started reading me poetry. He was halfway through a sonnet when he just leaned down and kissed me, out of the blue. It was even better than I'd ever imagined it would be. We kept kissing and kissing all afternoon, until it looked like a storm was rolling in.

"As we were heading back on the ferry, I cuddled up to him and said, 'Won't it be funny when we become a public success story next Monday?' He looked all confused, and I reminded him that the results of your program would be announced on election day. He pulled away from me and said he hadn't known our relationships had to become public." Chloe's lips trembled.

"But he must have," I said. "That's part of the contract Jelena made him sign."

"He said that she rushed him through the details to get his signature and he never saw that part. I asked him if that was a problem and he went all silent. I said I thought he'd be happy to share how we'd fallen for each other. And then he replied . . ." Chloe took a shaky breath. "'Well, there's no need to go rushing in, Chloe.'

"I felt hurt, so I went silent, and then he didn't say anything, either, and the rest of the trip home was awful."

"Why didn't you call me?" I asked. "I could have called him and found out what was going on so you didn't have to have a painful conversation. Maybe he's a little shy about people knowing about his personal life?"

"I held off calling because Hunter told me we'd talk about it later and I was hoping we'd work it out. I didn't want to panic too early. But then his messages got sporadic. On Monday, I got two texts. Normally, I'd have had about forty. And then, last night, when I was on Facebook, I noticed he was online, so I asked him a question via Chat. The next minute, Chat was saying that he'd gone offline. I texted him, asking if I'd done anything wrong.

"And then, all through the night, he sent me these texts about his ex and how messed up he was from that relationship. The texts are really intense, Aurora—like, all the details of his breakup and his therapist. I know he thinks that will put me off, but I understand what a breakup's like and I want to prove to him that it's safe to trust again. But he point-blank avoided me when I tried to talk to him at lunch today."

"That cad! After kissing you and chasing you for almost two weeks?" Jeffrey smacked his fist against his palm. "I can sort this out for you, Chloe. I don't know much about you or this guy, but that's not gentlemanly behavior."

"Jeffrey, I don't think violence is the best option," I said quickly. "Chloe, I'll talk to Hunter. Like you say, we can get cautious if we've been hurt. I'm sure he'll realize you're a risk worth taking."

I was unable to find Hunter anywhere during study break. He definitely wasn't taking calls; all of my attempts were met by his voicemail. I ended up asking the orchestra members if they knew where he was. Finally, a trumpet player told me he'd seen Hunter heading for the school gate.

"He was with a dark-haired girl," he said.

It couldn't be Chloe. I knew she was still back in the library with Jeffrey. He couldn't be involved with another girl, could he?

My heart beating faster, I ran for the school gate. Thankfully, all potential candidates had had to give their address when they'd filled out the questionnaire, so I had Hunter's in my phone. I Google Mapped the location; it was apparently a ten minute walk from school. I broke into a sprint. I had a very bad feeling.

As I approached Hunter's place, I stopped running. I needed to catch my breath to conduct a conversation. As I bent over, trying to steady my breathing, I realized I could hear voices. There was a veranda that ran the length of the front of Hunter's house, partially obscured by the trees on his front lawn. As I walked up the drive, I realized one of the voices was Hunter's. The other was female, but since Hunter seemed to be doing most of the talking, I didn't recognize it.

I dashed up the steps and onto the veranda. If Hunter was playing around, I was determined to catch him in the act. Hunter, who was standing at the railing, whipped his head around at the sound of my footsteps. There was definitely a dark-haired girl standing next to him, but his head obscured her face.

"Aurora?" the girl said.

"Lindsay? What are you doing here?"

Thank god! For a moment I'd been terrified I'd have to tell Chloe that Hunter was two-timing her.

"We're hanging out," Hunter replied. "What are you doing here?"

"I'm here because Chloe's confused about why you've pulled back from her after a successful date on Sunday."

"You told me that you'd stopped seeing her after camp," Lindsay said to Hunter.

"Lindsay, you're totally out of the loop." Why was she looking so shocked? "Hunter did the shout-out to her during the assembly. You were there! He called her up and played a violin sonata over the phone on Friday night, then took her to Indigo Bay on Sunday. Of course he's still been seeing her."

"Well, that's news to me," Lindsay said. "I was under the impression that the assembly performance was for me."

My mouth dropped open. "What?"

"I told you *and* Chloe the story of Hector and Berlioz." Hunter was entirely focused on Lindsay. "Both of you assumed the shout-out was about you. Neither of you actually asked me to verify that."

"Well, I don't know about Chloe, but you and I definitely had a conversation about it." Lindsay's eyes were snapping. "I told you I thought it was inappropriate, because I had a boyfriend and you were supposed to be seeing Chloe. You just shrugged."

"Wait a minute. The reason you couldn't work with Hunter and Chloe anymore was because you were freaked out by that performance being dedicated to you?" I asked Lindsay. "And you thought by stepping away you'd prevent Hunter from messing things up with his match?"

"Temporarily," Hunter answered for her. "Then she started coming over here every time she had a problem with her boyfriend."

"That is not the story. You told me you wanted to see *Bright Star*," Lindsay spluttered. "I brought it over so we could watch it together. And then you read me that poem about swooning upon a lover's breast and told me you wished that was us!"

"Lindsay?" I stared at her. "Tyler would be crushed if you did anything—Tell me you didn't."

Lindsay started crying. "Of course I didn't. But Hunter confused me. This whole thing started as a friendship, after you paired us up at camp. It's only been the last week that he's started sending me romantic quotes and pictures of lovers from famous paintings."

"He's been doing exactly the same to Chloe." I couldn't believe what I was hearing, but I wanted Lindsay to have all the facts. "Stuff about soul mates, quotes from *Romeo and Juliet*."

I felt disgusted.

Hunter shrugged, looking unaffected by either Lindsay's shocked face or my revolted one. "Material used by a long line of seducers before me. Girls lap that stuff up. That's why men who say they aren't into poetry are idiots."

"You're the idiot." Lindsay looked as sickened as I felt.

"Sweetheart, let me remind you that, a few minutes ago, you were debating whether to break up with your boyfriend and throwing little hints in to see if I'd promise to be all yours if you did." Hunter laughed. "I loaded that gun ages ago. I knew exactly what it would take to get you to pull the trigger."

Lindsay looked like she was about to collapse on the floor—or strangle Hunter. Before she could do either, I stepped in front of her.

"Why?" I asked Hunter. "Why cause two girls, both of whom you had a special connection with, all this pain and confusion?"

"Women are fickle," Hunter said. "You know, when I was dating my ex, I had to study Shakespeare's sonnets. You presumably know about Shakespeare's Dark Lady—the woman whom scholars claim to be his inspiration? Well, it was pretty obvious to me that, whoever this woman was, she took advantage of Shakespeare's sensitivity. If you go through the sonnets, you can see how many references there are to unfaithfulness.

"I found out that my ex was a modern-day version of that Dark Lady. She cheated on me and broke my heart, so I learned pretty quickly that limiting myself to dating just one girl was the easy way to wind up a fool. After all, if women are going to work on my emotions like I'm a puppet, why shouldn't I get in first?"

The words came out like a river of poison.

Hunter had a twisted smile on his face. There was a hard and flinty edge to him now, like a knife, and I didn't want it near us any longer.

"Lindsay, we should go." I grabbed her hand and headed for the veranda steps.

"And, just so you know," Hunter called after us, "I'm transferring to a music school in another state. I start on Monday, and I'm not attending the last two days of school this week. So if you're planning to start a smear campaign, I won't be there to see it."

"Why bother with Chloe or me if you were leaving anyway?" Lindsay asked him, even though I was now dragging her down the driveway.

"I figured I'd get a kick out of hooking up with you both and knowing neither of you had a clue." Hunter's chuckle floated down the path toward us, like a noxious cloud.

"That never would have happened!" Lindsay was furious.

"Keep telling yourself that, Lindsay," Hunter said, his voice dry. He went inside and slammed the door behind him. I yanked Lindsay down the drive and onto the street, both of us still reeling.

"Thank god he's leaving Jefferson," I said. "He's a destructive person. I wish we knew which school he was transferring to so we could warn the girls there."

"I wish I could go back in time." Tears were streaming down Lindsay's cheeks. "I'm mortified, Aurora. I don't know what I was thinking. I honestly saw it as a friendship at first. I was really upset about Tyler not coming to camp, and while we were ropes buddies, Hunter asked what was troubling me. It all came spilling out, and then, the more I talked to him, the more my doubts about Tyler seemed to grow."

"That was all deliberately and carefully done, Lindsay. He never actually said that your relationship had no passion, but he asked you if you knew what passion was. He's smart enough to have known what effect that would have on you."

"I should have tried to fix my relationship instead of letting him build up a case for me leaving Tyler."

"Were you going to?" Part of me wondered if I was pushing things too far by asking this, but I was involved now.

"I don't know." Lindsay's voice shook. "That's what scares me, Aurora. My self-esteem was crushed when Tyler dumped me. I know it seemed like I was moving on and following my dream of being a designer, but underneath I felt like a quivering mess, praying that he'd take me back. And then, when he did, the anger started. All I could see was how he took me for granted and how easy it had been for him to throw me away. And then along came somebody who told me I was beautiful and made me feel like I was the most fascinating person to spend time with.

"I admit it: I was tempted, even though I love Tyler. I convinced myself that I wanted to end the relationship because it wasn't working, but there was a tiny whisper at the back of my mind telling me there was another reason for considering a breakup. That's what's making me feel sick. I'm scared I'm as fickle as Hunter says all women are."

I took her hands. "You can't listen to someone like him," I said in my fiercest voice. "He's twisted. You can't let him win."

"You aren't judging me?" Lindsay's face was drenched with tears as she looked at me. "I know how highly you respect love. How can you be okay with the way that I disrespected it?"

I hugged her. Who was to say, situations reversed, that it couldn't have been me bowled over by poetry and supposed romance? "I can see where you're coming from, Lindsay. And you didn't cheat on Tyler, even though Hunter was doing everything he could to persuade you to. You *do* respect love."

"How can I tell Tyler what happened?" Lindsay pulled away from the hug. "I know Jelena or Sara would tell me not to. But I can't lie to him."

"Do you want to stay with him?" I asked.

"I want to try," Lindsay whispered. "What all of this has proved—even though I shouldn't have needed proof—is that Tyler's a good guy. The type of guy who means what he says and proves it with what he does for me. He might not understand poetry, but a relationship is more than that."

"I think you need to be prepared for the possibility that he might react badly," I warned her.

Even though she'd stayed faithful, I knew Tyler would be devastated by her confession.

"I know. I'm going into this aware that I could lose him. After all, if he was breaking this type of news to me, I might dump him. I'll head over to his place now—he deserves to know the truth."

30

“So one of our matches has not only dumped Chloe and left the program but also changed schools?” Jelena said to me and Lindsay, the next morning.

We both nodded. Lindsay’s eyes were red around the edges. Tyler had had a fit when he heard about what had gone down with Hunter and had told Lindsay he needed till Monday to think their relationship over. Lindsay had been up half the night crying.

“So now I only have one fake couple to present on Monday?” Jelena went on.

Lindsay and I nodded again. Neither of us knew what to say. We were still shell-shocked after the grenade Hunter had thrown at us.

“Stop it. You look like bobbing babushka dolls!” Jelena put her head in her hands. “There was no way to prevent this?”

“Hunter was rotten to the core.” Lindsay’s jaw was tense as she said his name.

“The chemistry calculator is supposed to screen the matches! I’m going to have a serious chat with Hayden!”

Jelena stormed off before I could stop her. She returned ten minutes later, still looking angry.

“He says he can’t help the fact that people misrepresent themselves," she said. "The calculator only analyzes the information it's given." She sighed dramatically, sounding like Sara. "Thank god for One Hour Later. I knew this Find a Prince/Princess program was a liability."

"That's enough, Jelena!" I cried.

Not only did I have to watch my program collapsing from the inside, but now my friend was trashing it, too. It had meant the world to me to be able to put my theories into practice, and now it had all gone to waste. I'd lost Jelena's faith, and soon I'd lose the faith of everyone else at school.

I headed off to get a drink from the cafeteria before I completely lost my cool. After consoling Lindsay yesterday, I'd then had to break the news to Chloe. I hadn't told her who the other girl was that Hunter had been simultaneously wooing. That was Lindsay and Tyler's business. Not even Jelena knew the girl's identity. Chloe had been completely devastated, and when I'd seen her this morning, her eyes had matched Lindsay's.

The hardest thing for me to face was that my program had done this to them. For all my attempts to play cupid, it appeared I was hopeless at it. Like Jelena had said, the grand total of weeks of effort was one fake couple. I was a failure. I brushed away a tear.

My phone rang. Mom.

"Why don't you come over for dinner on Sunday, darling?"

I agreed, desperate for a distraction from my own thoughts. If I sat around all weekend thinking about my failures as a matchmaker, I'd go crazy.

As I hung up, Hayden came over.

"Why didn't you tell me what happened with Hunter and Chloe?" He sounded hurt.

"I was worried you'd say *I told you so*, after you warned me that they were rushing in."

"Oh, Aurora." Hayden's face looked sad. "You don't really think I'd gloat about that, do you? I know that program is close to your heart."

For some reason, his pity made me feel worse than if he'd gone on about being right. I felt my chin tremble.

Hayden must have seen it, because he enveloped me in his arms. "There will be other chances for your candidates, you'll see. You just need more time. It was a hard ask of anyone to get results that quickly!"

"I don't want to talk about it," I said, my head buried in his shoulder.

I knew he was trying to make me feel better, but I didn't have any more time. The program would be shelved by Jelena and Alex on the reasonable assumption that it didn't work.

"What are you doing on Sunday night?" Hayden said, stroking my hair. "There's a funny movie showing that I thought we could see."

"I promised to have dinner with Mom."

I felt him tense. "Aurora, I know you're excited about having her back in your life, but I'm worried—"

"She's my mother. I'm tired of feeling guilty about the fact that I want to see her!" I realized, as the words came out, that my frustration with Dad and Ms. DeForest, as well as my disappointment over the program, had made them more aggressive than I'd intended. "After four years, you might want to make up for lost time, too."

"We're only trying to protect you."

"By *we*, I assume you mean you've been talking to Dad and Ms. DeForest?"

They'd arrived home last night, but thankfully had been too tired after the drive to attempt a conversation.

"They're concerned—"

I cut him off. "They weren't concerned about how their sudden commitment ceremony might affect me, so I don't see why they should be worried about Mom. It's just because she hurt Dad, and Ms. DeForest is taking his side."

"What your mom did to your dad is pretty hard to get over," Hayden said seriously.

"I know the situation, Hayden. I lived it. Of course Dad has a right to feel hurt. But should I completely write my mother off because of that?"

Hayden couldn't understand. His parents were picture perfect.

"You don't have the answers," I said. "So let me struggle with finding my own."

Around seven p.m. on Saturday, my phone rang. I could see from the caller ID that it was Jelena.

"Hey!" I said. "Only about forty-one hours till voting starts. Are you pumped?"

I was hoping to keep her focused on the positive. I couldn't take another session of analyzing why the program had failed. I knew Jelena wanted to identify the holes in the original model so we could move it forward, but it was still too painful for me.

"Aurora?" Her voice was a whisper. "I need you to come over to my place right now." Her voice broke. "The others too. Please hurry."

She hung up. I immediately texted Cass and then Sara.

Something's wrong with Jelena, something serious, head to her place right away.

The three of us could handle this. Lindsay had been pushed to her maximum, emotionally, in the last few days.

I called a taxi, scribbling a note to the NAD. He and Ms. DeForest had gone for a dinner at some macrobiotic friend's place. It was only as the taxi pulled away from my place that I realized I'd left my phone in my room. Well, I wasn't going back for it now. Jelena needed us.

When I rang the bell, Sara whipped the Cantrills' front door open. "She won't talk to us," she said. "She's curled up on her bed, crying."

I took the stairs two at a time.

Cass was sitting on the bed, stroking Jelena's hair and making soothing sounds. Jelena was wearing a black triangle bikini.

"Jelena?" I said softly as I approached the bed.

"You were right. I should have remembered what happened to Josephine," she sobbed.

"Alex." Sara made his name sound like a swear word.

"Pride before a fall." Jelena's voice was almost lost in her pillow as she cried into it.

"What's he done?" I asked.

"I did it!" Jelena wailed. "I set myself up. I walked straight into the trap!"

I put my hand on her shoulder. "Please, Jelena. Whatever it is, we can get through it together."

Jelena sat up and took a heaving breath. "Like Sara said, he's been flirting with me since last weekend. Full on. I encouraged it because I thought it meant I'd be able to control him. When I texted him today that I was home alone, swimming in the pool, he told me he was coming over. I let him in and we swam for a while. He kept complimenting me on my bikini and my body. I felt like Cleopatra with Mark Antony, knowing he was at my mercy.

"Then we swam to the shallow end, and he grabbed his phone, saying he should add me as a friend on Instagram. We were sitting on the edge of the pool, looking at a bunch of my photos, and then the next minute he launched into this speech about how I was not only a goddess to look at but also a formidable leader and an intelligent woman. He said he'd made a terrible mistake, not recognizing that earlier in the term. He said part of the reason he'd wanted to run with me was so he could get close to me again, that he just couldn't help himself when it came to me, when it came to . . ."

Jelena's voice got shaky.

"When it came to what?" I asked softly.

"Passion." Jelena made the word sound broken. "He put his arm around my waist and started kissing me."

"And you *resisted* . . . *Right?*" Sara asked.

"Sara, let her finish." I looked at Jelena's expression; it was fragile. Her brows were pushed together as if she was in pain. She couldn't have kissed Alex back after everything he'd done to her the first time around . . .

"No," she said. "I let him kiss me. *I know*, Sara. At first it was because I saw it as an opportunity for some power play, but then . . . with him kissing me, I let myself feel things again. You know, I really fell for him that first time, before he dumped me." Her voice had become a whisper. "I didn't notice his fingers undoing my bikini top until I felt the air on my chest. And when I realized, I freaked out and told him to stop, but—"

"He stopped, didn't he?" Cass and I asked in the same second.

I felt like I might throw up. This couldn't be why she was so upset . . .

"He took a photo," Jelena whispered. "It happened in a split second, I swear. I'd told him to stop and I was trying to pull my top back from him, and then I heard this tiny click. He took a photo on his phone—a shot of me without any top on . . ."

Now Jelena was crying so hard she couldn't talk.

"I'm calling my dad." Sara's father was a police officer at the local station.

"No!" Jelena grabbed the phone out of her hand. "I don't want my parents to know. I don't want them to see me this way. Alex said if I told anyone, he'd text the photo to everyone he knows."

"Jelena, you're under eighteen," Sara said. "It's underage pornography. The police will destroy the photo before he can send it to anyone."

"Sara's right," I said. "Jelena, I know you don't want to tell your parents, but this is serious. You know how the internet is—once an image winds up there, it's permanent. It'll be around for the rest of your life."

I hated to drive home how bad this was, but she needed to see that it was vital we tell the police.

"You think I don't know that?" Jelena said. "He knows it too.

That's why he told me that he's going to save the photo somewhere that no one can trace it back to him. He can upload it to the internet the same way—it can go out to all the teachers, students, and parents, and nobody will ever know it was him. He said the only way to guarantee it not being made public is if I drop out of the election."

Jelena blew her nose on a tissue Cass passed her.

"That's blackmail," Sara said. "If you won't go to the police, then I will."

"Sara, please!" Jelena begged. "This is my issue."

"You asked us around to help you. This is the only way we can," Sara shot back.

"Guys!" Cassie glared at Sara as Jelena started crying into the pillow again.

I waggled my eyebrows at Sara, signaling that the two of us should leave the room to talk. We headed down the hall and into the bathroom. I shut the door.

"If she won't budge on calling the police, we need to move fast," I said. "The only other option is to intercept Alex before he gets home and transfers the image onto something untraceable. We know he's on foot, and his place is pretty far from here, so there's still a chance we can do it. We need an interceptor to get his phone off him. I think it's time to get a guy we trust involved."

"Hayden?"

"We need someone Alex won't suspect. He knows Hayden can't stand him, so he'll be wary if Hayden approaches him. It has to be someone Alex knows—but not too well. I'm thinking Johannes."

Sara and I spent the next few hours on edge, waiting to see if our plan would work. Jelena had begged us to stay the night, because she didn't want to be alone, so Cass shared her queen-size bed while Sara and I shared the blow-up mattress on her floor. For hours we tried to persuade her to report Alex, but she only shook her head and told us she wanted to think about it first.

After she fell asleep, the three of us continued to whisper. Sara and I filled Cass in on the plan. We were all praying it would work, but if it failed, we needed to make a stand and go to the police to report the incident.

This wasn't simple high school nastiness. What Alex had done was harassment. He could do the same thing to countless girls in the future.

At around 12:30 a.m., Sara's phone rang. She answered, and gasped at whatever the person on the line was telling her.

"Thank god! Johannes, I owe you a kiss for sure!" Sara hung up and punched the air.

"Success?" I sat up, every muscle tensed in the hope that we'd pulled this thing off.

"You guys don't have to keep up the act of loving couple," Jelena said grumpily, woken by the call. "I've lost the election."

"He wasn't calling to whisper sweet nothings; he was calling with your salvation," Sara said. "Johannes stole Alex's phone right out of his back pocket. Alex thinks it's been taken by someone at the bar."

"Wait a minute . . . Johannes and Alex were at a bar?" Jelena sat up too.

"I called him earlier, right after you told us what had happened. Aurora and I made a plan of attack," Sara explained.

"You guys! It was private!" Jelena sounded furious.

"Shut up, Jelena. Desperate times call for desperate measures. I told Johannes what had happened and he said he'd intercept Alex on his way home. Johannes spun some story about how he'd been forced to date me because of Jelena's campaign, but he wanted a real hot chick, not some man-hater—"

I let out a laugh. "He didn't really say that?"

"He had to!" Sara said. "If he didn't lay it on thick, Alex would have suspected something. Anyway, Johannes convinced Alex to be his wingman tonight. He wouldn't even let Alex go home first, in case he did something with the picture. They went to a bar where Alex's friend is the manager and had a few drinks. Johannes pretended to be drunk and stumbled on his crutches, grabbing on to

Alex from behind. At the same time, he took Alex's phone from his back pants pocket. Alex didn't notice for a while, but when he did, he assumed it'd been stolen. He made a complaint to the bar staff, but he didn't want them to call the police because he's underage.

"Anyway, he was so angry he stormed off to get a cab, and meanwhile Johannes ran to the bathroom to check the phone. He told me there's no record of any sent messages or any image sent to Alex's email accounts or uploaded from the phone. He's dead certain. He's something of a tech whiz," Sara said proudly. "Alex will probably keep bluffing to you that he's backed the photo up, but don't say anything to him or it'll be traced back to Johannes. You're in the clear now."

Jelena threw her arms around Sara, Cass, and me. "He's a freakin' hero! You guys are, too."

"That's what best friends do," I said. "You can count on us to bring the bad guy down."

Even though the other girls fell asleep quickly after Johannes's phone call, I was still uneasy. For the second time in a week, someone had used passion to deceive one of my friends and manipulate her into a position of vulnerability. Three times, if you counted Chloe. Who were these people who played with emotions to gain control over others, for no greater purpose than their own self-satisfaction? I felt shocked by the darkness lurking inside people.

If we couldn't see through the facades of these would-be Casanovas, how could we protect the people we cared about? How could we stop these liars and cheats from doing it again and again, leaving a chain of broken hearts behind them? How could we stop the hearts of their victims from turning to stone after they'd been broken?

This was obviously what had happened to Hunter. He'd loved once and he'd been hurt, and then his heart had become something impenetrable.

I barely slept. The next day, after brunch, when I walked down Jelena's driveway, I felt like everything was different. Something had changed inside me. Hayden had said my heart was innocent—but it didn't feel that way anymore.

Cass and Sara had woken up with big smiles, thrilled that Jelena was in the clear. Try as I might, I couldn't see it the way they did—as a problem solved. Yes, we'd managed to save Jelena, but the events of yesterday could have had a very different outcome. Next time something like this happened, we might not be as fortunate. Look at Lindsay and Chloe. The idea of having to be on constant alert against possible betrayals and broken hearts was frightening.

I shivered. Above me, the sky was the cleanest, sharpest blue I could ever remember seeing. And yet I felt like night had fallen on everything. All that I looked at was marred by sinister shadows.

Suddenly, I didn't want to grow up. I didn't want to start viewing everyone around me with suspicion in case they were potential Hunters or Alexes. I'd always thought of love as a fairy tale—a Disney-like confabulation of colors and fireworks and everlasting love. Now I realized that the charming prince could be a wolf waiting to consume you instead of kissing your hand.

Like a child who'd stumbled upon the wrong storybook and was frightened by what they found in its pages, I wanted my mother. Instead of turning left at the end of Jelena's drive, I went right, toward the bus stop that would take me to Mom's apartment.

31

I raced up the stairs to the entrance of Mom's building. Movers were carrying furniture down the courtyard stairs. I dashed past them. As I exited the elevator and approached her apartment, I saw that the doors were open.

"Mom?" I called out as I walked in.

Two men looked up at me while they were in the process of lifting the black-and-white-striped chaise longues that Mom and I had sat on last weekend while drinking tea. With them was a neatly dressed woman.

Mom was moving? She'd mentioned that she and Carlos were intending to give up this rental apartment, but I hadn't known that they'd actually started looking for a new property.

"Mom?" I called again. She was probably somewhere in the apartment with Carlos, directing the moving team. "Carlos?"

The woman came up to me. "You're looking for the couple who were residing here?"

"They're moving out?"

"Yes, it's all rather abrupt." She didn't look pleased. "They've paid out the remainder of their lease, plus a bonus settlement, so I suppose I shouldn't be complaining, but it's a little bit much to expect a real estate agent to supervise the removal of rented furniture."

"Are they taking it to their next property?"

"Goodness, no." The woman laughed. "It'd cost a fortune to ship all of this to Ibiza."

The message was on my phone, of course, when I got home. It had been left while the girls and I had been having brunch with Jelena and her parents. It was short and to the point: There was an emergency with Carlos's commercial properties group in Ibiza, which would take months for him to sort out in person. Mom was going back with him for support, and "Besides, little Jefferson can't really compare with the European lifestyle!" She said she'd call once they touched down in Spain.

I wasn't going to wait; I called her. A crazy part of me wanted to jump in a taxi and go to the airport.

"Aurora—our plane's about to board."

I could hear them announcing the details in the background.

"You didn't say good-bye."

I would have expected something like this, when she'd initially come back into my life, but not now. Not after coming so much closer to a real relationship.

"There wasn't time, Aurora." Mom sounded stressed. "We only learned of the difficulties back home late last night, and all of this morning I was frantically packing. By the time we got into the car, I knew we wouldn't make the flight if we stopped at your father's."

How could she sound so practical? Suddenly switch off, as if I'd never existed? I'd wondered this countless times after she'd first left, and here I was, asking the question all over again.

"Don't be sad," Mom continued. "We'll be flying you out for the wedding. We're thinking August. You'll love it!"

"You aren't coming back?"

I hadn't even considered that. Wasn't Carlos launching a major development here?

"No immediate plans, but you never know. The developers that

Carlos put in charge here are more than capable, but they might need a visit from him every so often."

"But I thought you came back because you wanted to reestablish a relationship with me? Because you love me . . ."

"Of course I love you," Mom replied. "Have I told you how proud I am about how self-sufficient you are?"

"Self-sufficient?" I hated the word. Basically, it meant she felt she had a guilt-free ticket to exit whenever she pleased.

Mom sighed. "I can't make my life all about you, Aurora. And yours shouldn't be all about me, either. We get on so well when you don't need me for all those mothering things."

"But I do need you. I know I'm self-sufficient, and I know you like that, but I do want a mother, or something like one."

I started crying softly and was immediately furious with myself. Breaking down was no way to prove to her that I wasn't needy.

"Don't be silly, Aurora. You're sixteen, not a baby, so stop blubbering like one. I have to run for my flight. Ciao, darling."

And then there was silence. I sat on my bed, stunned. Once that plane took off, I was out of sight, out of mind for her, I knew it. Without my physical presence as a reminder, the calls would only come every six weeks or more. What killed me was that each time she called, the exact amount of time that had gone by would be tattooed inside my heart, whereas she wouldn't have registered the loss of time and connection.

I'd actually believed that things could be different this time, that now that I was becoming an adult, we'd form some kind of lasting friendship and she wouldn't be able to put me aside so easily.

Well, I wasn't going to fool myself again.

I got out my laptop and sat down at my window seat. I'd start an assignment. After all, I really did need to be self-sufficient now. What was my alternative? To lie sobbing on the floor? She was gone anyway.

I almost didn't hear Hayden's voice when he came into my room. "Aurora? You're sitting here in the dark, you silly thing."

He flipped the light switch and crossed over to the window seat where I was sitting. "Your dad said you were working on your assignment."

I hadn't dared to go downstairs. Sitting in my room, I could hold myself together, but I hadn't put on enough armor yet to tell the NAD and Ms. DeForest the news that would confirm what they'd believed about my mother.

"Mom left." I wanted to say it before he said anything.

He looked confused.

"As in, left the country," I said. "Back to Ibiza. Like you guys told me she would."

Hayden's face dawned with understanding, and he immediately reached for me. I pulled back so that I was almost pressed against the windowpane. It was cold against my skin.

"I'm fine."

I wanted to say *Don't touch me—I'll dissolve*, but I couldn't. Anything beyond the matter-of-fact, I didn't trust myself to pull off.

"Of course you're not fine." Hayden looked upset.

He reached for me again, and this time I couldn't move away. Before I knew it, we were both sitting on the window seat, his arms around me like a cloak. The light outside the window was dark blue.

"You don't have to pretend with me," he said, stroking my hair. I wasn't aware that I was struggling to breathe until I realized that the gasping sound in the room was me.

"I can tell you're trying not to cry," Hayden whispered into my ear. "But you can. I'm not scared of tears, and you shouldn't be, either."

"I don't want to cry."

I didn't. I wasn't going to, even if my body seemed to be betraying me.

"You don't have to be brave all the time," Hayden said. "You are incredibly strong, Aurora, but some moments of vulnerability aren't going to make me love you any less."

I felt like my heart had flatlined. He'd just made what I had to do even harder.

"Don't say that, please." I moved out of his arms and stood up. I stared at the windowpane, trying to compose myself. "In fact, let's pretend you never did, okay? I don't want you walking away and knowing it was all for nothing."

"All for nothing?" Hayden stood up. "Aurora, you don't have to say anything back. I know what I just said is intense; it came out by accident. I didn't intend to lay that kind of thing on the line for *months*—and you shouldn't feel pressured to, either."

"You shouldn't say it to me, because I'm not worthy of it."

Hayden laughed. "Are you crazy?"

"I'm not worthy of it," I repeated slowly, "because I have to break up with you."

"Okay, now I know you're not yourself," he said seriously. "This has been a horrible day for you, but there's absolutely no reason why we should break up."

"You have the most wonderful heart, Hayden, but mine's broken. I always thought a heart could only be broken by romantic love, but that's not true. Nobody ever warns you that your parent can break your heart too."

It wasn't just my heart that hurt; it was my whole body. To say someone broke your heart was only the tip of the iceberg—they broke all of you.

"She left, Hayden. She didn't go involuntarily, because she was dying, like in fairy tales. Sure, she went away once to find herself—maybe that's forgivable. But this time she had every opportunity to stay with me. And she didn't. She chose to go. She *chose* to leave me."

Hayden moved toward me, as if he was going to hold me up. "Aurora, you're not the reason she keeps leaving. It's something in her—"

"Her, me, it's the same outcome." I put my arm up to keep him at a distance. "At some point she decided to leave me. And it might sound dramatic, but it's the honest truth that if someone else did the same . . . I feel like it would kill me. I'd shut down completely."

"You wouldn't." Hayden grasped my hand. "The Aurora I know is standing right here, intact, in a situation that most people wouldn't be able to handle. You're scared now, but that won't last. Like I said, you're so strong."

"Hayden, I'm not. You don't know how hard it is for me not to jump to the conclusion that you're going to want out of my life. I assumed it before you gave me the necklace; I assumed it after you gave me the necklace. It's ridiculous. One day it's going to drive you crazy, or push us to the point of breakup. You deserve better than that."

"Not everyone leaves. Let me prove that to you. All I need from you is a little faith—"

"I have faith in you. I don't have faith in me." It made me feel sick to voice my doubt out loud. "And that's why I need you to walk away from me."

"I'm not going to let you do this." Hayden stared at me with fiery determination. "You're someone who feels things. Part of the reason I fell for you so hard is how much you *care*—the way that you look out for your friends, your dad, the people you're trying to matchmake. You're always stretching yourself to the end of the earth for everyone, wanting them to feel loved and happy. You're a *feeling* person, Aurora. You can't cut yourself off from that."

"I can. I love you . . ." My voice shook as I said the words that should have been full of joy, but were now bittersweet. "But I—"

"Don't say that right now," Hayden choked, echoing my earlier words.

"I'm sorry . . . I . . . I can't be with you any longer."

I'd held it together so far, but Hayden's red eyes and the rapid rise and fall of his chest were tearing at my composure. If I got upset, he wouldn't do as I asked. I forced my face into its most emotionless expression.

Hayden stared at me, searching my face for feeling. "If you love me, how can you not be upset at losing me?"

The words nearly broke me. They were what I wanted to say to my mother.

"Because I don't love you as much as I love my mother," I said. "Yet. You might see that as a bad thing, but for me it's huge to know that I could care about you just as much. I never thought that anything could hurt me as much as losing Mom, but I know that losing you once we've gotten even closer would. And that's why I'm cutting it off now." I turned my back on him, hating myself. "Please . . . leave."

I heard Hayden trying to control his breathing for a minute or two. Then, like any good knight, he fulfilled my request.

I cried after he left, of course. Not sobs but tears that flowed like a continuous stream, as if there were no end to them, as if they ran from some eternal source of sadness. Hayden might think that I wasn't hurting as much as he was, but that wasn't true.

By the time the NAD and Ms. DeForest came upstairs (Hayden must have filled them in), I couldn't even form words. I barely heard what they said to me as they put me to bed and then sat with me until I drifted away.

32

I slept as if I was in a trance, my body too heavy to lift from the mattress. I slept so long that I barely made it out the door in time for school. I raced into the assembly as they were about to shut the auditorium doors. I could see my friends in the third row, anxiously looking around for me.

"Where were you?" Sara asked, when I slipped in beside her. "Jelena's backstage. It's election day, remember!"

"She's still running?" I asked. "With Alex?" She couldn't be. Not after everything that had happened.

"Shh . . . We don't want him clueing in that anything's up." She nodded her head toward Alex, who was sitting a row over. "Jelena needs us backstage. Have you checked your phone?"

I hadn't wanted to know about any messages, after the one from Mom. What had I missed? I felt really guilty about not being there for Jelena when she'd needed me.

Sara yanked me along with her as she ran backstage. Jelena was standing there with Chloe, Jeffrey, and Johannes, who was still on crutches.

"You guys! This is nerve-racking enough without having to stress over your whereabouts," Jelena said.

Despite the agitation in her voice, Jelena looked the picture of confidence and composure—a stark contrast to the girl she'd been on Saturday night.

Mr. Quinten headed out onto the stage to announce the start of the assembly.

"I'm sorry, I didn't get your messages," I said. I didn't want to get into the story of Mom's rapid flight back to Ibiza quite yet. I didn't trust myself to be able to talk about it without dissolving into tears, and today was about Jelena, not about me. She needed strength and positivity in the final few hours before voting time. "What's going on?"

I didn't know whether I was supposed to play a part in what was about to happen. Obviously we were going onstage, but for what exactly?

Jelena sighed. "Aurora, I don't have the time to explain it all again. We're due on, any second. I'll be doing the talking, so all you need to do is stand there and look supportive, like these guys." She gestured to Chloe, Jeffrey, Sara, and Johannes.

"Is this to do with the program or the election?" I asked.

"As far as Alex knows, I'm announcing my withdrawal from the election. He thinks he's won this. But we all know pride comes before a fall."

Mr. Quinten announced her name and Jelena marched onto the stage, gesturing for us to follow her. Jeffrey took Chloe's hand as we walked out. It seemed like he was still in comforting mode. She smiled at him.

"Good morning," Jelena said to the rows of students, who still looked half-asleep. "What I have to tell you may come as a shock." She took a deep breath, and people sat up straighter in their seats, curious. "I'm here to announce my withdrawal from the election."

There were gasps around the auditorium. Alex was looking smug.

"That is, I'm withdrawing from the election as Alex's teammate," Jelena went on.

There were murmurs as people tried to make sense of her statement.

"I've decided to run alone, like I originally intended to."

Cassie and Lindsay, sitting down in the crowd, let out a cheer.

I was so proud of Jelena for stepping back into the ring. So many other people would have given up after going through such a traumatic experience, especially knowing they'd be fighting against the popular vote.

"I realize this is quite confusing," she said, "especially because the election vote will take place between twelve and one today. However, certain circumstances over the weekend showed me that Alex West and I do not share the same values. A joint campaign would mean a presidency that goes against my beliefs in a particularly repugnant way."

Some of the audience gasped in reaction to her comments. Alex shrugged his shoulders. He obviously wasn't worried.

"I realize I'm taking a huge risk by running on my own," Jelena continued, "since Alex has a particularly compelling campaign with One Hour Later."

There were cheers from some sections of the audience.

"But, from the start, I've been committed to running a campaign with heart. As you will remember from my speech at my launch party, I see teenage love as a battlefield, a place where self-confidence can be blown apart. Well, that metaphor goes beyond dating. High school is also a battleground. A place where good and evil hang in the balance, where the strong attempt to bully the weak. To be honest, until recently, I'd been lucky enough never to have experienced this. I'd never been a victim of bullying. I'd never felt ridiculed, or embarrassed, or sick to my stomach about coming to school."

The auditorium was deathly silent now. To hear Jelena, queen bee of Jefferson, talk about bullying was a historic moment.

"I knew this happened to other people, of course. I'd heard girls using gossip like a weapon against other girls they didn't like; I'd heard guys talking about beating up 'losers,' as they put it. I knew, of course, that the student council has been trying to implement effective antibullying tactics for years, and struggling without sufficient funds. But none of that really hit home until this weekend, when I found myself completely vulnerable after being bullied by another person here at Jefferson High. What I'm about to show you demonstrates how devastating an impact bullying can have."

Suddenly, the photo Alex had taken of Jelena appeared on the giant media screen behind us. Her chest had been pixelated, so you couldn't see the details, but it was obvious that she was topless. The room became chaos as people pointed and commented.

"This photo was taken while I was defenseless, without my permission, and at my own home," Jelena said. There was a slight tremor in her voice. "The person who took it threatened to make the image public if I didn't do as they said, which was to drop out of the race for school president."

The chatter grew louder. Even though Jelena hadn't named anyone, people were looking at Alex.

Jelena's voice grew more confident. "I was completely devastated, and I actually contemplated giving in to this bullying, because I felt like I had no other option. I wanted you to see the picture so you can understand how horrendous the situation was. This person wanted to take my power from me. Well, unfortunately for him, I decided to do what had seemed unthinkable on Saturday—to let you all see it. If I have to suffer, to stand naked and vulnerable in front of you, then I want it to be for a purpose.

"I want you to ask yourselves this: How would you feel if this was your photo, or a photo of one of your best friends? Imagine how powerless you would feel. And I ask you to support me in a new campaign strategy: a comprehensive antibullying program for Jefferson High, which will provide students with resources to deal with both physical and online bullying. A program that will identify the bullies and stop them from crushing those they choose as victims."

"Smoke them out!" someone in the crowd shouted.

"Stop the oppression!"

Jelena smiled. "Thank you for your support. At the start of this election, my slogan was 'Think with your heart. Vote Jelena Cantrill.'" She pointed at the photograph of herself, which was now emblazoned with the slogan in gold letters. "Today, I'm urging you to do that again. Sure, you can vote for One Hour Later—that's the popular option, I know. But if this school becomes a more positive place for us all, those hours are going to go by pretty quickly anyway. So I ask you again: think with your heart and vote for the candidate *with* heart—Jelena Cantrill."

Jelena gave a bow. One by one, rows of students stood up and cheered, until the entire room was on its feet applauding. Except for Alex. He'd stood, too, so as not to draw attention to himself, but his face was stony.

"To end this on a positive note, I now give you the triumphant results of the Find a Prince/Princess program," Jelena said, and gestured toward Sara, Johannes, Jeffrey, and Chloe.

At her cue, Johannes grabbed Sara by the waist and pulled her to him. His crutches fell to the floor with a crash, but he paid no attention as he kissed Sara in front of everyone. Jeffrey raised his hand, which was still holding Chloe's, into the air like a fist punch, then brought it down and placed a tender kiss on the back of her hand.

Hugging was the theme of the day. As we filed off the stage, Sara and I swept Jelena into one of our own.

"I'm so proud of you!" I cried.

"I'm even prouder!" Sara enthused. "Jelena, that was inspirational! And, Johannes, you are the most amazing guy ever for swiping that phone."

She pulled away from Jelena and threw her arms around Johannes's neck, kissing him again and again.

Jelena was smiling. "You guys don't have to pretend anymore, you know."

"Don't be silly, Jelena." Sara turned to us, her cheeks flushed. "Like I was ever going to resist Johannes. I was just trying to give you an extra challenge during your campaign—I know you thrive on them."

Jelena raised an eyebrow, but her mouth was amused.

"Oh, really?" Johannes pretended to be put out. "So all my sweating over winning your heart was just a game to you? My ankle, a casualty—"

"Hey, less complaining, more kissing." Sara pulled him to her again.

"Babes, I really think that's our cue," Jeffrey suggested wryly to Chloe.

She laughed and gave him a kiss on the cheek. They both turned and gave me a thumbs-up.

"You know, Aurora, you could have saved yourself a lot of effort if you'd set us up from the start," Jeffrey joked.

I motioned for Chloe to come to one side with me. "You and Jeffrey?" I asked.

The kiss Chloe had given him had looked promising, but I wasn't sure whether Jeffrey's joke was an accurate evaluation of their situation.

"Well, at first he made me laugh when all I wanted to do was cry," Chloe said. "Then, over the last few days, I realized that I wanted to hang out with him. I'd kind of always thought dates had to be deep and meaningful, but I've never felt so at ease with someone. Plus, he's kind of a cutie."

I looked over at Jeffrey as he grinned at Chloe again. His blue eyes were twinkling with fun.

"I'm going to see how it goes, take it lightly at first. No diving in," Chloe said with a laugh, and skipped back over to Jeffrey.

Who would have thought? Opposites did attract, after all.

As Jelena and I left the auditorium, I realized I hadn't asked her something that had been pressing on my mind since Saturday night.

"You're not going to let Alex get away with the photo in a larger sense, are you?"

"Of course not," she said. "You guys were right. What he did was serious. Whether I win or not, I'm going to Mr. Quinten—and the police—to report it. After all, the image is still on Alex's phone—it's indisputable evidence. The only reason I didn't take it to Mr. Quinten first thing today was because I don't want Alex to be able to claim that I won—if I win—because I blacklisted him. I want to win on my own terms."

The positive feedback following Jelena's emotional speech was overwhelming, and not just for Jelena. People kept coming up to me and asking when the next round of the Find a Prince/Princess™ program would take place. Apparently, they were hanging out to be matched by yours truly, after seeing the happy endings of Jeffrey, Chloe, and Sara.

"I knew choosing those three would pay off," Jelena said, as we watched another group of girls heading to the voting booths, determined to vote with their hearts.

"*Choosing* them?" I stared at her.

"Crap. I never meant to tell you that," she said quickly. "Okay, to be honest, I looked through the list of people who'd put down their names to be matched up. I knew that if voters were going to believe that our campaign could work miracles, we needed three people who seemed like lost causes in terms of love. So, come announcement day, I ensured there were only three names in the hat—Jeffrey, Sara, and Chloe."

"That's a little sneaky, Jelena," I said, with a disapproving look.

"Hey, I sensed you were lacking in the confidence department yourself," she said pointedly. "I knew that if you managed to pull the matches off, you'd be totally convinced of your love guru powers." She gave me a charming smile. "Because you *are* a love guru. I hope you start believing that. Especially if we get elected."

I gave Jelena a big hug. "*When*, not if, we get elected. There's a good vibe in the air right now, and I think it's because people are voting with their hearts."

They were. Three hours later, the votes were in, and Jelena was officially next year's school president.

When Mr. Quinten announced the result, Cass, Scott, Lindsay, Tyler, Sara, Johannes, Jeffrey, Chloe, and I, along with dozens of supporters, all started screaming. Lindsay threw her arms around me, seconds after Tyler had done that very thing to her.

"You guys are okay, then?" I asked her in a low voice.

"We're working through a lot of stuff," she said. "Some of it's far from nice, but we really love each other, and I'm hoping that'll pull us through."

Hayden emerged from the student council office and came over to give Jelena a hug. He high-fived Johannes, Scott, and Tyler and looked like he wanted to come over to Lindsay and me. But he didn't. I wondered if what Lindsay had said could be true: that love, if it was strong enough, could pull you through anything.

When I got home that afternoon, I wandered up to my room and sat down on my bed, trying to sort through my feelings from the day. There was a tap on my door, which was open. I looked up and saw Ms. DeForest.

"I wanted to speak to you."

Was she still upset with me after the commitment ceremony?

She came in and perched tentatively on the end of my bed. "You wouldn't know this, because it's something I keep pretty close to my chest, but I've had a similar experience to you. A soul challenge, as we call it in group sessions. Don't worry, I'm not going to make this a sharing circle. I just wanted to tell you that a fundamental person in my life also left me at a very young age."

She paused. I opened my mouth, wanting to ask a question, but then she continued.

"Not my mother. My father. He was very much like what I know of your mother, from your father's descriptions—charming, charismatic, handsome. But also controlling and often cold-natured. He left my mother and me when I was nine. Unlike your mom, he didn't go overseas, just to the other side of the city, although it felt like he was continents away because I saw him so infrequently." She sighed. "It was only as I got older that we managed to develop a relationship, but to be frank, it worked best when I did what he wanted me to. Including a master's in business, graduating with first-class honors."

I looked at Ms. DeForest's wild hair and the crystals draped over her flowing bohemian dress. She'd been a business major?

"I even unconsciously chose a fiancé who was just like him. The type of man other women were jealous over. The type of man who broke off the engagement when my mother died from breast cancer."

Ms. DeForest paused again. I was beginning to understand why she seemed distant and cold at times. I felt broken from losing one parent; if I'd lost both, I'd probably be kind of standoffish, too. It was a protection mechanism.

"I'm not telling you this because I'm hoping a sob story will make you like me better or bring us closer," she said. "Whether that happens is yet to be seen, and essentially it comes down to you and me and how we reconfigure this dynamic in the future. I'm telling you this because I want you to know why I was concerned about you spending more time with your mom. In my experience, more time with my father never actually made me feel better about myself. It usually left me feeling pretty wounded when he chose to pull away, which he did a lot."

I nodded, my eyes meeting hers. After this most recent blow, I actually felt like I'd gone backward in terms of my self-confidence and strength. The second betrayal had hurt worse than the one I'd experienced at twelve. Maybe it was because it had torn at existing scar tissue.

"There's another thing," Ms. DeForest said. "Your experience of love within your family can make you believe that you need to earn love." She nodded at me, emphasizing her statement. "That's not true. You are worthy of love—lasting love—and you need to hang on to that. You may always be a little wary. I know I am. I realized, on the day of the ceremony, that you might be concerned about my intentions toward your father because of our previous breakup."

"Why did you end it with him?" I still felt protective of the NAD.

"Self-preservation," she said. "I was also concerned that he might still be wounded from his marriage. That ceremony the other day was about two rather terrified but determined people trying to show that they're moving forward." She shrugged. "Which you need to do in life to keep growing."

"How do you know that it won't happen again?" By "it," I meant abandonment, pain, loss. Everything that currently held me in suspended terror.

"It might. But as someone who's lived with the same hurt and fear you're experiencing, let me assure you that not everyone who loves you is going to leave you. It's easy to fall into the trap of believing that, but if you do, you're going to miss out on some pretty special people."

She smiled and headed for the door.

"Dana?" I'd never used her first name before. "I know our relationship didn't start out the best way, but like you say, I hope we can change that."

She smiled and left the room, her skirts billowing after her.

I felt slightly stunned by how much of what she'd said made sense to me. I'd always felt pretty alone when it came to the situation with Mom—after all, none of my friends' moms had abandoned them—so, to have someone talk about the same hurt and fear was reassuring.

Obviously, there was a history between Dana and me, but I had to admit that I was glad the NAD had found someone who was sensitive to his wounds. Now that I understood her a little better, maybe she and I would become closer, especially now that she and Dad had become a more permanent thing.

However, even as my stepmother, I knew she would never be a replacement for my own mother. No one would. That relationship would always be a piece missing in the jigsaw puzzle that was my life. Part of me would always be looking for it, wanting to fill the gap so my life felt complete, but it wasn't to be. I'd never stop feeling that sadness, but if I wanted to live a happy life, I had to realize that one missing piece couldn't detract from the overall beauty of the picture. Mom might have left me, but I couldn't let her take all of my joy and positivity with her. I needed to focus on the relationships I did have.

I thought about Jelena's determination to fulfill her dreams, even after someone had tried to steal them away. Chloe's vow to not be the wounded woman again. Lindsay's ability to stick with someone who'd once hurt her and whom she'd now hurt back, and to try to work things out until they were made right. The NAD's and Dana's bravery in standing up in front of everyone and trying again. None of it was easy. All of it took courage. And I admired them for it.

And, all of a sudden, I wanted to be brave, too.

I ran out the front door and toward the fence between the Parises' house and ours. Hayden was already standing there, like he'd been holding a constant vigil. I leaped over the fence, and his mouth dropped open in shock.

"Please, don't say anything yet," I begged him. "I know last night I asked you to walk away from me, but that's the exact opposite of what I want now. You remember the Leap of Faith at camp? You held your arms out and I leaped into them. I think I can do that again. I'm not saying I won't teeter at the edge sometimes and feel like my fear is getting the better of me, but I know that your voice will always cut through the terror.

"I couldn't do it last night, I know. But like I told you, I didn't have the faith in myself. I do now. I know I can take that last step and launch myself out. After all, it takes two—you can't catch me if I don't jump."

"Show me," Hayden whispered. "I'm standing with my arms open right now. I want to know you can do it."

His arms were wide, waiting for me. Taking the remaining two steps that separated us, I launched myself into them. Our bodies entwined, I put my lips to his, kissing him over and over, each kiss a pledge to stay with him, to not let fear get the better of me. I put everything I was feeling and hoping into my kisses, desperation and conviction all jumbled into one crazy, nonverbal promise that had to win him over.

"Are those kisses supposed to convince me?" Hayden asked, when I finally pulled away.

Supposed to? Was he saying they hadn't worked?

He grinned. "You'll never need to convince me. Like you said, I have faith in you. My arms are open 24–7. In fact, I had this made today, in the hope of convincing *you*."

He pulled something from his back pocket—a T-shirt with "Love is my religion" scrawled across it in gold letters.

My favorite quote from Keats. He knew me better than anyone. My eyes smarted as I realized how steadfast his belief in me was.

"And now you can wear it with pride. My champion of love, and cupid's copilot." He touched my cheek tenderly. "My Princess."

Hayden pulled me to him again. Both of us knew that this was the beginning of a very happy ending.